Taking Heart

ALSO BY CAROL DOUMANI

NOVELS
UNTITLED, *Nude*
Chinese Checkers
Indiscretions

COOKERY
Good Enough To Eat

Taking Heart

a novel by **Carol Doumani**

WAVE PUBLISHING VENICE

MANUFACTURED IN THE UNITED STATES OF AMERICA

FIRST EDITION

PUBLISHED BY WAVE PUBLISHING
POST OFFICE BOX 688
VENICE, CALIFORNIA
TSUNAMI@PRIMENET.COM

DOUMANI, CAROL.
TAKING HEART: A NOVEL / BY CAROL DOUMANI, -- 1ST ED.
P.   CM.
ISBN 0-9642359-1-9
I. TITLE.
PS3554.O86T35   1999
813'.54--DC21   99-23893
                              CIP

DUST JACKET PRINTED BY GARDNER LITHOGRAPH
BOOK DESIGN BY JOHN DEEP

10/9/8/7/6/5/4/3/2/1

In memory of Larry Thrall,
and for Beverly,
always in our hearts,

and for Jon and Carol Pugh

Precious friends all.

ONE

I

*L*ater she remembered hearing the scream of brakes, the urgent thud of impact — metal to flesh. But at the time she was so absorbed in her pre-workout routine that it had only registered as distant music, one instrument in a symphony of neighborhood sounds.

Still, maternal instinct is triggered to respond to such warnings, so unconsciously she took stock of her family: Jonah was at school. He had called an hour before from the dorm phone at Oceancrest, his voice splintered with teenage angst as he made lame excuses why he couldn't come home for the weekend (she had ultimately wormed the truth out of him — his father, her ex-husband Matt, had proposed a camping trip in the Sierras, the first Emily had heard of it); Jack, husband number two, had left thirty minutes before to go golfing with his foursome at Palm Ridge Country Club, so he was probably on the first green. The spice of his aftershave still clung to the air, and she breathed great comforting gulps of it as she stretched; Fiber, their adored Wheaten Terrier mix, rescued from the pound as a puppy, was lying on the window seat, basking in the first warming rays of winter sun, which filtered in past the branches of the great coral tree in the front yard; her parents were a thousand miles away in a retirement home in Boulder, Colorado; Jack's parents were on a Princess Cruise to, of all places, Belize.

Satisfied that her loved ones were safe in their respective lives, Emily dismissed the sound and concentrated on her stretches. The six-mile run on Saturday morning was not only a matter of exercise but of self-discipline, her personal imperative to start the day in control of herself, since there were so many other things she couldn't control.

Like the fact that her young marriage to Jack seemed to be stagnating, and nothing she said or did seemed to help. Oh, they loved each other, of that she was certain. But their relationship had stopped growing, the initial heat turned tepid. They seemed to be going through the motions, mimicking the passion they'd felt during their courtship in an unconscious attempt to reignite the spark that had issued between them in those first months.

The truth was, they were opposites, and their idiosyncrasies, which had seemed endearing in the beginning, had become annoyances. Jack was impulsive, competitive, volatile; she required orderliness and routine and was prudent in the nurture of body, mind, and spirit. Jack played sports for the sheer exhilaration of the game and watched them obsessively on TV; she exercised for fitness, not for fun, and tuned out whenever Jack tuned in to the NBA, the NFL, or the NHL.

Despite their differences, they did try to make it work. They'd gone to the County Fair just last week — her suggestion for a neutral outing which would satisfy both their ideas of a good time. She had waited patiently while Jack rode the roller coaster four times in a row. On the last go-round, he had vomited his lunch of hot dogs and beer, but still, he would have gone a fifth time and a sixth, had she not insisted that he ride the Ferris wheel with her instead, to hold her steady as the carriage slowly circled, while she took pictures of the view. That about summed up their differences — he craved a wild ride, she was happy to observe and record from a safe place.

And when they'd argued on the ride home, the word *divorce* had erupted from Jack's mouth, bursting like a kernel of corn from a hot air popper. "I suppose divorce is the only solution," he'd said, or something to that effect. It had been a sarcastic remark, but the power of the word had surprised and silenced them both, and had left a nagging unease between them, like a fragment of popcorn stuck between two teeth.

She bent to touch her toes and exhaled, the long rush of breath becoming a sigh. By now she and Jack should be comfortable and complacent in their relationship. Was it her fault? Some vital flaw in her nature? That she might be the architect of her own misery made her lean further into her stretch, until the taut hamstring of her left leg burned.

Even Jonah was aware of the tension in her relationship with Jack — or perhaps her son was part of the cause. After four years, despite Jack's fervent attempts to get close to him, the boy had remained distant, preferring the company of his real father, Matt's second wife Lauren, and their infant son, which all three called J.B. — short for Jonah's Brother (Matt wasn't a child psychologist for nothing). This was Jonah's second year at Oceancrest Middle School for the Arts, and recently he'd devised all manner of excuses to avoid coming home on weekends. Emily hated to pull parental rank and insist, but she sometimes did, aching to regain the sense of family that had been an unavoidable casualty of the divorce.

She straightened and took a sip of water, sloshing it around in her mouth as though to flush out the taint of this subject.

"Fiber — okay, boy, let's hit the road!"

She smiled, watching the terrier snap to attention, his bright black eyes riveted on her as she crossed the bedroom and started down the stairs. When was the last time Jack had responded to anything she'd suggested with half as much interest?

"Let's go!" she called as she descended, knowing Fiber wouldn't yet budge. He would remain motionless in anticipation, barely daring to breathe, until she spoke the magic mantra, *Jack's back*!, which would trigger a flat out rush for the door. It worked every time, whether Jack was indeed back or not.

"Fiber, Jack's back!" she called at last, and sure enough, the dog raced past her down the stairs and was at the door before she was, his tail wagging, neck extended to receive his collar and leash.

Dogs were so satisfying that way, thankful for routine and willing to listen. *Not like 13-year-old sons or second husbands,* she thought, *challenging you at every turn, asserting their independence as though each issue were a contest, and at all costs they must win, or simply ignoring you as though you were a head cold, an irritant that must be endured, but would eventually go away.*

This morning had offered a perfect example. When Jack had shouted his good-bye, she'd called down to him, "I left that letter from the Club on the ledge. Don't forget, it's got —"

"I'll read it when I get back. Bye hon," he'd interrupted, slamming the door.

"— the new key card for the gate in it," she'd finished quietly to herself. "You won't be able to get in without it."

The first year of their marriage, no question, she would have jumped up and run after him, catching him before he'd driven off, proffering the key card as evidence that his needs were foremost in her mind. The second year, at the least, she would have stuck her head out of the window and tried to flag him down before he'd turned into the street. The third year she might have called the Club and warned them of his imminent cardless arrival. Or at least the thought would have crossed her mind.

But this was the fourth year, and what was the point anymore?

Jack would probably be able to wangle his favorite groundskeeper or guard into breaking the key card rule and letting him into the members' parking lot. That was something she both loved and resented about him, his ability to bully life into submission through sheer charisma, even if it meant breaking the rules. In contrast, she was much more submissive to authority and always did what was expected of her. It was just easier that way.

She walked through the kitchen to the back door, and as she picked up her house key, the one attached to a stretch band she wore on her wrist when she ran, she noticed that the letter from the Club and the new key card were gone. But she'd seen them just ten minutes before when she'd taken the trash out to the back alley, luckily beating the garbage truck on its weekly rounds, but unluckily running into their elderly neighbor Laverne Lawrence, who kept her standing in the damp cold without a jacket, jawboning about the relative merits of incineration versus recycling.

Had Jack returned to get the letter and the green plastic card while she'd been in the back? She smiled to herself as she followed Fiber out the door, imagining Jack's reluctance to return for them, and then his relief at having been able to retrieve the card without having to admit his oversight to her. She'd casually bring it up at dinner, not so much to say "I told you so" as to make sure he knew *she knew* he'd tried to sneak by her. And after that, she'd smile and tell him she loved him — no, not just *tell* him, she would mean it. And she would try harder to make this marriage work — through patience, tolerance, respect, and generosity. Starting tonight!

Uplifted by her resolve to make things better, Emily zipped her jacket and adjusted the earphones of her Walkman, flipping on the audio book cassette. She always listened to Books on Tape when she ran — it was more efficient to exercise her mind and body at the same time. And she relished the luxury of being read to, the story insulating her from the noise of the street, and the constant nattering of her brain. She was currently halfway through *Sense and Sensibility*, finding the measured predictability of the characters' nineteenth century lives a steady metronome by which to set her jogging pace.

At the foot of the driveway Fiber veered right toward the ocean, which was 1.2 miles away. From there they'd head south on Adams to the park, run once around it and out on Covington, through the neighborhood village and right on Jessup to Pleasant, and home again. The busy part of town — the access road to the highway, the Club, and the distant civic center — was to the east, and both Emily and Fiber preferred the scenic, less traveled route. This was their ritual and, like most of Emily's habits, it never varied.

But had she broken with routine today and turned left out of the driveway, she would have seen the accident, just blocks away at the on-ramp to the freeway. She would have recognized the red 1965 Mustang with silver racing stripes, now crushed like an empty cola can against the unforgiving bulk of a Pepsi delivery truck, and the set of Big Bertha golf clubs, splayed across the highway like swizzlesticks.

If she had delayed her run just fifteen minutes, she would have still been home when the police car pulled into the driveway and the two deputies got out, adjusting their holsters and securing their hats before pressing the bell one, two, three times, then finally slipping a business card into the doorjamb with a message to "please contact Sgt. Ray Wilson as soon as possible."

But as it was, Emily jogged her six 10-minute miles, stopping only to let Fiber mark the trail four or five times along the way and to change tapes in her cassette player. By the time she circled back down Jessup to Pleasant, the squad car was long gone. Because she always entered the house through the back door, she didn't see the officer's card stuck in the front doorjamb, and she went blithely about her business — giving Fiber his kibble and filling his water dish, and drinking a 20-ounce glass herself, then taking the stairs two at a time and heading for the shower.

The running water drowned out the ringing of the telephone, and Jack's casually discarded pajamas were covering the answering machine, so when she got out she didn't see the red light flashing, indicating that a message had come in while she showered. In half an hour she was down the stairs and out the back door to her car, again turning right toward the local village, to make a quick stop at the office, then to do the weekend's errands and marketing.

Her mind was occupied with itemizing the grocery list as she backed down the drive, so when she saw Laverne Lawrence trying to flag her down, she just waved absently and kept on driving. After all, she'd more than fulfilled her neighborly duty for the morning, and she wanted to keep to her schedule so she would be back from shopping before Jack returned home from his golf game.

○

"Yes, Mrs. Rhodes, I told her what you said about the ice. Yes, 80 pounds sounds like a lot for 50 people, but you don't want to run out, do you? It's only frozen water. It's not like a rental that has to be returned. If you don't use it, it'll melt."

Rolling her eyes, the receptionist handed Emily two pink-slipped messages as she walked by.

"But the cost is minimal, Mrs. Rhodes," Nancy continued. "I don't know, maybe three or four dollars...."

·Party Line's office was chaotic, as was usual on a Saturday, the biggest day of the week for party planners, with frenzied hostesses panicking about last-minute details, purveyors confirming deliveries, and waitstaff checking schedules. Emily waved and nodded to the seven people she worked with as she walked to her office, unaware that the timbre of their conversations lowered as she passed and that their eyes were following her. She sniffed the air as she neared her own cubicle at the end of the building near the kitchen. It was heavy with the perfume of baking cookies, Party

Line's famous bittersweet chocolate coconut crunch bars, Emily's recipe.

She nudged the door shut behind her with her heel, but immediately it burst open again, nearly knocking Emily off her feet. Party Line's co-founder Ann Smith poked her head in. Ann's frizzy red hair was tightly coiled around rollers the size of orange juice cans. A closer look revealed that they *were* orange juice cans.

"I've heard of the Pillsbury Doughboy," Emily said with a smile. "But what are you, the Sunkist Sweetheart?"

"I've got a headache Demerol wouldn't put a dent in, so don't mess with me," Ann snapped, tottering into the room on three-inch platform wedgies that increased her height to all of five feet two inches. "Giselle promised this will make me look like Nicole Kidman. Of course, she's eight feet tall, but I believe in the power of positive thinking."

"Isn't the point of putting your hair in rollers so that it looks good when you go out? Or is wearing them to work a fashion statement?"

"If you ever slept on orange juice cans, you wouldn't ask that question."

Ann perched on the edge of Emily's desk, looking, but trying not to show that she was, at the pink message slips in Emily's hand. "Hey, I thought you finished last night," she said. "I didn't expect you in today. What'd you do, rob a bank?" Ann asked, changing gears in mid-thought.

"Huh?"

"Two guys from the Police Department were here looking for you, but they wouldn't tell us why."

"Looking for me? When?"

"About half an hour ago. I told them you were off today, to try your house. I never would have given them the address, I swear, but they already had it. Said they'd been by and you weren't home. I figured you were either jogging or on your way — "

"Wait a minute, back up," Emily demanded. "There were policemen? Here? Today? Looking for me?"

"Would I kid you?" Ann raised her eyebrows. "They were really studly too, and boy, did they know it. At first I thought they were those male strippers who dress up like cops — like the ones Stacey Silvester had us hire for Ellen Bartlett's 50th. She ended up taking one of them home with her, didn't she? Or maybe both! Anyway, I knew it wasn't *your* birthday. Or your anniversary. So I figured these guys must be for real. Nice belt. Is it new? It would go great with my Versace jumpsuit. But I'm never wearing that thing again, not since I saw the exact same one on Marcia Lennox at Chez Charles. Wanna go there for lunch? Do you have time today?"

This was typical AnnSpeak, mouth outpacing brain, a mynah bird on speed. Emily didn't bother responding. She often didn't. People said Emily and Ann were like the two sides of the brain: Ann, creative, spontaneous, emotional, and Emily structured, pragmatic, rational. But they understood each other. It worked. Maybe that's why Emily had thought the same sort of "opposites attract" partnership would work in her marriage to Jack.

"They called too," Ann persisted.

"Who?"

"The police. See?" She motioned to the message slips Emily was holding.

Sure enough, on one was written "Sgt. Ray Wilson." The "please call" box was checked twice, with a phone number beside it. The other message was from Laverne Lawrence. Again! The poor old widow lived alone, and sometimes she just got desperate for human contact.

"So what's up?" Ann prodded. She took a cigarette out of her pocket and tapped it against Emily's desk.

"Ann, what are you doing?" Emily sighed.

"Oh, I'm not going to smoke it." Ann avoided Emily's eyes. "I quit, remember? This is just a, like, a nervous thing. I've already bitten my nails down to the cuticles. Connie is furious with me. She says she refuses to manicure stumps." Ann removed one of the orange juice cans from her hair and tested a strand. It was still damp, but springy with curl. "Nicole Kidman, right?" She began to rewrap it. "So what gives with the Hill Street Blues?"

"I don't have a clue," Emily said, falling into her desk chair. "I just came in to pick up the glue gun so I can work on the Turner invitations tomorrow while Jack watches golf. You know how focused he gets."

"That's because you make him watch with the sound off."

"He wears earphones!"

"So let him turn on the volume."

"But then I'd have to listen to it too."She flipped through the mail piled on her desk. "Maybe that jerk down at the beach sent them. Remember I told you? The one who swore Fiber bit him when we were jogging down to your house. You know how he *hates* strange men, and this guy was definitely strange."

"Yeah, but how would he have gotten the number? Did you give him a card?"

"I was jogging. I don't carry cards with me!"

"Really? I thought you kept one under the insole of your shoe in case of emergencies," Ann teased, "along with $10, a copy of your driver's license, and a Xerox of your address book."

"I did not give him a card. I didn't even give him the time of day."

The phone rang, and both Emily and Ann jumped. It rang a second time. "Want me to get it?" Ann asked.

"Of course not," Emily said, and picked up the receiver. "Hello? Yes, it is." And then she just listened.

Ann watched her partner's face flush red, then just as quickly drain of color. "Emily, what?"

Emily did not reply, continuing to listen, her expression frozen.

"Oh," she said at last, just that one word, nothing more. Then, slowly and deliberately, she laid the receiver down on the desk and picked up her purse. "I have to go," she said, and she walked out the door. She didn't look back.

"Emily! What's the matter? Where are you going?"

Ann could hear a male voice still talking on the open phone line. She picked up the receiver and tried to hold it to her ear, but one of the orange juice cans was in the way. She quickly stripped it out. "Hello? Who is this? Me? I'm Annabel Smith, Emily's partner, and, well, I'm a very close friend, I assure you. Mrs. Barnes just dropped the phone and ran out of here like a bat on fire, I mean a house from hell, oh, you know what I mean. What is going on?" she asked.

Listening, she pulled out the remaining cans, one by one.

○

The drive to Westside Medical Center was interminable and fleeting at the same time. Emily's brain kept pounding, *Jack, Jack, Jack,* like the beat beneath a melody you hear once and can't get out of your head. She tried to picture him in her mind, but she couldn't even remember what he'd been wearing when he'd left the house that morning, even though it had been less than two hours since he'd kissed her good-bye. Instead she saw the pigeon nesting on the cylindrical shade around the red light at the street signal on Main, and she wondered why it had chosen the red canister instead of the yellow or green lights. Her eye caught a glimpse of a kid on a skateboard shooting out of a Taco Bell, and she flashed on the fact that Jack *loved* Mexican food. Burritos were his favorite food, another difference between them.

Jack, Jack, Jack, her brain repeated, as though reciting this litany would make it all a mistake, would ensure that no matter what she'd just been told, there had been no accident at Jessup and Dover, and that Jack was out on the golf course with his cronies as he was every Saturday.

How bad was it?

She hadn't even waited to ask.

She realized that she was driving very fast, nearly twenty miles an hour over the posted limit, and she started to move her foot to the brake, but changed her mind and hit the gas instead. "Oh, Jack," she moaned aloud, as the car shot forward.

She'd never been to the Emergency Room at Westside, and as she saw the building up ahead, she felt a tickle of panic. Which entrance should she use? Where would she park? Did they have valet parking at this hospital? How far would she have to walk? She shook her head, appalled at her mental meltdown. How could she be worrying about something as trivial as parking when she'd just found out her husband had been in an automobile accident and then rushed to the hospital? Of course she knew the answer: she was trying to avoid thinking about what she would find when she went inside.

To compensate, with flagrant and uncharacteristic disregard of convention, she pulled up at the red curb next to the entrance, turned off the engine, and jumped out of the car. She wouldn't have even pressed the "lock" button on the remote, but it was a habit, and the Toyota chirped its three-note good-bye as she raced through the automatic doors into the hospital.

2

hey told me my husband ... Jack, Jack Barnes." Her words came out in a choked, hoarse cry, directed at the first staff member she saw. She didn't even notice that the Emergency Room receptionist was helping one patient fill out a form and that two people were standing in line, waiting.

With studied patience, the nurse receptionist picked up a clipboard and skimmed the list of names. Then she turned to a computer terminal and tapped a quick entry. She was wearing a royal blue cardigan over her uniform, and in a rush of memory, Emily now recalled that Jack had been wearing a blue shirt of that exact shade when he'd bent to kiss her good-bye that morning. She'd noticed a small tear next to the second button and had made a mental note to mend it before sending it to the cleaners. Because Jack loved the shirt. It was more than his favorite shirt, it was his lucky shirt, and he would want to wear it at the tournament next weekend. *Please God, don't let the blue shirt be ruined,* she prayed silently.

"Emily Barnes?"

"Yes. How did you know my name?"

"Your husband's insurance records. We accessed them from his car registration."

So it was not a mistake. Jack had been in an accident, and they'd brought him here. *Okay,* Emily said to herself, *okay.*

"He's already in surgery, Mrs. Barnes," the nurse continued. "They took him right in." Her eyes had a kindly droop to them.

"Surgery? I didn't even know — How badly was he hurt? Is he going to — "

"If you'll just have a seat, dear, I'll get one of the volunteers to escort you to the Surgical Waiting Area." She reached across the counter and squeezed Emily's hand, nodding toward the folding chairs which were lined up auditorium style, facing the nurse's station.

"But, how is he? What happened?"

"I'm sorry, dear, I honestly don't know. But I will call someone immediately to come out and speak with you. All right?"

"May I just see — " She tried to look at the computer screen, but the nurse quickly tapped a button and the screen went blank.

She didn't want to sit. She didn't want to *be* here. But then who did? The nurse smiled with compassion so sincere that Emily could feel it, and she gestured again to the chairs. She seemed so relaxed and warm, unlike those hustling, self-important interns on *ER*, or the harried nurses on *60 Minutes* who complained about the health care crisis. *Surely if there were something terrible in that computer file she would not act so calm, would she? Of course not, it would be inhuman.* Grasping a tenuous thread of hope, Emily did what she was told and sat in the nearest empty chair, front row center in this theater of crisis.

To her right an Asian woman was cradling a small child with a splint on the index finger of her left hand. The splint was made out of a pair of chopsticks bound with a piece of raffia. The child stared at Emily through mournful almond eyes, then held up her bandaged finger for inspection and sympathy. Emily's eyes flooded with tears, and startled, the child began to wail. Emily turned away, unable to acknowledge any pain but her own.

To her left an elderly man was hugging himself and rocking gently, his eyes clamped shut, his mouth slightly agape, revealing decaying dentures. Next to him a heavyset man balanced a magazine on the folds of his lap. He coughed, spraying mucous and spittle into the air.

Suffocated by free-floating misery, Emily clutched her purse to her chest, trying not to breathe or see or hear or feel or think. *Jack, Jack, Jack*, her brain continued to chant in time with the rocking motion of the man with the rotted dentures.

"Mrs. Barkley?"

Emily looked up. A teenage boy was standing before her. His body was lean and spindly, and his arms dangled loosely at his sides, too long for his still-growing body. He was wearing a pink polo shirt which was untucked at the back. When he saw her notice this, he reached around and self-consciously tucked it in. "Barnes," she said.

"Oh yeah, right. My name's Greg. I'm going to take you to the Surgical Waiting Area. Then one of the physicians will come out to tell you what's happening with your husband." Emily stood, and he turned to lead the way. "I'm really sorry," he added, the words tossed over his shoulder as an afterthought.

Did he know something? "About what?" she asked.

The boy looked perplexed. "That you're here. That your husband is in surgery. Like, I'm sorry," he repeated. "That's it."

His casual disregard was a slap in the face. Emily wanted to shout at him, "*How can you be sorry? You don't even know Jack or me.*" But he was only a kid. What could he know of life and death and the confusion of terrifying emotions crowding Emily's heart? Biting back her anger and fear, she followed him down the hall to a bank of elevators. He pushed the call button, whistling through his teeth as they waited.

His face was blank, a mass of freckles. She imagined taking a pencil and drawing lines from dot to dot — would an image appear? A horse? An airplane? A rose?

"Did you see my husband when he came in?" she demanded.

"Um, no ma'am. I didn't."

"When did he get here? Was he conscious?" she persisted.

He shrugged. "I don't know. They don't tell me that stuff."

"But I need to know!"

"Like I said, I'm sorry," he repeated, and ducked his head, embarrassed by her tirade.

It was an outrage — to be left in the hands of a mere child who couldn't possibly tell her anything about Jack! Somewhere within these walls, perhaps close enough to hear her voice if she cried out to him, he might be going through a crisis, and he was going through it alone. Frustration welled up within her. She felt like she was dying of thirst while standing next to a well — she could smell the water, almost feel it trickle down her parched throat. But when she bent over to drink, she could only graze the surface with her fingertips.

The elevator was agonizingly slow in coming. No doubt trying to distract her from the wait, the boy, Greg, said, "I'm a candy striper."

"What?" she asked, baffled, trying to make some sense of the non sequitur.

He motioned to his pink shirt. "A candy striper, you know, a volunteer. I work here two days a week after school and on Saturdays. We get credit for it."

"Oh." Emily fumbled for a response. "I didn't know candy striping was co-ed," she said dumbly, the first thing that came into her mind.

"It isn't really. That's why I signed up. You know, I figured there'd be a lot of Sheilas."

Did he think she knew someone named Sheila? Did he have her

mixed up with someone else? Maybe it was a mistake after all.
"Who?" she asked.

"Sheilas. You know, *girls.*"

Then she remembered, she had heard Jonah use that term. God knows where it came from. But how obscenely inappropriate, cruel even, that the *child* the hospital had sent to be her escort into this terrifying netherworld was bragging about the fact that he worked here not out of compassion nor an urge to help people, not because he had some special skill nor a devout desire to learn one, but in order to pick up girls! She stared at him, furious, unable to speak. Behind them a dozen more people had gathered. They were all chatting amiably, waiting for the elevator. Would it never come?

"Are there stairs?" she demanded.

"What?"

"Stairs. You know, to walk up to the next floor."

He looked perplexed. "But ... we're not going up. The Surgical Waiting Area is down, off the lower lobby."

"*Down* then." She was almost shouting now, her voice trembling with rage. "Can we take the stairs *down*, please, instead of waiting here for the damn elevator? At this rate *we're going to die standing here!*" She didn't realize that her raised voice had silenced the crowd of people around them, and that they were now all staring at her.

A man's voice broke the stillness. " 'Die' is not a particularly good word to use in a hospital. I think the preferred euphemism is *pass on.*"

Emily whipped around, ready to spit fire. But when she saw the speaker, she caught herself.

He was withered and wizened, as though someone had siphoned all of the air out of his body and strapped the carcass into a wheelchair. His skin was the color and texture of a very old tortilla — white and flaky with uneven brown splotches and creases. He could have been twenty-eight or eighty-two — she couldn't tell because he had a UCLA cap pulled low over his face and was wearing dark glasses. He smiled at her, a death's grin, his lips cracked, his teeth large and even, but cast in dull yellow. A three-day growth of beard prickled his chin, and clear, narrow tubes protruded from each nostril, meeting under his nose and running down and around to the back of the chair in a single snake of plastic, to an oxygen tank. Beside him a metal tree blossomed with brightly colored plastic bags, each funneling fluid into or collecting it out of his body. The odor of decay cloyed at her senses.

"I'm sorry, you're right," she mumbled, indignation transformed into contrition by the man's ravaged appearance, and the sudden horrifying thought that Jack could end up like him. Was it possible? She fought to dispel the image.

"No, no, you're right. Some of us *could* die waiting for this elevator. People probably have." The man caught a ragged breath. "But unfortunately, the ol' Otis has no conscience, does it, Jimmy?"

"Nope," the orderly behind the wheelchair replied. "Not that I've seen."

"By the way," the man continued, "I've been told there are stairs just through the door around that corner, but I can't say for sure." He cracked a grin. "They made me leave my Nikes at the door when I checked in."

At last the elevator door opened. Emily stepped back to allow the man to be wheeled to the rear of the car. Then she, Greg, and the others squeezed in.

They rode down in uncomfortable silence. Emily felt the man's eyes on her and could smell his disease. She glanced over her shoulder. He was staring at her with eyes that held a trace of sadness, and a dim spark of humor. Without smiling he winked at her, and she quickly looked away.

Mercifully, the elevator stopped on the next floor, and when the doors opened, Greg stepped out. She followed him, exhaling. Until that moment, she had not realized that she had been holding her breath.

"Good luck," the man in the wheelchair called after her. "It's all about luck in this place. Not skill, not science, just timing and luck, right Jimmy?"

"You got that, Tin Man," the orderly agreed.

Emily followed Greg down a low-ceilinged hallway, until they came to a small, empty room that looked like an air raid bunker left over from the '50s: white-washed concrete block walls, fluorescent lights flickering with age, a scarred, Lysol-scented linoleum floor mopped to a high gloss. Orange vinyl chairs surrounded the perimeter of the room, their line broken by an occasional low table, and in the corner, a metal cart holding a coffee urn, Styrofoam cups, those thin red stirring sticks, powdered milk, and Nutrisweet packets. The place stank of shock and sorrow. What good news could possibly be delivered in a room like this?

She couldn't make herself step through the doorway.

"This is just temporary. They're remodeling the real waiting room on the main level," Greg explained, misunderstanding her hesitation. "It's supposed to be done next week."

"Hopefully, I won't still be waiting by then," Emily replied sourly, and she forced herself to walk in.

"No way," Greg assured her. Then he realized her comment had been sarcastic and bit his lip. "I'll go find the Surgical Liaison," he said, deserting her.

And so Emily sat and waited some more.

Jack, Jack, Jack, her brain chanted, the words becoming a prayer. She wondered when the accident had taken place, and what time it had been when she'd gotten the call from the police. Was it thirty minutes ago? An hour? More? It seemed a lifetime that she had borne the weight of this tragedy — or *potential* tragedy. No one had yet told her that Jack was in serious danger. A small light flickered inside of her, the hope that Jack was okay, that whatever surgery had been undertaken had been minor — a small gash, a broken bone, a twisted ankle.

Her lips twisted into a smile. Jack would love to have a scar to show off to his golfing buddies. She could imagine him wearing it with pride, like a medal won in battle, and telling the boys the story of the accident in excruciating detail over beers in the clubhouse after a game.

Then time stopped.

Part of Emily wanted to scream with impatience — Jack's life might be hanging in the balance while she sat waiting in utter ignorance and frustration. Wasn't there something she could do?

But part of her welcomed the slow passage of the minutes, because when this time was over, she knew there was a real possibility that Jack's life and her own might be changed irrevocably. What if he did end up like the man in the wheelchair?

Think of the positive side, she told herself. First, Jack was *alive*, that much was certain, because they were operating on him at this very minute. Second, the chances of him having had a serious accident were slim, because there couldn't have been many cars out that early on a Saturday morning, and because the stock brokerage where he worked was closed on the weekends. So it was unlikely that he had been distracted by his cell phone, a worry that plagued her during the week.

Footsteps echoed in the hallway, heavy, booted steps, slowly drawing closer. Instinctively, Emily glanced around the empty room looking for a way to escape what was coming. But there was nowhere to run, nowhere to hide. She felt humbled by the profound helplessness of her situation, her vulnerability. Any second now she would discover Jack's fate — and her own. Unconsciously, she rose to her feet.

A police officer appeared in the doorway. He was a big man, too tall and bulky for this underground bunker, and he looked out of place, like a grown-up entering a child's playhouse. He held his hat and a clipboard. "Mrs. Barnes?" he asked. Emily nodded. "They told me you'd be down here. I'm Sgt. Ray Wilson, Clearview Police." He hesitated, stiffening as though he, too, dreaded this confrontation.

They stared at each other awkwardly, until the silence that held them captive was broken by a low rumble emanating from Emily's stomach. She pushed against her abdomen with her fist to muffle the sound, but it only growled louder. She blushed. He smiled. The ice was broken.

Sgt. Wilson ducked under the low overhang of the door and walked into the room. "Can I get you something to eat, ma'am? A donut, some tea?"

"No, thank you, nothing. What about Jack? Is he all right? Please, nobody's told me anything."

Sgt. Wilson gestured to the bank of seats. "Let's sit down, Mrs. Barnes. I'm going to start at the beginning and tell you what I know. Then I'll want to ask you some questions. But ... we should sit down."

Emily sat. Sgt. Wilson sat next to her, carefully arranging his long legs so that they did not touch hers. He held up his clipboard and flipped back the first page. His voice was a low monotone. "The incident occurred at 8:53 A.M. on Saturday, the sixteenth of February, at the intersection of ..." He stopped and looked at Emily. "Aw, hell, why don't I just tell you in my own words?"

She nodded. "Please."

"Well, according to the driver of the other vehicle —"

Emily gasped. So there had been another car, another person involved, someone with whom they would now be intrinsically bound.

" — who was uninjured in the impact, by the way — your husband was driving east on Jessup, just coming up to Dover, where the on-ramp is to 138. He may have been going a tad over the limit, the other driver wasn't sure. But in any event, it seems a dog ran into the street in front of the vehicle, and the driver, your husband, swerved so's not to hit it. He must have lost concentration, thinking about the animal, because instead of braking at the stop there at Jessup and Dover, he hit the gas and collided with the second vehicle."

He looked down at his notes. "It was a sixteen-wheel Pepsi delivery van, in motion at the time, and, well, it doesn't look like your husband was wearing his seat belt because he was thrown through the windshield. Paramedics were called by a witness, the owner of the dog, I believe, and they arrived at 9:07."

Emily remembered having heard the distant sound of a collision just before she began her morning run, and a whimper of animal agony escaped her throat, echoing in the tomblike room. She quickly put both hands over her mouth, pressing hard to keep her heart from bursting out. Had that been Jack's accident? Could fate be so cruel? It seemed like one of those grisly stories on the evening news — palatable as curiosities because the media transformed them into entertainment.

But this was no news story. This was her life. And Jack's.

"I'm sorry to be having to tell you this, ma'am," Sgt. Wilson said softly. "Believe me, it isn't easy. My 82-year-old father was involved in a collision last year. A bad one. And he hasn't fully —" He stopped himself. "Sorry, you don't want to hear about my personal life." He laid his hand gently on Emily's knee. "Now you just nod when you're ready, and I'll tell you the rest."

A look of horror flashed across Emily's face. There was more? She took two shallow breaths in quick succession, then nodded.

"Okay then." He flipped to another page on his clipboard and read, "The paramedic's report states that when they arrived at the scene, they found the victim's body on the pavement, partially wedged beneath the rear right wheel of the van. He was unconscious but breathing. They said ..." he stopped again, unsure whether or not to continue. "Maybe you should hear this from the doctor, Mrs. Barnes. Why don't we wait for him? I don't want to give you any wrong impressions."

"What? What is it? I still don't know — I mean, he's alive isn't he? They brought him here, they're operating on him, so he must be alive! Tell me!" She was on her feet and screaming at him now. "Tell me!"

"Yes, Mrs. Barnes, your husband is alive," a voice said softly.

Both Emily and Sgt. Wilson turned. A doctor stood in the doorway, head, body, and feet swathed in surgical greens. The only clue that the doctor was a woman was the feminine tone of her voice.

Her face was expressionless. She shuffled across the room in her paper surgical slippers and held out her hand to Emily. "I'm Dr. Leventhal. Andrea Leventhal, Mrs. Barnes. I was on duty when your husband was brought in."

"You operated on him?"

"My team is working on him now. They're still in the O.R. I came out to tell you what's going on." Although the doctor spoke softly and with an edge of fatigue, her voice did not falter. Emily understood that she was used to talking about life and death and injury and surgery, the way other women discussed dress designers and recipes and children's play habits, and she was grateful for this.

The doctor sat down beside Emily so that they were at eye level, woman to woman. "I can tell you that he *was* breathing independently when he was brought in, although of course we have him intubated during surgery. And despite the trauma of the injuries and the loss of blood, his heart seems to be undamaged, pumping strongly." Seeing the hope welling up in Emily's eyes, she continued, "That isn't necessarily good news, Mrs. Barnes. The fact is, the right limbs of your husband's body are gravely damaged. His spleen and his right kidney were ruptured, and he sustained a fracture to his skull. We don't know yet if there has been any injury to the brain, because we are completely occupied with damage control. He is in a coma. If we are able to keep him alive, and that is *if*, the coma could be temporary, or it could be permanent. I'm very sorry." She paused. "Is there anything you want to ask me?"

"How bad is the damage to his limbs? He loves to play golf...."

The doctor looked startled. She turned away, composed herself, and then faced Emily again. "I'm sorry, Mrs. Barnes. I guess I wasn't clear enough. His right arm and leg were crushed. There was no possible way to ..." she trailed off. Then she began again, "What we're trying to do is keep him alive. When he stabilizes, we'll salvage what we can."

Salvage? What a horrid word to use, as though Jack were a piece of furniture or an old appliance in a junkyard. Emily's mind was reeling. She needed to focus on something else. "What about the driver of the truck?"

"To my knowledge, he wasn't brought here. Officer, do you have any information?"

Sgt. Wilson skimmed his notes. "He was treated at the site of the collision for minor abrasions and released by paramedics. I'll give you his name and number. Your insurance company will want it."

The doctor stood. "If there's nothing else, I'd better get back in there. A nurse will be along shortly to get some information from you, your husband's medical history, health insurance, that sort of thing. If there's anyone you want to call, just ask the nurse and she will find you a phone." She looked around the room. "I'm sorry they've brought you down here. It's terribly depressing, I know. They're remodeling the real waiting room upstairs. It's going to be very nice."

"Can I see him?"

"Not yet, I'm sorry. We have a lot of work to do. Let's see how the surgery goes, Mrs. Barnes. Let us do what we can for him right now."

"But what if ..." Emily was unable to finish the sentence.

"You wouldn't want to see him the way he is right now. I know it's very hard, but I am going to ask you to trust me on this. I understand how you must feel, truly I do. I will come to get you, I promise, as soon as he's stabilized, or if he seems ... to be slipping. Why don't you go up to the cafeteria and have something to eat? I'll have the nurse find you up there."

"Thank you, Doctor, no. I'll wait here. I'll be all right," Emily replied.

Sgt. Wilson stood and adjusted his holster. "Dr. Leventhal, can I have a word?" He turned to Emily. "I'll be getting along too, Mrs. Barnes." He took a card from his shirt pocket. "I'm going to be at the station writing up my report. If you want to talk to me, please feel free to call me at this number."

"Thank you, Sergeant. I appreciate it."

He nodded and followed Dr. Leventhal out the door. As their footsteps receded down the hall, their voices were muffled by the cement walls. Still, Emily heard the words "shock" and "damn sad" and "tragedy." Or did she just imagine it? She looked at her watch. It was twelve minutes after eleven. Impossible. She shook it and held it to her ear. Sure enough, it was ticking. She looked around the room for a clock, some confirmation that in the space of a few hours, Jack's life and her own had altered irrevocably, more dramatically than in all of the thirty-eight years that had proceeded them. But there was no clock on the wall. No art either. Nor any windows. Nothing in this cell to distract or reassure her, except a low table, strewn with tattered copies of *Fishing World* and *Health Care Today,* and a Mr. Coffee burbling with stale caffeine. Again, she hunkered down to wait.

At two-twenty, she called Ann.

By then, with the help of a highly efficient and kindly nurse, Emily had filled out half a dozen forms, drunk four cups of coffee, visited the ladies room twice, and gotten word from Dr. Leventhal that Jack was still in surgery, that they were doing everything they could to keep him alive.

At one point an orderly brought in a small bag containing Jack's personal effects. The blue shirt was not there, but miraculously his watch, the Seiko chronograph she'd bought him for their third anniversary, was, and it was still ticking. The crystal was covered with dried flecks of blood which had now turned black. She picked at them with her thumbnail, concentrating her mind and energy on this task, as though Jack's survival depended on it. And in this way, she maintained an outward semblance of her usual controlled, quiet demeanor, while inside her emotions churned.

But the moment she saw Ann's frizzy red hair — the orange juice cans had apparently not worked — she broke down. The tears came slowly at first, a trickle out of one eye, then the other.

"Oh, honey," Ann wailed, "I am so desperately sorry. In my whole life, this is the worst thing I've ever heard!" She ran across the room and threw her arms around Emily, pulling her close, squeezing hard. The pressure seemed to rupture something inside of Emily, and her weeping escalated into gut-wrenching sobs, the trickle of tears into a torrent.

"I can't believe this," she managed to sputter.

"I know! It's incredible! I mean, accidents happen a million times a day, but when it happens to someone you love — my God! Let it out, Em, just release it, let it go."

The two women clung to each other, rocking slowly, until Emily's tears were spent. She was exhausted. "Oh, God, look what I've done to your shirt," she sighed. "It's probably ruined." She patted the spot, which was wet and streaked with mascara. "I'm sorry."

"It's okay. I've been wanting to get one of those DKNY button-downs, but I couldn't justify the expense while I still had this one. So now I can go for it." She smiled bravely, but frowned again when Emily didn't smile back. "How is he? What does the doctor say?"

"I don't know. He's been in surgery all this time. Ann, I am so scared. She said the right side of his body was ... crushed." Her voice caught. "It hurts just to say that," she whispered. "And what does it mean? How badly can he be hurt and still be alive?"

"All I know is that the human body is pretty damn amazing," Ann said firmly. "And you know Jack. He's not going to take this lying down. Oh, for God's sake. You know what I mean."

Emily nodded, clinging to the hope Ann was offering. "No one's more of a fighter than Jack."

○

But as she stood next to his bed later that night, she realized that all the fight had gone out of Jack. He was alive, yes, but at what cost? Only his head, neck, and shoulders were visible above the bedsheets, and most of what she could see was swaddled in tight white bandages. Under the sheets, the lump that was his torso appeared obscenely off balance, his neck and head gruesomely closer to the right side than the left, and from the middle down, the lump became so very, very narrow.

How much of a human body could you hack away before the essence of "self" was destroyed?

Tubes and wires connected him to a bank of machines, their monitors displaying the only proof that Jack was actually living. Emily ached to touch him, to shake him out of this nightmare into wakefulness, but at the same time she was repelled and afraid. Who would tell him what had happened? Or deep in his sleeping soul, did he already know the drastic toll that had been extracted to save his life? She wished Ann were here, but Ann still belonged to the real world, the one where people ate and slept and interacted with others. She had gone to pick up Fiber and take him to her condo at the beach. Then she'd promised to make a few calls to Emily's and Jack's closest friends, to let them know what had happened. Emily had thanked her, but without emotion. The world outside of the hospital had ceased to exist for her. All that mattered was Jack and this stark room, and waiting for him to open his eyes.

"Mrs. Barnes, you're still here."

Dr. Leventhal stood in the doorway. She was now wearing a blue blazer, turtleneck, and jeans, and she looked as tired as any other 45-year-old woman who'd had a long, hard day at work. Without the identifying mantle of surgical greens and stethoscope, she seemed less formidable. Emily's heart leapt at the gentle sound of her voice, and she smiled bravely.

"I want to be here in case he wakes up," Emily whispered.

"He's so highly medicated, he'll be out for at least twenty-four hours," Dr. Leventhal said. "And we'll try to keep him out longer than that if we can. We've given him a strong cardiac medicine to try to get his heart to pump blood into his brain. But there's so much swelling in the cranium that the pressure is keeping the blood out. At this stage, the best thing is for him to be completely still, and for the machines to do the work, so his body can use all of its resources to heal. We won't know anything for at least a couple of days. Please go home and get a few hours of rest."

"Dr. Leventhal, what are his chances?"

The doctor sighed. "I'm always reluctant to answer that question. If I'm optimistic, the family gets their hopes up, so if the patient doesn't pull through it's even harder for them. But if I'm pessimistic, everyone loses faith, and I sometimes think the patient *feels* that, and he or she loses the will to live.

"What I can tell you is this — he lost a great deal of blood; we had to give him five liters. And the trauma from the amputation of an arm and a leg —"

Emily cringed. She couldn't help it. The doctor had already told her that they had been forced to remove Jack's limbs, but she couldn't get her mind around that thought. Even if he lived, he would be horribly disfigured, an invalid, the kind people pity and turn away from, literally half a man.

" — is severe. As far as his head injury, we still don't know very much. It's remarkable that his vital signs are as stable as they are. He's a very strong man. I hope you are strong too."

○

Time forgotten, Emily sat staring at Jack, willing him to live. But it was the old Jack she wanted, and she had to come to grips with the fact that he no longer existed. Who would this new, diminished Jack be?

She tried to form a mental image of him as an invalid. To be sure, some people rose to the occasion — the headlines were rife with stories about paraplegics and physically challenged survivors who accomplished miracles, who were grateful for their salvaged lives and made the most of each second. But would Jack be so heroic? She couldn't visualize him in a wheelchair, nor herself pushing one.

She felt a gentle hand on her arm and looked up. A young doctor stood in front of her. Who was he? How long had he been there?

"Hi, Mrs. Barnes," he said. "I'm Danny Delany. I'm a resident and I was on duty when your husband came in, so I scrubbed in on his surgery."

Emily said nothing, so he continued. "Dr. Leventhal paged me and asked me to sit with your husband tonight so you can go home and get some sleep."

"No, thank you, I couldn't leave him."

"That's what Dr. Leventhal said you'd say. But you should go, just for a few hours. Tomorrow will be an important day. You'll want to have all of your energy, maybe a fresh change of clothes. I won't leave his side, I swear. And we'll call you right away if there's a change."

Emily looked at him searchingly. "I promise," he said. And something about the way he said it made her believe him.

She bent down and kissed Jack's forehead, letting her lips linger there until she could no longer abide the coldness of his skin, the lack of response. " 'Night, darling," she managed to whisper. "Hey, I'll stop by Sergio's in the morning and bring you a breakfast burrito, okay?"

She lingered another minute, then turned and left the room, feeling she should not go, but going nevertheless. She walked slowly down the hall toward the bank of elevators. Once away from Jack, fatigue struck her with the force of a blow across her back. She willed herself to put one foot in front of the other, promising herself that she could rest while she waited for the elevator to arrive.

But this time, the car appeared as though on cue. Emily stepped in and automatically turned to the front. She stared at the floor buttons for a long moment, unseeing.

"Believe it or not, it can't read your mind," slurred a voice behind her.

"What? Oh, sorry," she mumbled. She couldn't think where she wanted to go, or why.

"What floor?" the voice asked. It was breathless, vaguely familiar. She turned her head, and there was the man in the wheelchair, the same one she'd spoken with earlier when she was that other person, the woman she was before Jack's accident. What had the orderly called him, the Tin Man? He was wearing a shirt which was unbuttoned and hung open over his gaunt frame, pajama bottoms, and slippers.

"My car's at the Emergency entrance," she managed to say. Would it still be there, or had it been towed? Just as well if it had. Emily did not relish the idea of driving; she doubted that she would ever enjoy riding in a car again.

"Then you want One. Turn left out of the elevator, go to the end of the hall, and you'll see the signs."

"Thank you," Emily mumbled, and pushed the button for the first floor.

"How'd it go today?" the man asked. His speech was oddly thick. Could he be drunk? As though in response to her unspoken question, he said, "The damn medication. Mouth feels like I've been eating cardboard, so dry, y'know?"

She didn't answer. She had no energy to waste being polite to this tragic man. She had her own tragedies to think about.

"Not so good, eh? This is a tough place, very tough," he commiserated, his words seeming to bubble out of his mouth. "My heart goes out to you." Then he laughed, a giggle really, which ended in a sloppy gasp. "My heart goes out to you," he repeated, throwing his arms open wide. "As though it'll do you any good."

Emily stared at the man's exposed chest. Every rib was visible, his pale skin drawn tight against each. But just below his rib cage, beneath a grotesque tapestry of scars, a monstrous growth bulged as though about to erupt from his body. She averted her eyes.

The elevator door opened on the fifth floor and two orderlies got in, shaking their heads. "Hey, Tin Man, what's up?" one of them asked. "You know, you should be in your room. It's after midnight. What are you trying to do, kill yourself?"

"No," the man snorted, "that's *your* job. I'm just trying to make it through the night."

"Don't mind him, ma'am," the orderly said to Emily, punching the button for the fourth floor. "He's just a little ornery."

"Wouldn't you be if you were in my shoes, or should I say slippers? Came into this place, I was 6'2", 200 pounds, and now look at me!"

The orderly rolled his eyes at Emily. "Sure, you were, Tin Man, and I'm Tom Cruise."

"Yeah? And here I thought Tom Cruise was a white guy."

"Say what? Then you must be color-blind," said Jimmy, grinning.

The elevator doors opened on Three. "I got 'im," the second orderly said. "I'll meet you in the cafeteria when I get 'im strapped in."

"Ooh," the man gurgled, "he's going to tie me up! I love it when they do that."

The orderly rolled his eyes. "Come on, Tin Man, out you go," he said. He tried to push the wheelchair out the door, but the man was using all of his strength to hold down the hand brake.

"I just want to ride a little longer, talk to this nice lady. Have a heart," he wheezed.

"That's a good one, Tin Man. I sure do wish I had one to give you," the orderly said, prying his hand loose from the brake and finally wheeling the chair out the door.

"*Good night, Irene, good night, Irene, I'll see you in my dreams,*" he sang in gasping breaths as the elevator doors slowly closed.

"Our resident character," Jimmy explained. "Sometimes they get him so drugged he don't know which way is up. You're lucky. One night last week we found him in this here elevator naked as a jaybird. And lemme tell you, that's a sight you can do without! But it's just the drugs. He's harmless really, a good-hearted guy." He smiled sadly and shook his head. "A good-hearted guy," he repeated.

Emily was silent. The man and his troubles were of no consequence to her. She had enough to think about.

The elevator doors opened again. "You gettin' out on One, ma'am?"

○

She didn't consciously plan it, but somehow she ended up parked on Jessup at the on-ramp to 138. She watched the intersection for some minutes, her warm, tense breath drawing misty designs on the windshield. The streets were deserted at this early morning hour, only an occasional car emerging from the sleeping neighborhood, streaking by to join the night traffic on the highway. What did she hope to find in this empty intersection? The Mustang and the Pepsi van had been towed away, the street itself cleared of debris. There was no sign of the tragedy that had taken place here, no trace at all.

Emily knew she should go home, tried to will her hand to reach up and turn the key in the ignition. But it was as though some vital synapse had been broken. She could only sit there, staring at the street, her pragmatic nature demanding that she process every detail firsthand, to try to fill in the blanks and force it all into a formula that added up.

Because in her mind, it made no sense. Jack was not connected to the broken body lying motionless in that hospital bed. He was still the whole man he'd been when he'd bent to kiss her good-bye that morning, full of energy and the elixir of aftershave. They had planned to have an early dinner out and to go to a movie, their usual Saturday night entertainment. Monday he was scheduled to fly to Scottsdale for a meeting, and they had talked about her going along, but she had been reluctant to take the time away from her own work. Thursday he was supposed to meet his parents' cruise ship when it docked in San Diego and then drive them to their home in Oceanside.

Jack's parents. Somebody had to tell them what had happened.

And her own parents.

And Jonah.

Ann was making calls to a few friends, but Emily would have to tell the family herself. How would she find the words? Was it better to wait and see if Jack survived and risk their anger at being denied such portentous news? Or should she tell them now and force them to bear the grief that much longer? And how could she possibly tell Jack's mother that her son was hovering near death? Amelia Barnes was a frail eighty-one. She would probably have a stroke.

A car swept by, and as it passed, its headlights reflected a fragment of light, glimmering like a jewel in the gutter. A shard of glass? A bit of broken fender or dashboard? Certain that it was some talisman of the accident, a clue as to why it had happened, she leapt out of her car and ran to retrieve it. But by the time she got to the spot, it was lost again in the darkness.

Falling to her knees, she groped for the shard, desperately sifting through the debris, muddying her clothes, her shoes, her hands, becoming more and more frantic with each passing moment. But without light, it was invisible. She had to wait until another car passed before she saw it again, revealed in the glare of headlights. There! She leapt toward the spot where it gleamed, and she knelt to grasp it.

It was the new plastic key card for the country club gate. She pressed it to her heart.

○

Emily pulled into the driveway as dawn was breaking. It was her favorite time of day. On a normal morning she would be up by now, going through her pre-workout routine. Jack would be in the kitchen, preparing his orange that funny way he did— slicing off both ends first, then cutting the rest into smile-size sections, so he could put each segment in his mouth and rip the pulp off of the skin. As she passed him on her way out to run, his good-bye kiss would be tart and fresh with citrus. The memory of it made her mouth water.

Maybe she would go for a run. She certainly wasn't going to go to bed at this hour, and the exercise would clear her mind. Her spirits rose in anticipation of the endorphin rush of exercise and the comfort of ritual.

The phone began to ring just as she unlocked the door. Caught off guard, she picked it up without thinking.

"Hello?"

"Mrs. Barnes? This is Marlee Masterson at Westside Medical Center. There's been a change in your husband's status. We think you should come right over."

"What kind of change? What is it? Tell me!"

"He opened his eyes, Mrs. Barnes, and he asked for you. This is highly unusual so soon after surgery. We thought you'd want to know. Please hurry."

3

*T*wenty minutes later, when Emily reached the hospital, breathless and bursting with hope, she was told that Jack was back in surgery.

"How can that be?" she railed at the floor nurse. "They called me. They told me his eyes were open and that his condition had improved!"

The nurse took Emily's hands in both of hers and squeezed them with professional compassion. "Mrs. Barnes, we are doing all we can for him. I think you'd agree that the fact that your husband is still alive is an indication of that. He is in one of the finest hospitals in the country, with a team of some of the most brilliant doctors in the world at his side. They are doing whatever is humanly possible."

"I'm not stupid," Emily cried.

"No, dear, I don't think you are," the nurse said evenly.

"Then why won't you tell me the truth? Where is Jack? Where is he?"

"I *am* telling you the truth. Your husband is in surgery."

The room began to spin, the nurse's face fading in and out of focus. The thin lifeline of optimism that Emily had been clinging to suddenly snapped, leaving her suspended in midair like a cartoon character who runs off a cliff, then realizes her feet are still moving, but there is no ground beneath her. "They made me go home," she wailed. "I would have stayed. I wanted to be here." Bright lights, snatches of conversation, the smell of antiseptic, and the vision of Jack's diminished body all flooded Emily's senses. "I don't think I can do this," she heard herself whisper. And then, merciful darkness.

$\circlearrowleft$

The pillow beneath her head was deliciously plush and firm. She burrowed her face into it and tried to pull the protective blanket of sleep up around her. But relentless fingers of yellow light were prying at her eyes, and pain pounded an alarm in her head. Reluctantly she allowed herself to wake, blinking hard to bring the room into focus.

She was facing a window, but through it saw only sky and clouds. Where was her beautiful coral tree, the one she and Jack had planted full grown when they'd bought the house, as an extravagant paean to their marriage? They'd chosen to buy the tree which they loved, rather than the living room furniture which they needed, because it symbolized the growing life force which was their relationship. They had planted it so it would be visible from their bedroom window, and Emily had started every day of her marriage to Jack looking at it.

She rolled over on her back and looked around the room, trying to get her bearings. It was a square and starkly furnished white space, with just a bed and a nightstand, two drab green leatherette chairs under the window, and a small television bracketed near the ceiling of the facing wall. That was the dead giveaway. She was not in her own bed, and this was no hotel or guest room. The only place she knew where televisions were suspended from the walls was a hospital.

The instant the word "hospital" formed in her brain, she remembered Jack, and the weight of despair pressed on her heart. *Jack! Was he still in surgery?* She looked at her watch. One o'clock. When had she fainted? It couldn't have been later than six o'clock, because it had still been dark when she'd arrived at the hospital. Was it possible that she'd slept for seven hours?

She leapt from the bed and her stockinged feet slid on the polished floor. She struggled to keep her balance. Where were her shoes? Clutching the bed frame for support, she looked around the room. No shoes, no jacket, no purse.

Still in her stockinged feet, Emily pulled open the door and ran out into the hallway, so focused on finding Jack that she didn't see the wheelchair parked there. Its side arm caught her in the groin, and with a grunt, she fell across the lap of the occupant.

"Nice running into you again," a man said as she struggled to right herself. The voice was familiar. It was the patient the attendants called the Tin Man.

"Three times in twenty-four hours," he observed. "I've got to think that this is more than a coincidence."

His presence was merely an obstacle, a blur in Emily's consciousness. She looked down the hall in both directions.

"Can I help you find what you're looking for? It's a pretty simple system — "

"My husband was in surgery when I got here this morning. I need to find out where he is."

"There's a big board by the nurse's station, kind of a flow chart to keep track of the patients. Come on, I'll show you."

"It's okay, I'll find it."

Emily jogged up the hall, trying to ignore the fact that the man in the wheelchair was keeping pace with her. Somewhere along the line he had shed the metal tree that had slowed him the day before.

"What happened to him?" he panted.

"Automobile accident," she replied.

"Bad one?" He caught himself. "As though there's such a thing as a good one! Poor guy. What's the prognosis?"

"Look, mister," Emily said, slowing to navigate past a food cart blocking the hall, "I don't mean to be rude, but I can only concentrate on one thing, and that's my husband, Jack. So just let me be."

He stopped pushing and sat up straight. The chair slowed to a stop. "Sorry," he said. "I didn't mean to be heartless, but ... it's a problem in my condition."

Emily wasn't listening. Ahead she saw the nurse she had spoken with when she came in. "Nurse, excuse me!" she called.

"Mrs. Barnes! I was just coming to wake you." The nurse smiled. "Are you feeling better?"

"What about Jack? Is he out of surgery?"

There was a barely perceptible pause before the nurse spoke, and in that instant of silence, Emily's world began to implode. "I believe the surgery is over, yes," the nurse said carefully. "Why don't you come into the lounge, and —"

"No! I waited all day yesterday. I'm not — " Her voice quavered with the effort it took to maintain control. "I can't wait any more. Do you understand?"

"Yes, I do," the nurse said kindly. "I understand. I'll just page Dr. Leventhal and she will be here as soon as she can," she continued firmly. "She asked me to call her the instant you woke up. Please, Mrs. Barnes." She gestured across the hall. "There's a nice room just over there. Do help yourself to a cup of coffee or some juice. I'll get the doctor right now." And she hurried off.

Having no other choice, Emily dragged herself into the lounge. It was a patient room with the bed removed and a few of the green leatherette chairs installed. A doorway led to a bathroom, and suddenly Emily realized how badly she needed to use it.

After she had relieved herself, she washed her hands in the sink and looked at her reflection in the mirror. The face that stared back at her had her features, but they were distorted by anguish into the visage of a stranger — hair mashed against forehead, lips cracked and dry, skin sallow, mouth drooping. Her teeth were so filmy, she imagined she could see decay beginning to eat away at them. Her eyes were dull with exhaustion, puffy from crying, devoid of hope.

Emily splashed cold water on her cheeks, then smoothed down her hair with her wet fingers. She was still wearing her clothes from the morning before, and they were wrinkled, sweat dampened, and dirty from her hunt in the gutter at the accident site. She did what she could to make herself presentable and stepped back into the lounge.

The first thing she saw was the Tin Man, stationed next to the window, a magazine open on his lap. He held it up so she could see the cover. "*People,*" he told her. "The hospital only gets one copy, so every week I have to track it down. I read it to remind myself that there really is a world out there. I've been in for fifteen issues this round."

Emily didn't respond.

He held out a roll of candy. "Lifesaver?"

"No."

She wanted to scream at him to go away, but she didn't have the energy. And besides, she didn't want to *be* alone right now. So she sat in the chair furthest from him and rested her head in her hands, staring down at the floor between her stockinged feet.

The man began to drum his fingers against the armrests of his chair, beating a staccato rhythm. Emily was wound so tightly that even this slight sound, a vibration really, was an impossible irritation. She glared at the man, and he stopped abruptly.

"Sorry," he said. "Nervous habit."

Emily wondered what *he* had to be nervous about. She was the one climbing the walls. Staring at him, she noticed the odd bulge in his abdomen, still protruding, but now covered by a loose shirt, and she thought about Jack's mangled body and amputated limbs. What kind of prosthesis would he have to be fitted for ...

"Mrs. Barnes."

Emily recognized Dr. Leventhal's gentle voice and turned, searching for her future in the woman's eyes. All she could see was fatigue, faint lines of it drawn at the corners of the doctor's eyes, and smudges of mascara under her lower lids.

The doctor looked at the man in the wheelchair. "Do you mind giving us some privacy?" she asked quietly.

He shook his head and rolled the chair toward Emily. He took her hand and put something into it, a hard cylinder, and closed her fingers around it. "Good luck," he said, and wheeled himself out the door.

Dr. Leventhal sighed and lowered herself into a chair as though her body ached. She met Emily's gaze unflinchingly. "He didn't make it, Mrs. Barnes. His brain activity has ceased. He's gone."

Her words seemed to hang suspended in a crystalline arc, the way a wave holds its shape for a split second before crashing on the shore.

"Are you sure?" Emily blurted out stupidly. Her voice trembled. "I thought ... they called and told me he was better, that he had opened his eyes and asked for me."

"We wanted to be hopeful, Mrs. Barnes, but I will tell you now, it would have been a medical miracle if he had survived more than a couple of days. The injuries were catastrophic. I am so very sorry if I ... if we led you to believe otherwise. Do you want to hear the details?"

Emily thought for a moment, then shook her head. "No. Not now."

That was all she could say. The earth's orbit had ground to a halt. She couldn't see or hear or think or feel. A kind of numbness overtook her, as though in sympathy for Jack her heart and mind were mimicking his death.

Then, surprisingly, she felt Dr. Leventhal reach into her lap and take her hands, squeezing them firmly between her own, rubbing them, drawing her back to life. Emily didn't speak, she just held on. Instead of thinking about Jack, she concentrated on how elegant the doctor's fingers were, how delicate and dry, slender and strong, and scrupulously clean, with nails trimmed down to the quick. Her own fingers were short and stubby, the nail polish cracked, the cuticles dry.

They sat like that for a long time, neither woman speaking or moving, emotion flowing between them. Emily didn't cry, and later, when she tried to recall her thoughts at that moment, her only memory was of space. It was as though her soul had gone in search of Jack.

A nurse appeared at the door. "Dr. Leventhal — " Without taking her eyes off of Emily, the doctor shook her head briskly, and the nurse went away.

Finally, after a space of time that could have been five seconds or five thousand years, Emily took a deep breath and sat back in her chair. "Thank you," she said. "I think I'm okay, for now." Dr. Leventhal nodded and let go of her hands.

"What do I do?" Emily whispered.

"Just sit here for a while. I'm going to send someone in to talk to you, to explain the options, to help you make plans. There are some decisions you'll have to consider immediately."

The doctor stood and looked down at Emily. "Maybe I shouldn't say this, but I have a feeling you're a strong woman, Mrs. Barnes, so I will. It is very easy for any person, but particularly for a caring person to be overwhelmed by tragedy, especially when it strikes so suddenly. I've seen death completely destroy the lives of those who are left behind, and I hope that doesn't happen to you. As a doctor, and as a woman who has also lost a husband, I want to tell you that it will ultimately be your decision, something you consciously choose, whether or not this ordeal defeats you. Life should go on,

Mrs. Barnes, as hard as it may be to believe it now. I sincerely hope yours will."

She reached into her pocket and took out a card. "This has my office and home phone numbers on it. Call me if you need to talk." When Emily took it, the doctor held her hand an extra second, and looking into her eyes said, "I am profoundly sorry that our best was not good enough to keep your husband with you."

And then she was gone.

○

"Mrs. Barnes? I'm Elaine Greenberg. My sincere condolences to you."

Emily looked up, into the sympathetic eyes of a woman in her early 50s. She was plump, motherly, and attractively dressed in a loose-fitting wool dress and low-heeled shoes. Her glasses hung from a chain around her neck, and she was carrying a three-ring binder. "I see you've met our Tin Man," she said.

"What?"

She gestured to Emily's hand. Emily opened her fingers and saw she was holding a roll of Lifesaver candies. "He's not very subtle. But then, neither are we." The woman handed Emily her business card. It read, *Elaine Greenberg, Donor Liaison, The Organ Bank.* "Have you heard about TOB?" she asked. Emily shook her head. "Most people haven't, until they find themselves in your situation. That makes our job all the more challenging."

Was this the person Dr. Leventhal had sent to talk to her? "I'm not following you," Emily said. "Are you here to help me ..." her voice trailed off. To help her do what? Plan Jack's funeral? Plan the rest of her life without him?

"I'm here because *you* are in a position to help others, people whose lives depend on a gift you can give them. May I speak with you about it?"

Emily recoiled as though she had been struck. "Are you looking for a donation of some sort? Because if you are, your timing stinks! There's no way I can think about money. Don't you realize — "

"I'm not talking about money, Mrs. Barnes," Elaine Greenberg cut in. "I'm talking about your husband's body, his organs, his eyes, his skin. In the next few minutes, you need to make a very important decision, and that is whether or not you will give us permission to harvest the parts of your husband's body that are still vital, so that other critically ill patients can utilize them."

Understanding washed over Emily, and the color drained from her face. "My God, Jack just ... it's only been five minutes!" she sputtered. "Can't this wait?"

"As a matter of fact, no, it can't. We only have minutes from the time of brain death to do this work. A team is standing by now."

"A team of vultures?"

Elaine Greenberg persisted. "Mrs. Barnes, as grim as it must sound to you now, when a patient's brain — "

"His name is Jack Barnes!" Emily cried.

Elaine Greenberg composed herself. "I know it seems cruel to speak of this now, but we have no choice. Jack's brain is not functioning, which means *he* is dead. But his organs are still alive." She let the weight of this sink in, then continued in a softer tone. "Through you, your husband can save the lives of some and improve the lives of others. Perhaps it seems like a desecration; it's understandable if you think so now. But in fact, since the beginning of time, this is the way things have worked; in death, through decomposition or as sources of food, our bodies have contributed to the renewal of life. Consider the patient who has been existing on a dialysis machine. No matter how much money he has, he can't buy back good health. But *you* can give it to him by making your husband's remaining kidney available. And through that donation, a part of Jack will live on."

Emily hugged her stomach, bending forward so her head almost rested on her knees. "How can you ask me to make a decision like this?" she choked out.

"How can I *not* ask you? I'm sure it is the last thing you want to think about right now," Elaine Greenberg acknowledged, "but unfortunately the window of opportunity is very short. We can only keep some of the organs alive for four to five hours. That means we have to begin immediately in order to find recipients who match, and get them here and prepped for surgery."

Emily looked at the card. "Mrs. Greenberg, I haven't even seen Jack yet. What you're asking ... it's too big a decision for me to make right now. Besides, how could I? It doesn't seem like it's my right. It's Jack's body," she whispered, "not mine."

"But it's not a choice he can make now, Mrs. Barnes." Her voice was firm but gentle. "Whether or not it was his wish, it is now up to you as his next of kin to make the decision. I urge you to sign this paper. Please, Mrs. Barnes. I'm sorry to put it like this, but either way, as tragic as it is, your husband is not coming back. But because of his death, others can live."

Emily could not speak.

Mrs. Greenberg leaned closer to Emily's ear, her voice barely above a whisper. "If you could see the suffering — young people, children even. Mrs. Barnes, wouldn't you like to live the rest of your life knowing that your husband did not die in vain, that in dying he gave the ultimate gift? The last person I spoke to had just lost a daughter who was eight years old," Elaine Greenberg said softly. "Can you imagine how priceless her organs were to another child, and to that child's family?"

Still Emily did not respond.

"I'll give you a moment to think about it," Elaine Greenberg said. She stood, smoothing down her skirt. "I'm going to make a phone call. Then I'll be back."

As she left, the resident named Danny, who had spent the night with Jack, entered. His expression was somber, his eyes downcast.

"Mrs. Barnes, I just wanted to tell you how damn sorry I am," he said. Emily covered her face with her hands, but a sob escaped. He sat down next to her. "I don't know if it'll help or not, but I wanted you to know that I didn't leave your husband alone for one second last night. Not one. While I was with him we talked, y'know? He didn't say much, but I'm pretty sure he was listening. Sometimes you can feel it when they're listening."

He swallowed hard and continued. "I tried to explain to him all the procedures, what we were doing for him, so it wouldn't be a shock. And I told him that you and all the people who love him were waiting for him to get better. I asked him to hold on tight, to try as hard as he could to stay with you."

His voice broke, and he continued in a whisper, "But then later, I told him that if the fight was too rough or if there was too much pain, that you would understand and still love him, even if he let go. I'm pretty sure he heard me. I felt that he did. I hope that was okay. I hope I said the right thing."

"Yes, you did," Emily said softly.

"It was after that, about an hour later, that he opened his eyes. I couldn't believe it! Nothin' like that ever happened to me before. They told me he was ... nobody expected him to come out of it so soon. I rang for the nurse, and while I was waiting, he was moving his lips — it looked like he was trying to say something. Your name — it's Emily, something like that, isn't it?"

Emily nodded.

"I thought I heard Dr. Leventhal call you that. Anyways, it sure looked like he was trying to say it! So I told the nurse to call you. She didn't want to. I don't think she believed me. She said it was probably just a nerve spasm. But I thought we should give your husband the benefit of the doubt. So I insisted she make the call."

He looked bewildered, unsure. "Maybe I was wrong. But I just thought you should know what was going on." Emily nodded. She couldn't speak.

"After that," he lowered his head, "everything stopped. When Dr. Leventhal came, they took him into surgery again. And well, you know the rest." He breathed a heavy sigh. "I'm sorry we got your hopes up. It's my fault. I feel ... responsible. Like I made it worse for you."

Emily squeezed his hand in both of hers. "No. I'm glad you made them call me. I should never have left last night. I'm just glad ... I'm just glad he wasn't alone, that someone who cared was with him. Thank you so much."

Danny looked relieved. "All right then," he said, and he rose and left the room.

Alone again, so very alone, Emily tried to focus on what Elaine Greenberg had asked her. What would Jack want? What would he do in this situation?

There was no question. Jack was the most generous person she'd ever known. Some people were hoarders, some liked to collect things. But Jack was a giver. Once on a rainy night he'd literally taken the jacket off his back and given it to a homeless woman who'd been camped beneath the marquee outside the local theater, trying to keep dry under a sheaf of damp newspapers. There had been no motive for the gift, nothing to gain. It had been a spontaneous gesture of humanity. The woman did not thank Jack, and he had not mentioned it afterward. But Emily had never forgotten it, and she had loved Jack even more for his instinctive benevolence.

"Mrs. Barnes?"

Elaine Greenberg was back. She said nothing, just stood expectantly in front of Emily.

Emily sat up straight and looked into her eyes. "If I sign, who will get Jack's organs?"

"We keep that information confidential. Emotionally, it's better for both the donor family and for the recipients. I have a packet here for you that will explain everything."

"And if I don't sign?"

"Then I say thank you and leave you to make whatever arrangements you prefer for the disposal of the body."

Disposal of the body. Emily looked away. A minute passed, then another.

"Mrs. Barnes, please." Mrs. Greenberg said, her tone gentle but insistent.

"I need to see him first."

Mrs. Greenberg exhaled and her expression softened. "That can be arranged. I want you to know that we will take very good care of him. If you agree to the donation, we can still prepare the body for an open casket. No one will be able to tell."

Emily put her hands over her ears. Then she took a deep breath. "Please. I just want to see him."

Emily stared at Jack's face. It was the first time she had ever seen a dead body, and she was surprised that although it looked like Jack in every way, she did not feel him there. Physically, his body still existed, but psychically, he was no longer present.

His eyes were closed, and he was still bandaged, still hooked up to a multitude of machines. His body was hidden by a thin sheet. Part of her wanted to throw back the cover, to see for herself the extent of Jack's injuries. That was why she was here, wasn't it, to convince herself that Jack was dead? And then to say good-bye to him?

But she couldn't force her hand to grasp hold of the sheet. Instead, she felt an overwhelming need to protect him, to preserve his right to privacy, and to dignity.

She gasped — she'd seen movement, she was sure!

"OH MY GOD!"

There, again! She watched the sheet covering Jack's chest rise slightly, then fall, as he expelled air. Relief surged through her with the force of a tidal wave. "Nurse!" she bellowed. "He's alive!"

Her mind was racing a million miles a minute. *What I almost did!* she thought. "Jack? Darling, can you hear me?" She took his hand, her eyes focused on the rhythmic rise and fall of his chest.

"Mrs. Barnes? What is it?"

"He's alive — look! He's breathing! You were wrong — it was a terrible mistake! Oh, I can't believe this. How could you … I'm so glad that — " she stopped in mid- sentence. The nurse was shaking her head.

"I'm sorry, Mrs. Barnes. It's the machines. Your husband isn't breathing. He has suffered brain death. It's the respirator, it's keeping his body alive so the organs can be harvested."

"No, you're wrong. See? He's moving. I know he's alive — " Emily could not tear her eyes off of Jack.

"I'm terribly sorry, dear," the nurse said, shaking her head. "You should have been warned. Look here." She put her hand on Emily's shoulder and gently turned her so she was facing the bank of machines beside the bed. "Look at this monitor, Mrs. Barnes. It registers brain activity."

The monitor registered a thin, straight line.

"NO!"

"Yes, Mrs. Barnes. He is gone. There is no question about it. I'm so very sorry."

Emily turned back to Jack. Her legs trembled as the adrenaline rush subsided. She felt stranded on the brink of a precipice. What if they were wrong, with all of their sophisticated monitors and tests? What if Jack were still alive, still struggling valiantly to reach out to her through the cloying rapture of a coma?

But in her heart, she knew he wasn't. And more, she knew that as damaged as his body was, it was best that he wasn't. With sudden clarity, she knew she was making the right decision.

All that was left was to say good-bye.

But how could she? If only she could *talk* to him and know that he had heard her. One last time! The realization that she had missed the chance to say good-bye, to send him off with love, tore another ragged gash in her badly rent soul. What had been her last words to him when he'd left the house Saturday morning? Something about the key card for the gate at the Club. "Don't forget ... you won't be able to get in without it."

Why hadn't she told him that she cherished him, or thanked him for the love he had given her?

Now all she could do was stroke his pale face with a trembling hand. His expression was serene, the fine lines about his eyes and on his forehead now etched into a waxen mask. But he was cold to her touch, his skin the texture of an apple that had fallen from the tree, soft with imminent decay. She wanted to bring her lips down to kiss his, to caress the familiar cheek, but there was nothing familiar about the sensation of her fingers on his skin. And she understood with a certainty that transcended rational thought that the soul of the man she had lived with for four years, the husband she had loved and laughed with, cooked, cleaned, and cared for, wrapped her arms around on some nights and on others pulled away from, the essence of the man who had given her his name and free access to his body and heart, was not inside this empty hull lying before her. She did not know where Jack's valiant spirit had gone, but it was not here.

There was a tap on the door. Elaine Greenberg stuck her head in. "I'm sorry, Mrs. Barnes, but if you've said good-bye, we need to get started." Emily nodded, and with dry eyes, turned away.

4

*R*emarkably, the rest of the afternoon passed smoothly. There was a great deal of paperwork to get through, but the hospital staff was as adept in dealing with death as it was in saving lives. Wrapped in a cocoon of grief, Emily felt like a patient herself, and she silently she felt the world shift under her. She made no effort to think about what had happened, nor did she think about the future. Instead, she let herself drift on the current of the day, like a leaf borne down a rushing stream toward a waterfall.

Just after three o'clock, Ann appeared, her face for once pale and without makeup, her hair tamed into a severe ponytail. She was wearing a somber black jersey dress that Emily had never seen and high-heeled black Prada boots.

"Thanks for coming back," Emily said as Ann bent to hug her. She smelled of expensive perfume, Opium perhaps, or Joy. The scent cloyed at Emily's senses, and she had to stifle the reflex to gag.

"Are you kidding? Where else would I be?" Ann asked, squeezing Emily carefully as though she had been made physically frail by Jack's ordeal.

Emily clung to her, savoring the life force that flowed from Ann.

She touched the fabric of her dress. "I never saw this before," she said. "Is it new?"

"This? No, I've had it for years. There's hardly ever the right occasion to wear it, it's so funereal, but I thought it was perfect...." She caught herself. "Ohmygosh, I can't believe I said that!" She clapped her hand over her mouth.

Emily smiled weakly. "It's okay, Ann. I've been through death certificates, autopsy consents, organ donation agreements, undertaking contracts. Nothing's going to set me off now."

"It's a good thing," Ann chirped, "because you know me. My mouth is bigger than my brain, or at least it works twice as fast." She dumped her oversized handbag onto the table and sat down next to Emily. "I went by your house to get you some supplies. I didn't know what you'd need, so I brought a little of everything."

She reached into the bag and extracted a bottle of Evian and a packet of Kleenex, a makeup kit and hairbrush, Emily's address book, a bran muffin, a gray cardigan sweater, a pair of warm socks, and shockingly, a pair of black bikini panties. Emily looked at her questioningly. "I don't know about you," Ann whispered, "but sometimes it makes me feel better to wear sexy underwear."

She opened her notebook and uncapped a Mont Blanc fountain pen. "Now, we should start planning. I called Jerry's Cleaning Service and scheduled them to go to your house tomorrow. They would have gone today, but since it's Sunday, there would have been an extra charge, and I thought, why waste the money? There's plenty of time.

"Mary's started on a menu. Depending on what time the service is, we should have fairly substantial food, a buffet and some passed hors d'oeuvres. For some bizarre reason, funerals make people ravenous.

"Do you want it inside or out? Rain is a consideration, but your yard can accommodate a lot more people than your house. We've still got the heat lamps we used at the Hadley wedding. I'm sure

Crown Rents will let us keep them a few more days, in light of the circumstances. I'll put a call in to Mel. If not, Party Line will absorb the cost...."

Emily put her hands over her ears and lowered her head between her knees. Ann stopped in mid-sentence. "Em?" she gasped. "Are you all right? Shall I call a nurse?"

Emily sat up. "My God, Ann. I can't ... I haven't even ... I should ..." She took a deep breath. "What I'm trying to say is, I need to go to our safety deposit box tomorrow and look at Jack's will. I don't even know if he wants a funeral, let alone a *party* afterward."

"You can't go by what a document like that says! Maybe it sounds crass, but who knows what kind of mood he was in when he wrote it? It's up to the living to make those decisions. It's what *you* want. I know we can do a great — "

"Stop!" Emily interrupted, her voice shrill, and Ann did.

She collected herself, then said in a quieter voice, "I'm not a prospective client, so quit trying to sell me."

"But I'm only — " Ann started.

Emily waved her hands in front of Ann's face. "It's me, your partner! I appreciate what you're trying to do, but I'm not going to make any decisions about this today. I need to go slowly, to think it through. We can talk about it after I find out what Jack's will says."

Ann shook her head. "You know how hard it is to get a good staff together on short notice, and we have to give Sammy plenty of notice to make the burritos. Jack loved Sergio's. You have to have them."

"Jack won't be there, Ann. It's a funeral. *Jack's* funeral. I don't want to think about burritos right now, if you don't mind. I want to think about how my husband wants to be remembered. I want to think about how I'm going to cope with his death. Is that all right with you?" She regretted the shrillness in her voice, but her emotions were charting their own swift course now. It was all she could do to hang on for dear life.

Ann bowed her head, finally contrite. "I'm sorry, kiddo, you're right. You're absolutely 200 percent correct. I guess it's just easier for me to think about food than about Jack. Oh, Emily, he was such a great guy. I loved him too, you know, even if he did think I was an airhead. It's not like he was wrong in that department!" She burst into tears. Emily put her arm around her, and Ann nestled into them.

"Look at this," Ann sobbed. "I came here to comfort *you*!"

"You know what?" Emily said. "You are." And in a funny way, she was.

$$\circlearrowleft$$

Ann insisted that Emily spend the night at her condo, and Emily didn't object. The less she had to think about, the better, and what was the point of going to her own empty house where she would be besieged by ghosts in every room?

Before she and Jack married, on the nights Jonah spent with his father, Emily often stayed at Ann's. For one thing, her condo was right on the beach in San Mare. Although it was only a few miles away from Emily's house, waking there to the sound of crashing waves and the vistas of wide sandy beach inspired fantasies of far-off places — the coast of Mexico perhaps, or Portugal.

And that was what she needed now, a little time in fantasyland before she faced the reality of her new life.

When they walked in the door, Fiber ran to her, springing straight into the air as though his legs were pistons, kissing her right on the nose, then running circles around her, investigating the new batch of smells clinging to her body. It was his typical response, and it usually warmed Emily's heart. But tonight it made her cry. The dog had worshipped Jack, and he would miss their macho roughhousing and nightly games of catch. But more, Emily's tears came because she realized the dog had no idea that Jack was never coming back. Dogs had no concept of time. In their world, humans came and went without explanation. So to Fiber, Jack's death was no different than a trip to the supermarket.

Maybe that was the way to handle this new grief, to tell herself that if she waited, someday, sometime, Jack would return, carrying a load of groceries and some takeout food.

They sat on Ann's porch with glasses of white wine and a box of mini rice cakes between them, watching the winter sun drop into the ocean. The night was balmy for February, but still Emily and Ann wrapped blankets around themselves, more for comfort than for warmth. Fiber lay snuggled close to Emily, raising his head to watch each dog that passed on the path below them.

"What are you thinking?" Ann asked.

"That it's a relief not to have to explain this to Fi. He loved Jack so much." She stroked his head, and he looked at her appreciatively. "But how am I going to tell everyone else?" She cupped a hand to her ear as though it were a telephone receiver. "Hello, Judy? This is Emily. I'm fine, great. Well, actually I guess I'm not so great. See, Jack was in an accident yesterday, and to tell the truth, he died today. Yeah, really. Totally dead. Thanks, yeah, I'm sorry too. Well, gotta go. Let's do lunch soon." She looked at Ann helplessly. "How can I?"

"You can't, and you don't have to. All you have to do is make a list. Lew and Nancy will make the calls from the office. In fact, you don't even have to make the list. We can just go down the names in your address book. Do you have it on mail merge on your computer? Or better yet, we could e-mail the death announcement. I wonder what Amy Vanderbilt would say about that."

Emily frowned. "I still have to tell our families — Jack's parents are due back from their cruise on Thursday. Do I wire them on the ship and ruin their last four days, or do I wait until they dock and hit them with it then?" She set her wineglass down. "Can you imagine making that call? Either way it's going to be impossible."

"I see what you mean." Ann looked off at the horizon, and Emily knew what she was thinking, that she was glad *she* didn't have to make that call.

"And then my parents. Mom is in constant pain with her polymyalgia, and Dad's Alzheimer's is getting worse. Plus, he just had cataract surgery last Thursday. They're probably already wondering why I haven't called them since Friday to check on him. And what about Jonah?"

"At least Jack wasn't Jonah's real dad. If it were Matt, it would be much harder for him, don't you think?"

"Of course, but it's still going to upset his life. He's just at that age where he'll worry about me and be embarrassed if his friends treat him differently when they find out. And speaking of me, I have no idea where I stand. Financially, I mean. Jack took care of our joint affairs." She sighed and looked at the ocean. "This is so unreal. I can't help thinking it's a dream, and pretty soon I'll wake up with a raging headache, and my life will still be in one piece."

Ann reached for the cell phone and put it in Emily's lap. "You probably won't get through to the cruise line's office on a Sunday night anyway, so that just leaves two calls, Jonah and your folks. Why don't you bite the bullet and get them over with?"

"I suppose I should." Emily looked at the phone.

"I'll thaw us some dinner. Is Weight Watchers lasagna okay?"

"I'm not hungry," Emily replied, but Ann had gone in.

She looked at the phone. Her parents or her son, which would be less painful? She dialed her parents' number.

One ring.

Two rings.

Three rings.

And then, mercifully, the answering machine picked up. "Eunice and Edward can't come to the phone right now." Her mother's voice spoke the words as though she were reading the words from a book. "Please leave your name and telephone number, and we'll get back to you as soon as possible." Emily hung up. This wasn't the kind of message you could leave on your parents' answering machine.

She cleared the line and dialed again. "Oceancrest Middle School for the Arts, good evening," a voice answered.

"Yes, could you connect me to Winchester Hall please?"

"Thank you, hold on."

○

When Ann appeared again, holding two steaming plates of lasagna, paper napkins, and forks, the portable phone was back on the side table, and Emily was leaning against the railing looking out at the ocean. "Did you get through?" Ann asked.

"Nope." She took the plate Ann held out to her. "I got my parents' answering machine, and I forgot that Jonah is camping with Matt this weekend. He won't be back until curfew. Maybe I should drive up there and tell him in person. If I left now, I'd be there when he got back, and — "

"No way! I absolutely forbid it. You're exhausted. You need to rest. There is no reason Jonah needs to know tonight. Now, come on, I slaved over a hot microwave to cook this lasagna. Eat!"

"I don't feel very — "

"Eat! And if you finish it all, you can have one of the white chocolate chip brownies left over from the Steinman bar mitzvah."

○

Ann's guest room was comfortingly feminine and familiar. Emily had helped her pick out the knotty pine dresser and woven rug, and the rocking chair in the corner had been Emily's own, from the time Jonah was an infant. She remembered spending nights with Ann when her romance with Jack was new, staying awake until all hours, babbling as excitedly as a teenager. Now she lay in the dark without words, drained of all emotion and eager for sleep. The bed was queensized, with a navy gingham canopy and matching down comforter — much smaller than the four-poster king she was used to at home. Jack had never slept with her here, so with Fiber stretched out next to her, she didn't feel his absence.

In fact, she was surprised how little she felt at all. Because she had not experienced it herself, Jack's accident seemed like a terrible story she had been told, or even a rumor. And she had only seen him twice after it had occurred, on Saturday night when he lay so still, bandaged and inert after the grueling hours of surgery, but still alive, and on Sunday, when he lay even more still, in death, with his chest rising and falling in a mockery of life.

"I can do this," she thought. "I'll survive."

Then, just as she was beginning to relax, fragments of memory streaked across her consciousness — the look on Dr. Leventhal's face as she said the words "he's gone," the waxen feel of Jack's skin, the frigid air at the hospital morgue, the dizzying odor of chemicals. These recollections were hazy, like flashes of a nightmare, and they quickly passed, leaving her exhausted, empty, floating.

Her own life, too, seemed distant, a vague recollection. Had it been less than two days since she and Fiber had gone on their Saturday morning run? She felt like she was out of sync, detached from her daily routine. But, in fact, she always took Sundays off from exercise. It was her day to be with Jack. He would forgo his golf game, and she would put aside her lists, and they would be together, even if "together" meant that he was watching golf on TV while she worked on a Party Line project. At least they were in the same room, sharing space.

Well, in a manner of speaking, they had been together this day too. Only when she had left the room, Jack had remained behind.

To clear her mind and to entice sleep, Emily began to make her lists. Since the long-ago day she'd given birth to Jonah, each morning had begun with a jolt of recognition that no matter how early she rose, how much she planned, how hard she worked, she would never be able to accomplish all that was expected of her — or rather all that she expected of herself.

So she had started making lists of everything she and Matt, and ultimately Jonah, had to do each day, an insurance policy that nothing important got overlooked in the mad scramble of the day.

After Matt had moved out and it was just Emily and Jonah, she quickly learned that raising a child without a partner was as demanding emotionally and physically as a full-time job. And by then, she and Ann had started Party Line, which *was* a full-time job, so her need to make good use of every moment was even greater.

She kept two running lists of all that needed to be accomplished each day, her own version of a double entry system. One she pinned to the refrigerator so Jonah could refer to it; the other went with her wherever she went — into the bathroom when she showered, into the kitchen while she cooked, into her car, her office, and finally next to her bed at night. Instead of listening to the radio when she drove, she recited her list — *take Jonah's boots to the shoemaker, go to City Hall to pay parking ticket,* she'd murmur as she merged into the traffic on Jessup. *Buy glitter for the Turner invitations, pick up stamps for the Manderbach bar mitzvah thank-you's,* she'd say out loud as she waited at the crosswalk for the children from the Montessori school to cross at Washington.

She prided herself on her ability to get things done, crossing off each item with a sense of accomplishment and relief, until one day she realized that the lists themselves had become more important than the tasks, and that she was adding items to them for the sheer satisfaction of having more things to cross off.

Jack had been amused by her obsessiveness and liked to tease her about it. One day, next to her list of *groceries, iron shirts, order new running shoes,* she'd found he'd tacked on his own list: *watch sun rise, take a steam bath, eat a burrito.*

All of a sudden it struck her that Jack would never again leave her another list, another note, or a message of any kind.

She forced her mind away from this thought, focusing on organizing the next day of her life — it was as far ahead as she could think. At dawn, she and Fiber would go for their run, three miles on the soft sand, a tough workout. Then a hot shower, fruit and coffee with Ann, and while they were eating, she would make lists for Ann and the staff, of the people to inform of Jack's death. She would begin the calls only she could make at eight o'clock sharp.

When the bank opened at ten, she would retrieve Jack's will from the safe-deposit box. Once she knew his wishes, she could start planning his interment. Then the drive up to Oceancrest to tell Jonah face-to-face that his stepfather had died.

And after that, what? Without the safe harbor of her marriage to Jack, the rest of the day, the rest of her life, stretched bleakly before her, impenetrable as the night, unfathomable as the ocean crashing on the nearby shore.

○ ○

Sam awoke in a dark, windowless room. As his vision cleared and adjusted to the darkness, he read the time on the glowing hands of a clock on the wall. Two-twenty — or was it ten past four? He could barely make it out. And was it morning or night? He had no way of knowing.

He had been warned that after surgery his arms would be restrained and his voice blocked by a tube down this throat — the anticipation of this had been chilling. But, in fact, his arms were unbound, resting comfortably at his sides, and although there was a tube in his throat, it was not the terrifying, choking thing he had feared. The blue plastic resting between his circled lips felt more like a pacifier, and he took comfort from it.

He felt a tightness in his chest, but no pain. Had it been another false start? There had been two already in the fifteen weeks he had been waiting at the hospital. The first time he had only gotten so far as to have his chest shaved and washed with antibacterial soap, before being informed that the surgery had been canceled due to a positive crossmatch, an indication that he and the donor were incompatible. The second time the crossmatch had been negative, so he had actually gone into surgery. Awakening in a room similar to the one he was in now, he had been ecstatic thinking that it was over, that he had survived and was finally on the road to recovery, only to learn that the operation had been aborted mid-surgery, when the doctors realized that the new organ had been injured in transit. Fortunately this discovery was made before they had removed Sam's diseased heart, but unfortunately it was after they had cut him open. So he still had that incision to recover from.

"Mr. Sampson, how do you feel?"

A nurse stood over him. She was gowned and masked, but he could tell she was the Irish nurse, the one with the flame of red hair knotted at the nape of her neck. She was not an attractive woman, but she was his favorite because she was scrupulously honest with him — he'd been through far too much in the past five years to tolerate anything less. Still, the fact that the concern on her face was only partially masked by experience and professionalism made him wish for the little El Salvadoran nurse who never gave him a straight answer, who only kept repeating *Dios te esta viendo,* God was watching out for him.

The nurse handed him a pad of paper and a pencil, and he wrote, "No pain. False start?"

"Didn't they tell you?" Her stern face brightened with the pleasure of being the one to impart the good news. "Glory be — you have a new heart. And it's beatin' like a wee one with a new tin drum! Congratulations to ya, sir!"

He felt a flare of exaltation, a firecracker's burst of joy. Then, depleted by the surge of emotion, he lapsed into unconsciousness.

When he opened his eyes again, magically, the Irish nurse had morphed into Dr. Greshom, the chief of surgery and reigning heart specialist in this hospital. He was a small, compact man, but he gave the impression of someone much larger because of his stature in the medical community — or perhaps because his patients saw him most often as Sam did now, when they were prone and he was towering over them.

The doctor sat on the edge of the bed, cupping his palms together like a thirsty man holding the weight of precious water. "I held your old heart in my hands," he told Sampson, "Just so you know, it was definitely shot to hell. Working at about 20 percent capacity. Astonishing, that. Eh? You should have been dead months ago!"

Sampson was unable to speak, but this time it wasn't because of the tube blocking his air passage — that had been removed, he couldn't remember when. Now his throat was constricted with emotion. Tears stung his eyes, and for the first time in what seemed like years, they were tears of joy and relief, not grief and pain.

Dr. Gresham smiled at him. "Hey, none of that! We don't want people to think I gave you some kind of a sissy heart, do we? Let's take a look at my handiwork, see what kind of a scar you're going to have."

He pulled down the sheet, and the nurse gently untied Sampson's surgical gown from behind his neck, stripping it to his waist. The bandages on his torso were soggy with blood and ooze. Sampson shifted uncomfortably, anxious that this might signal a problem.

"Not to worry, just your average drainage," Dr. Greshom assured him, snapping on rubber gloves and removing sterile tweezers from his pocket. The nurse held out a pan, and piece by piece, Dr. Greshom peeled off the strips of soiled gauze from Sampson's chest and dropped them into it. "Some colleagues of mine are testing a procedure now where they can do a bypass arthroscopically, like they do for gall bladder, without even opening the chest cavity. Y'know how they do it, for the gall bladder, I mean? First they cut the organ free, snip, snip. Then they stuff a little bag in there through a hole the size of a pea, and skooch the organ over into it." He made a pushing motion with his index finger to illustrate. "Then they put a little miniature egg beater-type thingie through the hole and into the sack, and blend it all up like paté. When they're finished, they pull the bag full of goop out through the little hole, and voilá! Pretty soon I'll be treating most of my patients on an outpatient basis. Amazing, eh? 'Course we'll still have to cut in order to transplant, because even though we can get the old organ *out,* there's no other way to get the new one *in.* At least not yet."

He accepted a sterile wipe from the nurse and dabbed it against Sampson's chest, then another, and another, until the wound was clean. He rose and smiled. "Look at that incision, straight as an arrow. A masterpiece. I should have been an artist."

"... or one of those gents who paints the yellow lines on the roadway," the nurse teased in her Irish lilt. It was music to Sampson's ears.

He dared a glance down at his chest and tried not to gasp. The sight of his own flesh, cleft from the sternum to the bottom of his rib cage, was shocking. The lips of the wound were raw and uneven, the skin around it red and puffed with outrage, and dotted with darkening clots of dried blood. A neat row of thin gray staples, about thirty of them, was all that was keeping his organs from spilling out of his body. He had been told about this, but seeing it now, comprehending the trauma that his body had endured, was horrifying. He lay very still, afraid that the slightest movement would cause the staples to rupture.

"You are doing just fine. All indications are positive. I think you've got a winner." Dr. Greshom stripped off the rubber gloves and handed them to the nurse. "Now you do what these nurses tell you. This surgery puts me at 83 percent — I haven't lost a patient in eleven months. So don't screw it up for me."

"I'll do my best," Sampson said. They were the first words he had spoken, and to his ears, his voice sounded unfamiliar, as though someone else were speaking, someone he didn't even know.

"There's a good man," the doctor said heartily, squeezing Sampson's shoulder so hard that he winced. "You've got to stay in this sterile room for three days. But when I come by tomorrow, I want you to be sitting in that chair over there." He nodded toward a green leatherette straightback chair, now pushed into a corner. "If all goes well, you'll be home by the end of next week."

When the doctor left, the nurse rebandaged Sampson's incision and rubbed a bit of cream onto his shoulders and arms. The lotion was a balm on his skin, her strokes like a lover's caresses. But when she pulled him upright to thread his arms into a fresh gown, he gasped as though he'd been struck in the chest by a sledge hammer. He was positive the doctor had been exaggerating to buoy his spirits — there was no way on earth he'd have the strength to get out of bed tomorrow, let alone the courage to go home by the end of next week.

"That's all right," the nurse said in a soothing voice, as though sensing his concern. "Don't think about anything now but rest. You'll be surprised how fast you'll bounce back, a young man like yourself, with a healthy new heart. You're living for two now, him that died and you yourself. Why, you'll see, it's going to feel as though you've been reborn!"

He had the dream for the first time that night. It was not unpleasant, but startling in its intensity, as vivid as a memory. He was walking on a strip of beach in a sun-dazzled, crescent-shaped cove. The sand burned the bottoms of his feet, and though he knew, even in the dream, that relief was only inches away in the waves which lapped at the shore, he did not move into the water.

Instead, he continued trudging through the sand. Suddenly he broke into a jog, running faster and faster, milliseconds of relief coming each time his foot left the ground. He could feel his heart rate increase until it was a thrumming drumbeat inside of his chest. And even though his breath was coming in ragged gasps, the muscles in his legs aching, he did not stop. Faster and faster he went, until he rounded the curving arc of the cove and then —

And then he woke up. It was the morning of the second day.

TWO

5

Jack's wishes, recorded in a codicil to his will, written just months before, had been explicit: absolutely no religious service commemorating his death. Instead, he wanted a party, a joyous celebration of his life. Much to Emily's surprise — and admittedly, relief — he had even set aside the money to pay for it.

He had also composed a guest list which, in his typically expansive style, extended past immediate family and closest friends to include neighbors, business associates, and his golf buddies. He'd included suggestions for the menu and the directive that he was to be cremated, his ashes buried under the tallest eucalyptus tree in the rough off of the eighteenth fairway at Palm Ridge Country Club.

"Jack always had a unique sense of theater," Ann had murmured, reading this over Emily's shoulder. It was true, some of Party Line's best ideas had originated with Jack.

"I'm surprised he didn't demand that his favorite caddie be buried with him," one of the staffers quipped, but nobody laughed.

"It is a little macabre, that a man under forty would plan his funeral in such detail, don't you think?" asked Lew, himself a man under forty.

"It was my idea," Emily told him. "I thought we should plan ahead. But to be honest, I didn't expect all this."

It wasn't what she would have chosen either, but the more she thought about it, the more appropriate it seemed for Jack, to have his friends remember him as he'd lived, not to mourn his death. So she threw herself into the preparations, grateful to be too busy to think about what had happened, or what her life would be like without him.

Her first concern was getting permission from the Club to actually dig up the beautifully tended land — she doubted that such a thing could be done. But she found that Jack had already cleared the way by making a substantial donation to Palm Ridge's "Re-Greening Fund" in exchange for the right to select a final resting place.

A city permit was necessary, too, and Emily knew that there were strict rules relating to burials. But a call to the local Department of Public Heath revealed that Jack had already paved the way there as well — one of his foursome worked in the Mayor's office and had gotten the approval. "We had a bet," the man explained to Emily. "Jack didn't think I could pull it off. I won."

All that remained was to hire several of the Club's gardeners to do the actual digging and replanting, and for a modest retainer, they were happy to comply.

Once the major issues were dealt with, Emily went into high party-planning gear. If Jack's wish had been to have a celebration, she would give him one nobody would forget! Through the dictates of his will and his choice of a final resting place, Jack had already set the tone, so she decided to elaborate on the golf theme and to design the memorial service around that.

It was a colorful event. Although a few traditionalists did show up in funereal dress, the majority of guests were appropriately attired in khakis or pastels, tweed golf caps, and argyle socks. Everyone had been cautioned to wear low-heeled shoes, but a selection of spiked golf shoes was available to anyone who had forgotten. A dozen golfcarts waited to transport those who preferred to ride out to the burial site, and the flag on the eighteenth hole had been replaced by a banner which read *Jack Kensington Barnes, June 16, 1961 - February 2, 1999.*

Just as the service was beginning, Jonah surprised her by coming to stand at her side. He hadn't said much when she'd told him about Jack's death, but then neither had many of the other people to whom she'd told the news. She thought she understood — words were inadequate. What could you say about a tragedy so profound?

Jonah wore a new sport coat and tie. He was fidgety but remembered his manners. He even allowed her to hold his hand, a dutiful son. He was already taller than either her or Matt, his body lean and muscular from hours of practice with the swim team, and his hair, though longer than she would have liked it, was handsomely streaked blond by the California sun. She was so proud of him! It made her heart swell that he was so attentive to her in front of all the guests.

The ceremony was personal and brief. Instead of religious rhetoric, Jack was remembered through anecdote. "He always wanted to be a jazz musician," his older brother remembered. "When he was a kid, Buddy Rich was his idol — tho' when he got older, he dropped the 'buddy' part and just idolized the 'rich.' " That got a good laugh from the crowd.

Jack's boss at the brokerage firm told how the staff had once voted Jack "most likely *not* to return to the office after lunch." "It was just as well. With some guys, you couldn't stand the beer on their breath. With Jack it was those damn seafood burritos. I swear, he tried to get the firm to take that little taco stand public. He said we wouldn't even have to pay cash dividends, we could compensate the shareholders in Szechuan burritos. Frankly, I was beginning to wonder what they were putting in that secret sauce."

One of his golf partners chimed in, "I don't mean to say he

wasn't smart, but we used to tease him that his handicap was higher than his I.Q. — although that may have said more about his golf game than it did about his intelligence. And by the way, Jack always insisted that our foursome be politically correct; so we didn't say he had a double digit *handicap,* we simply said his score was *stroke impaired.*"

The ceremony ended with a nod to golf's beginnings in Scotland: a trio of Scottish pipers played *Amazing Grace* as Jack's ashes, fitted inside of a specially designed golf bag, were lowered into the ground. Each guest was given a golf ball with Jack's initials and the date on it, and a gold-plated tee, which they dropped on top of the golf bag. Then one of the pipers separated from the other two and strode off across the eighteenth fairway, somber strains of music drifting away on the light breeze.

Throughout the proceedings, Emily was well aware of the grim expressions that Jack's mother and father wore beneath their cruise ship tans. They had been adamantly against this frivolity, even after she had shown them Jack's will and explained that the idea for the ceremony had been his. Grief had taken its toll on them, and as soon as the last gold tee had been thrown into the grave, they took their leave. Emily offered to walk them to their car, but they waved her away. "Stay with your guests," Jack's mother said. "We'll find our way on our own." The bitterness in her voice weighed heavily on Emily. She watched them walk away slowly, clutching each other for dear life. She doubted that she would see much of them anymore.

Her own parents had been reluctant to make the trip to Los Angeles for such a tragic event, and she had not encouraged them. Neither of them was in good health, and they had never approved of Emily's divorce from Matt, let alone her remarriage to Jack. Although they would never have said it aloud, she knew that they hoped she would now find her way back to Matt — this in total denial of the fact that Matt was happily remarried, and was a new father to boot.

"Mom, can I go now?" Jonah asked, snapping her back to reality.

"Go where?"

"To hang out with Dad and Lauren. This part is over, isn't it?"

As much as she wanted him with her, Emily gave him a quick kiss on the forehead, which he carelessly brushed off. "Sure, you go on," she said. "I'll be fine." And with a pang of envy, she watched him join Matt and Lauren and walk with them toward the clubhouse, a happy family.

The guests gradually dispersed, and she was alone on the fairway. A few people looked over their shoulders at her, perhaps wondering if they should wait, but she ignored them. She stood by the mound of earth that covered Jack's ashes, rooted to the spot, as though in lieu of flowers or a tombstone she would mark the gravesite. A sudden gust of winter wind whipped around her, but though her legs were bare and her hands ungloved, she didn't feel the chill. The cold had already settled in her heart.

A lavish buffet had been set up in the clubhouse dining room, replete with upscale versions of Jack's favorite foods: instead of hot dogs, Emily had ordered sausages on homemade baguettes with a dozen exotic mustards; thick French fries were served with sour cream and caviar instead of ketchup; miniature pizzas were topped with duck and goat cheese instead of pepperoni; and, of course, there were platters of Sergio's Szechuan burritos, which could not be improved upon, but which she had cut into quarter-sized portions.

"Great party," a stranger said, as she passed.

"I can see Jack's hand in this," one of his golfing buddies remarked, piling two of everything onto his plate.

"Jack's, and Wolfgang Puck's," another agreed, taking advantage of his open mouth to stuff a whole pizza in. He chewed savagely, a thin drool of plum sauce trickling down his chin.

Emily excused herself, thinking how glad she was that there would be no reason for her to socialize with these men after today. She had nothing in common with them, had never met their wives or families. She didn't even know their last names. They had been Jack's sporting companions, inhabiting a part of his life from which she had been excluded.

And what had she been? The woman who washed his polo shirts and waited for him to come home when he finished his daily game.

Home. She had not been back to the house since Jack's death, six days before. But now that the memorial was over, she realized that she was yearning for familiar things — the sight of the light filtering through the coral tree in the morning, the sound of the trash trucks in the alley, the scent of her childhood in the heirloom oriental carpet in the den. She was ready to go home and start picking up the pieces.

But the party wasn't over. She scanned the room with the detached eye of a professional, to see that the platters on the buffet table were replenished, that empty glasses and used plates were cleared from side tables and counters, that guests were mingling easily.

"Excuse me, Mrs. Barnes?"

Emily turned to find a young man of about twenty-five standing behind her. He was burly and hirsute, wearing faded jeans and a leather jacket. His shirt was unironed, but clean, and buttoned to the neck. She saw that he was clutching a bouquet of wilting flowers, the kind sold by itinerant workers on busy street corners.

"You must be one of Jack's golfing friends," she said, although she couldn't imagine him fitting in with the plaid pants crowd.

The young man looked stricken. "Me? Oh, gosh no, I'm ..." He shuffled from foot to foot, at a loss for words. He swallowed and began again. "I'm ... I didn't know your husband, not really."

"Then ... why are you here? I don't understand."

"I was driving the truck. The Pepsi truck." His expression implored her to grasp the connection, without requiring him to say more.

"Oh my God," she gasped. "I — " Her eyes filled with tears.

"Shit!" The young man backed a few steps away, and he looked furtively from side to side to see if anyone had overheard. "I'm sorry, I guess I shouldn't have come. But I had to, in a way. Meet you, I mean. Tell you how bad I feel. This is the worst thing that's ever happened to me. In my *life!*" He ran a hand nervously through his hair. "Not as bad as what happened to him, I'm not trying to say that. Geez, no. But like, I don't even want to *drive* anymore, and that rig used to be my world. I got everything I own sunk into it, and now ..." He exhaled heavily, and his whole body seemed to deflate.

"Anyway, I just wanted to come, to pay my respects to you, and him, y'know?"

Emily took a deep breath, tried to steady herself. She knew what he wanted, needed to hear, but it was hard enough for her to look at him, let alone to speak the words with conviction. This young man had been a victim of the accident as much as Jack had been. But he was still here, and Jack was gone. Forever.

At last she found the voice to whisper, "It wasn't your fault. I know it was an accident. It just ... happened. There was nothing you could have done."

He was visibly relieved. Tears welled in his eyes. "Thank you," he said, "thanks," and he backed away, forgetting that he was still clutching the flowers, stumbling into Emily's neighbor, Laverne Lawrence, and spilling her drink. He quickly mumbled his apologies, then turned and fled the clubhouse.

Grateful for the distraction, Emily found a napkin and helped Mrs. Lawrence dab at the wet spot on her dress, a floral print of pink daisies on a black background. She wore a pink belt around her ample waist and matching pink shoes. In one hand she held a plate full of food, in the other a wide-brimmed glass, now only half full of frothy strawberry daiquiri, the cocktail Jack's will had specified. The fruit, imported from Chile because it was out of season in the Northern hemisphere, had been a gift from Party Line's produce purveyor.

"Oh, my dear, this is quite a send-off for your dearly beloved," Laverne Lawrence chirped to Emily, in her high, birdlike voice. Her cheeks were flushed the same rosy shade as her shoes and belt. "I've never seen such a jolly throng at a funeral." She gestured to the crowd with her glass, and Emily caught her hand, steadying it before the liquid arced over the rug. "I'll have to retain you to plan mine," she chuckled, "which shouldn't be too far off now!" She took a sip of her drink.

"Careful, Mrs. Lawrence, those are very potent!"

"Nonsense, it's just fruit juice with a dash of 'naughty' in it. I must have the recipe."

"I'll see that you get it," Emily said, moving away.

"Don't be a stranger now that you're alone," Mrs. Lawrence called after her. "We widows have to stick together."

Widow. Is that how people would label her now? The word sounded more dignified than "divorcée," but it conveyed the same image, of a woman alone, someone who had loved and precipitously lost. Mrs. Lawrence spoke the word with pride, wore her own widowhood like a badge of honor. But to Emily the word screamed of grief and loss. It was a mantle that she was not yet prepared to wear.

"He was a real pro," a man in lime green pants and a plaid windbreaker said, thrusting out his hand to be shaken as she walked past.

"Kept his eye on the ball," another added, an enormous Cohiba clenched between his tobacco-stained teeth.

"Sorry for your loss," someone else murmured.

"Sorry."

"Very sorry."

Emily nodded at each person and kept on walking. Sorry! The word was inadequate, condescending, and overused, like the word "love." She was sick of hearing it. All she could think about now was getting out of this place, away from these people and their suffocating, smug pity.

"Emily, are you okay?"

It was Gary Forrester, one of Jack's old friends from college. He put his arm around her, his brow furrowed with concern. "Come on, you look like you need some air."

"You've got that right," she said, and let him steer her toward the patio overlooking the golf course. When they were outside, he tightened his arm around her as she breathed in great gulps of the cold evening breeze.

"You okay?" he asked.

"Better. Thanks. It was just overwhelming...." She shook her head, "I can't stand all of this pity, you know?"

"I wonder if Jack considered what it would be like for you," Gary said, "having to be both the gracious hostess and the grieving widow at the same time. Probably not, knowing our Jack," he finished with an affectionate smile.

Widow. There was that word again. But it sounded different coming from Gary. Less like "alone," more like "available." Emily smiled at him, knowing he meant to be supportive, not seductive. Gary was one of her favorites of the friends Jack had brought into their marriage. He and his wife Marcia were CPAs, with successful careers and a twelve-year marriage. They were adults, and they had brought out what Emily thought was the best in Jack.

She fell easily against him, allowing herself the comfort of being held by a strong, tall man. "Thanks, Gary. I'm okay now, I just got a little claustrophobic in there. Sometimes I'm fine, other times, I feel like I'm drowning."

"Well don't!" Gary said. He turned to grip her by the shoulders, tilting her face up so their eyes met. "We all loved Jack, we still do. But the best way we can honor his memory is to go on with our lives. That's what our pastor at Unity Presbyterian tells us. The death of a loved one is a wake-up call, reminding us to live our lives to the fullest each minute, to make sure we tell the people we cherish that they are important to us, to reach out and grasp the things that matter."

"Amen," she said, half-mocking his sermonizing tone.

He gave her a squeeze. "Sorry, babe, I didn't mean to go all preachy on you. I just want you to know that you are loved." He pressed his lips to her forehead.

Emily stiffened slightly. Jack had always called her "babe." It sounded odd and at the same time disconcertingly familiar, hearing the endearment in Gary's baritone.

"We'll need to go over some paperwork together," he was saying. "Not right away, but as soon as you're ready. I'll give you a call." He winked at her and walked away.

"I didn't know Gary was such a snake," Ann muttered, coming up behind Emily. "And since when does he call you 'babe?' "

"Come on, he was just trying to be a friend."

"Yeah? It doesn't appear that his Mrs. Forrester thinks so." Ann nodded toward the bar, at Marcia Forrester, who was shrugging off a proffered arm from her husband, turning a cold shoulder. "I've got a hunch Gary wants to come over and 'do your books,' so to speak, and she knows it," Ann said.

"That's ridiculous. Gary was Jack's friend. That's all."

"In case you've forgotten the drill, now that you're single again it's best to steer clear of married men," Ann said. "Hold it!"

She reached past Emily to stop a passing waiter. "Spit it out," she commanded, holding a napkin under his mouth.

"*Que?*"

"The gum, Jose. Never, ever chew gum when you're working a party. Spit!"

"*Madre mia,*" the waiter growled, but he coughed it up like a dutiful child. Ann crumpled up the napkin and threw it on his tray. "Go now, *vamoose!*" She shooed him away. "If he were one of ours, I'd fire his ass, I swear. And did you notice the way they double staffed the ladies' room? You can't pee without tipping *twice*. And there's *no one* in the men's room. It's an absolute pigsty."

"You were in the men's room?"

"Of course not! I asked Lew to check it out. He told me to give you his sincere apologies, by the way. He had to go to his daughter's harp recital, which I thought was rather appropriate."

"I want to leave too. Do you think that would be rude?"

"Hey, you're golden right now, kiddo. You could get away with murd — sorry! Me and my mouth. Should I stay and play hostess, or do you want company?"

"Stay, thanks. I just want to curl up in my own bed and sleep."

"What about Fiber? Want me to keep him at the condo until you get settled?"

"God, no, I need him. I'll stop by and pick him up on my way." She looked around the room. There were about twenty people left, mostly club members who had overindulged on daiquiris. They might linger for hours yet. "You'll cover for me?" she asked.

"Don't I always?" Ann teased.

"Thanks, Ann." Her eyes flooded with tears. "I don't know how I could have gotten through this without …"

"Shhh. Go on, go! Before your mascara runs. I'll call you tomorrow and we'll do a post mortem." Ann put her hand over her mouth. "Oops. Sorry. You know what I mean."

↻

Emily drove away from the clubhouse slowly, wanting to go home, but already apprehensive about turning the key in the door. She stopped at the automatic gate and withdrew the green plastic key card from her pocket. She'd been carrying it with her ever since she'd found it, all that was left from the accident. Now she slid it into the slot in the lockbox. The iron gate slowly swung open, allowing her egress, then slowly it slammed shut behind her, closing the door on a chapter of her life. She opened her glove compartment and gently laid the card inside.

As she drove home, she mulled over the events of the day, doing a *post mortem*, as Ann had aptly dubbed it. It had been a strange sensation, to be celebrating Jack's life and mourning his death, while at the same time acting as hostess and party planner. She hadn't particularly felt Jack's absence, but that wasn't such a surprise. She was used to being at parties without him; it was her job. And even when they did go out together socially, he liked to mingle, flitting from person to person like a hummingbird, pollinating each conversation with a joke or an anecdote, then moving on, while she preferred to stand in one spot and have long, meaningful, one-on-one conversations. Often, by the time Jack was ready to leave, she hadn't even gotten as far as the buffet table.

No, it hadn't been Jack's absence that had made the day strange. What troubled her was the fact that the ultimate event in Jack's life hadn't seemed sad. The mood had been upbeat, and actually, except for Jack's parents, everyone appeared to have had a good time, despite the reason for the party. That had been the point, hadn't it? But what did it say about Jack, and his friendships? What did it say about their marriage, that she could describe his memorial service as "a good time"?

Emily recalled images glimpsed on the evening news of lives ravaged by the sudden death of a loved one. Almost every night there was a story and an accompanying video portrait: a mother in a black shroud, propped up on both sides by somber, sobbing friends; a puffy-eyed widow wailing and throwing herself on a lowering casket; men raging and threatening vengeance on murderous perpetrators; children stunned into silence by the tragedy of a lost parent. Why was she feeling none of these emotions? Shouldn't she be weeping uncontrollably?

Instead, she found herself thinking about the mail — Ann had picked it up several times, so there wouldn't be stacks overflowing the mailbox, thank goodness; and the newspapers — Laverne Lawrence had collected them each morning. Marnie, her weekly housekeeper, had let herself in on her usual day, so the house would be spotless. It would be nice going home to a clean house.

But how could she be thinking these petty, self-centered thoughts when Jack was dead?

Maybe it was still too soon. Only a week had passed since the accident, and in that week, she had numbed herself with work, devoting every waking minute and all of her resources of energy to the planning of the memorial service and party. But now that they were over, she realized that she was thinking about anything but Jack. Was there something wrong with her that she wasn't immobilized by anguish?

She pulled the car to a stop in front of the garage and sat staring at the house as though seeing it for the first time. It was a bungalow built in the Craftsman period of the mid-1920s, with a shingled brown wood exterior, a slate roof, and a meandering brick walk leading over a sloped lawn to the street. Its lines were clean and strong, with no frills, a reactionary statement toward the ornate Victorian architecture predominant in that period. Its eloquence was in its simple details: Tiffany-style stained glass panels set into the front door, dark, wide, tongue-and-groove plank floors throughout, mahogany beams fitted together and secured with leather strapping instead of nails.

Courtesy of an automatic timer, a warm light beamed from the windows, welcoming waves of it filtering out through the branches of the coral tree in the front yard. Because of the tree, it would be difficult for anyone to see into the master bedroom, but the gardener had finally trimmed the bottlebrush hedge surrounding the house, as she had been asking him to do since January, and he'd cut it so severely that the living room was visible from the street. A chill shot up her spine. A single woman living alone in an upscale suburb — would she now become a target for burglary, mugging, carjacking — and what was the term they used now, *home invasion*?

She had never worried much about her physical safety. Jack had entered her life soon after her split with Matt; his sturdy, confident presence in her life had made her feel safe even when he wasn't physically with her. But now ... perhaps it was time to invest in an alarm system.

And then there would be the issue of men. She was only thirty-eight. Surely at some point she would start to date. Was Ann right about Gary? Had he been flirting with her? Sometime in the last fifteen years, she'd lost the instinct to know.

Fiber whined softly at her side and scratched at the window. "Okay boy, you're right. We might as well go in." Emily turned off the engine and opened her door, letting the dog jump out first, then getting out herself. She beeped the car alarm and slowly walked to the house.

The door opened with a sucking sound, as though Jack's death had created a vacuum. The air inside was stale and heavy, so despite the chill of the night, Emily left the door ajar to let in some of the crisp night breeze. Then she remembered her earlier thoughts about intruders, and she closed and locked the door, instead opening the narrow slatted louvers over the sink.

There was a bowl of fresh fruit on the counter, a meager assortment of oranges and apples, and a note from Marnie, the housekeeper, expressing sympathy and saying that there were some casseroles and cakes in the fridge, offerings left by friends and neighbors.

Emily opened the refrigerator, curious, but doubting that there would be anything to whet her appetite. Sure enough, there was an unfamiliar pink Tupperware container of pasta salad — a sniff told her that it was laced with pesto, a cold roast of pork, a cheesecake in a Pyrex dish. She closed the refrigerator, trying not to be annoyed. She knew in her heart that people meant well, but it was obvious that the gifts had been offered by friends to assuage their relief that they did not have to experience Emily's loss, rather than given to soothe her. For anyone who knew her well would have remembered that she had an allergy to garlic, hence pesto was out, and that she ate no meat or dairy, so the pork roast and cheesecake were also taboo.

It didn't matter. Although she hadn't eaten a bite at the funeral, she wasn't hungry. A dry bagel would do for tonight's dinner, and she always kept a bag of them in the freezer. While it thawed in the microwave, Emily took a tentative walk through the house. Why did it look and feel so different? Nothing had been altered — Marnie never dared rearrange Emily's careful placement of furniture, never even threw away the newspaper unless it was in the recycling pile. How could Jack's death make everything seem so changed? He was often absent; could the mere fact that he wasn't coming back this time make such a difference?

When the microwave chimed, Emily put the bagel on a plate and carried it upstairs. Fiber ran up ahead of her and was waiting at the foot of the bed, his eyes riveted on the door to the bedroom. He knew Emily's habits, that she took a handful of crackers or a slice of bread up to bed as a late-night snack, and she always shared it with him. That was, after all, how he'd earned his name.

The bedroom.

The bed.

Why was she shocked to see Jack's nightstand still piled high with what he called his "reading material" — business papers, sports magazines, catalogues, and notes to himself, scribbled during evening telephone conversations? A gum wrapper lay crumpled next to the pile. Marnie hadn't dared touch even this.

Emily picked up the wrapper, but she left the stack of papers untouched. She would ultimately have to go through them herself, ferret out what might be important and throw the rest away. She would also have to pack up Jack's clothes, his toiletries, the contents of his desk. There were whole areas of the house she had always thought of as his — the garage, the guest room he'd converted into an office, the back porch where he kept his sports equipment. She would have to tackle these one at a time.

Like emotional acupuncture, this mental tabulation of Jack's space and personal effects elicited the first real pinpricks of loss. But in a way, it was a relief to feel something, even if it was pain. She hoped that, as with traditional acupuncture, this small discomfort would keep the true pain at bay.

As a distraction, and also for company, Emily reached for the television remote control. But even that reminded her of Jack. It had been a running joke between them, how he had commandeered it early in their relationship and had maintained dominion over their programming choices ever since. Emily had not put up much of a struggle; she preferred to read or do paperwork for Party Line rather than watch the sitcoms and sports shows Jack favored. Yet, by the end of each season, she would nevertheless be weary of Jack's obsessive channel surfing and of hearing the shrill voices of the commentators in the background of their lives.

Well, now she could watch whatever she wanted— or nothing if she desired. She pressed the "on" button. No surprise, the set was tuned to ESPN, a basketball game, the Lakers versus the Chicago

Bulls. She stared at the screen, mesmerized by the frenzied action. Hearing the familiar screams of the fans and the blare of the referee's whistle allowed her the comfortable illusion that Jack was somewhere in the house, just out of view. Without looking at the screen or adjusting the volume, she set the remote on her own nightstand and walked into the bathroom.

Mercifully, Marnie had done the laundry, so Emily was not forced to deal with Jack's soiled clothes, the last he'd worn before the accident. Even the towels were fresh, the sink, shower, and tub scrubbed clean. The sting of ammonia hung in the air, erasing all but the memory of the last odor Emily remembered smelling that Saturday morning, the intimate spice of Jack's cologne.

She stepped out of her clothes and dropped them into the hamper to be taken in for dry cleaning. Then she got into the shower. The water was hot, too hot. She was glad for the sting of the scorching water on her bare breasts and stomach. Even pain was better than the numbness she had felt since Jack's death. She stood directly under the spray, hoping the water would wash away her guilt for committing the sin of continuing to live when Jack was dead.

Later, lying in the too-wide bed, grateful for Fiber's small body stretched to its full length along her side, Emily fell into her routine of making lists. Tomorrow morning, Saturday, she would get up as usual and take Fiber for a six-mile run. Afterward, she would spend some time in the kitchen, preparing food for Jonah's afternoon arrival, and then begin planning a party for his birthday next month.

Jonah.

Her tall, strong son had taken the news of Jack's death with surprising disinterest. In fact, despite his attentiveness at the funeral, he had tried every excuse he could think of to flee when it was over.

"I've got two tests next week," he had told her. "Since I had to blow off Friday for the funeral, maybe I should just go back to school afterward so I can study." It was the first time he'd ever used that one!

"Nonsense," Emily had insisted, wounded. "You're only thirteen. No test is more important than being here. Anyway, I can help you study."

"For computer science?" he'd whined. "Right. Like you've got a clue."

"Hey, I know my way around a modem," she'd replied. But that wasn't the point. She knew Jonah wasn't lobbying to go back to campus early in order to study. It was simply that he didn't want to be around her now. She was tainted by Jack's death, a pariah, and he wanted to put distance between himself and her pain.

Their relationship had changed drastically after her marriage to Jack. Jonah had resented Jack's intrusion in his life, but stubbornly, Emily had pushed them together, standing in the background herself, eagerly watching them interact.

But although Jack did his best, they remained as different and distant as a basset hound and a borzoi — the same species, but completely different breeds, and most often they sniffed around each other warily, then went their separate ways.

With the crystal-clear vision of hindsight, Emily realized that what she should have done was maintain her own bond with Jonah, exclusive of Jack, and not press the "new family" thing so hard.

Well, that's what she would do now. She hoped it wasn't too late to win him back. She drifted off to sleep, itemizing her shopping list for the next morning, the ingredients she would need to prepare Jonah's favorite dish, chicken pot pie.

6

She spent Saturday morning sifting through the sympathy notes that had arrived during the previous week. Most of them were unreadable. Either they sounded like they had been copied from an old version of Amy Vanderbilt — " ...We are so sorry to hear of your tragic loss ..." or they were long and flowery tributes that seemed to have nothing at all to do with Jack — "... He was a great man and he will be remembered forever by all of us who loved him ..."

So instead of actually rereading the notes, she merely organized them into groups by sender: family/work/neighbors/Jack's friends/ Emily's friends. Since neither of them had large families, and they hadn't been married long enough to cultivate a wide circle of friends, the majority of the notes had come from her own working associates and friends, and from Jack's old chums, most of whom she didn't know well. But these notes she pored over carefully, hoping she would glean some wisdom about Jack, some personal truth she could cling to.

She was just starting on another list, this one of the people who had sent flowers or food, or had otherwise gone out of their way to be thoughtful, when she heard Matt's car pull up in front of the house. She looked at her watch. It was after three.

From the window over her desk, Emily watched father and son emerge and tried to temper her annoyance. She didn't want to get off on the wrong foot today, of all days, but they were intolerably late, and her plans for the afternoon were shot. The month before, against her objections, Matt had signed up Jonah for a karate class which met on alternate Saturdays at ten o'clock. They had agreed that after today's class he would take the boy for an early lunch, then bring him straight over. By Emily's calculation, that should have been before one o'clock.

But here they were, two hours late, sauntering up the walk as though they had all the time in the world. Matt's arm was hiked up around Jonah's taller shoulder, and Jonah was laughing, butting against his father with his hip to nudge Matt off the path and into the bottlebrush. How long had it been since Jonah had been this playful with her?

Biting back hurt feelings, Emily turned away from the window and shut down her computer. She would not make Jonah feel guilty by letting him know he had caused her pain, and she would not give Matt the satisfaction of seeing her anger.

"Hello," she called with forced gaiety, as she heard the front door open. "Jonah?"

"Hi, Mom," he replied, and then she heard his size twelve feet stomping up the stairs two at a time. She rose from her chair and made it to the hallway in time to see his untied sneakers disappear at the top of the staircase. A moment later, the door to his bedroom slammed shut. Was the slam intentional or accidental?

She walked into the foyer. Matt was kneeling, trying to pet Fiber. But the dog would have none of it. He ducked his head and backed away, growling softly. Fiber had been utterly devoted to Jack, but he was aloof with other men. Despite how hard Matt tried — and he had made it his personal mission to befriend the dog — Fiber had never warmed to him. It pleased Emily to see how this frustrated Matt, who prided himself on his ability to tame person and pet alike.

He stood when he saw Emily, trying to work his slow charm on her, an easier mark. "Hey, how's it going?" he asked softly. He was a small man, no taller than Emily, and like Jonah, he was dressed in jeans and unlaced yellow and white running shoes. His eyes were blue, and they penetrated her defenses with practiced ease.

He brushed the hair from his forehead and took a tentative step forward, his arms open to embrace her. Involuntarily, she stepped back. "Nice service yesterday," he said. "You did good." Conciliatory, a bit awkward, the compliment caught her off guard.

"Thanks," she said, disarmed and suddenly teary.

"I mean, it's not every day you can bury a guy and get in a round of golf at the same time." He mimed taking a golf shot and grinned at her.

The sarcasm was a slap in the face, more so because he had couched it in false sympathy. She should have seen it coming.

"What's wrong with Jonah?" she demanded, striking back with the first thing she could think of.

"Nothing," Matt replied, ever infuriatingly placid. At least in her life with Jack, despite its failings, there had been drama.

"Then why are you so late? The afternoon is shot." Damn, she hadn't meant to snap, but Matt's nonchalant attitude created a void, an emotional trap that she invariably fell into.

"I thought we discussed this," Matt replied, stuffing his hands into his back pockets. Emily wasn't a psychologist, but she knew this was body language for "don't blame me, my hands are tied." "Jonah's karate class is at ten and afterward we took him to lunch."

Emily didn't ask who the "we" referred to. She assumed it was Lauren and J. B., since Matt and his new family always spent the weekends joined at the hip, a '90s version of Robert Young and family in *Father Knows Best*. "The class is forty-five minutes, right?" she asked instead. "And how long does it take to grab a burger, fifteen minutes, twenty tops? That would have put you here by twelve-thirty at the latest."

"The class went long today, almost two hours, because they're getting ready for a competition," Matt explained patiently. "Then Jonah didn't want a burger. We went for sushi at Yama, and you know how long that takes on a Saturday. We weren't even seated until nearly one-thirty."

"Sushi? At Yama? God, Matt, he's only thirteen. What kind of lunch — "

"He'll be fourteen in a few weeks, and sushi was his choice, Emily, not mine. Not that it should make a difference. God, you're tense." He put his hands on her shoulders and gave them a squeeze. "Look, maybe we should just keep Jonah with us this weekend, let you have some time to heal."

"Don't patronize me. I'm not one of your patients," Emily said shrilly, and instantly she was sorry, because once again, she'd let Matt goad her into spilling her anger, and in the process, she'd given him the upper hand.

She lowered her voice an octave and tried to keep her temper in check. "I was planning to take him to the Museum of Flying — there's a new show — and then maybe to a movie. Now it's too late to do anything. And he'll be bored stiff just sitting around here with me until dinner."

"Let me give you some advice," Matt said. "And I'm sorry if I sound like a shrink, but that's what I am. Don't structure every minute of his life. You're smothering him. He needs to be free, to build his inner resources. Let him just 'be.' "

"You're a fine one to talk — giving him karate lessons and sushi." She glanced out the window at Matt's car. There was Lauren, sitting in the passenger seat, bouncing baby J. B. on her lap. "And making a family affair out of it," she couldn't help adding.

"No wonder he doesn't like to be here. How can I compete with that?"

"Hey, it's not a competition," Matt said.

"No? Then why is it Jonah never wants to be with me any more? I'm his mother. I need him!"

"Don't you see, Emily? You have to let him need you, not the other way around."

"What neither of us needs is a lecture from you," she snapped.

"I don't mean to lecture you, but Jesus, whenever he's here, you've got a list of things a mile long for him to do."

"Did he tell you that?"

Matt sighed. "Don't go there, Em."

"Why? Doctor-patient privilege?"

"Jonah is not my patient. He's my son."

"And mine!"

"What I'm saying is, I don't want to go behind his back, reporting everything he tells me about you," Matt said.

"So he *does* talk to you about me," Emily said triumphantly.

"Of course he does. Doesn't he talk to you about me?"

"Only to tell me that you bought him new Nikes for $125, and that you want him to go to Colorado with you for a month this summer, which is out of the question, by the way. He has to go to summer school."

A car horn honked. Matt pulled back the drape and motioned to Lauren that he was coming. "Look, Emily. I know you're out of balance right now — "

"*I'm not out of balance*!" she declared through gritted teeth. "How dare you!"

"Okay. You're not out of balance. You're just fine. Perfect. All I'm trying to say is, don't lean on Jonah, don't try to make him take Jack's place."

"That's crazy. I wouldn't do that."

He said nothing, but cocked his head and raised his eyebrows, an expression of disbelief that spoke volumes. He edged toward the door. "You two have a good weekend. I'll talk to you next week."

"Fine." Emily closed the door on Matt's heels, careful not to slam it, although she would have liked to punctuate his exit with a resounding thud.

From the window, she watched him hurry down the walk, his untied laces slapping against his shoes. She saw him get into the car, reach over to nuzzle Lauren, then give the baby a peck on the cheek before driving away. He made her so angry, with his superior attitude. It was her *job* as a mother to make sure Jonah applied himself, to see that his life was filled with more than just karate and sushi. This had always been a sore point with Matt. He thought Emily was too controlling and cautious. He was always telling her she needed to loosen up.

Well, she would show him she could be loose. Loose as a goose.

She charged up the stairs, with Fiber on her heel, and knocked at Jonah's door. "Jonah?"

"Yeah."

"May I come in?"

"Do I have a choice?"

She opened the door. Jonah was lying on his bed, head at the bottom, feet on the pillow, bouncing a basketball against the headboard. Seeing him there in his childhood bed she realized how much he'd grown. He was taller by a head than either she or Matt and outweighed her by twenty pounds. No longer a little boy. But still not a man, still in desperate need of a haircut.

There were other things about him that were changing too: his vocabulary seemed to be shrinking in direct inverse proportion to his growth spurt; he was spending more and more time playing with his computer; and his interest in sports was declining. At the beginning of the quarter, he'd announced that he'd given up the swim team, saying it took too much time away from his schoolwork. He was no longer fascinated by insects and dinosaurs. In fact, she couldn't think of what *did* interest him these days, beyond the three m's — music, movies, and money. Maybe that was normal.

"Hey!" she said, tapping the soles of his shoes. "Feet off the bed. You know the rules." She bit her lip — she was being controlling already, without even thinking.

"Sorry." His voice was cracked too, torn between boy and man. He sat up and held the ball on his lap, studying it so he wouldn't have to look at her.

"About this afternoon's plans ..." She saw him tense and felt a stab of anguish. So Matt was right, Jonah did dread her "lists." "Um, if you want to just hang out, or do something on your own, that's fine."

"Are you serious?" he asked. Then cautiously, he added, "What's the catch?"

"No catch. I've got a lot of stuff I need to do, so I won't bug you."

He looked up with undisguised surprise and delight. "Can I go to Joey's?"

He was testing her, she knew. Joey was the neighborhood bad boy. He lived two blocks away, and he had become Jonah's best friend when they'd moved in three years earlier. The two of them had never gotten into serious trouble, but they'd come close a few times. She had always known Joey was the instigator of their pranks, saw that he bullied her son into situations Jonah would have never gotten into on his own. But Jonah had always been overly susceptible to peer pressure, desperate to be liked, traits he'd inherited from his father, who had become a psychologist because he wanted to be everyone's confidant and best friend.

Switching Jonah to a boarding school had been predicated in part by Emily's desire to separate him from Joey — or at least to put him into an environment where there would be good influences as well. There had been other reasons for sending him away. The school she had chosen, Oceancrest, had an accelerated arts program, and she hoped to foster Jonah's creativity. And Jack had supported the idea of boarding school; he'd gone to one himself. "All boys need to get away from their moms at this age," he'd said, "or else they grow up to *be* their mothers."

She didn't want Jonah to go off and leave her today; she was desperate for his company. But when she saw the eagerness on his face, what could she do but say yes.

"You'll be home for din — " She stopped herself. "Oh, go, have a good time. Call me and let me know what you're going to do for dinner. I made chicken pot pies if you decide to eat home."

"Thanks!"

"You're welcome."

Jonah bounded to his feet and lunged for the door, not taking a chance that she would change her mind.

"Wait — before you go — "

"Aw, Mom," he whined, sagging against the doorjamb.

"Don't panic, I just want to ask you one quick question. About Jack."

"I knew it was too good to be true." Jonah plopped back down on the bed, facing away from her, and began bouncing the basketball between his feet.

"Jonah," she caught the ball mid-bounce, and she sat down beside him. "What do you feel about ... about his death?" She sounded just like Matt and hated herself for it.

"What d'you mean?"

"I mean, are you angry, or sad, or scared? Are you curious about the accident?"

"I dunno. None of those, I guess," he mumbled.

"You've got to feel something," she prodded.

"Why?"

"Because he was — " What was Jack to Jonah? His stepfather, yes, but only technically. Matt was still very much his father; Jack had been merely a recent and an occasional stand-in. "He loved you. You know that, don't you?"

"I guess."

"Don't you even care that he's dead?" she demanded in exasperation.

"Yeah, I care, okay?" Jonah mumbled, gnawing on a hangnail, clearly uncomfortable. "Can I go now?"

"No! If you care that he's dead, you must be able to give a name to what you're feeling." This was something else Matt always said, *give a name to it.* She hated that she kept using his words.

Jonah was mute. Then he turned and looked at Emily, dead on. Without expression, he said, "Okay, here it is. What I feel is like I'm off the hook because I won't have to hang out with him anymore just to make you happy. Satisfied?" He got to his feet and started for the door.

Stung, she threw the ball at him, a bit harder than she meant to. He caught it and eyed her warily, knowing he'd stepped over a line. "Jack was a wonderful man! He was joyful and strong and kind. And he was honorable. Everyone knew it. He wasn't perfect, but he knew who he was, and he accepted the good and the bad in himself. And he was that way about the people he loved too. When you refused to meet him halfway, he never got angry, did he? He just backed off and let you be. He was tolerant. Do you know how rare that quality is? Do you?" she persisted.

"I 'spose."

She gave up. "Oh, phone me later," she said, trying to keep the resignation out of her voice. "Let me know if you'll be here for dinner. And start thinking about what kind of party you want for your birthday. The invitations should go out next weekend."

"Mom, I told you. I really don't want any big deal," he said.

"But it's your — " she began, but he was already gone. She was alone again.

"And tie your shoes!" she called after him.

◌

Emily stripped off her clothes and lay down on the bed without getting under the covers, without putting on her nightgown, without caring about anything but sleep. She closed her eyes and lay utterly still, waiting, wanting the release, but then unable to give in to it. Her body felt damp and heavy. She was having trouble breathing, and her heart was racing.

Her thoughts shot back to another time when she'd felt like this, on one of her first dates with Jack. He'd suggested that they go scuba diving at his favorite spot in Palos Verdes. She had never gone diving before, but she was a strong swimmer, and at that early stage in their relationship she had been eager to please him, to be a cheerful companion and a good sport. But still, it was her nature to be cautious. Don't you need some sort of license, she'd asked.

Jack had scoffed at her concern. Diving was easy, as simple as riding a bicycle, and he would teach her. So she'd gone along with it, had let him rent the full complement of equipment, and was waiting outside for him at dawn, a time of day when she normally — and preferably — would have been preparing for her morning run.

On the drive south, he'd pointed out some of his favorite haunts: the little market where he always stopped for coffee, the gas station where they would go after the dive — the owner was a diver himself and would let them use his hose to rinse the salt water from their gear, the taco stand where they would have lunch. She would be starved, he had assured her, and this place had the best burritos north of Tijuana.

They had been in such good spirits! The secluded cove was a breathtaking, crescent-shaped strip of sand beneath steep cliffs. And she had felt like they were a team, a couple! After having agonized over the decision to ask Matt for a divorce — after having dealt with Jonah's confusion and fury, the messy details of separation, the hassle of legal proceedings, the dissection of their joint property — but mostly, after having faced the reality of single life, the prospect of finding a new partner so soon made Emily buoyant with optimism.

So despite the fact that Jack's instructions to her had been brief and vague, she'd stood next to him on the rocky spar of land which jutted out into a deep bay, let him strap the tank on her back, and pull the mask down over her nose. And on his command, she'd plunged into the water feet first.

When she hit, the frigid shock had put her whole body on alert. She'd tried desperately to remember Jack's sketchy instructions about breathing underwater: *suck in through the nose and blow out through the mouth, like you have a head cold.* But doing this on dry land had been one thing. Under ten feet of water, it was quite something else. Plus, he had not explained to her that there were currents to deal with, that while she was concentrating on breathing, she must also think about swimming, or else her body would be hurled against rocks.

Not only that, but despite the thick skin of the wetsuit, the water was freezing. Wasn't its job to keep her warm? If the wetsuit wasn't performing as promised, who was to say the tank of air wouldn't fail as well?

She had felt her anxiety level rising. Fear was a weight on top of her, an invisible force holding a heavy pillow over her mouth and nose, pressing down just hard enough to immobilize her. She forgot Jack's instructions to breathe "in through the nose, out through the mouth," and her body slowly sank to the bottom.

Despite the fact that he had been remiss as a teacher, Jack was watching her closely, and as she'd started to sink, he'd rushed to her side, swimming furiously, all flippers and flailing arms. Emily had allowed him to scoop her up and pull her to the surface and then to shepherd her toward the beach.

"What were you afraid of?" he'd asked, once they were safely on the sand and she was bundled in a towel. "Why did you give up? You were just ten feet under the surface."

She had only been able to shake her head dumbly. How do you explain fear? Maybe she wasn't a fighter. Maybe she was weak or just stupid. She'd thought she'd blown it, that it would be the end of their relationship. But she'd been wrong. Jack had continued to call her for dates, and they had become good friends, then lovers, then husband and wife.

Months later, when she dared broach the subject, he'd admitted that yes, he'd been a little disappointed that she had not proven to be a good scuba companion. "But this is the way I look at it — it meant a hell of a lot that when I said go, you jumped into the ocean. I knew you were afraid, but you trusted me. When the chips are down, that's what I want in a partner. Besides," he added with a grin, "I saved your life, so you owe me. And I plan to collect for the rest of our lives!"

Now she was drowning again, grief pressing the air out of her lungs. But this time, Jack was not there to save her.

7

She finally admitted to Ann that something was wrong. "I tell myself I'm grieving, that I have to go through it. But it's not what I thought it would be like. I could deal with being sad, but I'm not, really. Not sad. At least not how I thought I'd be. What I am is nauseated and exhausted, depressed, lethargic. My concentration is shot. And look at my skin. I've got teenage acne. And my hair is so limp all I can do is put it in a ponytail. Do you think I should see a doctor?"

"What you need is therapy," Ann insisted, flipping through the pages of her filofax. "And I know just the woman to send you to."

"Wait a minute! I don't want to tell some stranger all of my personal problems," Emily protested.

"Marilyn Macy isn't a stranger. She lives in my building, right down the hall. You remember her, tall, mid-forties, wears Jungle Gardenia perfume. Much too much Jungle Gardenia perfume, if you ask me." Ann wrinkled her nose. "Sometimes I want to gag when I open my door. But I think she's an excellent therapist."

"I don't believe in therapy."

Ann responded with a knowing smile. "You can't possibly say

that unless you've tried it," she'd said. "And once you do, you'll see that it's very comforting, a great way of releasing the inner demon."

"That's what I have you for," Emily teased. "To release my inner demon."

"And that's why *I* have to go to a shrink," Ann countered. "Seriously, try it. You'll be glad. I promise you."

"Why this Marilyn Macy? Why not your doctor?" Emily asked. "You seem to think so highly of him."

"I don't think Dr. Janz would be right for you," Ann said hastily.

"Why not?"

"Well, for one thing, he just listens. He doesn't say anything, which is fine for me because I'm such a motor mouth. But as resistant as you are to spilling your guts, I think you need someone more responsive to coax you through it. Also, I think you'd be better off with a woman."

"Why?"

"Because you're very vulnerable right now, and you don't want to fall in love with your shrink."

"You mean you — "

Ann looked away. "Just trust me on this."

"That's not going to happen to me."

"Don't be so sure," Ann cautioned. "You'd be surprised how easy it is to fall for someone who hangs on your every word like you're the most fascinating person in the world. All of a sudden, you forget you're paying him to listen. Pretty soon, well, you're already prone, so nature takes over. And then what do you do? Of course the good doctor is feeling nada, or at least it's unethical for him to admit it if he is feeling anything close to reciprocal. So it's a one-way street, which is bad enough. But if anything happens, it's worse, because then you lose your therapist — so who do you tell about the torrid affair you're having with your shrink?

"You're better off with a woman. I guarantee it."

◯

Emily stood in the hall outside of Dr. Marilyn Macy's office, trying to summon the courage to enter. She looked at her watch. It was two minutes after two, so she was already tardy, which annoyed her on general principle — she hated to be late! But also, it meant that she was wasting money, because Dr. Macy operated on a payment-in-advance/no refund system.

The elevator door opened, and a man got out. He walked past Emily, paused, then turned around and came back. "The numbering in this building is a little confusing," he said politely. "Can I help you find an office?"

"Oh, no, thank you," Emily stammered. "This is where I'm going." And she quickly opened the door and stepped in.

The anteroom was tiny, only big enough for two chairs and a low telephone table. The door leading to the inner office was ajar. Should she wait, knock, or just walk in? "Hello?" she called out tentatively.

Marilyn Macy appeared at the door. "Emily? Yes, of course, I recognize you," she confirmed. "You used to stay at Ann's a few years ago."

"Before I married Jack — " His name caught in her throat, and there was an awkward silence.

"Well, I'm glad to see you again. Come in," Marilyn said. She stepped aside for Emily to enter.

"I almost didn't come," Emily admitted. Then, apologetically, she added, "I'm not sure I can do this."

"We're just going to have a friendly chat, Emily. If you find it uncomfortable, we'll stop. Don't be concerned," Dr. Macy reassured her. "Nothing you can say or do here is 'wrong.' It's just a process, a discovery, a way of helping you find the tools to deal with your life. Come on in."

Emily looked around the room. She had expected a black leather couch with a straight-back chair next to it, a serious desk, framed diplomas on the wall. But Dr. Macy's inner office was decorated in chenille and chintz. Instead of the leather couch, there was a very inviting chaise lounge covered with needlepoint pillows, each depicting a different breed of dog. A canvas-in-progress was lying on the table between two wing chairs a few feet away from the chaise, and beside it sat a basket mounded with colorful skeins of fine, thin wool. There were no diplomas on the wall, just some tastefully framed abstract watercolors.

"This is beautiful," Emily said.

"But it isn't what you expected?" Dr. Macy asked.

"Not really."

"My philosophy is that the more comfortable and *comforted* my patients feel, the more willing they'll be to open up. To be honest, this Laura Ashley look isn't exactly my style. At home, my furniture is Knoll and Le Courbousier. But this seems to help my clients relax. Is it working?"

Emily nodded. "All you need is some homemade cookies."

Dr. Macy turned to the table beside the lounge and reached for a plate. "There's a *Mrs. Fields* in the cafeteria of this building. She's a much better baker than I am, so I let her do the work. Help yourself."

"Thank you, maybe later," Emily said. She looked around the room. "Where do you want me to sit?"

"Wherever you want. You can stretch out on the chaise and put your feet up, or we can sit in these two chairs and talk face to face. Some of my patients prefer to pace. I've got one who likes to stand on his head!"

"If I had my choice, I'd rather we were outside, going for a run."

"I'm open to some exercise," Dr. Macy said, much to Emily's surprise. "But we'd have to keep it to a fast walk. Since neither of us is dressed for it today, why don't we just stay here? We've only got thirty-five minutes left as it is, not much time for a first session."

Emily looked around, then chose one of the wing chairs. It was comfortable without being too soft. Dr. Macy took the other.

"Do you mind if I work on this while we chat?" she asked, picking up her needlework.

"No. The pillows are beautiful."

Dr. Macy held up the canvas for Emily to see. "I'm doing a series." She pointed out the various pillows. "Boxer, Collie, Saluki, Samoyed. This one's a Rottweiler." She held it at arm's length and eyed it critically. "Although at this point it looks rather more like a deformed black pig! Do you have a dog?"

Emily nodded. "A Wheaton Terrier mix. The love of my life. I can't believe how dependent I am on him. He's become very protective of me since Jack died." She paused and looked at Dr. Macy. "Well, I guess I jumped in feet first, didn't I?"

"Nothing wrong with that." The doctor looked up from her needlework. "Ann told me about the accident. I'm so sorry for your loss." Then in a quieter tone she continued, "I'd like to hear about it in your own words, if you feel comfortable telling me, that is."

○

Precisely thirty-five minutes later, Emily left Dr. Macy's office through a side door which led directly into the hall. She looked at the slip of paper in her hand. On it was the name of an internist, Dr. Evelyn Marshall.

"From what you've told me, it's conceivable that the cause of your symptoms is physical, not emotional," Dr. Macy had told her. "Why don't we rule out the possibility of something corporeal before we blame it on your psyche? Not that you don't have every emotional reason in the world to feel lousy. But let's take it one step at a time."

Emily dialed Party Line from her car phone. "Was she any good?" Ann asked.

"What do you mean 'was she any good?' You're the one who recommended her!"

"Yeah, but I only know her as a neighbor. That time the police caught those two kids spray painting graffiti on the building, everybody wanted to put them in jail except Marilyn. She suggested putting them in an art school and letting them learn how to express themselves on canvas. That showed me a lot of class."

"Did it work?"

"We didn't *do* it. The vote was unanimous against Marilyn and me. I just liked that she had the idea." Ann's voice through the phone became distant. "Lew! Something's being cremated. Can you check the pies for Simington? Christ, where is everyone! We've got a three-alarm fire going here. Look sweetie, I gotta go before the pecan pies for tonight turn to charcoal. You coming back in?"

"No, Dr. Macy wants me to see another doctor. I might as well get it over with."

"What other kind of doctor?"

"An internist. She thought I should get a physical before we started ripping my psyche to shreds. I suppose it's a good idea. I haven't had one for years."

"Well, I'll leave for Simington by six. Party's at seven. See you there."

○

Forty-five minutes later, after a battery of preliminary tests, poking, prodding, measuring, and questioning, the doctor called Emily into her office. "I think I know what's causing you this distress, Mrs. Barnes," she said.

"Is it serious?" Emily asked.

"Yes, very," she replied. Then she smiled. "Congratulations, you're pregnant."

◯

"YOU'RE WHAT?" Ann screamed. The platter she was holding tilted precariously, and Emily lunged forward to catch the pecan pie before it slid onto the floor. The other Party Line staffers who were crowded into the small space of the Simington kitchen stopped working and turned to stare.

"Ann," Emily hissed between clenched teeth. "I told you I didn't want anyone else to know right now."

"What are you, Emily?" Lew asked. He was arranging copper-and gold-painted vegetables in a silver bowl, the centerpiece for the Simingtons' fiftieth anniversary party. "In love, in debt, or," he held up a cucumber dill, "in a pickle?"

Nancy, her arms plunged in a sinkful of soapy water, chimed in, "Or are you up to your elbows in hot water?"

Stephen, the bartender, stopped chopping limes and lemons and said, "Sounds juicy, whatever it is."

"Go back to work, you cornballs!" Ann shooed them back to their jobs. "You three are worse than the audience at a *Rosie O'Donnell* taping."

"She's going on *Rosie*?" Nancy asked. "My next-door neighbor's cousin was on once. It was a show about psychic healers, and this woman had one remove a fibroid from her uterus without surgery. They showed a film clip. I swear, the thing was the size of a grapefruit! But it was dripping blood and ... "

"Thank you so much for sharing that appetizing tidbit with us just before we serve," Lew said, as Ann and Emily pushed through the swinging door into the dining room.

"I just wish my bra size was as big as my mouth," Ann said apologetically. "Sorry, you took me by surprise."

"Which is exactly how I felt when the doctor told me!"

"How far along are you?"

"Five weeks."

"So it is — "

"*Of course it's Jack's.* Who else's would it be?"

"Well I don't know what you do in your private time!"

"Yes, you do."

"Yeah, you're right," Ann admitted. "Are you going to keep it?"

"I don't know." They set the pies on a burlwood sideboard. "These days I can't even decide which running shoes to wear. How am I going to decide what to do about this?" She spent a moment putting the proper utensils on each platter. "When I found out I was pregnant with Jonah it was such a happy time. Matt was ecstatic. He went out the next day and bought an entire roomful of baby furniture on credit. We were paying off that Visa bill for three years!"

"What would Jack have thought?"

Emily sighed. "I've told you how much he wanted us to have a child."

"But you didn't do it."

"I have Jonah. I didn't really need to go through all that again. Now ... I could look at this as a gift Jack has given me, a parting gift. But I can't imagine going through pregnancy and childbirth alone, to say nothing of raising a child as a single parent, can you?"

Ann was silent. "I've thought about it," she said softly.

"You have?"

"Well, sure, hasn't every woman? The problem is, I could never go to a sperm bank." She shuddered. "I'd want to at least know the father and the genes. And the older I get, the more picky I am about potential candidates."

♲

Emily didn't go straight home. Instead, she turned right on Jessup and pulled to a stop just before the intersection at Dover, the place where Jack's accident had occurred. She turned off the engine, letting the darkness surround her. It had become a habit to visit this spot at least once a day. What drew her here? If she wanted to remember Jack, why not go to the grove of eucalyptus trees at the country club where his ashes were buried?

Because this was the last place Jack had been fully *alive*. If there were such a thing as a spirit, Jack's was still here — and along with it, the unfinished business of saying good-bye to him.

"Jack," she said aloud, her breath steaming the glass of the windshield. "I have news for us. I'm pregnant. Are you glad? Do you want a child? Is this all part of some grand plan? What should I do?" She rested her head on the steering wheel and closed her eyes. "What should I do?"

A rapping on the window startled her. She jerked her head up, and though her eyes were blurred with tears, the window fogged, she could see a man peering in from the passenger side. At the same instant, she realized that the door was not locked. A cry of surprise caught in her throat.

The man was speaking, but his voice was muffled by the heavy glass of the window. Fear was a bird caged inside her chest, beating its wings to escape. *Get out of here. Drive away!* she thought. But the urgent message wasn't getting to her hands. Instead of moving to turn the key in the ignition, they remained locked around the steering wheel.

Then the handle of the passenger door was turning. Her purse was open on the seat next to her. There was money in it and a fine snakeskin wallet her parents had given her for her birthday. Maybe that would satisfy him, and he would let her drive off, unharmed.

The door swung open, and the man stuck his head in. He was wearing a knit cap, and the skin on his face was mottled with the evening chill. In the dim light cast by the street lamp, his smile seemed sinister.

"What do you want?" Her voice came out a whisper, and he

leaned further into the car, perhaps to hear her better, perhaps because he sensed her fearful awareness of her own vulnerability.

"I seen you sittin' here most every night when Arthur and I take our late walk." He nodded downward, and hearing his name, a Jack Russell terrier leapt onto the car seat. Startled by the sudden movement, Emily gasped and drew back against the door. The dog wagged his tail and thrust out his snout toward her, sniffing the air.

"Geez, Arthur, get the hell down from there. The lady don't want you in her nice clean car." The man reached in and jerked roughly on the dog's collar, trying to drag him from the car. But the terrier wiggled closer to Emily, obviously soliciting a second opinion. "Arthur, damn you! Sorry 'bout this. He gets me into a hell of a lot of trouble, this little guy. Other day, early Saturday morning, coupla three weeks ago, he runs out into the street, to do his deed in the gutter, y'know, like he's been taught. He's good about that. Most dogs are, you give 'em a chance. Anyway, a guy comes haulin' down Dover, smokin' a cigar the size of a knockwurst. He musta seen Artie here squattin' in the gutter, 'cause he swerves like hell, not that he needed to. Artie was just takin' care of business. Next thing I know this guy guns it and *wham*! Damn car barrels smack into a Pepsi truck."

The words tore at Emily like lashes of a whip. "Was he badly hurt?" she asked.

"Badly hurt? I mean to tell ya ... his body flew outta that car like it was in an ejection seat, like those fighter jets have, y'know? Only this guy don't go soaring through the air 'til his parachute deploys. No sir, he sails through the windshield and slams into the Pepsi truck — *Bam!* — and drops like a stone." The man gestured with his shoulder against the dashboard to illustrate the impact. "It all happened in a flash. But the sound of it! Good thing he didn't hit his head. I mean he would have been dead meat!" He shook his own head, remembering the scene. "Most gruesome thing I ever saw." He gestured out at the intersection. "You can still see the bloodstain on the street," he added.

Emily lowered her eyes and wrapped her arms around herself, keening. She couldn't look at the man, but she wanted to hear the rest. "Then what happened?" she asked in a whisper.

"I grabbed Arthur, ran back to the house, and called 911. By the time I got back the police were here already, couldn't have been more than three, four minutes. Musta had a patrol car in the area. An ambulance pulls up maybe five minutes later. Got him out of here in no time flat. That guy was some lucky sonofabitch, excuse my French. Don't mean to get so carried away, but you don't see one like that every day."

Emily stroked the small dog who was watching his master with rapt attention. Surprisingly, she felt no anger at the animal who had unknowingly precipitated Jack's death, nor at his master. Clearly, by retelling the story to anyone who would listen, the man was struggling to exorcise the guilt he felt for the part he and his dog had played in the accident. She wondered how he would react if she told him who she was, if she picked up the story and recounted Jack's eleven hours of surgery, the extent of his injuries, his death the next day.

"Maybe you shouldn't let your dog off the leash," she said finally.

"T'weren't his fault. The guy — "

"But the dog could get hit by a car, don't you think?"

The man shrugged. "He won't take care of his business on a leash. What am I supposed to do?"

He gathered up the dog and got out of the car. "Sorry ta disturb ya. Have a nice night."

THREE

8

To Sampson's surprise, the doctor's timetable proved uncannily accurate. He did sit up briefly the second day after surgery, and he was walking — well shuffling — down the hall on the fourth. On the tenth day, they'd brought an exercise bike into his room, and on the eighteenth, he was dressed, at the door to his room, waiting in a wheelchair for the orderly to bring him his discharge papers. He'd lost a tremendous amount of weight. The jeans and polo shirt he'd arrived in four months earlier now draped his body in exaggerated folds. Even his shoes and socks seemed too large — could his feet have shrunk? But he'd been told to expect a dramatic weight gain due to the steroids they were pumping into his system to ward off rejection. He didn't like the idea of getting fat, but it was a lot better than getting dead.

"Good-bye, Mr. Sampson," the red-headed nurse said, as the orderly wheeled him past her station. "I wish you the luck o'the Irish."

"Good-bye to you too, Nurse O'Shea. I can't exactly say it's been a pleasure being here," Sampson said, "except I have enjoyed seeing the sun shining in your face each morning. I'm going to miss that."

"Well, glory be," she beamed, her face reddening to almost the color of her coiled hair. "He must've got the heart of a real gentleman!"

Dr. Greshom caught up to him as he waited for the elevator. "Feeling good?"

"Never better," Sampson said, surprised at how good he did feel.

"Sam, listen, you've done great, but you've got a long road ahead."

Sampson braced for bad news. "Don't tell me. The new heart is a lemon. It's being recalled for repairs."

"No, no. Nothing like that. Nothing you haven't heard a million times. I just want to go on record once more. First of all, you've had *major* surgery. That in itself is a shock to the system. Second, you've got a new heart. It's a strong one, but as far as your immune system is concerned, it's a foreign object and your body wants to get it out of there."

"I thought that's why I'm talking the cyclosporine and the steroids to put a lid on my immune system."

"True," Dr. Greshom admitted, "but our experience is that most recipients still go through at least one episode of rejection. It will take your body time to adjust. And because we've depressed your immune system to practically zero, you're at an incredibly high risk for infection. Don't let anyone who's sick get within a hundred feet of you. Avoid drafts, germs, and bacteria. And for now, by all means, forget you even heard the word sex. Even an innocent kiss could be the kiss of death."

"That's encouraging," Sampson said grimly.

"The encouraging news is you've got a healthy heart, which is more than I could have said for you last month. And my patients have a very high survival rate. The odds are in your favor. Just take it easy, okay?"

◯

Gracie peeked through the curtains of the old house, which were drawn to keep the heat in on the cold and rainy winter day. "He's here, Mom!" she called, her voice shrill with excitement. "I can see him!"

"Finally!" Diana said. She wiped her hands on her apron and looked out the window at the Medivan pulling into the driveway. She regretted that she hadn't been able to pick Sam up herself, but someone had to supervise her mother and the kids, that was just the way it was. The attendant got out and walked around to open the passenger door, and a gaunt, pale man emerged. If she hadn't known it was Sam, she wouldn't have recognized him.

Despite the steady rain, or perhaps because of it, Sampson took his time coming up the walk. It had been more than four months since he had been in a climate other than the regulated hothouse temperature of the hospital, or set foot on anything besides drab industrial carpet or waxed linoleum. He savored the sensation of actually *feeling* the conditions outside of his body, and he wanted to make it last.

"Why doesn't he hurry?" Gracie whined.

"You're so spacy, Gracie," Kevin snarled. "Doncha remember?" He grabbed his younger sister roughly and slashed at her chest as though his hand were a knife. "They slit him open and yanked out his heart. He's a mutant now. And he's gonna come and get you while you're sleeping and rip your fingernails out with his bare teeth. Grrrrr!"

"Mom!" Gracie screamed, pulling away.

"Kevin stop it, you're scaring her," Diana warned, biting her lip to keep from letting it show that he was scaring her too. She'd begged Kevin to be here for Sam's homecoming, and for once the boy had acquiesced. But that morning she'd noticed a new bruise on Gracie's forearm. Now it was turning a vicious shade of purple. She wondered if Kevin had purposely hurt his younger sister, or if the two had just been playing, as both had insisted. "Please don't ruin this for all of us, Kevin," she said.

"What did I do?" he implored.

She ignored him and looked out the window. Sam was waving good-bye to the driver of the Medivan. He started up the path, but only went a few steps, then turned and pulled a small branch off of the camellia bush. He held it to his nose and inhaled deeply. Diana could see that the rain was soaking through his light jacket.

She flung open the door and called, "Sam! Hurry up and get your derriere in here! You'll catch your death." She bit her lip. Damn, she hadn't meant to say that word.

"Hasn't caught me yet," Sam beamed, meandering up the walk at a snail's pace. She watched him approach, struggling to hide her concern behind a smile. What happens to a man's soul when he endures what Sam had endured — not just the surgery and the transplant, but the chronic proximity of death? She remembered friends of her high school steady, Charles, who had been drafted and shipped off to fight in Vietnam. They had left as boys with their bright innocence worn as carelessly as the sweaters looped around their necks. But they had returned as men, with furtive eyes and war tattooed on their arms.

Without realizing it, she had expected the same of Sam: surviving a life-and-death ordeal meant coming out the other end changed. But she could read no outward difference in Sam, no bitterness. He looked thinner, to be sure, scrawny in his sweatshirt and jeans, but he had been thin before this illness had begun to consume his life. His long hair, a casualty of months of radical medication, was buzz cut close to his head, making his ears appear to stick out at right angles. But his color was better than before, pale, but no longer a sickly green. And his eyes, naturally droopy at the corners like her

own, did seem to have a touch of the old sparkle back in them —
or was that the glint of tears?

He was coming up the stairs, not taking them one at a time as he
had for months before he went into the hospital, when they were
still all in denial about how serious his heart condition had become,
but barging straight up them to the porch, without even stopping
to catch his breath. Diana ran out to meet him, and he threw his
arms around her, hugging her, and they were both crying — then
laughing, like maniacs.

"Jesus, Sam, you're drenched!"

"And it feels glorious! Where are the kids? I've got presents!"

"Here!" Gracie shouted. Giggling, she ran out into the rain and
threw her arms around him. Kevin hung back, self-consciously
kicking the floor molding with the heel of his filthy, torn sneaker.

"Ohhh!" Gracie's voice was shrill. "Uncle Sam, you're as wet as
a mad hen," she cried, and snatched at the small stuffed bear he
held out to her.

"That's mad as a wet hen, you dingbat," Kevin growled from the
cover of the doorway.

"Hey, guy, come on out and get doused like the rest of us." Sam
reached out a hand, but Kevin folded his arms across his chest,
scowling.

"No way, man. I'm not nuts."

"Kevin, for heaven's sake," Diana scolded. "It won't hurt you."

"Who asked you?" Kevin muttered.

"Kevin — "

Sam dropped his hand. "Let it go, Diana," he said softly. "It's no
big deal." But the joyful mood was broken. They all trooped wetly
into the house, and Diana hurried off to get towels.

"So how's it goin'?" Sam asked Kevin.

"It's cool," Kevin shrugged noncommittally.

"Brought you something for your collection," Sam said. He

patted both pants pockets, then dug his hand into his coat pockets, one, then the other, finally finding what he was looking for. He held up a long, thin, shiny pin for Kevin to see.

"What is it?" Kevin's voice was slack with disinterest.

"It's a pin they use to hold bones together after a bad break. The shopping opportunities were kinda limited at the hospital, and I didn't think you'd want a stuffed animal," he said. "But this, well, I thought maybe you could make an earring with it or something."

"Thanks." Kevin grunted and started up the stairs to his room.

"Great, Sam," Diana sighed, handing him a towel. "Just what he needs is encouragement." She helped him out of his wet jacket. "You know he opened a charge account at *Piercing Kingdom*. I don't even ask where he gets the money to pay for what he buys."

"What's the big deal? You pierced your ears when you were his age," Sam reminded her.

"Yeah, but not my eyebrow, my nose, my tongue, or God knows what other body part. Sometimes I think I can hear him *clanking* when he walks!" She shivered involuntarily. "Gives me the creeps."

"That's part of the point, don't you think, to send old mom around the bend? How's he been otherwise?"

She shrugged. "The same — remote, hostile, nasty to everyone."

"Your typical teenage boy."

"As though you, who aren't even married, would have a clue!" She shook her head. "You know what I found in his room?"

"I'll take a wild guess. *Playboy*."

"Close. This one's called *Tattooed Lust,* or something like that." She shuddered. "I couldn't even stand to touch it."

"Just like I said, your typical teenage boy."

"Well, I don't like it."

"You're not supposed to. You shouldn't be snooping around in his room anyway. A mother's place is in the kitchen and in the laundry room."

"Speaking of moms — ours is waiting to see you," Diana said.

"And how is she?" he asked.

"Some days are better than others. On the bad ones I have to watch her like a hawk. It's a good thing she's in that chair, though, or I'd be chasing her all over the neighborhood." She dried Sam's short hair with a fresh towel. "Yesterday I went in her room and she had put on every sweater in her dresser. Every single one! I asked her if she was cold, pointed out that she was sweating like she was in a steambath, but she couldn't seem to equate the two things, that wearing all those sweaters would make her so hot. Fortunately, today she's in prime form. I'd better warn you, though, she's got this whole party planned for you."

Sam froze. "Party? Oh, man," he groaned.

"She wanted to surprise you the minute you walked in, but I convinced her we should let you get home and get settled first, and have the party this evening."

"Good thinking. The surprise probably would have given me a heart attack."

"That's an awful thing to say."

"It's true. I'm not supposed to be in crowds. Doctor's orders."

"Well, the doctor is going to be here too, so I guess it's okay."

"But I hate parties."

"It's not for you, silly, it's for her. And she's got her heart set on it. You're not the only one who's been through this crisis, you know."

Sam said nothing. He knew his long stay in the hospital had been a strain on everyone.

"And I've been cooking for a week. You could at least act a little grateful."

"Grateful is one thing I am, Sis. I just wish there was some way to show it besides being the guest of honor at a damn party!"

◌

From his bedroom on the second floor, Sam could hear the sounds of the guests arriving, but he didn't get out of bed. Over the past few years, *bed* had become more than a place to sleep, it was his refuge. As he lay still, resting his body, his mind worked, replaying the well-known refrain of the progression of his illness, from the time it had been diagnosed, to the present, a meditation that calmed and terrified him in equal measures. But like an irritating advertising jingle, it kept replaying over and over.

Most of the doctors agreed that the damage to his heart was congenital, but it had only been discovered five years earlier. He'd been at a gig in Newport, playing drums with a band from San Diego, subbing for their regular drummer who, without warning, had split for Mexico. Sam had felt fine when he'd taken the stage. Actually, he hadn't *been* fine, but it wasn't until later that he'd learned that the way he'd been feeling — exhausted, breathless, depressed, symptoms he'd been blaming on too many late nights and the lack of love in his life — were indications of heart disease. Sure, getting up in the morning had taken a supreme act of will, and even the most fundamental physical exertion had left him gasping for air. But he'd assumed it was because he hated to exercise and was in lousy shape.

He'd even had an excuse for the most telling sign: the swelling of his lower extremities, which made it uncomfortable even to stand. This he'd blamed on his diet: too much salt. In truth, it was his body crying for help: his dying heart was too weak to pump his bodily fluids, so they pooled in his ankles and feet, even in his testicles, which swelled to the size of grapefruits, a very odd sensation that gave him a good excuse to not test his luck on any of the sweet young things who hung around backstage.

They'd been playing their second set that night, in the middle of his solo on *In-A-Gadda-Da-Vida*. He was in the thrall of the music, feeling the beat reverberating through his body when, without warning, he'd felt a numbness in his arm, a mild sensation which quickly turned into a sharp pain. Then he'd blacked out, fainted dead away.

Someone had called 911, and the paramedics arrived in minutes, which had probably saved his life. What drama — and he'd missed the whole thing! He'd regained consciousness at Hamilton Hospital, and the young emergency doctor there had run a battery of tests on him, then called in a cardiologist who'd arrived in a tuxedo, smelling of cigars and expensive brandy. The upshot was he'd learned his heart was a piece of crap, leaking where it should have been tight as a snare drum, clogged where it should have been flowing freely, and practically double its normal size. They'd said it was a miracle he'd reached the ripe old age of twenty-nine without a doctor ever diagnosing the problem, and they pumped him full of medication — a waste to be force-fed drugs he couldn't even enjoy! They'd told him he would still be able to play the drums once he got his strength back, but being able to and wanting to were different things; he'd vowed to give up his music then and there. Everyone had thought it was a phase he was going through, that he was just concentrating his energies on getting better. But it wasn't that. Why did he need to play the drums when the rhythm of his heartbeat was so damn loud that it drowned out any sound he could make on his set?

When he'd come home, he'd stashed his drum kit in a closet in the back of the old house. It was of no use to him, because the only paradiddle he could hear was the one beating on his internal snare. And that one was too erratic to follow. It terrified him to try. Everything terrified him. Because he didn't know when he might fall over the edge again. Each time he sensed his heart beginning to race, he was consumed by panic, wondering if it would eventually slow on its own accord, or if it would take off on a riff that would cause his whole damn body to explode.

So he'd changed his lifestyle — taken the medication they'd prescribed, eaten right and exercised a little, and tried to ignore the black cloud of doom hanging over his head. He'd even tried alternative forms of therapy: acupuncture, meditation, visualization, herbs, homeopathy. But his health hadn't improved. In fact, it had gotten consistently worse, and worse, and still worse, until finally the judgment was made: he needed a new heart, or he would be dead before his thirty-fifth birthday.

And he'd begun the agonizing wait: four months in the hospital. For a lot of that time before the surgery, he'd felt pretty good, well enough to go home. But the doctors had told him his chances of getting a replacement heart would be better if he were in the hospital, making a case for how serious his condition was.

Truth be told, his health hadn't improved that much since the surgery. Yes, he was alive. But getting a transplant hadn't been the miracle cure he'd expected — not that he'd admit it to anyone. Breathing was still hard, and now he had to deal with the side effects of the drugs he was forced to take in mind-boggling quantities, up to 84 capsules a day. The cyclosporine and steroids, which were crucial in helping his body adjust to the new organ, caused fatigue, nausea, and irritability, to say nothing of the hidden damage they were doing to his eyes — causing cataracts, to his joints — osteoporosis, and to his sex drive — not just the drugs but the whole process had taken its toll on his libido. He had to be vigilant about cuts and small injuries, and he certainly had to keep out of the trajectory of viruses and infections, not the easiest thing to do while trying to live a normal life.

He'd tried to explain this to his mother, hoping she would call off the party. But she had refused to listen. Confined to a wheelchair by her arthritis and tortured by the onset of dementia, she coped by denying the existence of her own illness, so she applied the same surreal logic to his.

"But Ma, I can't be around people," he'd told her. "If I catch a cold, it could kill me."

"What cold could catch you?"

"I'm serious, Ma, the doctor told me — "

"Nonsense, darling, look at that scar on your chest. If you can survive that, you can survive anything."

She did have a point. If the miracle of modern medicine could give him a new heart, why couldn't it protect him from the common cold?

○

Sampson looked at the clock. It was six already, almost time for his entrance. When he'd been in his prime as a musician, he'd loved mingling with strangers, lived to get up in front of a crowd and perform. But since his heart trouble had been diagnosed, he'd begun to dread being with strangers or being forced to put up with people he didn't like — and there were so few that he *did* like. The last thing he wanted to do on his first night home from the hospital was to be nice to a houseful of doddering old fogies. But how could he disappoint his mother? She and Diana had hung in there with him throughout his ordeal, and one of the things he'd learned in the transplant support group sessions he'd been required to attend as part of his rehabilitation was that the process was almost as arduous for the family of the transplant recipient as it was for the recipient himself. So how could he deny them their celebration, just because he didn't want one himself?

He rose slowly and cautiously, to let the heart become accustomed to the change. Since the surgery, when he moved too suddenly, he'd had the horrifying sensation that the scar on his chest would rupture and all of his internal organs would spill out. When he'd dared mention this to Nurse O'Shea, she'd assured him that it was impossible, that it was just his brain playing tricks on him, a way of warning him to be careful.

So careful he was, in private anyway. But as soon as other people were around, he assumed an air of nonchalance and confidence about his body. He had been an invalid for so long, it was crucial to his self-esteem that people now perceive him as whole and healthy. When they told him how much they admired his strength and determination, he would shrug it off and reply, "What was my alternative?"

Sampson stood in front of the mirror, wondering if he would ever *feel* normal again after what he had been through. During the 106 days he had been in the hospital waiting for a new heart, he had done a lot of reading and a lot of thinking. The heart was the seat of all human emotion, the eye of the soul. What did it mean that his own heart was gone and a new one inserted in its place? Had he lost his soul as well?

He thought about the alien organ beating inside of his body, and of the nameless, faceless person who had died in order for him to live. What had he done to deserve such a gift? So far, his life had been unremarkable. He was only marginally talented as a drummer, certainly not brilliant. He had not achieved greatness in any conceivable way, nor had he made any lasting impact on the world. Why had he been worth saving? In some ways, it was a burden to have been given this priceless treasure, something he would now have to earn. Just the thought of it made him weary.

There was a knock at the door.

"Uncle Sam?"

"It's open."

Kevin opened the door just a crack. "She says it's time," he mumbled, without looking at Sampson, and started to close the door.

"Hey, hold on." Sampson called. "Come in. I want to show you something."

Kevin shuffled into the room, as though it pained him to do so, and stood awkwardly next to the door. He was huge for a 15-year-old, but his features had remained little-boyish, and his head appeared too small for his body. He compensated by wearing his hair long and uncombed, and decorating — or mutilating, depending on one's perspective — his face with multiple piercings. Between the facial jewelry and the raging acne, Kevin was not easy to look at.

He twitched uncomfortably, pulling at the frayed collar of his shirt. Obviously, he'd made some effort to dress for the occasion — it was a pretty safe bet that Diana had demanded it — but the tails of the shirt were untucked and, Sampson smiled to see, he was still wearing his grungy, torn sneakers.

"Come in, all the way," Sampson said. "And shut the door."

Kevin didn't move.

Sampson started to unbutton his pajama top. "I want to show you something."

"Hey man, cool it with the striptease. In case you forgot, I'm no pervert," Kevin sneered and started to back out the door.

"Shut up and look at me." Sampson's tone was sharp enough to halt Kevin's retreat. He walked over to the boy and held open the front of his pajama top. He didn't know why, but he knew it was important for his nephew to actually *see* the surgical scar. "Look at me," he repeated.

"Fuck that," Kevin said softly, eyes downcast, steadfastly studying the laces of his sneakers and twirling the skull-and-crossbones stud in his left ear.

Slowly, Sampson reached out and lifted Kevin's chin so that the boy's line of vision was even with the crusty wound on his chest. His touch was as tender as a lover's, and like a lover, Kevin finally allowed himself to be drawn into this intimacy, taking a shallow breath as he gave in to curiosity, gawking at the rent in Sampson's torso.

Sampson knew the wound was grotesque, especially since the staples had been removed. Now, in addition to the crimson slash of the incision, which ran from sternum to navel, there was also a line of black-scabbed holes on either side of the scar. And though he'd gained some weight, his skin was still drawn as tightly as the head on his Slingerland maple shell snare drum, and his shoulder blades still protruded like the Collarlock rack that held his hi-hat cymbal stand.

Sampson looked down at his chest and pointed at the place at the lower end of the incision where the line went all squiggly. "Damn doctor, you'd think he could've at least cut me straight," he grumbled with a grin.

Kevin said nothing.

"You can touch it if you want."

Kevin met his eyes curiously. "Why would I want to do that?"

"You know you want to. Give me your hand."

"No, hey man, I — "

"Give it to me!"

Reluctantly, Kevin let Sam guide his hand over the ridges of the incision. Although the nerves around the scar were numbed by trauma, Sam could feel the tremble in the boy's touch, an almost erotic sensation, and he felt his own emotions stir. Aside from the professional hands of nurses and doctors and the hug he'd received from his sister that morning, this was the closest physical contact he'd had with another person in months.

"What does it feel like to you?" he asked the boy.

"I dunno."

"Give me a word. Anything," Sam demanded sharply.

Kevin squirmed, but he did not pull away. "Cruddy." His voice was a reverent whisper.

"That's the healing, same as when you get a cut yourself and then it scabs. The body regenerates from the outside in. Kind of a miracle, don't you think, how it knits itself back together?"

Kevin jerked his hand away. "Thanks for the anatomy lesson. But can I go now?"

"Sure." Sam watched the boy retreat. Then he sighed, buttoned up his shirt, and followed the boy to the door.

Diana was walking up the stairs. She watched Kevin slouch past her without a word. "I was just coming to get you," she said to Sam. "What were you two doing?"

"Nothing. Just talking."

She raised an eyebrow. "That's a first. Did you get him to say more than two consecutive words?"

"Not exactly."

"I didn't think so. He hasn't been willing to make that deep of a commitment to human communication since Rod died." She put her hand to her mouth. "There I go. I promised myself I wasn't going to mention him. At least not on your first day home."

"It's okay. He's on my mind too. We're both *thinking* about him, we might as well *talk* about him."

"The holidays were so awful, Sam, with Rod only ten months in the ground and you in the hospital, getting weaker every day. I don't know how any of us got through it." Diana's eyes flooded with tears.

He put his arm around her shoulders. "I hope those are tears of joy, because we've both already tapped out our supply of sorrow."

"You sound like a country-western song," she said. "A corny, two bit country- western song. My favorite kind of music."

Sam rolled his eyes. "Yeah, I know. Just promise you won't admit that around anyone I know."

Using the back of her hand, Diana brushed away her tears. "Do I look okay?"

CAROL DOUMANI

"Beautiful." He reached for his bathrobe and put it on.

Diana straightened the collar and tied it shut for him. "How are you really, Sam? How about the pain?"

He shrugged off the question.

"No, really," she insisted. "Tell me."

Sam sighed. "I wouldn't call it pain. But I can feel the heart. It's uncomfortable, like someone reached inside of me and wrapped it in a bag. Like it's not me."

Diana's face clouded. "Should we call Dr. Greshom to come up? He's downstairs already, shaking hands with everyone like he's running for president. I guess he figures with the median age of this crowd hovering at around seventy-five, he can sign up a few more prospective patients. Shall I get him?"

"There's nothing he can do. It's not really a physical thing, at least that's what they tell me. It's more mental, or emotional, I guess. Come on, let's get this over with."

Diana picked a piece of lint off of his bathrobe. "Is that what you're wearing?"

Sampson looked down at his tattered robe, his uniform for the past five months. "Nothing else fits. Anyway, as long as I'm supposed to be the patient, I thought I'd dress the part."

○

"Mom's not so good at keeping a secret," Sampson told the assembled guests, once their polite applause had died down. He stood midway down the staircase, trying not to look at the faces below, concentrating on enunciating his words through the baffle of the sterile mask he had to wear over his mouth. "In fact, she told me you all were coming tonight, which is why I got all dressed up." There was laughter from the guests, and he relaxed a little.

"I'm touched that you've come, really, although I suppose you're here to make up for the fact that so few of you sent flowers or visited me in the hospital during the 130 days and 7 hours I was there." Groans from the crowd.

"Now, now," he continued. "The truth is, I can't blame you. Nobody likes hospitals, except for doctors — and they like them because every time they walk in the door, it costs someone's insurance company a thousand bucks."

He waited for the laughter to die down again. "But also, they know what a hospital really is. It isn't a place where sick people go to suffer and die, even though that sometimes happens, and to be honest, that's what I thought would happen to me when I checked in last November. No, a hospital is a place where miracles happen. And one happened to me."

Nobody spoke. The room was completely still, so silent that Sampson thought he could hear his new heart beating.

"Let me tell you what it's like to have a dying heart," he went on. "First of all, you're wiped out all of the time. Talking to you like this, well, I couldn't have done it last month because I wouldn't have had the strength. I wouldn't have had the desire either, because I was also depressed. All the time. No matter whether it was a beautiful day, or if the woman of my dreams showed up at my door, or if I'd just won the lottery —well, maybe that's the same thing."

Laughter again, and he waited until it got quiet. "Lying there, sick as a dog, nothing made me happy. I didn't want to work or eat or play my music. All I wanted to do was, well, I hate to say it, but it's true. All I wanted to do was die, because then at least I'd have relief.

"When Dr. Greshom told me I needed a new heart, I didn't believe him. See, I thought you'd be able to *feel* that your heart wasn't working — like having a stomach ache. And even though I felt like hell, it didn't seem like the pain was in my heart. So I ignored what he said and waited until I had a heart attack. Then I believed him.

"Okay, fine, doc, I need a new heart. Get me one. But that wasn't so easy. There are thousands of people out there who need new hearts and lungs and corneas and kidneys, and in most cases, the only way a guy like me is going to get one is if somebody else dies.

"Isn't that the pits? To think I was in the hospital for sixteen weeks, just waiting for some poor stranger to die and give me the greatest gift anyone can give another person? Whose heart is it, you ask? Well, they don't tell you that. I don't know what the wisdom is, but they are pretty hard-nosed about it. It could have been a man or a woman or a kid, well a *big kid* anyway, someone who died from an illness or an accident or a disease. It's kind of like the Lone Ranger: you ask yourself 'who was that masked stranger?' Well, I'll never know. But in any case, I'd like you all to join me, and raise your glasses to the person whose heart is beating in my chest."

"Here, here," someone called.

"And to the doctor who put it there, Gerald Greshom!"

"To the doctor!"

Dr. Greshom beamed and took a small bow.

There was silence as the guests sipped their drinks. "Now, let's get on with the party," Sam said. "I don't know about any of you, but I'm starving. Anybody got a burrito?"

"A burrito? I thought you never ate junk food," someone called.

"I know. Weird, isn't it?" he replied, perplexed at his own words. "For some reason I have an incredible craving for a nice greasy, cheesy, messy, totally-bad-for-my-new-heart burrito. Don't tell my doctor!"

9

*S*ampson slipped behind the wheel of the old Volvo and pulled the door shut. It closed with a satisfying metallic clank, sealing him in. He grasped the steering wheel in both hands, reveling in the sensation of being in the driver's seat after, what had it been, five months? Six?

Before his heart had tanked, he'd practically lived in this car, his drum kit stashed in the back, drifting from gig to gig, sitting in with bands for a single performance or a tour, or just bumming around until his money ran out. Impulsive, compulsive, erratic, undependable — he'd been all of these — before fear of dying made him prudent, restrained, careful, and rooted back home, on a street just heartbeats away from the hospital.

The question was, how would people describe him now?

He inhaled deeply, expecting to smell the familiar scent of worn leather, but instead got a nose full of the sugary perfume of the cookies Diana had baked for him to take to the hospital.

"What is this?" he'd asked when she'd handed him the red-and-white gingham box tied with a polka dot ribbon.

"A little thank-you for all the wonderful nurses who put up with you for so many months," she'd told him. "Believe me, they deserve it."

"I can't walk in there with this. I'll feel like a fool."

"You *are* a fool, Sammy, but it never stopped you before. Go on, everyone will love you for it. Trust me."

"I don't want them to love me," he'd whined. "I want them to forget they ever knew me, and that goes both ways."

But he'd taken the cookies anyway, thinking he might tuck into them himself now that his appetite was back with a vengeance. Strange that it manifest itself in a voracious hunger for junk food. He salivated just watching TV commercials for Jack-in-the-Box and McDonald's, and he had added tortilla chips, ice cream, and mayonnaise to Diana's marketing list.

Seat belt buckled, gearshift in park, left foot on the clutch, right foot on the brake, he turned the key in the ignition, and miraculously the old wagon chugged to life. A sense of elation washed over him, as though his life was beginning again.

"Hey, man!"

Sam turned and saw Kevin hurl himself down the stairs of the front porch. How the kid managed to move so fast without tripping on his low-slung Levis was one of the mysteries of youth. Sam rolled down his window. "What's up?"

"Drop me at the mall?"

"It's about five miles out of my way, but sure, if it's okay with your mom."

Kevin scowled. "Y'mean I need, like, *written permission* to go to the damn mall?"

"No," Sam replied evenly, "I just think she'd like to know what your plans are, don't you?"

Kevin sighed, then turned and yelled, "Hey, Mom! I'm going to the mall." He looked back at Sam impatiently.

Sam gritted his teeth. "Hop in."

Kevin hitched up his baggy pants and shuffled around to the

passenger door, taking his time now that his ride was set. Sam tapped a beat on the steering wheel, trying to keep his temper in check. It wasn't just the boy's mouth that troubled him; most kids his age had attitudes. It was the combination of the attitude and the ass-riding pants, ragged shirt, the slouch, the scowl, the shock of unwashed hair, the rash of acne competing with the scraggle of nascent beard, the piercing on ear, eyebrow, nostril, lip, and who knew where else that set him on edge. Even worse, Kevin smelled, a rank odor that seeped from his pores, seeming to emanate from something fetid *inside* his body.

The only positive thing, the one skill Kevin had that could pull him through this troubled puberty, was his aptitude with computers. The kid was a geek, manipulating the technology with amazing mastery. He loved to lose himself in the Internet, in a way that reminded Sam of how he used to lose himself in music.

Kevin pulled a pack of Death Cigarettes from his pocket and lit one. Sam coughed. "Hey, secondhand smoke kills," he said.

Kevin held the pack up to Sam's face. "That's why they call them Death." He took another long drag of the cigarette, watching Sam, waiting. Sam felt his pulse quicken, and he fought to stay calm by inhaling through his nose, exhaling through his mouth, the way the physical therapist had taught him.

"You know what it feels like to smoke marijuana, don't you?" Dr. Greshom had asked him soon after the surgery. Surprised at the question, since at that point his medical history was hardly a secret, Sam had admitted that he did have more than a passing acquaintance with the effects of weed.

"I'm not telling you to smoke it now, God forbid," the doctor had said. "Don't smoke anything! Ever! But think about the feeling it gave you, what did they used to call it? Mellow yellow? Like you were detached from reality and nothing could affect you? That's what I'm talking about. You should live the rest of your life as though you're high as a kite. Don't let anything piss you off. No big ups and no big downs either. Nothing should be as important to you as maintaining a sense of equilibrium. Because now your life depends on it."

So Sam kept breathing deeply, as Kevin put on his shades and settled back against the seat, his feet up on the dashboard. The boy turned to him, frowning. "C'mon, man. Let's boogie."

"Lose that butt first."

Without looking at him, Kevin took a long drag, then flicked it out the window, onto Diana's immaculate lawn.

"Thanks," said Sam, and threw the car into reverse. The Volvo responded with a jerk as the transmission locked into gear, and Sam eased it down the driveway, backing into the street and turning south, toward the mall.

They drove in silence for a few moments. Then Kevin leaned over and snapped on the radio. Static screeched out of the speakers. Kevin punched a few buttons, but the reception did not improve. "What's the story?" he asked.

"No antenna," Sam said. It was the first time an act of vandalism had ever proved a positive thing: he hated the noise Kevin considered music.

"Got any CDs?"

"Nope. Don't even have a CD player. But y'know what? It's only ten, fifteen minutes to the mall. I think we'll survive."

"Jeez." Kevin slid further down in the seat and stared out the window. Hostility rose off of him in palpable waves, neutralizing the joy Sam had felt minutes before. He wondered how someone so young could be so angry.

"Where're you off to?" he asked pleasantly.

"Didn't we already play this tune?" Kevin asked with exaggerated patience. "Like, we're going to the mall, remember?"

"Where *in* the mall, I mean?" Sam asked, still polite.

"What's it to you?"

"Well, as a matter of fact, it would help me know where to drop you. It's a big place."

"Wherever. I can walk."

Then why don't you, Sam wanted to snap, but didn't. There was nothing to gain from baiting the kid.

"I'll be done by five. Do you want me to pick you up?"

"Nah. I'll get someone to drop me. Or else I can hitch."

"That's not acceptable."

Kevin sneered, and Sam could see that his teeth were filmy and stained the dull yellow of straw. He just stared at the diseased teeth, and then into the boy's eyes. Finally, Kevin shrugged and turned back to the window. "Whatever, man."

They rode in silence for a few miles, Sam watching the road, Kevin staring at the passing cityscape. "So, what are your plans for spring break?" Sam asked at last.

"Huh?"

"What are you going to do with yourself this week while there's no school?" Sam repeated patiently.

"I'm not *doing* anything, man," Kevin said.

They rode in silence for a few miles. Then Sam felt the boy's eyes on him.

"What?"

"So whose ticker did you get?"

The question took Sam by surprise, not that he hadn't thought about it endlessly and exhaustively, but this was the first time Kevin had asked him anything about his surgery, about anything personal for that matter. "I dunno. They don't tell you."

"Why not?"

"Well, it's a pretty sensitive subject. Obviously somebody had to croak for me to get their heart. What if their family resents me, or feels I owe them something? Think how you'd feel if, say, Gracie died and your mom gave her heart to a stranger."

"Poor suck. He'd get a wimpy, runt heart." Kevin paused. "How d'you know *you* didn't get some pussy heart?"

"I don't. For all I know, I could have the heart of a 15-year-old delinquent or a 35-year-old school teacher. It depends on the size and the match, not the sex."

"I know how I'd find out what I got."

"How?"

"Check the obituaries for that day and time. See who died."

"I've thought about it. But in a city this size, a lot of people die in one afternoon. Plus they have med-vac planes to fly in organs from other places. They keep them packed in ice in these special coolers. I think they can keep them for something like four or five hours. So it could have come from practically anywhere in the United States. You couldn't check the obits for the whole country."

"Yeah you could. The Internet, man. The Net has all the answers."

"Maybe so," Sam mused. The question was, what would he do with the information if he got it?

"How'd you know they gave you a good one?"

"That was Doc Greshom's call, and anyway, it's not as though I had much of a choice. If I hadn't gotten this heart, I would've bit the big one by now. So however flawed it might be, it beats the one I had."

"What if it's a clunker and it conks out on you?"

"I suppose I go back on the list and hope to get another one," Sam said quietly. But the kid had put his finger on it. The donor's sex didn't matter, but his or her health profile did, and the more specifics Sam knew, the more he could prepare himself for the future.

They drove in silence again. "I'll tell you, going through it makes you appreciate every heartbeat. Each one is like a gift, and I'm damn thankful just to be alive." *It should happen to you, kid,* Sam thought, *teach you a little gratitude.*

He pulled the Volvo to a stop at one of the mall entrances. "Listen, Kev, do me one favor. Please. Just call your mother, let her know where you are. And tell her you'll be home for dinner." Kevin started to object, but Sam raised his hand signaling for silence. "Hey, what's the difference? It's free food. Just do it, okay?"

Kevin said nothing. He flung open the car door and started to get out.

Sam grabbed his sleeve and roughly pulled him back in. "Do it," Sam insisted.

Kevin plucked Sam's fingers off of his shirt. "Gimmie five bucks and I will," he replied calmly.

"What? You want me to pay you to call your mother?"

"I'm broke, man. Please? Besides, you're the one who wants me to do it."

Sam dug into his pocket and slapped a five dollar bill in Kevin's hand. "Just be home by six."

"Right," the boy said. And stuffing the bill into his pocket, he got out, slammed the door, and slouched off.

○

Sam parked the Volvo in the blue zone near the hospital entrance, the space reserved for patients, and he sat for a moment staring at the imposing building. It was eerie to be returning of his own free will to the site of such prolonged agony and apprehension. When Diana had brought him to this hospital all those months ago to await a new heart, he'd barely been able to walk unassisted. He'd been terrified to enter the building, afraid that the big glass doors only opened in, that he would never walk out. In the long months of waiting on the cardiac floor, his terror had been justified: there were only twelve beds, each occupied by a person like himself who was clinging desperately to life. And not all of them had survived.

The rhythm of his days had been set by his fickle heartbeat: bouts of tachycardia, when his heart felt like a time bomb, interspersed with the chemical calm provided by drugs: propafemone, amiodarone, propranolol. He had lived from dosage to dosage, welcoming the pain and the discomfort, the bad food and the lack of privacy, because they were all indications that he was still alive.

He'd tried not to hear or smell or see the disease and death all around him. And he'd kept a polite distance from the other cardiac patients: they were all competing for the same prize. To win it yourself might mean that some new friend would die.

In the daylight hours, he'd lain still in his bed preserving what meager energy he had, watching his pulse on the monitor. But at night, he'd roamed the hospital corridors in his wheelchair, raging against sleep in terror that his heart might not last the darkness.

Friends had tried to get him back into his music, bringing him CDs by his favorite bands, new Regal Tip hickory drumsticks, copies of *Modern Drummer*. But he'd rejected the gifts, indifferent to their hurt feelings. Couldn't they understand? He was completely consumed by the cadences of his body. Synthetic music, music that did not come from inside of him, was a superfluous and dangerous temptation. The twenty-six essential rudiments in a drummer's repertoire mattered not at all; the beat of his heart was the single rhythm that engaged him, and it held him rapt day after day after unending day.

Because if he let down his guard for one instant, lost focus on his organic rhythm, he feared he might not be ready for the most important rhythmic change of all.

Despite this vigilance, his bad heart continued to deteriorate. Ultimately he'd agreed to allow the doctors to cut him open and install an internal metronome, a "cardioverter," they called it, to monitor his heartbeat. Its job was to deliver a mild electrical shock to halt the tachycardia when his heart took off like a runaway train and to stun it back into an even rhythm. They had made the installation sound like a cakewalk, a minor surgery which, they assured him, was absolutely necessary, and which would give him control over his heart. No one had warned him that in his depleted state the surgery would be horrific, the recovery would be lengthy, and that the device that they were implanting would be the size of a Stephen King novel, bulging obscenely and painfully from his chest, like something *in* a Stephen King novel, a constant visual reminder of his dying heart.

Nor had they been honest about the force of the electrical shocks it would deliver. "Mild," they'd told him, just an instantaneous zap, nothing to it. Oh really?

BAM! Try having your whole body sent into spasms by a bolt of electricity.

BAM! In every cell.

BAM! Choking for air. No control.

BAM! Pain. Boiling acid running through your veins.

BAM, BAM, BAM!

Make it stop….

As his strength had waned, his brain had expanded, bloated with chemicals and hallucinations of death. Thinking became his only form of exercise, and caged by his decaying body, he felt like Gracie's pet hamster, forced to run endless circles in the wire wheel of his mind. Although his mental exertion further depleted his strength, he could not silence the beat that was constantly pounding in his mind's ear, jammed on a broken record, pithing his psyche with a diamond needle.

Finally, when even death seemed more desirable than the incessant wakeful days and anxious nights, his guard would collapse, and sleep would trickle around the edges of his awareness, anointing him in blessed and utter peace. Thus, days passed, and weeks, and months, until the call came the first time: a heart had been located for him. Twice he had gotten this call before fate had found the heart that was to be his. But the third time proved to be the charm. In a matter of hours after he had gotten that call, he was sedated and rolled into surgery. And when he woke up, everything was the same, only it was all different.

Since the transplant and his return to the world outside of the hospital, he had not picked up his drumsticks. The tapes and CDs given to him by friends remained in their plastic wrappers, his drum kit stashed in a back closet. Why? Probably it was superstition. Deep, deep down, in a place he didn't allow himself to go very often, he knew he was afraid that the music he had listened to and made with his instrument had tempted his heart away from its job as conductor to his body, inspiring it to dissonant and dangerous rhythms. Maybe it was silly to think this, but he wasn't taking any chances, just in case. As far as he was concerned, the music in him had to die in order for the rest of him to live.

If music weren't an option, what would he do with the rest of his life?

↻

Cookies in hand, he got out of the car and walked toward the hospital entrance, taking it slow not because he had to but because he now had the choice. The air was crisp on this March day. He inhaled deeply, and he was suffused with the optimism of the coming spring. He had been afraid to think about the future for so long now that it seemed odd to contemplate whole months and years and decades ahead. His life might not even be half over yet. What a concept!

Although he was surrounded by the ill and afflicted who were coming and going from assignations with the purveyors of hope inside of the hospital, he realized that he no longer felt like one of them. In fact, their presence made his own feat of survival all the more miraculous. He had fought the same battles as these people, and he had come out alive!

But for how long?

Within minutes, Dr. Greshom's nurse would be running him through a battery of tests, any one of which might reveal a crisis. He remembered the doctor's warning, the day he left the hospital after surgery, "You've got a long road ahead."

And he never would be out of the woods, as long as he lived. Because at any moment, his body might reject the new heart. If it did, the end could be swift. Or, he might survive in a diminished state and once again become an inmate of this medical prison, playing the same refrain, only this time not staccato, but *lentamente*.

"Stand aside, please," a voice commanded.

"Sorry." Sampson hadn't even realized that he had stopped walking, that he was blocking the entrance to the hospital. He stepped aside and a man pushed a wheelchair hurriedly past him through the double glass doors. The boy in the chair could not have been more than ten years old, but his red-ringed eyes held an adult's knowledge of pain. His legs, thin as matchsticks and too short to reach the footrests, stuck straight out from the seat of the chair, and Sampson could see that the tennis shoes on his small feet still had the price stickers on the bottoms, that even after this outing, the rubber soles had not touched the ground.

The boy was wearing a Dodgers cap and jacket that were sizes too big for him, making him appear all the more diminished. And in his lap, nestled in the folds of the jacket, lay a baseball. The boy was too weak to even grip the ball, but his tiny hands rested protectively on top of it.

When the wheelchair passed Sampson, it hit a crack in the tile flooring, and the baseball rolled off of the boy's lap and bounced onto the ground. The boy raised his hand in a feeble attempt to retrieve the ball, but distracted by dread and grief, his father was heedless of the fallen trophy, and he continued to push the wheelchair into the hospital's lobby. The ball rolled down the ramp, and a careless foot accidentally kicked it into the shrubbery.

Sampson backtracked and rooted around in the bushes until he found the ball. He stooped and scooped it up. On it were scrawled the signatures of a dozen or more players. One had written, *For John, a real champ.* Sampson knew something about luck and superstition and talismen, so he understood how much John needed this one. He charged through the double doors and jogged into the entry hall. Ahead he saw the wheelchair round the corner to the bank of elevators, so he picked up speed, running now, hoping to reach the boy before he disappeared in the maws of the elevator.

The doors were just closing as he got there. He held the ball above his head. "Wait! John! I've got your ball!" he called, but the car was already rising. He leaned unsteadily against the wall, panting with exertion, trying to catch his breath. The world around him began to spin, and he clutched the ball to his chest.

"Hey Tin Man!" a voice called. "What'd you do? Go out for a long fly to right field?"

Sampson saw the orderly he recognized and started to smile, but his expression turned into a gasp for air. Just as his legs started to crumple, he felt the orderly's powerful hands grip him. Then everything went black.

↻

When he opened his eyes, he was lying on an examining table, an oxygen mask strapped over his nose and mouth. Dr. Greshom's balding head gradually floated into focus. Sampson pulled the mask down so he could speak. "What's up, Doc?" he asked.

The doctor frowned. "What the hell did you think you were doing?"

"Just testing the equipment," Sampson said, trying for a light tone. But speaking was still difficult, and his words came out in a wheeze.

Dr. Greshom pulled the mask back up over Sampson's face. "It's not a game, Sam. Or if it is, you're playing for damn high stakes — life and death."

Sampson ripped off the mask again so he could speak. "I thought you told me exercise was good, that I'd be able to run a marathon."

"I believe my exact words were that the new heart had the *capacity of a marathon runner's*. Your body, however, would need months of training to be anywhere near conditioned to actually run one. In any event, that would be a long-term goal, and Christ, it's only been five weeks. Damn fool!"

He checked the monitors strapped to Sampson's body. "You're in luck. Everything's stabilized now." Sampson tried to sit up, but Dr. Greshom put a restraining hand on his chest. "But don't push your luck too far. I want you to lie here for at least an hour. Just relax, let your body recover."

"Can't, Doc, I've got a hot date," he lied.

"Cancel it."

"You wouldn't say that if you saw her."

He gave Sampson a mock-stern look. "Listen, buddy, I've got a lot invested in you. Don't screw it up by being dumb. If you lie here for a couple of hours and everything still seems okay, I won't insist that you stay overnight. But I warn you, I've got a bed waiting."

Sampson held up his hands. "All right, I hear you. I'll take a nap. But could I just get some water first. Man, I'm parched."

Dr. Greshom nodded to his nurse, and she left the room to get Sam a drink. "Any other complaints? Pain, shortness of breath, dizziness, nausea?"

All of the above, Sampson thought, but didn't dare admit it. Aloud, he said, "My God damn hair's falling out, and I didn't have that much to begin with. You didn't tell me getting a new heart would make me go bald."

"Happens to the best of us," Dr. Greshom said, smoothing down the sparse wisps of gray spread over his own pate. "In your case, it's due to the drugs not to the new heart. But wait and see. Some-times the new organ will stimulate the host body to produce new hair. You might end up with a head of red ringlets, like Shirley Temple, depending."

"Depending on what?"

"The donor."

"Speaking of which ..." Sampson reached out and took hold of the doctor's arm. "What if I want to know who the donor was."

"You know the rules, Sam. We don't give out that information. It's hospital policy. Don't take it personally."

"I've got another person's heart beating in my chest and you tell me not to take it personally? How else can I take it? This guy saved my life!"

"Well, he'll never know."

"So then, at least you're telling me that it was a 'he.' "

Dr. Greshom sighed and gently pried his arm from Sampson's grip. "All right, you caught me. Yes, your heart came from a male, a Caucasian man in his thirties. But that's all I'm going to tell you. Let it go, Sam. It's your heart now. Take good care of it. No more of this craziness." He walked toward the door. "I'll see you in two weeks for the biopsy."

"*Take another little piece of my heart,*" Sam sang, mimicking Janis Joplin's raspy voice. Dr. Greshom walked out of the room, shaking his head.

Sam closed his eyes, the Joplin song ricocheting through his mind. They'd told him the biopsies would be regular occurrences for the rest of his life. They would literally be snipping out pieces of the heart muscle to test it. Not a happy thought. But better than the alternative.

There was a knock on the door. "Come in," Sampson called, and the nurse entered carrying a paper cup of water. She was an Asian woman, young and attractive. Her uniform molded neatly to her body. Everything about her was ordered, immaculate, and invio-late.

"Does this belong to you?" she asked. She handed Sam the signed baseball, the cause of this near crisis. "The orderly said you dropped it when you fell."

"Thanks, Ada." He closed his hand around the ball, savoring the smooth feel of the leather, remembering the boy, John. "It's not mine, it belongs to a patient, a little boy named John. I don't know his last name, but I'm sure he'd like to have it back."

"I'll take it by Lost and Found," she said. "Probably he'll check for it there. And thank you for the cookies, by the way. They were delicious. Did you bake them?"

"No, my sister did. Her way of saying thanks." He finished the water and held out the cup.

"Well, please tell her we enjoyed them." The nurse reached for the cup, but instead of giving it to her, Sampson took hold of her wrist. It was thin and cool. He could feel the delicate bones beneath the skin. For some odd reason, he had a fleeting impulse to crush them.

"Ada, can I ask you a question?"

"Let go of my wrist, please."

"Sorry." He released her. "If someone saved your life, wouldn't you want to thank them?"

She narrowed her eyes. "Mr. Sampson, I know very well what you're leading up to. Doctor has already told you that we cannot divulge donor information."

"Please," Sampson said, "just think about it. If someone else's heart was beating in your chest, wouldn't you like to know where the damn thing came from?"

She softened, then sighed. "Yes, I probably would."

"All right. Thank you."

The nurse walked to the door, took the handle in her hand, but did not open it. Without turning around, she said quietly, "My husband's a lawyer. He'd probably tell you to go to The Organ Bank and threaten to sue if they didn't tell you. They're probably as afraid of malpractice and nuisance suits as the rest of the medical profession, and they'd do anything to avoid a lawsuit. But don't you dare tell them I said so!" She opened the door. "The receptionist has their card," she added. And then she was gone.

○

It was nearly six-thirty by the time Sam was given permission to leave. Diana liked to serve dinner at the ungodly hour of six, so he knew she would be worrying why he was late. But lying on the table for three hours had given him time to think. And he'd resolved one thing: he wanted to learn the identity of the person who had given him this heart.

He dressed, and on his way out, he stopped at the reception desk. The cards were there, just as the nurse had told him. Sam took one, even though he'd been to the office several times before his transplant. *The Organ Bank*, it read, *Giving the Gift of Life*. The logo was two hands outstretched, as though in offering.

The office was not far from Dr. Greshom's, just a small suite of rooms with a glass entrance, etched with the same logo as the card, two outstretched hands. A woman he didn't recognize was locking up for the night.

"Excuse me," Sam said. "I'm wondering if I could get some information."

A look of mild annoyance flashed across her face, but then she smiled. It was her job to be available to answer questions. "We're closed for today, but I'd be happy to get you a brochure. Oh, maybe I have something here." She fumbled around in her bag and withdrew a slightly crumpled leaflet. She thrust it at him. "Mrs.

Greenberg, our donor liaison, will be in at ten o'clock tomorrow. I'm sure she would be happy to explain our services at that time...."

"You don't understand," Sam said. "I don't want to make a donation. I mean I would if I could, but ... I'm a recipient. I got a new heart five weeks ago."

"Oh, well then congratulations." Unconsciously, the woman looked down at Sam's chest, as though she could see through his clothes and skin to the organ beating inside. "Then what do you want to talk to Mrs. Greenberg about?"

"I'm curious about ... the donor."

The woman nodded wearily, as though she'd heard this before. "It's not our policy to divulge ..."

"I know that, but — "

"Mrs. Greenberg will be happy to explain it to you in more detail tomorrow, but what we suggest is that if a recipient wants to contact a donor's family, they write a letter — without putting their name on it of course — and we see that the family gets it."

"I was hoping ..." he began.

She was starting to walk away. "I'm really sorry, but I'm going to be late picking up my daughter from ballet."

Sam watched her go, overwhelmed by helplessness and fatigue.

○

It was past seven when he pulled the Volvo into the driveway. The old house was glowing with light, and before he even opened the door, Sam identified the tempting aroma as Diana's Moroccan couscous.

She came to the door to greet him, her face tight with worry. "You're so late! I was just about to call Dr. Greshom's office." Her eyes searched his face. "Are you okay?"

Sam shrugged out of his jacket. "Yeah, sure," he said. "You know how doctors are. If they don't make you wait at least an hour, they don't feel like they're giving you your money's worth."

"Next time, call," she said. "I was a nervous wreck."

He kissed her lightly on the forehead. "Hopefully, there won't be many more 'next times.' Kevin home?"

"Upstairs," she said, stepping back into the kitchen but not taking her eyes off of him. "Do me a favor. See if you can pry him away from that damn computer. Tell him dinner's ready in five minutes."

"Sure thing."

Sam took the first few stairs quickly, then when he was sure Diana couldn't see him, he slowed his pace, just to be safe. He stopped outside of Kevin's room. *Do Not Disturb on Pain of Death* was written above a skull and crossbones. Sampson knocked anyway. There was no answer. He tried the knob, and it turned in his hand. For once, the room was not locked. Cautiously, he opened the door.

Kevin was staring at his computer screen, his back to Sam. He had on earphones, and his body was hunched forward. Sam could see characters in a game bounding across the screen.

He walked up behind Kevin and threw a business card onto the keyboard. Startled, Kevin ripped the earphones off his ears. "What the fuck ..."

"I have a job for you. A good way to earn a few bucks," Sampson said. "We'll talk after dinner which, by the way, is in five minutes. And nothing about this to your mother."

Without waiting for a response, Sam turned and left the room.

Kevin watched the door close. Then he looked at the card on the keyboard. *The Organ Bank*, it read, *Elaine Greenberg, Donor Liaison*.

10

Sampson picked at his food — another of Diana's tour de force efforts to save his life through good nutrition. Instead of meat, the couscous was made with tofu and vegetables. It wasn't bad, just bland, and he was craving something greasy and spicy — a chili dog, a slice of pizza, a burrito. Where did these cravings come from?

He looked around the silent table at Diana's family, each of them lost in their own thoughts. Although he loved them, he yearned for privacy and solitude. But for the past five years, he had been too preoccupied with illness to support himself financially, devoting most of his physical and emotional energies to just staying alive.

Living in Diana's and Rod's home — his mother's house actually — what little extra money he had earned had come from a variety of sources: one-night gigs in clubs, session work in recording studios, and once, from a job substitute teaching drums at a private secondary school. Not all of his jobs had been about music. He'd worked as Santa at Christmas, Mr. Bunny at Easter, and even as his namesake, Uncle Sam, on the Fourth of July. He'd sold mattresses and espresso machines, and Avon door to door. He'd taken tickets at Magic Mountain and distributed leaflets for a local Thai restaurant. Once he had started his own business, selling colorful hand-knit sweaters from Guatemala off of a pushcart in the mall.

But the jobs never lasted long. Inevitably, he would wake up one morning, knowing it was over. "I've got a bum heart," he would explain to his employer. And he never needed to say more. Sometimes when his final paycheck arrived in the mail, it would be fatter than expected. A pity bonus, he called it, and he'd hand it over to Diana just to get rid of it.

Diana had never pushed him to get a steady job, nor did his mother, even when she was more lucid. Instead, they had made allowances. And he'd let them, even though money was a scarce commodity, and anything he did donate to the family coffers went to good use. The old Victorian house where he had grown up and lived his whole life was a bottomless pit that swallowed up every bit of every family member's income — his own meager contributions, his mother's Social Security, and of course Diana's and her husband's, until Rod's recent death. Unless they could convince their mother to move to smaller quarters or into a retirement community — and so far she swore she would only leave the way her husband had, feet first — or until her dementia became unmanageable, they all had to pitch in to pay for the upkeep of the family homestead.

True, they had all benefited from the arrangement: Mom felt secure and safe here, and Diana could care for her and her own family without having to oversee two households. As toddlers, Kevin and Gracie had loved the spaciousness of the old house and the grounds — most of their friends lived in tiny condos or tract houses with small fenced yards, which would have been all Diana and Rod could have afforded had they tried to make it on their own. And Sampson, ever a bachelor with a small, sporadic income, here had the benefit of free rent, a housekeeper, a cook, company — and most important, a secure home to return to.

All in all, the pluses had far outweighed the minuses — but did they still? As Sampson looked around the table, it occurred to him that perhaps the living arrangement had molded them into the people they were, and not the other way around. If they put his mother in a nursing home, she might now enjoy the companionship of her peers instead of retreating into silence as she so often did. If the children lived closer to town, it's true they would miss the spacious house and yard, but they might make more friends. Kevin might not be so angry, Gracie so timid.

And Sampson himself? Even before his heart problem was diagnosed and the search for a new heart had begun, he had been pale and fragile, chronically short of energy and enthusiasm. And the family had come to expect that of him. It was his role to be sick, and he'd learned to play it to perfection. But without the built-in support system Diana provided, might he have found a permanent job, even a wife and family of his own, rather than lazily living as an invalid on the fringes of his sister's life in his parents' home?

Taking a bite of tofu, he mused over the word *invalid*. In addition to meaning "a sickly person," it also meant "null and void." Was that what the first thirty-four years of his life had been? He certainly didn't have much to show for them. And how many years did he have left, even with the new heart? He turned to Diana and caught her staring at him. She averted her eyes and took a small bite of rice, pretending not to see him.

"Hey, sis, I'd like to look over the household accounts tonight, if it's okay with you."

That got her attention. Slowly she finished chewing what was in her mouth and swallowed. "What for?"

"I'm just curious, that's all. I'd like to see where we stand financially."

"You don't trust me with the books?"

"Of course I trust you. You're more thorough than the IRS," Sampson said patiently, trying to lighten the tone. She had studied accounting at night school after she and Rod had married, and she was actually a whiz at bookkeeping; it was a talent of which she was duly proud. "But I'd like to know the particulars," he said.

"Why?"

Sam looked around the table. All eyes were on him now. Even Gracie stopped her careful segregation of the peas from the carrots on her plate to listen to his answer.

"Well, now that I've had my surgery, I'm thinking about getting a job. A real job. Can you believe it? And maybe it's time for me to be on my own too."

"Oh, Sam!" Her voice fell heavily, like a downstroke at the end of a stanza.

"Can I be excused?" Gracie asked, sensing by her mother's tone that she might be allowed to escape without finishing her vegetables.

"Three more bites."

"Mom ..."

"Grace Claire ..."

Petulant but obedient, Gracie speared a cube of carrot and slowly lifted it to her mouth, carefully pulling it off the fork with her teeth, so her lips did not even touch the vegetable. She tried to swallow without chewing, but gagged, and had to take a big gulp of milk in order to get it down.

Diana turned her eyes back to her own dinner, distractedly probing the couscous with a fork. Sampson could tell that her hackles were up, her suspicions aroused. "You know how glad I would be if you picked up your music again," Diana began. "But we've talked about this — after six months of disability, Social Security will kick in, and it'll cover all medical procedures and most prescriptions. If you go back to work, you won't be eligible for Social Security benefits, and you know you won't be able to get affordable insurance. Sam, we need that check. I haven't wanted to worry you, but our budget is balanced like a hippo on a high wire," she said. "What with Rod gone, and all the extras these past months ..."

She didn't have to enumerate the "extras." He was well aware of the hidden costs of his illness and treatment, things neither Social Security nor insurance would cover, such as additional laundry bills for sheets and towels stained by his oozing wounds, or the salary of the handyman who had been hired to do necessary repairs while Sam had been in the hospital. And who knew what his mother's medical bills would be in the coming years as her dementia progressed? The only certainty was that the costs would escalate.

But Sam held firm. As hard as it was now, it would only get harder if he waited. "I know how the system works. But I need to carry my own weight for once. I've been leaning on you too long," he said.

"You're not leaning," Diana protested.

Of course she didn't see it that way. This was what they called codependency: how could she be a martyr without an invalid brother who required her to sacrifice herself for him? "We can talk about it later," he said. "It's no big deal." To appease her, he took a bite of eggplant and, like Gracie, gulped it down without chewing. He had such a craving for Mexican food!

○

While Diana cleared the table, Sampson got their mother settled in the den and turned on the television to NBC. Tonight's offering was the second half of *Extra!*, then more entertainment gossip disguised as news on *Hard Copy*. The rest of the evening would be filled with sitcoms, until *Homicide* at ten and her bedtime at eleven.

"Mom, don't you want to see if there's something else on?" he asked, as he always did. "Maybe there's a movie on one of the other stations."

"This is fine, dear," she replied, her eyes fixed on the set. "You know I enjoy my programs."

But was she really seeing what was on the screen? He doubted it.

For her, television was a hypnotic, a way to tune out reality. All she wanted in life was sameness, routine, to get through the days.

If he stayed in this house, would he end up the same way?

"You okay, Mother?"

She nodded, already mesmerized by the small screen. "Thank you, dear," she said without taking her eyes from it. "Just make sure I've got my knitting." Her hands were always moving, but since her decline had begun, there had been no finished product.

"It's in front of your left foot, Mom. So don't stand up or you'll step on it," he joked. The last thing she would do would be to try to get out of her chair without help — although he was fairly certain that she was capable of it. Immobility, illness, and pain had become her friends, and she used them as a shield from the world. He well understood how easy it was to fall into that trap.

Stealing a glance into the kitchen to make sure Diana was still occupied — she was loading the dishwasher — Sampson went upstairs and knocked on Kevin's door.

"Yeah?"

"It's me," he said.

"Okay."

Sam opened the door and looked in. Kevin was lying on his bed reading *Wired*. Sam's eyes swept the room and he saw that *The Organ Bank* business card he'd given Kevin earlier was still resting on the keyboard, exactly where he'd left it. Had the boy even looked at it?

"Got a minute?"

"I 'spose."

Sam picked up the card and brought it over to the bed, sitting down next to Kevin. He slipped it in front of the page of the comic so Kevin had to look at it.

"So?" Kevin asked.

"So, I've got a job for you, a *paying* job. Want it?"

"What do I have to do?"

"Find out whose heart I got," Sam said, without missing a beat.

Kevin's jaw dropped in surprise, then he caught himself and tried to look disinterested. "What d'you mean?"

"This afternoon you said it would be no sweat to go on-line and find out whose heart I got. I want you to do it."

Kevin considered this. "And you'll pay me?"

"That's what I said."

"How much?"

"Depends on the results. If you get me a name, it's worth … what's fair? A hundred bucks?" Sampson could almost see dollar signs lighting up Kevin's eyes. It would mean selling one of his drums to pay the boy, but they weren't doing him any good gathering dust in the closet. "A hundred bucks for a name and an address. But there's a catch. If anyone finds out you're doing this — that goes for your mom, Gracie, anyone here, *or* Dr. Greshom or any of these *Organ Bank* people — you get zip."

"How come?"

"Because I want it that way, and the guy with the money makes the rules, in case you haven't learned that yet. What d'you say? Want to give it a try?"

"Big deal. An idiot could do it."

"Good, then it won't take you long. Today's Monday. If you can get me the info by Wednesday night, I'll throw in … the CD-ROM of your choice."

"How come you wanna know so bad all of a sudden?"

Sam shrugged. "Talking to you this afternoon, I just got curious. Do we have a deal?"

"I 'spose." Kevin's voice was noncommittal, but Sam could tell that he was hooked.

"Let me know when you find something." He stood and tousled the boy's hair. It was greasy to his touch and as matted as an old sheepskin rug. "And take a shower," he said. Kevin groaned and jerked his head away.

Sam pulled the door closed and stood outside, listening until he heard the electronic three-note melody the computer made when it booted up. Then he smiled and started down the stairs.

Diana was waiting for him in the dining room, with the household books spread on the table. "What were you talking to Kevin about?" she asked.

"Man stuff," Sam hedged.

"Like what?" she probed.

"Like it's between the two of us, okay?" Sam sat and pulled the nearest of the ledgers toward him.

"It's fine with me. It's great, in fact, to think that someone in this household might actually be able to get him to utter more than two consecutive words."

"I didn't say he did. But he did grunt at the appropriate time." Sam smiled, and Diana relaxed a little. He flipped through a few pages and ran his finger down the page of a spreadsheet whose numbers were filled in by hand. "I've heard the term *frozen assets*, but why are these papers so cold?"

"I keep them in the freezer."

"Any particular reason?"

"In case there's a fire." When he still looked perplexed, she explained, "That's my only copy."

"Why don't you make a Xerox?"

"I could, I suppose. But it's such a pain schlepping down to Kinkos and waiting in line for three hours. Of course, if you're going to want to start checking my addition, approving every entry..."

"Diana, I didn't say that. In fact, we both know I'm helpless with numbers."

"At least you admit it."

"So if I'm going to understand this, I'll need your help." He pulled out a chair for her. "Please?" She continued to stand. "Don't be mad."

"I'm not mad."

Like hell, he thought. "I'm not trying to horn in on your territory," he assured her. "This isn't about my playing Big Brother."

"Then what is it about?"

"Sit down and I'll tell you."

Reluctantly, Diana perched on the edge of a chair, tensed, as though ready to spring to her feet at the least provocation.

Sam chose his words carefully. "I'm 34 years old. How many men my age do you know who aren't married and still live with their families?"

"Lots."

"Name some."

"John Barton."

"He's gay and afraid to come out of the closet."

She drummed her fingers on the books, thinking. "Rick Randal."

"Please. Rickie has Lou Gehrig's. He can't live alone." She opened her mouth to speak, but he interrupted her, "I know, I haven't been the healthiest person on the planet either. But that's in the past."

He took her hand. "Diana, I love you and the kids, but they're *your* kids. I love living with you, and I appreciate how you take care of me, but it's mom's house, and you have enough to do taking care of her and Kevin and Gracie. I think it's time I had my own life. Don't you?"

Her eyes were downcast. When she raised them, Sam could see that they were filled with tears. "I knew this would happen someday," she whispered. "I just didn't think it would be so soon after Rod ..."

Boy, she really knew how to wield the guilt. What could he say now? That like her husband, he was going to leave her, and even worse, that he was going, knowing she would be saddled with the possibly unmanageable task of financing the household and caring for their mother? What kind of man could do that?

But could he continue to live in this house for the rest of his life just to fulfill her expectations? Was guilt that much stronger a motivator?

"I'm not saying I'm going to do anything right now. At least not for the foreseeable future. I just want to get a better understanding of what it would mean to the family financially if I got my own place. Okay?"

"Okay," she said. But they both knew it wasn't.

○

It was nearly 2 A.M. before Kevin was able to get into the transplantation records. He probably could have cracked it faster, but he'd done a few lines of coke first, and with his brain wired, he had gotten sidetracked browsing through the network of organ transplantation websites. There were tons of them, with gory photos of damaged organs, grisly explanations of surgeries gone wrong, and survivors' horror stories.

With Smashing Pumpkins blasting on his earphones, he'd sent a few gag e-mail messages to various organ banks. He loved to get high and mess with people's minds on the Internet. After doing crystal meth, it was probably his favorite pastime. First he pretended he was a guy who had two hearts and wanted to donate one to science. Then he was a husband whose wife needed a new liver, writing that if they didn't give it to her, he was going to bomb the Mayo Clinic.

Finally, when the high peaked and he'd felt fatigue stealing up on him, he'd worked in earnest to crash the hospital's records. It turned out to be no sweat, just as he'd thought. Sure, the files were encrypted, it didn't take a brain surgeon — *ha, ha* — to figure out that he'd never get into them through conventional means. The best route, he reasoned, would be through the hospital's accounting department. He'd learned long ago that the way to get information about any company was to pretend you were someone who wanted to pay an outstanding bill. They'd lay it all out for you if you were promising to pay them something.

So he'd gotten in using a fictitious patient name and, quite brilliantly he thought, a departmental code number he found on a vial of his Uncle Sam's pills, which he'd found stashed in the medicine cabinet when he'd gone in to "borrow" a few assorted prescription drugs.

That gave him the idea to go downstairs and find Sam's medical file, which his mom kept on her desk, and then input some of the numbers off of it, as well as the name of his uncle's doctor. He got firewalled a few times, but he wasn't worried. That was one of the beauties of the Internet: he could hide his tracks, so nobody could trace the trail back to him. Well, probably the CIA could, or some geeky programmer at Microsoft. But why would they care about small shit like this?

Once he was in the billing files, he simply backtracked to the date of his uncle's transplant and looked for the name of the surgeon, Dr. Gerald Greshom. And there it was. No sweat. He booted up his printer to make a copy of the page, but "printer error" kept coming up on the screen. It had been doing this a lot recently. Maybe his board was burning out, or it could be a connection problem. So he jotted down the name and phone number of the patient who was listed as the organ donor: *Barnes, Jack.*

He wrote down the wife's name and phone number. They had a kid too, Jonah Keller, 13 years old. Now there was a mind he could mess with. He cleared the computer screen and accessed an e-mail yellow pages directory to see if the kid had an e-mail address.

Sure enough, when he typed in the name, *Keller, Jonah,* and the telephone number he'd copied from the transplant file, he came up with the Internet address: *jonahk@aol.com.* Perfect. He cleared the screen again and went into Hot Mail, and set up an anonymous mailbox for himself, one that couldn't be traced.

Dear Jonah, he typed, then he stopped. What could he write that would blow this chump's mind? Better yet, how could he use this kid to get something he wanted? And what did he want? He wanted what he always wanted, money to bankroll his highs. Crystal meth didn't come cheap. But how to get dough from this Jonah Barnes?

He deleted what he'd written and then typed in, *You'll be as dead as your Jack if you don't pay up what the fucker owed me.* No, that would just scare him away. He had to be more subtle. He deleted what he'd written and typed in, *Heard about Jack. Sorry. I got something of his, you might want it. Meet me at Piercing Kingdom Thursday at 10 and we'll talk.* He signed off with his favorite name, Crud.

FOUR

II

mily checked her watch. Matt was late, as usual. He joked
that it was genetic, that he'd inherited his faulty internal
clock from his father, and his lank blond hair and freckles from his
mother. Everyone laughed when he said this, because Matt had
curly dark hair and an olive complexion.

His habitual tardiness had been cute when they were dating, per-
missible because he compensated by being utterly attentive when he
did arrive. This was one of Matt's gifts: no matter how rushed he
was, or how full his schedule, he always focused completely on the
person he was with.

But after they had married, she had become less tolerant. She
prided herself on her own punctuality and came to resent the fact
that when they went somewhere together he often made them both
late. And although this wasn't the reason they divorced, it was a
symptom of the irreconcilable difference between them: Emily
played her life by the rules, and Matt ignored them. Matt and Jack
were alike in this way. Was it a coincidence or an unconscious
choice on her part to marry two men with such similar dissimilari-
ties to her own personality?

Through the window of the cafe, she watched Matt's Toyota Land Cruiser make an illegal U-turn and skid into a loading zone across the street. Instead of walking to the corner and waiting for the green light, Matt got out and ran through traffic in the middle of the block. If a policeman had been watching, he could have cited Matt for three violations. But there was no policeman in sight, and he got away with breaking the rules, as usual. Again, he was so much like Jack in this way.

Matt burst into the cafe, all energy and eagerness to find her, and when he saw her across the room his face lit up. Once, seeing that boyish smile would have made her heart melt. But over the years, she'd learned that it was just a contrivance, his way of getting attention, no different than his disregard for time. Jack's smile, though similarly boyish, had been genuine. Therein lay the difference between the two men: Matt was for show. Jack was for real.

Only Jack was dead, and here was Matt, living, breathing, thriving.

"Sorry I'm late," he said, sliding into the booth across from her.

"No you're not," she replied.

"I'm not?" She thought she saw disappointment flicker across his handsome face. "Great, I thought maybe you'd been waiting."

"I mean you're not *sorry*," she amended. "You're late intentionally. It's a power play. By making me wait, you're letting me know that your time is more valuable than mine. Which it's not, by the way."

"I can see that you've been making progress with your therapy."

"How did you know I was seeing a therapist?"

He grinned. "I didn't, it was just an educated guess. Who is it, if I may ask?"

"You may not."

Matt shrugged out of his jacket and signaled the waiter. "Well then, moving right along, let's eat. What's good here?"

"You tell me. This place was your choice."

"Oh, right." He picked up the menu and skimmed it quickly. "Let's see ... I usually have the salmon club sandwich and a Diet Coke." He nodded at the waiter, who wrote the order down. "Lauren likes the Salade Nicoise," he added.

She had been thinking about ordering the Salade Nicoise, but she closed her menu and said, "I'll have the Caesar Salad with chicken, dressing on the side, and an iced tea — no, make that a glass of non-fat milk."

"Since when do you support the California Dairy Council?" Matt lifted his water glass and took a sip.

"Since I found out I was pregnant," she replied.

He coughed, spewing water across the table. Calmly, Emily handed him her napkin. "You're kidding, right?" he chuckled hopefully.

"If I were going to tell a joke, I think I could come up with something funnier or dirtier than that," Emily said dryly.

For once, Matt was at a loss. "Well, I mean Jack ... did you, did he ..."

Emily let him fumble, enjoying holding the cards for a change. "Yes, Matt, of course Jack is the father. No, he didn't know. I just found out myself." Unconsciously she pulled a flower from the small vase of daisies on the table and started tearing the petals off it, one by one. "The odd thing is that Jack was the one who wanted us to have a child, not me. I have Jonah, I didn't need another baby. But Jack wanted one of his own, of ours." She sighed. "Funny how things work out, isn't it?"

"I'll say." Matt reached across the table and squeezed her hand, in a gesture that Emily found infuriatingly patronizing. She pulled her hand away and put it in her lap. "Have you decided what you're going to do?" he asked.

She shook her head. "I've always believed in a woman's right to choose — in the abstract. But I never had to consider it personally until now. I don't know, maybe it's the hormones, but abortion seems so cold-blooded, especially since this pregnancy is my only connection to Jack. On the other hand, I have my hands full as it is. The whole financial situation is difficult because his death was so sudden." She closed her eyes for a moment, overwhelmed by the thought of just how complicated it was. But her financial problems had nothing to do with Matt.

"Don't get me wrong. I'm not asking for help," she said. "But as you know, taking care of Jonah is kind of like baking bread: the more you want it to grow, the more you knead the dough." She laughed at her little play on words, but Matt did not. He seemed sobered by the subject.

"Does Jonah know?" he asked.

"No, I haven't had a chance to tell him. So please don't say anything to him — I want to be the one who tells him." Matt was silent. "Promise?" she demanded.

"Sure. It's your news," he said.

The waiter appeared with their lunches, and they both busied themselves with the food. Emily was ravenous, and she dug into her meal with gusto.

"How's the salad?" Matt asked after a moment.

"Good. Of course, cardboard would taste good these days, I'm so hungry. I don't remember feeling this starved when I was carrying Jonah. Maybe it's an age thing. I am kind of at the upper end of what's healthy. Although some people say that physically it's better to have babies later in life, because your body is completely formed and will bounce back to the way it was, rather than stretch out and stay stretched." She realized she was babbling, and took a sip of milk to quiet herself. It tasted thin and sour, and she swallowed quickly.

Matt put down his fork and steepled his hands over his plate. It looked to Emily as though he were praying for the right words. "In a way, it's good that this came up just now," he said.

"Oh? How do you mean?"

He stared at her, not speaking. Emily gritted her teeth. There he was, making her wait again. "What?" she demanded.

"Emily, Lauren and I want custody of Jonah."

Emily sat back, stunned. "That's not an option," she snapped. "No way. Forget it."

"Jonah wants it too," Matt said quietly. "In fact, he asked me. It was his idea."

Now she was angry. "When? He never said anything to me about it."

"He doesn't want to hurt you. Emily, it's the best thing."

"Best for who, Matthew? For Jonah? For you and Lauren? Because it certainly isn't the best thing for me!" She felt her eyes well up with tears and fought them back. "I'm his mother, for God's sake," she said in a choked whisper.

"And you always will be his mother, whether he lives with us or with you."

"Forget it. I need him with me."

"Emily, you sent him to boarding school. He isn't even with you now, except on some weekends."

"You were involved in that decision. We agreed because the schools in the area are lousy."

"In your area, but not in ours. There's a great high school in Stanton, and it's only a twenty-minute drive from our house, less than ten minutes from my office by bus. He can come to me after school, and we can go home together."

"What a great way for a teenage boy to spend his afternoons, watching his father deal with disturbed children."

Matt pushed his plate away, most of his sandwich uneaten. "He hates it at Oceancrest, Emily. You and I both know it."

"*I* don't know it, Matthew. He never said a word."

"He's afraid to, because —

"Because he doesn't want to hurt me?" she interrupted, mimicking Matt's voice. "Since when is he so terrified of my feelings?"

"You're a perfectionist. He's afraid of not being good enough in your eyes."

"That's ridiculous." She stood up. "I don't want to have this conversation with you. I want to talk to Jonah."

Matt sighed. "I agree. You two should talk. I just wanted to put our cards on the table." He stood too, blocking her exit. "Just think about it, Emily. It makes sense for him to be in a *family*."

"How dare you!" Her voice trembled with rage and hurt. "It's not my fault Jack died. He was in an accident."

"I know, I know. I didn't mean it to sound like that."

"You didn't?"

"Emily," Matt whined. He reached out to her, but she resisted. "The reality is both of our situations have changed since our divorce, and it's time to revisit the decision we made when we split up. All I'm asking is that you think about it and talk to Jonah. Will you do that for me?"

Emily gritted her teeth so hard they hurt. "No Matt, I won't do it for you." She picked up her bag and slung it over her shoulder. "But I'll do it for Jonah. Thanks for a lovely lunch."

↻

It had started to rain, and Emily had to pull her sweater up over her head and run across the street to her car, which was parked a block away. As she passed Matt's Land Cruiser, she noticed with annoyance that it did not have a parking ticket on it.

But her own car did. And she could see that she'd forgotten to lock it. What was happening to her mind?

She ripped the ticket off the windshield and threw it onto the passenger seat as she got in. Then she slammed the door shut and leaned her wet head back against the headrest, listening to the rain bombard the car, obliterating the noise of the street. She was soaked and shivering and breathing hard. Rivulets of water streaked down the windshield and side windows, and soon her labored breathing fogged the glass, obscuring the view and increasing her sense of isolation.

Was Matt telling the truth or was he fabricating the facts? In her litany of complaints against him, she'd never thought of him as dishonest. Manipulative, annoying, cloying, exasperating. But not a liar.

Or was he?

She had never felt so alone.

Finally, the dizzying flood of emotions began to ebb, at least for the time being. She reached into her purse for her keys, but they weren't clipped onto the inner pocket as they usually were. Anxiety flaring again, she groped desperately through the contents of the bag, certain the keys were inside somewhere.

But they weren't. She started to cry in earnest now, tears running down her cheeks in salty streams, mimicking the rain on the windshield. The thought of opening the car door, running back through the deluge to the restaurant to retrieve the keys, possibly having to face Matt again, then running back again to her car, seemed utterly undoable. Better to sit in the car and cry until she had spent all of her tears, or until the rain stopped, or until the police came and towed her away. She pressed her forehead against the steering wheel to wait.

A rapping on the passenger window startled her. Through the fogged glass she saw a bundled figure bending down beside the car. Probably one of the local homeless, looking for a handout, shelter, or pity. Normally she would have ignored such an overture, but her own lonely misery made her vulnerable to the needs of others. The man rapped again, and she leaned over and rolled down the window just a crack. Rain splashed in onto the car's leather seats.

"Yes?"

"Are these yours?" the man called through the small opening, dangling her key ring tantalizingly against the window.

"Oh, God, thank you *so* much," she cried, and unlocked the door. The man pulled it open, and before she could protest, flopped wetly into the seat beside her, slamming the door behind him. A frisson of terror shot through her. He could be a mugger, or a carjacker, or worse. And she had *invited* him into her car! What had she been thinking? Should she tell him to get out? Should she run? Encumbered by overwrought emotions, the intoxicating rush of prenatal hormones, and the devastation of Matt's revelation, her brain seemed to be working at half-speed, a computer with a memory too small to play so many applications at once.

The man turned and stared at her, and his mouth dropped open as though he were going to speak, but no words came out. He was dwarfed by layers of bulky, all-weather gear, his face half hidden, and he was soaking wet. A dank odor rose off of him, adding to her revulsion and fear.

He was holding the keys in his hand — should she grab them and run? If his motive was to steal the car, at least he'd have a harder time of it without the keys. But if he wanted the car, why was he offering her the keys in the first place? And why was he staring at her so intently?

"May I ... have them?" she asked.

"They are yours, aren't they?" he asked, sniffling to catch the dribble of mucus leaking from his nose. "There's no name on them or anything."

"Yes, of course they're mine." She was perplexed now, and wary.

"Well, they were just lying there on the sidewalk." He gestured out the window. "They could've been anyone's. But, I just thought ... I saw you sitting here and ..." a sneeze exploded out of his mouth, spraying phlegm on her extended hand. Horrified, she withdrew it and wiped it on her jacket, not even wanting to breathe with his germs hanging in the air.

"I'm sorry," he gasped. "Jeez, how embarrassing." He sneezed again, this time catching the mucus with both hands. He reached into his pocket. Even through the thick fabric, she saw a bulge there. Was it a knife? A gun?

"Look, I promise you the keys are mine," she said hastily. "There are three. They're on a silver chain with a little dog at the end." He held the keys up between them to confirm the description. "It's a Wheaten Terrier," she answered his unasked question.

"Nice breed?"

"Yes, as a matter of fact, they're wonderful. May I have my keys now, please?"

"Oh, sure, sorry." He coughed thickly, clearing his throat, and held the key chain out to her.

Quickly, she snatched it with two fingers and inserted the key in the ignition. "Thanks very much, I appreciate it," she said, hoping he would take the hint and get out of the car. But he didn't.

Instead he extended his hand and rubbed a clear spot on the windshield, then he leaned forward and looked out. "What a day, eh?" he asked conversationally, making no move to get out of the car.

"Excuse me, but I have a meeting and I'm late already," Emily said. She was breathless, pumped with adrenaline. "Thank you for finding my keys, but I've got to get going now." Surreptitiously, she put one hand on the horn and the other on the handle of her door, ready to honk and bolt if necessary. "I want you to get out of the car now," she demanded. Her voice was louder than she'd meant it to be.

He looked surprised, then embarrassed. "Oh, no," he began, "you don't — " but she cut him off.

"What do you want? Money?" She chanced taking her hand off the horn to reach into her purse. She pulled out her wallet and threw it at him. "Here! Just take it and go!" Her voice was quivering. "Please, I'm begging you!"

"Oh, no! You've got it all wrong. I don't want your money! All

I want is —" he took a big gasping breath. "I just want to talk—"
He dug into his pocket.

She didn't wait to see the weapon. She flung open the door, leapt
out of the car, and darted across the street. The traffic lights were
in her favor, and no cars were coming. But as she stepped up on the
far curb, the light changed, and the traffic streamed by in both directions, obscuring her view of the car.

Safely separated from the carjacker she stood in the pouring rain,
helplessly, hopelessly, trying to see across the street. The few pedes-
trians braving the weather hurried past, giving her wide, cautious
berth.

"Will you help me, please?" she asked a stranger with a huge
green umbrella.

"Help you what?" he asked, but did not stop to hear her answer.

"Please," she said to a woman jogging by in a Gortex anorak.
"Someone's trying to steal my car."

"No shit? Where is it?" the woman asked, jogging in place.

"Across the street." She gestured through the rain. "Will you
please call the police?"

"Lady, do I look like I have a phone on me?" the woman asked.

"When you get home then," Emily said.

"Yeah, sure, but that's like in four miles." She looked in both directions. "I think there's a restaurant around the corner, *Gulliver's*
or something. Why don't you call from there?" she called as she
jogged away.

Matt, Emily thought. *Maybe he's still at the restaurant!*

He wasn't.

But to her boundless relief, a metermaid was ticketing a van
blocking the alley. She listened to Emily's story and radioed in to
her precinct station. Barely a minute later, a squad car screeched to
a stop at the curb. Quickly, Emily explained what had happened.

"Hop in," the officer said. They made a U-turn and circled back
to the scene of the crime.

Only it appeared that there had been no crime. Emily's car was still parked just where she had left it, with the driver's door cocked open, blocking the flow of traffic. The carjacker had vanished — without taking the car.

"Looks like he's gone," the policeman observed, pulling to a stop in front of the Toyota.

"Crimeus interruptus," his partner observed as they got out.

"Maybe he couldn't get it started," Emily said. "I've got the keys."

"These guys don't need keys. I've seen 'em jack a Brink's armored car in three seconds," the first officer said.

"If they want it, they get it," the other one added, ducking his head inside of the car.

Emily could see that her purse wasn't on the seat. Perversely, she was glad that at least she'd been robbed. "Well, he got my purse anyway."

"You mean this?" the second officer said, holding up Emily's bag. "It was on the floor. Must've fallen off of the seat." He handed it to her. "Anything missing?"

She peered inside, shuffled a few things around. "My wallet."

"This it?" The officer leaned over to pull the wallet out of the space between the passenger seat and the door. He winked at his partner, who was shaking his head.

Emily took the wallet from him and counted the money and credit cards inside. "I don't understand," she fumbled. "He got into my car! He threatened me with a gun, or a knife!"

The two policemen looked at each other again. "Which was it, a gun or a knife?" one asked.

"I didn't see it, but he had something in his pocket. He was reaching for it when I got away."

"Can you describe him?" the officer asked patiently.

"Yes, of course. He was Caucasian, medium height and weight, wearing rain gear. Bulky, dark rain gear. And he had a cold. He was sneezing." She looked at the two policemen, the patronizing expressions on their faces. She slumped against the car. "You think I'm crazy."

"No ma'am, we don't think you're crazy. Just scared. You can come down to the station and file a complaint. But the fact is, without a witness or a good description — "

"Or an actual crime," the other officer put in.

" — there's not much we can do."

The other officer dug into his pocket. "Here's a card. If you remember anything else about him, or if he comes back after you, just give a call. All right?"

Emily took the card. "Thank you," she mumbled, her eyes moist with humiliation. "You've been very nice."

The policemen walked back to their car. "It's probably a good idea to stay out of this neighborhood too," one of them called back to her. "There are lots of creeps around here who'd prey on a woman alone."

Emily got into her car and slammed the door. She was still shaking, but now it was from cold and shame rather than from fear. She put the car in gear, turned the key in the ignition, and pulled into traffic.

○

From the shelter of a liquor store, Sampson watched Emily drive away. He wanted to kick himself for the stupid way he had blown their encounter.

Armed with the name and number Kevin had given him — given wasn't the right word, Sam had paid $100 for them — he had finally gotten up the courage to call, telling himself he could hang up if he got cold feet. But he'd gotten an answering machine, a woman's voice saying, *This is Emily Barnes. You can reach me during the day at 713-9901.* The voice sounded familiar, but Sam didn't know why.

"Party Line," the receptionist had answered when he'd dialed the number.

"I'm trying to reach Emily Barnes," he said.

"She just left for lunch."

"Do you know when she'll be back?"

"Let's see," the girl had said. "She's at Gulliver's in San Pasqual. That's ten minutes from here — I'd say about 2:30. Can I take a message?"

"No, thanks, I'll call back," he'd said, and hung up. As soon as the line had cleared, he'd called information to get the telephone number and address of the restaurant. At least he could see what she looked like, and if he felt bold enough ...

The maitre d' had pointed her out, sitting at a table with a dark-haired man. Her back was to him, the man facing him. The restaurant wasn't full, and through the ambient noises he had heard snippets of their conversation — *Jonah ... custody ... because Jack died.*

His initial plan had been simple: to wait until she left the restaurant, then "accidentally" bump into her, start a conversation, and see where it led. But then, abruptly, she'd stood and rushed out the door on the far side of the restaurant. He hadn't even seen her face.

He'd waited to be sure that the man wasn't following her — he wasn't. Instead, he'd calmly reached across the table and started to pick at the salad left uneaten on her plate. So Sam had gone after her.

And when he'd seen her drop her keys, it had appeared fortuitous, a chance to introduce himself and look like a hero at the same time. But he'd let it all go wrong. When he'd gotten into her car, turned and finally seen her face, he'd nearly lost his lunch. Because he'd recognized her as the woman he had met in the hospital the weekend of his transplant. He had been so stunned he hadn't been able to speak, and when he had finally opened his mouth, he'd blown it royally.

Obviously, she hadn't recognized him. And now her mind would forever be engraved with the impression of him as a would-be carjacker and mugger. If he tried to approach her again, she'd probably think he was a stalker and call the cops before he could get a word out. If he were smart, he'd forget the whole thing and let this woman go on about her business. It looked like she had enough unsettling influences in her life without meeting one more.

His throat felt scratchy. He pulled the roll of Lifesavers from his pocket and slipped two into his mouth. Cherry and orange, a nice combination. Then he pulled up the hood of his jacket and started to walk out of the store.

"Hey you," the clerk called to him. Sampson turned around. "Ya got something stuck to your butt."

Sampson swiped his hand across his rear end and pulled off a long, damp paper. A parking ticket. There was no name on it, but there was a car make, model, and year. Her car.

The bass guitarist in a band he'd jammed with a few times worked at the DMV. The guy used to have easy access to records. He could probably find out where she lived, maybe some other pertinent information. Sampson put the ticket in his pocket and left the store. Maybe he wouldn't forget the whole thing after all.

12

I want this to be over," Emily told Marilyn Macy at their next session. "I'm sick and tired of being sick and tired!"

"It's a natural response," the therapist told her. "Not only are you pregnant, with all the physical and emotional changes the condition involves, but you're still grieving for Jack. Healing is a slow, painful process, Emily, and unfortunately, nobody has invented a way to speed it up."

"But it just keeps getting worse," Emily complained. "Now Matt says he wants custody of Jonah. Marilyn, I can't give up my son, I can't! I'll be totally alone.... " She started to weep in great wrenching sobs. "See? Everything makes me cry these days. I hate my life being so out of control!"

Marilyn held out a box of tissues and waited while Emily wiped her eyes. "I thought you told me your ex-husband was a therapist."

"A child psychologist, actually."

"Then he is certainly well aware of the turmoil you're going through right now. It was unfair and manipulative of him to bring up this issue of custody while you're so vulnerable."

"He told me it was Jonah's idea."

"Do you think that's true?"

"Well, Matt *is* unfair and manipulative, but I agree, Jonah probably is unhappy at Oceancrest."

"Let him transfer."

"The schools around our house are lousy."

"Then move. Or let him go to a lousy school. What's worse? Losing custody of your son because you want to stay in a house you bought with a partner who isn't around anymore, or moving? And what's to stop you from putting him in a private day school here in town? There are plenty of them."

Emily stopped crying. "I guess I could." She sighed and looked down at the gnawed fingernails of her hands.

"So! Now that we've solved that problem," Dr. Macy said, "why don't we talk about what's really bothering you?"

"What do you mean?"

"You've mentioned a lot of specifics: your concern about possibly losing Jonah, your anxiety about your pregnancy, your loneliness. Have you thought about what emotion is driving all this negative energy? What does it all boil down to?"

Emily thought about it. "Just plain fear, I guess," she said at last. Oddly enough, this came as a revelation to her.

"Right. You're finding out how perilous it is to be balancing a life without a partner. It's pretty scary being up on that high wire alone, isn't it? Especially because from what you've told me about Jack, he was your safety net."

"Now that we both recognize that I'm scared witless, what do I do about it?" Emily couldn't keep the caustic edge from her voice.

"If I had all the answers I'd write a book and go on *Oprah*," Marilyn Macy said with a smile. "But I don't, so I can only give you a couple of suggestions. First, try not to cling to the past. I'm not saying you should forget who you are, shave your head, and move to Tibet. But clearly, some of the old avenues are closed to you: Jack is gone — you're not a wife, and for the first time in your life, no one's waiting in the wings; Jonah *may* become less a part of your life; you *may* not continue to live in your house. With all these variables, it's only natural that you feel dislocated. What you have to do is find *new* directions, new relationships — and I don't necessarily mean marriage — new roles, new interests. Do you think you can do that?"

"I don't know if I have the energy," she admitted. "What else?"

"Stop feeling sorry for yourself. Look around you, girl. Everybody's got problems and sadness and things they can't control. Nobody's perfect. It's not a contest with some omnipotent god handing out achievement awards."

"You mean there's no prize? Damn! And here I thought I was so close to winning," Emily said, smiling at last.

"Now you like lists, so we're going to make one. These are the things I want you to do before our next session."

○

Emily squeezed a drop of hot glue onto an invitation card and carefully pressed a swatch of denim cut in the shape of a "K" onto the sticky spot. The fabric sizzled, then stuck. She set the card aside and picked up another.

This part of her work was mindless, but she liked using her hands, creating things. Plus it helped her avoid thinking about Jack, and how empty her life had become without him. "Stop feeling sorry for yourself," she said out loud, echoing Marilyn Macy's words. "You're not the only one with problems."

She picked up another denim "K". The invitations were for a birthday party for a 10-year-old named Kristin, and Party Line was organizing an event for thirty preteens. The party would begin with a scavenger hunt at the mall (she'd contacted twenty stores; twelve had been willing to cooperate), then on to Rascals for a game of laser tag, and finally, dinner at the Hard Rock Cafe.

She had wanted to plan such a party for Jonah's birthday, but he had been unenthusiastic and unhelpful when she tried to enlist his help with the plans. So they'd agreed to have a simple family dinner instead — Jonah and Emily, Matt and Lauren — at Jonah's favorite restaurant, TGIFridays. She tried not to be disappointed that he didn't want her to do anything more than just show up at a restaurant, but it was hard to accept.

As she began to decorate another invitation card, the telephone rang. Normally, she would have let the machine pick it up; it was after six, and she was alone in the office — Ann and the Party Line crew were catering a baseball-themed fortieth birthday party for a mother of three Little Leaguers at a ball park in the Valley. But on the off chance it was Ann calling with a problem, she picked it up after the first ring.

"Party Line, may I help you?"

"Emily? It's Gary Forrester. How're you doing?"

"Gary! I'm good … well, as good as can be expected." She was surprised how glad she was to hear his familiar voice. "What's going on with you?" She put a dot of glue on the invitation and pressed another denim "K" to it.

"Same old thing. Just trying to get the numbers to add up. Which is one of the reasons I'm calling." He paused, then continued in a subdued tone. "Now that some time has passed, we should sit down and look at your financial situation. We need to file a few documents anyway, to change your marital status and get ownership transferred on the house, the car, the insurance. What do you say we talk about it over dinner, you pick the night?"

Emily felt a twinge of panic. This was the first dinner invitation she'd received in weeks. Immediately after Jack's death, friends and neighbors had been solicitous and concerned about her, asking her to dinner, to the movies, to sporting events. She hadn't felt like accepting, and most often, she hadn't. *We don't want to push you,* her friends had said to her, *just let us know when you're ready.*

But then the invitations had stopped. Cold. Her phone barely rang any more. It hurt, but she understood: people acted as though grief were a contagious disease they were afraid of catching.

Yet as much as she yearned for companionship, maybe what Marilyn Macy had said was true: she should not expect old relationships to sustain her. If she and Gary spent an evening together, they would just wallow in the sorrow of Jack's death. Did she really want to do that, or should she try to move on?

"Gosh, Gary, I'm buried here, and my desk is a mess. Let me get organized and call you when I unearth my calendar. Maybe we can get together for lunch one day. Okay?"

"Sure, no problem. Shall I call you later?"

"Who knows how long it will take me to find it. I'll get back to you. I promise. Love to Marcia," she said, and hung up before he could protest.

She breathed deeply, realizing that she was damp with perspiration. Since when did a dinner invitation throw her into a panic?

Since Jack had died, leaving her alone, vulnerable, awkward, just plain different.

Emily heard a key turn in the lock. Then the front door opened and closed. Emily's panic hit a new high note. It couldn't be Ann — the Little League party wouldn't be over for hours. Who else had a key? Who else would be coming into the office at this late hour?

She looked around for a weapon, some way to protect herself from the intruder. Her hands closed around a letter opener, and she stood, brandishing it, ready for a confrontation.

A head poked into her office.

"Lew?"

"Thought I saw a light," he said. "What are you doing here at this hour?"

Emily let out her breath and fell back into her chair. "Invitations for Kristin Bellwood's birthday party. What about you?"

The staff had nicknamed Lew and his wife Rachael *Ozzie and*

Harriet because they were so wholesome — when they married, they bought a house in the suburbs, a station wagon, and a sheep-dog named Moses. They had been high school sweethearts, and they had beautiful twin daughters who, like the angels they were, both played the harp.

He tapped the file folders he had under his arm. "Just tabulating the numbers from these old files," he said.

"Doesn't Gary do that? I was just talking to him."

Lew shrugged. "Yeah, I'm just making sure everything's organized for him. You know I prefer working with figures to working with clients — with numbers, two and two always makes four."

"That's great," she glanced at her watch, "but you know how stingy we are with overtime."

"Oh, this isn't overtime. I had to leave early yesterday for a dentist appointment. Damn crown fell out at the gym on Tuesday." He rubbed his jaw. "Anyway, I'd rather be here than home. There's nothing to go home *for* anymore."

"Come on, you've got a beautiful wife and two great kids."

"True, I just wish they didn't live in West Hills with Rachael's new boyfriend."

Emily deflated. "Oh, Lew, I'm sorry. I didn't know! How long ago did that happen?"

He sketched a circle on her desk with the tip of his finger. "It's been a couple of weeks." He gave an annoyed sigh, "more like three weeks and four days — " he looked at his watch, " — and six hours. Not that I'm counting. The house is so damn empty, I'm just bouncing off the walls."

"I know what you mean," Emily said.

"I can't stop thinking about her starting a whole new life with this guy just ten miles away, while I'm stuck with the shell of what we had together. The other day I was at Cafe Central meeting a client, and they were there having dinner. It was so damn humbling, to see them walk out together arm in arm — not only that, but she was wearing the dress I gave her for her birthday. How's that for a kick in the pants?"

Emily said nothing, imagining how painful it would be if Jack were still alive but living with another woman.

"Sorry, I didn't mean to go off on a rant. See, that's why it's better if I just work with numbers right now, not people. I'm not very good company these days."

"My therapist says the best thing to do when you're suddenly alone is to try to make a new friend, someone who didn't know you as a couple." Emily held up the "To Do" list she'd made at her session with Marilyn Macy. At the top of the list was written *1. Make a new friend.*

"Let me know if it works," Lew said with a smile, and got up to leave. "Meanwhile, if you hear a strange sound from my office, it's just me, bashing my head against the wall."

When he was gone, Emily considered the list in her hand. *Why not,* she said to herself. She picked up the phone and dialed.

"This is Dr. Leventhal's service," said the voice on the other end.

"My name is Emily Barnes. Dr. Leventhal treated my husband about two months ago, and … "

"Is this an emergency?"

"No, I — "

"Is it an insurance matter? If so I'll transfer you to — "

"No, no it's not about that. I just wanted to speak with her, that's all."

"Well, I can take a message for her, but I can't say when she'll pick it up."

Emily gave the girl her name and number and quickly hung up, regretting that she'd given the woman the Party Line telephone number. Now she'd have to stick around for God knew how long, on the off chance that the doctor would call back.

But the phone rang almost immediately.

"Hello, this is Andrea Leventhal returning a call from Emily — "

"Dr. Leventhal! "Emily broke in. "Thank you for calling back so quickly."

"I wish I could say I'm always so prompt," the doctor replied, "but it's the luck of the draw. I'm on duty today, and so far no crises in the E.R. How have you been, Mrs. Barnes? What can I do for you?"

How could she explain that she'd promised her therapist she'd try to develop a new relationship before their next session, and that she'd chosen Andrea to be her friend? "Please call me Emily — I'm doing all right, I guess," she replied. "I'm trying to do what you said, to go on with my life."

"It's hard, I know," the doctor said. "My husband Charles died fourteen months ago, and I still come home expecting to find him in the kitchen tossing a Caesar salad with his hands — he insisted it tasted better that way."

Emily thought of Jack, how he liked his Caesar salad so garlicky that she couldn't get near him for days after he'd eaten one. The memory was so distinct that she could smell the pungent aroma of garlic. "It changes everything," was all she could say.

"Yes, it does. Emily, do you have anyone to talk to?"

"You mean a therapist? Yes. I just started with her a couple of weeks ago when I found out ... when I found out that I was pregnant."

"Oh my," said the doctor. "Isn't it amazing how the life force insinuates itself in times of tragedy? I see it so often with my patients. It is indeed a mystery and a miracle."

"It was a shock, anyway," Emily admitted. "We weren't trying to get pregnant. I already have a son."

"Well, congratulations," the doctor said, ignoring the ambivalence in Emily's voice. "Are you looking for an OB/GYN? I know a very good one."

"Yes ... no, that's not why I'm calling," Emily replied. "I was just … I want to thank you for all you did for Jack, and for me. And I was wondering, would you be free to have lunch sometime? You probably don't take time for lunch, do you?" she added, answering her own question to fill the pause on the other end of the line. "Maybe we could meet for coffee. I'll come to the hospital if that would be easier for you."

○

There were directional signs to the hospital cafeteria in English, Spanish, Japanese, and what looked like Arabic, as well as the universal symbol of a fork and knife, so Emily easily found her way. She was early, as usual, and Andrea Leventhal had not yet arrived. With time to kill, she strolled down the buffet line and made mental notes — as a party planner, it was second nature for her to be curious about how other people handled catering and food service chores — the displays, the prep areas, the quality, quantity, and choice of foods.

She knew better than to expect much from a hospital cafeteria, but even so she was dismayed at what she saw. Although some effort had been made to appeal to contemporary tastes, the food was decidedly unappetizing. A salad bar offered only limp head lettuce, overripe cherry tomatoes, withered slices of red onions, and soggy, unpeeled cucumbers. There were two choices of pizza: greasy and greasier — actually pepperoni and vegetarian, the latter consisting of a solitary slab of fleshy, undercooked eggplant and a bay leaf atop a smear of blood-red sauce — not an appetizing choice in a hospital! And as she passed the grill, the rancid smell of fried lard was so strong that it turned her stomach.

It was too late for lunch and too early for dinner, so most of the diners were interns, recognizable by their white coats and their visible sun, sleep, and sustenance deprivation. They sat staring numbly into space, with Styrofoam cups of coffee clutched in their hands and the pseudo-sugary remains of torn Nutrisweet packets strewn on the tables before them.

Every so often a non-staff visitor would wander in, dazed with boredom or grief, the two emotions seeming to elicit similarly stunned expressions. One, a woman of Middle Eastern descent, entered the dining area carrying a tousle-haired baby with pierced ears and a patch over her right eye. Two other children, both under six, trailed behind her. The mother was short and stout and walked with a slightly bowlegged rolling motion. Although she was wearing an expensive designer suit, she had the hollowed look of a Holocaust survivor. The two older children were also well dressed and overweight, but unlike their mother, they were frolicsome and eager to sample the bounty of the cafeteria. They heaped their trays with runny chop suey and chipped beef, greasy French fries, and French toast drowning in syrup. For herself and her baby, the mother chose a wobbling slab of chartreuse Jell-O.

She must have sensed Emily's eyes on her, because she raised her head and stared back. Emily sent her a commiserating "I've been there too" look, but the woman did not return it. In fact, she did not seem to *see* Emily at all, blinded by her own misery and torment.

Is that how I look to people? Emily wondered, lowering her eyes.

"Her sister was raped, her husband and her brother-in-law were both beaten senseless," a voice behind her said softly.

As before, Andrea Leventhal seemed to appear without warning. "We don't know exactly what happened to the baby's eye, but the cornea is badly bruised. She will lose her sight in that eye unless we are able to find a compatible donor and do a transplant. And you can imagine how rare the corneas of a four-month-old infant are."

"What happened?" Emily asked in a hushed voice.

"The police report called it a home invasion robbery. The husband had just driven in with a new big screen TV sticking out of the trunk of his Jaguar. The thieves must have seen it and followed him. The wife was picking up the older kids from day care, and when she got back, she found the others."

"Are the husband and brother-in-law going to live?"

She shrugged. "We've done our best. It's like I told you about your husband, we can only do what's humanly possible."

"At least you can do something!"

Andrea smiled wanly. "Well, you can too. Buy their doctor a cup of tea. It's the only thing this cafeteria can't screw up. Come on, there's an alcove around the corner that's reserved for doctors. It's a little more private, and we can talk."

As they passed the Arab woman, Andrea bent and whispered something to her. The woman tried to smile. Her hand clutching the doctor's was white with tension. "Thank you so much, Madam Doctor," she said in English that was thickly accented and broken with emotion. "Thank you, thank you," she repeated, until Emily and Andrea were out of hearing range.

○

"So, how are you?" Andrea asked as they settled themselves at a table.

"Pretty good. Passable. Well, if you ask my family, not so great. Terrible," Emily finished. They both laughed.

"At least you admit it. From what I know about grief, that's a positive sign."

"In other words, feeling bad ... is good?"

"It's better than the alternative," Andrea said, "which is feeling nothing."

"I can relate to that, I've definitely been there," Emily agreed.

The doctor's beeper sounded. "Damn," she said. "Was I nuts to think I could sneak in an actual break?" She took out her pager and peered at the digital readout. "A cardiac patient. My husband's mother, as a matter of fact." She sighed. "Apparently it's nothing serious, or they would have coded it. Do you want to go up with me? Do you have time?"

"If I won't be in the way."

"If you are, I'll let you know."

As they waited for the elevator, a gurney rolled past, the occupant sobbing in obvious pain and anguish. "How can you stand seeing all this suffering day after day?" Emily asked. "Especially when you have your own loss to deal with."

Andrea looked at her thoughtfully. "I suppose you could say that what I've experienced has helped me to be patient with the grief of others. Empathy is a powerful teacher, as I'm sure you are learning. And as you pointed out, I do have some skills — using them to ease the suffering is very gratifying."

The elevator came, and they got in. The car was full, but out of respect for Andrea Leventhal's white coat, the passengers stepped back to make room. "But do you want the truth?" the doctor continued. "When I go home, I ache from all the emotion that pours out of me day in and day out. I guess you could call me a bleeding heart. Which is not to say I'm a liberal in the political sense, by the way," she hastened to add. "I believe in universal health care, but only if people are allowed to choose their own doctors. Can you imagine entrusting your life to someone you don't even like? Heck, I interviewed four veterinarians before I allowed one to give a rabies shot to my rabbit."

"You have a rabbit?"

Andrea reddened. "Oops. I usually don't reveal that little gem of personal trivia until I know a person better — I must *really* be tired!" She sighed. "The Rabbit Story: She belonged to a magician I hired to perform at a sixth birthday party for my daughter. Poor thing was scared to death — the rabbit, I mean, not my daughter — she wouldn't come out of the top hat. The magician was furious, started making jokes about rabbit stew, which was very upsetting to the children — and to me. So I rescued her and let her retire to greener pastures. I've got a pretty big back yard, all fenced. Last thing I needed was another animate object requiring care, feeding, and love. But my daughter adores her, and actually she makes a pretty good pet."

"What's her name?"

"Tricky."

"I meant your daughter."

Andrea laughed. "Oh. Jennifer. She's nine now. A great kid. Do you have a family?"

"A son, by my first marriage. He's thirteen, fourteen next week."

"That's right, you mentioned him."

$\circlearrowright$

They got out of the elevator on Eight. A nurse was waiting. "What's up?" Andrea asked her.

"She refused to take her meds. Said you okayed it. But it wasn't on the chart, so we — "

Andrea sighed. "I did *not* tell her it was okay to stop her meds. What I told her was she could stop taking them once the symptoms were gone, which they're not, not by a long shot." She turned to Emily. "This shouldn't take long. Do you mind waiting? There's a lounge over there." She nodded toward a small glassed-in space with the usual chairs and magazines and Mr. Coffee machine. "I'd say 'come with me' but Ruth demands my undivided attention, even if she doesn't agree with my diagnoses. It might rankle her to think she was sharing me with someone else."

"No problem," Emily said. "I have nothing but time."

"Good. Make yourself at home. I'll try to be quick."

Emily walked toward the lounge, but as she got closer, her steps slowed. She was overcome by panic — it was the same room in which she had been told of Jack's death. She couldn't go in. She turned and walked in the other direction.

It was dinnertime for the patients on this floor, and an attendant was pushing a cart of meal trays down the hall, checking his chart as he went, to match the right person with the right food. He stopped in front of Emily and took a tray into one of the rooms. When he was out of sight, Emily slid another tray out of the cart to examine the contents: a brownish, brothy soup, possibly mushroom or beef, a plate holding a crusty piece of fried chicken, a scoop of mashed potatoes, and a smattering of peas and carrots, and for dessert, a lemon meringue tart. Each dish was tightly covered with Saran Wrap, and all were the same tepid temperature. A hard, round roll was wedged between an empty coffee cup and a plastic water glass.

The tray itself was beige plastic, covered with a white paper doily. The napkin was cheap, white, and polyester, completely impervious to liquids, the plates disposable. Judging from the inferior quality of the utensils, patients would have to use their hands to eat the chicken, because it would be impossible to cut it or to stick the tines of the fork through it. For the cost of a hospital room, couldn't they do better than this?

"Those meals are for the patients," the attendant said. He took the tray from Emily and slid it back into place on the cart. "If you're hungry, there's a cafeteria down on Sub-One."

"I wasn't ... I was just curious to see what you were feeding them."

"Oh, everybody gets something different, y'see?" the attendant explained, showing her his chart, proud to be an authority on something. "Some got t'have low sodium, some low fat. Lot of 'em can't have nothing but liquids. Some you just want to feed 'em anything to put some meat on them bones." He grinned a crooked-toothed smile. "Best night of the week's Sunday. That's turkey night for them that kin eat it. With all the trimmins' too."

"How nice," Emily said, although she envisioned the thin, dry, white meat smothered with lumpy gravy, a stuffing made of stale crusts from yesterday's sandwiches, and gelatinous cranberry sauce. It simply wasn't right that the food was so bad. These people were sick, and they obviously needed good nutrition, appetizing food, *and* a pleasing presentation to raise their spirits. Maybe there was something Party Line could do. She walked on down the hall considering the idea. What would it take to operate a hospital food concession? All the equipment was in place, although new china and cutlery would help make the food more appetizing. But mostly it would be a matter of the proper personnel — knowledgeable cooks and a nutritionist to make sure each meal offered more than empty calories to the patients.

From an economic standpoint, it would be a winner, because there would be no need to worry about business; the clientele would be built in. But even more appealing was the idea that what she was doing would help people who desperately needed it. She would have to talk to Ann about it.

The hallway was wide, and most doors were open, the patients sitting up in bed or in chairs awaiting the biggest event of the day: mealtime. Some rooms were crowded with flowers, family, and friends, while in others, patients lay quietly alone in the darkness with only the strobing glare of the television to animate their faces.

As she passed one door she heard jazz playing, a piece with a strong but soothing drumbeat. She stopped by the door to listen. The patient was lying completely still. He was breathing in oxygen through tubes in his nose and was receiving intravenous medications from several colored pouches hanging on a metal tree. Behind him a bank of monitors registered his vital signs.

His face was puffy and full, but ashen, and very still. Oddly, there was something familiar about him. She came a step closer — and suddenly the man in the bed was Jack, not the man she'd married, but as she'd last seen him — his head bandaged, his body unnaturally narrowed, lying still, so very still. She stopped breathing, staring at him in horror and awe. The grief she had been struggling to keep in check flooded over her with such fresh force that she had to hold onto the door to keep from collapsing.

"Are you a friend of Sam's?" a voice asked.

"What?" Emily gasped. She squinted and tried to see into the darkened room. Finally she was able to make out the shape of a woman in the corner. Only her hands moved as she knit furiously from a mottled skein of yarn.

"Oh, no," Emily said. "He looked familiar is all ... I'm sorry. I didn't mean to disturb you."

"He caught a cold and it turned into an infection," the woman said. "With his heart ..." she swung her eyes back to the man in the bed. "We all *told* him to be careful. But instead he goes running around in the rain, like to catch his death. Literally," she added grimly. She knit a few stitches, seemed to compose herself, then added, "It's very kind of you to come. How did you know Sam was back in the hospital? I haven't told a soul. He wouldn't let me."

"Oh, I didn't ... I just happened to be here, visiting a friend," Emily stammered.

"But — " The woman looked confused.

"Like I said, I don't know your husband. But I'm sorry he is so ill," Emily said lamely.

"My husband?" The woman seemed startled. "Oh, no, he isn't my *husband*." She laughed. "Please, I have better taste than that! I'm Diana Harper. That's Sam, Stevie Sampson, my baby brother." She looked at him again. "And what a baby he is! Doesn't even know enough to get out of the rain. You should have seen him — "

Through the watery rush of his dreams, Sam heard the drone of his sister's voice. He struggled to open his eyes, but they were weighed down as though by the force of the sea. It was so comfortable there, floating there under the surface. Why should he fight it? But some inner force compelled him to rage against the heaviness, and he began to stir.

"Look, he's waking up!" he heard Diana say.

"Sam! Look who's here." Diana turned to Emily. "I'm sorry, what was your name again?"

"Emily. Emily Barnes."

Hearing the name, Sam tried harder to overcome the torpor that pressed him down, and finally he burst through to the surface. He blinked to clear his vision, and made out a figure standing to his left, at the foot of the bed. The indistinct, oscillating images he had been imagining now snapped into focus. It was her! Or was he still dreaming? What else would explain her miraculous appearance here? Although his facial expression did not change, the monitors behind the bed lit up, registering his internal excitement.

Diana rose from her chair, letting her knitting fall to the floor. "Oh my God, he's rejecting! Get the nurse!" she cried, and ran to the bed to press the "call" button.

"I was dreaming about you," Sampson said to Emily, but his voice was only a hoarse whisper.

"What is it? Is he okay?" Emily asked Diana.

"He's delirious. Go! Go now! Please get help!" Diana implored.

Emily backed away from the bed and ran from the room.

Sam saw her go, then closed his eyes and groaned. "Diana, I ... don't let her go. I need — "

"What do you need? Does it hurt? Can you breathe?" She put her hands on his chest and pressed her weight against them in a pathetic parody of CPR.

"Ugh!" Sampson grunted between pushes. "No! Stop! I'm fine!"

"Oh, God, oh God, what's wrong?" Diana picked up the pace of her pumping, tears running down her face. "Sam, Sam!" She looked at the monitors. The harder she pressed, the more erratic was their reportage of his internal stress level. "Somebody help!" she cried.

"You're — hurting — me!" Sampson gasped between blows. He flailed his arms wildly, trying to push Diana away. But he had no leverage, and she outweighed him by thirty pounds. His vision began to cloud over, the pain in his chest deepening into an unbearable searing heat. The ocean roared in his ears. He was going under again. The rip tide pulled him off his feet, and he sank beneath the surface just as two nurses rushed in. Emily was close behind them.

"Please help," Diana gasped, stepping back to let the professionals take over. Emily put her arm around her, and the two women clung to each other, watching Sam struggle to hang onto life.

Only Emily wasn't seeing this stranger. She was seeing Jack in the bed, remembering him in his last futile fight. It was horrible to watch, unspeakably brutal to see the scene reenacted.

"What happened?" one nurse asked.

"He opened his eyes, and all of a sudden the monitors went crazy," Diana said. She looked to Emily for confirmation. Emily nodded.

"Mr. Sampson, can you hear me?" The nurse shook him gently.

"Who's his doctor?" the other nurse asked.

"Greshom," Diana replied.

"Page him," said the first nurse.

"Code Red?" the second asked.

The first nurse looked at the monitors and considered. "He seems to be stabilizing now, but he might have had a rejection episode, or a minor heart attack."

Sampson mumbled something, his eyes still shut. The nurse bent low to him. "What was that, Mr. Sampson. What did you say?"

"I said, I'm fine. It wasn't my *heart* that attacked me, it was my sister!"

○

Emily slipped from the room, drained and shaking. All she could think about was getting out of the hospital as quickly as possible. It seemed to come over her more and more often these days, this fear, and the urgent need to flee.

As though she could run away from the realities of life and death.

As though she could escape to a place where Jack would still be alive, and Jonah would still want to be her son.

She pressed the elevator call button rapidly, three, four, ten, twenty times. Why did it not arrive? "Is something wrong with the elevator?" she asked a nurse who was also waiting.

"Nothing a complete overhaul wouldn't fix," the nurse replied. "Stairs are around the corner if you've got the energy. I certainly don't."

"Thanks," said Emily, and hurried in the direction the nurse pointed.

She flung open the door and ran into the stairwell. The door slammed shut behind her. Too late, she realized that the light was out. She groped in the dark for the door handle to get back out, but when her hands found it, it would not turn.

She was gasping for breath, dizzy with panic. Since childhood, she had always hated the dark. The walls were closing in. She needed air. She needed to get out of the enclosed space. Up? Down? Next to the door, a green emergency arrow glowed, indicating that the nearest exit was the roof, two floors above.

The metallic slap of her hard-soled shoes on the steel risers echoed in the stairwell as she ran up, a jarring cadence. She felt a flash of childhood terror, the sense of being chased by an unseen evil. Only when she was young, it had been a short distance to safety, a mere twenty feet from her own bedroom to the safety of her parents' room and the shelter of their arms. Now there was no safe haven, no one to turn to. All she could do was run.

She reached the roof door and tried to open it. The handle turned, but the door was jammed, swollen shut. Throwing all of her weight against it to break the seal, she pulled back on the handle with both hands, and finally she felt the door give slightly. Another strong jerk and it flew open. She stumbled backward, nearly falling down the stairs, but caught herself and ran out onto the roof.

Sobbing with relief and gasping for air, she leaned against the wall. The air was cold and breezy, and the sky was dark, but the roof was well lit. As she caught her breath, she noticed a group of people on the far side of the roof. They stood huddled together, watching the sky. What were they doing up here? She looked up, in the direction the others were looking, and saw in the distant darkness an approaching light, a tiny star moving closer.

Suddenly she was aware of a whirring noise, and the wind began to gust around her, whipping her hair into her eyes and pressing her clothes tightly against her body. The light in the sky was moving closer, and finally she saw that it was a helicopter approaching, preparing to land on the roof. For a moment, it hovered overhead. The whirring sound was deafening, and the rotors churned the air like a tornado, forcing her body flat against the wall.

She shielded her eyes from the bright lights on the helicopter's belly and watched as it slowly descended, growing larger as it neared the roof. The second its wheels hit the asphalt, two people ran forward, ducking low under the still-turning blades. One of them pulled open the door, and a stairway shot out. Immediately, a man emerged. He was wearing surgical scrubs and tennis shoes and was carrying a red-and-white cooler. Emblazoned on its side in letters so large that Emily could read them from where she stood were the words "HUMAN ORGAN."

Carefully the man carrying the cooler stepped onto the roof, and as a group, the three people hurried toward the elevator compartment, where a fourth person was holding the door open.

"How's it look?" one of them shouted over the whir of the rotors.

The man holding the cooler gave him a thumbs up. "What's our time frame?"

"They're ready and waiting," someone replied, and then the elevator doors drew shut.

13

*A*s Emily ran the morning of Jonah's birthday, she silently reviewed her lists. It was Saturday, so there was the usual round of errands — grocery store, dry cleaner, gas station, drug store. Then there was Jonah's gift. She was on her way to pick it up now. She'd thought long and hard about what to buy, ultimately deciding on a portable CD player, a safe but impersonal gift, something he'd said he wanted. But choosing which one would be difficult. Electronic equipment, anything that plugged in or operated on batteries, had always been Jack's area. Her mind just didn't work that way.

Damn it, Jack, why aren't you here when I need you? she thought. And once again, his absence struck her like a blow to the abdomen.

She stopped at a red light and jogged in place, trying to catch her breath. It always began in little ways like this, the debilitating realization that Jack was gone forever. She would be going about her day, enjoying the comfort of her routine, when she'd notice his razor in the medicine cabinet or see his name on a bulk mail advertisement. Then, suddenly, the bottom would drop out of her life.

But at the same time, her memory of him was fading, like a much-loved T-shirt that had been washed too many times. She could look at a photograph and see the vivid blue of his eyes, the strong curve of his biceps. But the deeper impressions were harder to hold onto — the sensation of his touch, the texture of his laughter.

What would it be like when she could no longer summon his spirit?

A little boy and his mother approached the corner and waited beside her for the red light to change. The child was clutching a green helium balloon in one hand and was holding tightly to his mother with the other. But when he saw Fiber, he let go of the balloon and bent to pet the dog. The green orb floated up and out of his reach, its tail flirting with the breeze. When the little boy realized he had lost his prize, he began to cry. "Mine!" he wailed. "Mine!"

The balloon caught a gust of wind and it sailed up over the street, then above the low buildings, bobbing higher and higher, until it became a mere dot of green against a backdrop of blue sky — still visible, but vanishing.

Just like her memory of Jack.

"It's all right, sweetie," the mother consoled her son. "We'll get another balloon."

"I want that one!" he keened, pointing upward.

Me too, Emily thought. *I don't want anyone else. I want Jack.*

"But it's gone. See? It's flying up to God." The mother glanced at Emily, a little embarrassed. "Say bye-bye to the balloon," she said to her son, and she waved at the slowlyl-disappearing disappearing speck.

"Bye-bye balloon," the child repeated, with tears in his voice.

Bye-bye, Jack, Emily said to herself, her own tears running down her face.

From his car, Sam watched the balloon vanish from sight. He had been trailing Emily since she'd left her house, driving at a snail's pace, making sure he kept out of her line of vision. It was perverse, he knew, his obsessive curiosity about this stranger. But it was something he couldn't — and didn't want to — control. Maybe it was a side effect of the drugs he was taking, or an emotional after-effect of the trauma his body had endured. Or was the heart beating in his chest sending an urgent message to his brain — *find her, know her, help her.* Whatever the reason, thoughts of her filled his mind during the day and his dreams at night.

The light changed, and Emily stepped off of the curb to cross the street. Her eyes blurred with tears, she didn't notice the motorcycle dart out from behind a car that was waiting to make a left turn. Her ears covered by the earphones of her Walkman, she didn't hear the harsh whine of its engine as it sped directly toward her. But watching Emily's progress from his car, Sam did see.

There was no time to think, so he acted on instinct, and jammed the gas pedal into the floorboards. The old hulk of a car surged forward, then stalled, blocking the intersection. It was too late for the motorcycle to stop, but the driver jerked the handlebars to the side, and the cycle swerved to avoid impact. For a split second, Sam thought it was going to career into the passenger door. He ducked his head, crossing his arms protectively over his heart, and waited for the thud of impact.

But the motorcycle pivoted on its rear tire, then scooted around the station wagon and sped off in a trail of noisy exhaust, as though nothing had happened. By this time, Emily had reached the opposite corner. She glanced over her shoulder, only subliminally aware of the commotion behind her and jogged on. She was safe.

Sam let out a long sigh of relief. He tried to start the Volvo, but the engine would not turn over. He craned his neck trying to keep an eye on her, ignoring the honking of the other motorists whose path he was blocking. He watched her stop in front of an electronics store, then open the door to go in.

Quickly, he tried the ignition once more, and this time the engine chugged, then caught briefly. Sam slipped the gearshift into neutral and let it roll forward until it cleared the intersection. Then he braked, affixed his handicapped placard to the rearview mirror, and got out. He was parked in the red, his rear bumper edging over the white line into the intersection, clearly violating at least two parking laws. But he left the car where it was and hurried down the street to the electronics store.

She had tied up her dog outside. It was a scruffy little thing, the color of whole wheat bread. Sam had never had a dog and he didn't know much about the different breeds. This one eyed him warily, so he didn't approach. But as he passed, he said, "Hey, you were almost one dead dog, you know that?" The animal stopped growling and cocked his head curiously.

Inside the store, Sam found Emily talking to a salesman. Atop the counter in front of her were several brands of portable CD players. He busied himself in the video section, keeping his back to her, but standing close enough to overhear the conversation.

"This Sony's got treble and bass controls, plus recording capabilities. That's why it costs a little more," the salesman was saying.

Try two hundred bucks more, Sam thought. *The JVC is just as good, and a helluva lot cheaper!*

"Well, which one would a 14-year-old boy want?" she asked.

"Can't go wrong with Sony," the salesman advised. He noticed Sam hovering by the video cameras and signaled to him, "I'll be right with you, sir."

Sam ducked his head, hoping Emily had not seen his face.

"Oh, go ahead if you've got another customer," she said to the salesman. "I want to just think about this a minute."

"What can I do you for?" the salesman asked, approaching Sam.

"I need a portable CD player for my nephew," Sam said.

"Sure thing. As I was telling the lady ..."

"I want the JVC 750," Sam said loudly. "I've shopped around, and it's the best sound for the money."

"It's good enough," the salesman allowed, "but you can't record off of it."

"So who needs to record? Most CDs have copyrights anyway. It's illegal to record them."

"Yes, but the Sony ... "

"You're just paying for the name with Sony. The JVC is top rated."

"Even so ... "

"And it comes with a one-year guarantee."

The salesman frowned, beaten at his own game. "Obviously you know what you want. Let me just finish with this customer, and I'll ring you up." He walked back to Emily. "So, is it the Sony for you?"

"No, I think I'll get the JVC after all," she said. "And could you please wrap it as a gift?"

Smiling to himself, Sam walked out of the store. He bent to pet the dog as he passed. And whistling, he strolled back to the Volvo, where a policewoman was just stuffing a parking ticket under his windshield wiper.

○

By seven-fifteen, Emily was furious. Matt knew the dinner reservation was for seven o'clock. He knew she would be waiting alone at the crowded restaurant — it was awkward enough for her, to share Jonah's birthday dinner with him and Lauren, let alone having to do so without a partner of her own for balance. At the last minute she'd asked Ann to join them, and Ann had agreed, until she learned Matt and Lauren would be there. "On second thought, it sounds like a family affair," she'd begged off, "I'd better pass."

"But you are family," Emily persisted. But Ann could not be persuaded.

Emily crossed her legs impatiently and felt the bag with the CD player at her feet. She was pleased with herself for buying something Jonah wanted rather than something she thought he should have. And thanks to the stranger in the electronics store, she'd saved a bundle on the one she'd bought. She hoped Jonah would be pleased.

Finally, she saw Matt across the room. When he caught her eye, he waved and started toward her.

"Sorry we're a little late," he said when he got to the table.

"A little? Try half an hour. If it weren't Jonah's birthday dinner, I would have left fifteen minutes ago." Where's my son?" She looked past him, trying to locate Jonah in the crowd.

"He's with Lauren. They're parking the car. I came in ahead of them because I wanted to prepare you."

"Prepare me for what?"

"For why we're late."

"All right. I'll bite. Why are you late?"

"We needed to make a stop on the way so Jonah could get ... a minor adjustment."

"What does that mean?" She finally turned to look at him.

He met her eyes and shifted uncomfortably, like his underwear was two sizes too small.

"Matt!" she said in exasperation. "What does that mean, a minor adjustment?"

He sighed. "He didn't say anything to you?"

"Jonah? About what?"

"About his new ... jewelry."

"What are you talking about?"

Matt took a deep breath. "He got his tongue pierced, okay? And we're late because he had to go to the place he got it and have the stud loosened a little because it was pinching," he said. He spoke quickly, as though saying it fast would make it less painful.

The words stung Emily, like air hitting a fresh wound. "Please tell me you're not serious," she gasped. "He wouldn't do that!"

"I didn't think so either. I thought it was just a lot of talk."

"What was just talk? You mean he *told* you he was going to do it before he did it?" she asked, incredulous.

"You know how kids are. He's been on this one for months."

"He never said a word to me!"

Matt said nothing.

"Of course you tried to talk him out of it," Emily persisted.

"I certainly didn't encourage him."

"Matt, what did you say to him?"

"I told him he needed to examine the reasons why he wanted to do it, and to be sure he understood the consequences — "

"That's not talking him out of it! Jesus Matt, you work with kids every day. You know you have to put your foot down."

"Not necessarily — there are other ways of handling this sort of thing."

"But our son put a ring through his tongue! Do you call that 'handling' it?"

"It's not a ring, it's a chrome stud."

"Whatever! Doesn't the fact that he ignored you and pierced his tongue prove to you that your method isn't working?" She sucked her own unembellished tongue, imagining a metal protuberance puncturing it. "It doesn't even sound sanitary, let alone comfortable. Jesus, why would he do it?" Emily asked. "It's so abusive!"

Matt cleared his throat. "Supposedly, it's, well, an erotic thing. An oral sex thing."

"Oh, Jesus," she interrupted.

"Apparently the little chrome ball rubs on — "

Emily put her hands over her ears, her face turning crimson. "Okay! I've got the picture!" she cried. They sat in silence for a moment. "He's only fourteen. Do you think he's already into kinky sex? He seems so shy around girls."

"I think it has to do with being shy. The piercing makes him appear cool, gives him status, like driving a certain make of car. It defines him."

"As what?"

"It doesn't necessarily mean that he's having sex. But if he is, well, that's even better — or worse, depending on your perspective," he added. "I really don't think we should blow it out of proportion."

"You would say that," Emily snapped. "What if he gets an infection? What if he loses his sense of taste? What if he never takes it out?"

"Try to think of it positively. It makes him cool with his homies, but he can also hide it when he needs to. So in a way, it's better than a nose or a lip piercing that everyone sees. And when he's had enough of it, which I hope will be soon, he can take it out, and the hole will close up. It's not even as bad as a tattoo, which would require laser surgery to remove."

Emily looked at him, incredulous. "You sound like you're happy about this."

"No, I'm not happy, but I don't think it's the end of the world either. Rebellion is part of growing up. Didn't you ever do something you knew your parents wouldn't like? Dye your hair? Wear miniskirts?"

"Maybe, but I never mutilated my body."

"You have pierced ears."

"That's different. They're decorative. Practically all women have them."

Matt shrugged. "It's still making a permanent hole in your body, and as far as everyone doing it, that's just my point. Piercing isn't exclusive to girls any more. Dyed hair either. Guys are getting into the act too."

"I noticed."

"What's that supposed to mean?"

"Your hair *does* seem darker than it was a few months ago."

"So does yours," Matt countered.

Emily opened her mouth to object, but instead started to laugh. Matt continued to glower at her, but finally he smiled grudgingly, and then he too started to laugh. They were still giggling when she saw across the room that her son and Lauren had arrived and were walking toward the table. Jonah looked unchanged, his mangled tongue hidden between rows of expensively straightened teeth. Lauren looked a little harried but lovely in a flowing green dress and matching jacket.

"There they are," Matt said. He rose to his feet. "Please don't say anything about it today. Not on his birthday. Not in front of his friend."

Emily stopped laughing. "What friend?"

Matt rose to his feet. "That was the other thing I wanted to warn you about." He reached to kiss his wife, then smiled unsteadily at the girl standing next to Jonah. "Emily, this is Laura. Laura, Jonah's mother, Emily Barnes."

The first thing that struck Emily about Laura was the color of her hair. It was shocking pink, the color of a flamingo. In fact, the girl resembled a flamingo in other ways too: her body was rail-thin and her legs long and bony. Even her nose was sharp and pointed, like a bird's beak.

But unlike a bird's beak, it was pierced with four tiny gold hoops, and she wore matching but larger hoops in her ears and through her right eyebrow. She was wearing a white leather mini-skirt and a vest with beaded fringe, which left her arms bare, revealing a two-inch-high tattoo of an angel on her right bicep. She eyed

Emily defiantly, as though trying to decide whether to be friendly or hostile. Finally she thrust out her hand. "Hey, Emily," she said.

○

Emily was silent throughout the meal, listening to the others make small talk which skirted the obvious issues of Jonah's pierced tongue, and of Laura — her hair color and body decoration, her crude table manners, and her relationship to Jonah. But as the entree dishes were cleared away, she sat up straight and cleared her throat. "May I ask you a personal question?" she said to the girl.

"I 'spose."

She gestured to Laura's facial piercings. "Doesn't it hurt to do that to yourself?"

"Mom!" Jonah groaned.

"I'm sure she's asked that often, Jonah, and I'm curious."

Laura smirked, displaying a mouth full of uneven teeth. "What d'you think it's gonna feel like if you shove a sharp piece of steel through your skin?"

"Did some hurt more than others?" Emily persisted politely.

"The most painful was my tragus, that's this little piece of ear right here." She leaned toward her and waggled her finger behind the triangular flap of cartilage guarding the entrance to her ear. "When Joanie, that's my boss at Piercing Kingdom, when she shoved the needle through, it was like, God! Childbirth couldn't be worse than this!"

"Then why do you do it if it's so painful?" Lauren asked.

"Don't you ever do anything that hurts?"

Lauren blushed and shook her head. "Not if I can help it. I'm kind of a wimp," she admitted.

"How about plucking your eyebrows? Doncha do that?"

"That's not pain, that's just ... discomfort."

"Well, a lotta times it's not much worse than that. Sometimes they use aromatherapy. Clary sage is almost a real muscle relaxant, so you hardly feel anything."

"You know in Spain they put rings in the noses of the bulls to control them because it's so painful when they pull them," Matt put in.

Laura leaned toward him seductively. "Wanna pull mine?" Matt flushed, and Laura sat back grinning, pleased with herself. She wet her finger and pressed it on the bread crumbs scattered across the table in front of her, then licked them off thoughtfully. She flicked one of her nose rings. "My friend Kevin did this one for me. I stuffed a carrot up my nostril so he'd have something to push into, y'know? So he shoves the stud through my nose and into the carrot, but we're so stupid, it was like, we couldn't figure out how to get the carrot out. There I was, walking around with a friggin' carrot sticking out of my nose!"

Jonah took a carrot from the relish tray and stuck it up one nostril. Emily quickly pulled it out. But she was smiling to herself. Despite Laura's metallic adornment, she rather admired the girl's self-deprecating humor.

"What did you do?" Emily asked.

"I finally pulled both the stud and the carrot out, but then the hole had closed up on the inside. So I had to have it redone professionally. Of course that costs more."

"You must have quite an investment in your ... jewelry," Matt commented, choosing his words carefully.

"You're not kidding. Like, I counted it up once and I think I've probably spent, God, more than three thou' on this stuff. I coulda bought a Geo Prism for that!"

14

On the way home, Jonah was sullen and exhausted, and rather than ignite an argument, Emily decided to wait until morning to bring up the issues of Laura and his pierced tongue. She still hadn't gotten a good look at the stud. Only once during dinner had she happened to time it right and glance at him just as he'd opened his mouth to laugh. Then she'd seen it resting there like a royal pea.

How could he tolerate such an alien object in his mouth? He'd rebelled against braces, wearing his tongue ragged worrying the wires and caps, loosening bits of food that got caught in them. And he had always been terrified of getting shots, a toddler's reaction which had nagged at him into puberty. Certainly puncturing his tongue with a hole large enough to accommodate a chrome stud would have required multiple shots of some anesthesia — which brought up the question of who had performed this travesty on her son. Surely no accredited doctor would mutilate a child's body, and since Jonah had done it at one of those grungy piercing studios, should she worry that he might have contracted a deadly infection? She looked at him, lazing against the seat back, eyes shut and feet propped against the dashboard, tapping time to the beat, and suddenly she remembered the CD player, still in the bag under the table at the restaurant. Damn! She'd been so disconcerted she'd forgotten all about it. Well it was too late to go back for it now. She'd call the restaurant in the morning.

Jonah had his eyes closed, mouthing the words to the song. He looked so achingly young — was it possible that Matt was right? Could a pierced tongue be a sex aid? Did her 14-year-old son know more about giving erotic pleasure than she did? And was Laura his partner?

"Mom," he said, breaking her reverie. "What time are you taking me to the bus tomorrow?"

"Six o'clock, so we can have the day together. I've got a whole list of things we can do."

Jonah picked absently at the laces of his Nikes. "I'm supposed to meet Laura at the mall in the morning."

"Sweetie, please, I know it's your birthday weekend, but I have the day planned for just us. Will you please make arrangements with this Laura for another day?"

"Mom ..." he dragged her name out into a whine. "I won't be down from school for two more weeks. I was with you tonight. Can't I have tomorrow off?"

"Have tomorrow off? Like it's a job to be with me?" Emily couldn't help but let the hurt creep into her voice. "The answer is no. We are going to be a family tomorrow. If you want, invite her to lunch at the house," she conceded recklessly, hoping to appease him.

"Why would she want to go there?" Jonah asked with exaggerated patience. "She's got her own place."

"She has an apartment?"

"Sort of."

"I didn't know you could rent an apartment at fourteen."

"She's older."

"How old?"

"I dunno."

"Jonah!"

"Seventeen, I think."

"Do you know her from Oceancrest?"

Jonah sniggered. "Right! Like she would be caught dead at that dork factory." He reached over and turned up the radio, making further conversation impossible.

They drove in silence for a while. There was so much Emily wanted to say, but she knew it would come out all wrong. She snuck a glance at Jonah. For the first time, she noticed the shadow of a beard on his cheeks and chin. He was changing so fast, no longer a child, but certainly not yet a young man. And somehow over the last few months, she'd lost touch with him.

She turned down the radio. "So where did you meet her?"

"Who?" Jonah grunted.

"Laura!"

"She's a friend of a friend."

"So when did you start seeing her?"

"Seeing her?" Jonah rolled his eyes. "Christ, I can't believe we're having this dumb conversation."

Emily bristled, anxiety and fatigue combining to push her over the edge. "Is that what you thought this was, a conversation?" she asked. "No, I don't think so. A conversation is a dialogue between two people. But that's not what's happening here. I'm asking questions, and you're just sitting there like a lump."

"Oh, man." Jonah scooted up straighter in his seat. "See, this is why I want to go live with Dad. He doesn't nag at me all the time. We're just like friends. We hang together."

There. It was out. Stung and needing to strike back, Emily snapped, "Oh? Was he *hanging* with you when you got your tongue pierced? If you're such pals, why didn't he have his done at the same time? That would be just about his speed."

Jonah's face turned beet red. "Here we go! Why are you so shitty to Dad? Why did you make him leave in the first place? Christ, I have to get out of here! I want out so bad."

It wasn't so much the words as the desperation in his voice that wounded her to the core. "Jonah, please, don't say that," Emily pleaded. "I'm sorry I sound so … shitty. I don't know what I'd do if you went to live with your father. I'd be so alone, especially now."

"It's not my fault Jack died," he said suddenly changing the subject. "Anyway, I can't take his place. So don't try to make me. Don't make me try! Why did he have to croak anyway? This whole mess is his fault," he finished with a strangled gasp. And to her astonishment, he burst into tears.

Immediately her own eyes filled with tears. She pulled the car to the side of the road. "What whole mess?" she asked. He did not reply.

She waited a moment to let him get control, concerned and confused by his outburst, but relieved that he was finally talking about Jack's death. Since the accident, he'd been so remote and unemotional. This was more the boy she knew, someone who felt deeply and cared about other people!

"Jonah, honey." She reached out to touch him, but he jerked away and huddled against the passenger door, turned so she couldn't see him cry. But she could hear the sound of his ragged breaths, and it made her heart ache.

"Darling, please. Nobody thinks it's your fault he died. Nobody expects you to take his place, or to take care of me. If I made you feel that way, I was wrong. I'm sorry."

His back was still to her, but she could see that he had stopped sobbing now, and was listening to her, his forehead pressed against the window. "I've never been through anything like this before, and I admit it's been very hard for me," she went on. "I know I haven't been the best mother in the world. And I'm sorry. But all that can change. It's going to change! I think I'm past the worst of it now. I'm ready to go back to the way things were before."

"How can it be the way it was before? You're pregnant." He spat out the words as though they were foul tasting in his mouth. "And you didn't even bother to tell me."

Emily recoiled in surprise. "I was going to. I meant to. I was just waiting for the right time. Your father never should have mentioned it."

"Like it's his fault you got knocked up."

"Don't you dare talk to me like that!"

On the seat between them, Emily saw Jonah's hand tighten into a fist, but she plunged ahead. "Look, I've been thinking about it, and well, maybe you should live at home next year. We'll start fresh, together. Not like it was before. Different. Better." She reached out again to stroke his back, but he whipped around suddenly, and her outstretched hand accidentally jabbed him in the face. He recoiled wildly, a savage look darkening his eyes.

"Don't touch me," he hissed, his anger flaring far out of proportion to the situation. "You're always doing that." A trickle of blood as thin as a pencil stroke sketched a line down his cheek. She longed to reach out to him, to stop its flow, but she knew better than to try.

"Don't you get it?" he stormed. "I don't want to start over. Even if Jack hadn't croaked, even if you weren't knocked up, I still would have wanted to move in with Dad. I want to go now. I don't ever want to go back to that dumb wooden house. I hate it there!"

Emily felt like she was the one who was bleeding. "We'll move to another house, in a better school district. You can help pick it out."

"No, Mom, it's too late. You're making this harder than it has to be."

"You mean there's an easier way to lose your son?"

"You're not losing me." Suddenly it was as though Jonah had

become the calm, reasonable adult, she the hysterical child. "It's like you and Dad told me when you got divorced, we'll still be a family, but we'll live in different houses."

"And you'll live in his."

"I've been at school for two years anyway."

"You *go* to school, but you *live* at home. Our home."

"It was never my home," he insisted. "It was yours and Jack's."

"Then we'll move to one that's ours, yours and mine. Anywhere you like. I'm sure we can find something near a good school."

"You're not getting it, Mom. I'm going to live with Dad. Next time I come up from school, I'm going to his house, not yours."

From the determined look on Jonah's face, she saw that it would be futile to try to reason with him now. Maybe she could force him to stay with her physically, but emotionally he was already gone. If he came back, it would have to be on his terms. All she could do was leave the door open and pray that he would find his way.

Sunday morning Sam parked the Volvo around the corner from the Barnes house, in a place where he could watch it without being seen. Feeling a little like a cop on a stakeout, he sipped cold coffee from a Styrofoam cup and nibbled on a Danish. It was a little after ten when the door opened and the boy stepped out. He was walking down the path to the sidewalk when Emily came to the door. She called something to the boy and he stopped walking, shaking his head in annoyance. Sam rolled down his window so he could hear.

"You're sure you don't want me to drive you?" she called.

"I already told you a million times — no!"

Emily leaned against the doorjamb, crossing her arms over her chest. "No, what?"

"No, I don't need you to baby me. I'm fourteen years old!"

"Jonah!"

"No, thank you," he conceded.

"Okay. See you this afternoon." She sighed and closed the door.

Sam waited a minute, keeping his eye on the boy. When he felt sure Emily would not come out again, he turned on the engine and pulled into the street. The boy cut across a vacant lot and came out on a busier street, immediately sticking out his thumb to hitch a ride.

Perfect, Sam thought. He swung the Volvo around the corner and slowed next to Jonah, leaning across the seat to roll down the passenger window. "Where are you off to?" he asked.

"The beach, or anywhere in that direction."

"Hop in."

Jonah settled into the seat next to Sam and eyed him briefly. Then he turned to the front window as though to say, *okay let's go.* Sam pulled into traffic, and they drove in silence for a while. Out of the corner of his eye Sam could see that the boy was tall and lean, with his mother's delicate features. But he had dark circles under his eyes and a dark expression — *like Kevin*, Sam thought. Only on this kid the sullenness was a mask, something he was working at achieving. With Kevin it was a manifestation of his soul.

Sam saw Jonah glance at the silent radio and said, "Sorry, antenna's busted. I gotta get that fixed some day."

"No sweat."

"Danish?" He held the box out to the boy. Jonah considered, then picked out a bear claw and took a big bite out of it.

"Thanks," he said with his mouth full.

"You live around here?" Sam asked.

Jonah nodded his head and swallowed. "My mom does. But I'm going to live with my Dad pretty soon, over in Blair Heights."

"This looks like a pretty nice neighborhood. Why d'you want to move?"

"It's a long story. My stepfather died a while back, and my mom's gotten really intense, always on my case. But my dad, he's cool. He pretty much lets me do what I want."

Sam waited before asking another question. He didn't want to appear too curious, but he knew from his own experience that kids who hitched rides felt it was part of the deal that they entertain the driver with conversation.

"That's too bad about your stepfather. Did you two get along?"

"Yeah, I guess. I mean, it was kinda hard because my mom wanted so bad for us to be a family. And she kept pushing us to do stuff together, which bugged me. Bugged him too. Mostly he liked to play golf."

"Did you play with him?"

"No way." He took another bite of the sweet roll. "But he said he would teach me how to scuba dive for my birthday." His voice grew wistful. "That would have been awesome, y'know? I always wanted to learn to dive. But he croaked instead. So anyway, I'm going to live with my dad."

"Then your mom will be alone?"

"Yeah, but she's pregnant. So she'll have the kid to keep her company."

When he heard the word "pregnant," Sam stepped so hard on the brake that they were both thrown forward. "Wow, that's heavy," he said, catching his breath.

"Yeah, that's what I said when my dad told me. Hey, this is where I get out. Can you pull over?"

Sam stopped the car at the curb, and Jonah got out. "Thanks for the ride, mister," he said. He held out his hand.

Sam took it, and they shook hands solemnly, man to man. "No problem. Good luck, kid."

"Yeah, thanks," Jonah replied, and walked away.

FIVE

15

Emily woke with a gasp, as though surfacing from dark water. She blinked rapidly, her vision still blurred from gazing inward at her dreams, her mind groggy with sleep.

As the room came into focus, she tried to sort through the images still fresh in her mind. She could only remember fragments of the dream — the weight of water pressing her down, the faint reflection of the sun creating a weak, dappled trail through the murky darkness, the palpable frustration of seeing salvation above her but being helpless to reach it. Like an abstract story, there was no plot to this tale, no urgency driving it to a conclusion, only endless yearning for release from a watery grave.

Grave. Was she thinking about Jack's grave? Or was some remote lobe of her brain trying to connect with him? But Jack's poor diminished body had been cremated. There could be no impression of life left in the dusky ashes — or could there be? How could one know?

Emily turned her head to look out the window at the coral tree. There had been wind earlier, but now it had passed. The tree's strong branches, verdant with spring growth, were completely motionless in the dark, unearthly still, as though time had stopped.

Straining to look at the clock on Jack's nightstand — she still called it *his,* even though two months had now passed — her eyes strayed to the papers still piled there. And she remembered why she had taken this afternoon nap: she had resolved to begin boxing up Jack's clothes and personal effects, a job she had postponed for so long that the knife-thrust of loss she felt each time she looked at the papers had dulled into a comfortable, earned ache, like a sore muscle after a long run.

But she knew she needed to remove Jack's things from her sight, her home, her mind, in order for the ache to heal. It made sense in theory, but when she'd mobilized herself that afternoon to go out to the garage to find some empty cartons, she'd felt an utterly depleting sense of exhaustion. Was it physical or emotional? She didn't know.

All she did know was that the feeling had ultimately consumed her. The mindless escape of sleep had been so seductive that she had embraced it like an illicit lover, not bothering to remove her clothes or shoes, or to turn the quilt down, so she had awakened with her head buried in the textured fabric. No doubt her face was crosshatched with indentations from the stitching — sleep scars her mother had called them when she was a child.

She felt like a child now, home from school with a fever. And she yearned for the sick-day comfort of ginger ale sipped through a straw, chicken pot pie, crackers spread lavishly with peanut butter, and Neapolitan ice cream. She remembered that these favorite foods had never tasted as good when she was ill, but that she'd savored them nonetheless because they'd represented the love and nurture of her mother's hand and heart. How crucial a part food played not only in health but in emotional well-being!

Her father had also nursed her when she was sick, bringing her candy and games, sitting on her bed to read Nancy Drew mysteries aloud. But who could nurture her now, a 38-year-old woman, ill with grief? Not her mother or father. It was clear from her recent conversations with them that they were expending all of their reserves of energy just staying alive. And though she knew they wanted to be there for her, wanted to console her, they no longer knew what she needed.

In their last conversation the only reference to Jack and his death had been oblique, a question from father to daughter. "Are you all right financially?" he had asked. "Because we will help out if you need it."

"No, Dad, I'm fine. Don't worry," she'd told him. She'd been touched by his offer, because she knew her parents lived frugally, but it also saddened her that he felt that giving her money was the only way he could help her, when what she desperately wanted was the comfort of his arms around her ... and perhaps the sound of his voice reading another chapter of *Nancy Drew*.

↻

It was after eight, so Emily decided to take a long bath before going back to bed for the night. As the tub filled with fragrant water, she peeled off her clothes and put them into the hamper. She was just about to step into the water when the doorbell rang. Wrapping a robe around her, she went to answer it.

Before opening the door, she looked through the peephole. Gary Forrester was leaning against the jamb. He waggled his fingers at the hole as though he could see her staring out at him. She felt a moment's confusion. What was he doing here? They'd talked about getting together to go over her finances, but had they made a date? She saw that he was carrying a bottle of wine, Stags' Leap Petite Syrah, Jack's favorite.

She pulled the robe tighter around her neck and opened the door. "Gary! What's up?"

His lopsided smile turned into a frown, and his hand dropped to his side. "Is that all the greeting I get?" The words seemed to stick to the roof of his mouth, and she realized he'd been drinking.

"I'm just surprised, that's all. Did I forget that we had a date?"

He sighed dramatically. "No, I was just at home, thinking about ol' Jack." He hefted the bottle of wine. "This was his favorite winery, you know. Stags' Leap. The old Stagaroo."

"Yes, I know." Emily remembered the trip to Napa, when they had discovered the small winery. It was off the beaten path, not well known at the time, a magnificent property with three perfect guest cottages for rent. She and Jack had fallen in love with the place and with each other. The bottle of wine Gary held in his hand seemed to symbolize all of that past emotion.

"He talked me into buying a case of it, remember? This is the last bottle."

They both stared at the wine bottle as though expecting Jack's spirit to float out of it.

"Hey," Gary said, "you look like you could use a hug."

He opened his arms, and after a moment's hesitation, she fell into them. Why not? What better balm for her loneliness. But when Gary enveloped her in a hug, she felt a rush of sadness so strong it was like a physical pain.

She needed air. She needed distance. But when she tried to pull away, Gary misunderstood, and tightened his hold on her. She began to struggle with greater urgency, but his grip was too strong. She could feel his heartbeat and, shockingly, his arousal. "Gary! Come on, let go!"

Sensing her distress, Fiber started to bark, circling them in a frenzy. He didn't let up until Gary released Emily and she stepped back, breathing hard.

Gary knelt to pet Fiber, but the dog ducked his head and backed away, growling softly. "Hey, little guy, I thought we were buddies," he said, his mouth twisted into a pout.

Emily gathered Fiber in her arms, using the dog as a shield. "He's been like that ever since ... he's just been more protective since we've been alone."

"Then he's a good dog." He tried to look Fiber in the eyes. "You've just got to figure out who's a friend and who's comin' to raid the pantry, pal."

"So where's Marcia tonight?" Emily asked, looking past Gary to the street as she closed the door.

"Denver," Gary said. "Her sister Jerri had a baby last week and phoned in an S.O.S. — 'send out sister.' " He shrugged off his coat and tossed it onto the banister. "It's fine by me. The alarm's been ringing on Marcia's biological clock." He made a face. "Hopefully once she experiences motherhood close up, she'll cool off."

Emily set Fiber down and wrapped her arms defensively around her belly, although it was still too early in her pregnancy for him to notice a physical change. "I thought you wanted children."

"Kids are great, don't get me wrong. It's all a matter of timing. Speaking of which — " he held up the bottle of wine. "This is a vintage whose time has come. Shall we?"

"No thanks. Look, I don't mean to be rude, but I've had a really rough — "

Gary interrupted. "You mean you're going to make me drink alone? After I came all the way over here? Come on, just one glass. It'll relax you, take your mind off things."

Without waiting for her to respond, he walked into the dining room and took two crystal goblets from the china cabinet. She followed him in. "Really, Gary, I'm not in the mood," she said.

"Why the hell not?" he asked, ignoring her objection and opening the drawer to get out a corkscrew. "It doesn't exactly look like you had big plans tonight."

"Well, for one thing, I was just going to — ohmygod, my bath! I'll be right back!"

The bath water was just starting to spill over the rim of the tub.

She sighed and mopped it up, trying to collect her thoughts. The tub looked inviting, but then so was the prospect of sympathetic company, a friend to lean on. More than just a friend, a warm, male body. And she hadn't had any alcohol since she'd learned that she was pregnant; could a few sips hurt the fetus at this early stage?

"Shall I bring it up there?" Gary called. "I could keep you company while you soak."

"No, it's okay, I'm coming down."

She quickly slipped into sweats and tied her hair back into a ponytail, avoiding the mirror. She probably looked awful, but the thought of putting on makeup at this hour and in her current frame of mind was exhausting. Besides, Gary was a close friend. Surely he wouldn't mind.

When she came back downstairs he was waiting in the living room, bent over the stereo. He pushed a button and Billie Holiday poured out of the speakers. "I never understood Jack's fascination with these old 78s. The sound quality is for shit."

"He didn't listen for the songs, he listened for the memory," she said, and took the glass of wine Gary held out to her. "This is the first time there has been music in this house since he died."

"Well, here's to first times," Gary said. He clinked his glass against hers, and they both drank. Then he put his arms around her again and pulled her into a slow dance. They moved awkwardly at first, but she loved to dance, and Gary was a good partner. So gradually she allowed herself to relax. By the time the song was over, they were moving in sync, her head on his shoulder, her eyes closed. They danced through the next song, and the next. Emily let herself drift, feeling safe and secure in Gary's arms.

When the record ended, they stood with their arms around each other, rocking slowly in the silence. Emily's eyes were still closed. She hardly felt Gary take the wineglass from her hand and set it on the table. But when he cupped her chin in his hands and lifted her face to his, she opened her eyes dreamily. She was about to tell him how much better she felt, when she realized he was bending to kiss her. Startled and flustered, she pushed herself back, out of his arms.

He gave her a wounded look. "Emily," he said, his voice resonating with emotion, "you don't have to be afraid of me. I'm not going to bite you. Unless you want me to," he added mischievously.

Emily stepped back. "I feel awkward without Jack and Marcia here. Don't you?"

"No, not at all. In fact, I think it's kind of nice, just you and me."

He gently ran a finger down the side of her face, rounding the edge of her jawbone, then lifting her chin so her gaze met his. "You're not going pretend that you don't feel anything, are you? Because all these years I've known you were attracted to me, right?"

Emily froze, not knowing how to react. She was fond of Gary, yes, but that fondness was friendship, not attraction. He was an old buddy of Jack's, nothing more. Over the years they'd laughed and teased each other, cooked meals together, had serious conversations, been squeezed so close together in restaurant booths that she'd practically been sitting on his lap. But always it had been as part of a foursome. Had he misconstrued a careless press of her thigh, some joking intimacy at a party?

Or was he just trying to hit on her now that she was alone and vulnerable?

She tried to sound nonchalant. "Come on, Gary — the husband dies and his best friend puts the moves on his wife. Talk about a cliché!"

Gary froze, then withdrew his hand. "Is that what you think? That I'm putting the moves on you? Geez! I suppose I should be flattered that you think I'm a player, but I'm not. Marcia would kill me!"

"But you just said — "

"Hey, babe, lighten up. I'm only trying to give you a lift. Anyone can see you're depressed and lonely."

"Thanks a lot," she said with a forced smile. Being described as depressed and lonely was hardly comforting; the fact that it was true didn't change things.

"Anyway, you're not the only one that misses him. He was my friend for nearly twenty years. The closest friend I had. I saved his life that time we were diving in P.V."

Emily frowned. She had heard the story a dozen times, although Jack told it with quite a different spin. Still, she felt chastened and embarrassed. "I know," she said, "I'm sorry. It's selfish, but I only seem to see his death in terms of how it affects me."

"Aw, hell. It's human nature. Don't beat yourself up over it," Gary said, changing gears again. "But don't lock out your friends either. We can help you. We *want* to help you. We're there for you." He pulled her down onto the couch and sat a respectable distance away. "Talk to me, babe."

With permission to unload her emotions, the words came pouring out. "I expected grief would be like having an injury — a broken arm or a deep cut. You know, a clear, clean kind of hurt. But it's not. It's more like having a low-grade infection, like I'm in this heavy fog." She went on, "It colors everything gray and depressing, and it's always there. It's smothering me! I wouldn't admit this to very many people, but sometimes I wish I could just get sick and die. I mean, I'm not suicidal or anything. But I'm so damn tired of having this weight on me. I want it to be over!"

"Think of it this way," Gary said. "There aren't many worse things that could happen to you than losing your husband. So after this, you've got it knocked."

"Maybe, but somehow I doubt it," Emily said, thinking about Jonah and the fact that she was losing him, too. "Anyway, thanks for listening." She gave Gary a chaste hug.

Gary hugged her back. "That's better. Now, shall we relax and have a drink like civilized people, or shall we just keep acting like strangers in a bar?"

"Not tonight," Emily said. "Honestly, I'm wiped out. Can we go over the books another time?"

"Okay, if you insist. But we should get to it soon. Jack left everything in pretty good shape, but sooner or later, you need to take charge."

"I know. I'll call you. I promise."

They walked to the front door, and Gary bent to kiss her good-bye. But he stopped himself and stepped back. "Oops," he teased, "I forgot. Don't want you to think I'm being too forward!"

"Then allow me," she said, and put her arms around his neck, planting a loud, wet kiss on his cheek.

"So that's it," he said with a smile, "You just want to be the aggressor. I kinda like that!" He started down the path.

She leaned against the doorjamb and watched him walk to the street. Her moods had been seesawing all day. But now, due to fatigue, the calming influence of the wine, and Gary's company, she was finally winding down. Fiber trotted over and stood by her side at the open door. He whined softly, looking out into the yard. She usually didn't let him out in front, both to preserve the lawn and because it wasn't fenced. But it was late, and except for Gary's car, the street was deserted. At this point, preservation of the lawn was low on her list of priorities. "It's okay, boy, go on," she said, and the dog bounded down the steps.

Gary rolled down his window and stuck his head out. "I'm there for you, babe. Let me know when you want to get down to business," he called as he drove away, his words making warm, gray puffs in the night air.

"I will," she replied, watching as the car disappeared. He was such a nice guy *and* a good friend. How could she have mistaken his overtures of concern for a romantic advance?

Suddenly Fiber began to growl, a fierce snarl she recognized as his warning of danger. He was staring into the hedge which separated the house from Laverne Lawrence's, frozen like a pointer with its quarry in sight. Then with a shrill yap, he plunged into the bramble. A dark figure darted out of the bushes on Mrs. Lawrence's side and ran down the street. Fiber scrambled through the shrub and bolted out the other side in hot pursuit.

"Oh, God," Emily screamed. "Fiber! No!" In her bare feet, she dashed across the lawn to the sidewalk and watched the dog race down the block at full speed. He was chasing something, but what was it? An animal? No, even in the darkness she'd seen something larger running away, a human form.

Heart pounding, oblivious to the cold pavement, she ran down the darkened street after her dog. "Fiber! Come boy! Fiber!" she shrieked. Her cries were shrill with anguish, but she didn't care if she woke the neighborhood. All she could think of was getting Fiber's attention, or if that failed, to warn any approaching motorists to stop. As she neared the corner, she saw him skid to a halt just at the curb and look over his shoulder at her. "Fiber!" she screamed again. "Here, boy! Look! I have a bone!"

The dog stared at her. He didn't come, but he didn't run away either. He stood in the street, facing her, his small body just a shadow on the dark pavement. Knowing he sensed her panic, and afraid he would bolt if she ran toward him, she slowed to a walk, calling him, trying to keep calm. She saw him look away, then back at her, unsure of what to do.

Emily heard the car approach. The whine of its engine and the blare of its radio were unnaturally loud, magnified by the stillness of the night. Even with her attention focused on Fiber, and before it came into sight, she knew it was traveling too fast, at least too fast to see a dog no taller than tire height standing stock still, three feet from the curb.

She knelt so that she was on Fiber's eye level. "Fiber, come!" she called again in what she hoped was a commanding voice. Confused now, he sat down, panting, anxiously cocking his head at her. He was only fifty feet away. She could see his white teeth and the whites of his eyes gleaming in the darkness. If only she'd thought to slip on his collar, the one with the reflective strip he wore when they ran at night!

The car's headlights arced across the asphalt. Fiber turned toward the light, then looked at Emily. But still he didn't move. Oh God, she thought, it isn't fair. Not both of them! Not my husband *and* my dog!

Then, like a gift, the answer came to her.

"Fiber, look! Here's Jack!"

Hearing the name of his master, the dog's head whipped around, and his eyes fastened on her. The car was nearly on him now. She had only a moment to save him. She stood up and shouted, "Fiber, listen — *Jack's back*!"

There was an excruciating screech of brakes, the smell of burning rubber. Anguish overwhelmed her. She covered her ears and closed her eyes, bracing for the horrific sound of impact, metal to flesh.

But it never came.

The car continued to screech as it careened into the turn. Then the sound diminished as it sped away and disappeared into the darkness.

And then, there was Fiber, loping up the sidewalk toward her, then running full out toward the house.

To Jack.

Jubilant, Emily tried to run after him, but her legs were watery and weak. The surge of adrenaline had taken her last store of strength. She struggled to propel herself forward, trying to see Fiber in the darkness ahead. When she reached her brick path, she stopped. There, in the open doorway to the house, was a human form, backlit by the glow of the interior lights. Her mind still reeling from Fiber's narrow escape from death, she wondered if by some miracle it *was* Jack.

The beam of a flashlight swept across the walk and landed on Emily. She shielded her eyes against the glare. "Emily, is that you?"

a woman called out.

She recognized the voice. "Mrs. Lawrence? Yes, it's me."

"Oh, for goodness sakes! Come, come." She beckoned with the light, and Emily hurried up the walk. "I was just getting back from my daughter's and I heard you shouting. Then I saw that the door was open, so I thought I should keep watch. Are you all right, dear? What happened?"

Emily was weeping now, relief and exhaustion pouring out of her in a flood of emotion.

"There, there, dear," Laverne Lawrence said. "It's all right now."

But Emily couldn't stop crying. Because for just an instant, she had really thought it *was* Jack standing on the porch of their home, waiting for her to run up the walk to join him.

○

Later Mrs. Lawrence helped Emily into bed and brought her a cup of tea. "Take it from an old biddy who's lived alone more years than she'd like to remember," she said, "don't leave doors and windows unlocked, and don't trust anyone, even people you knew before. Because they'll treat you different now. And don't think about how things were, or how they might have been."

"How can I not think about it?" Emily asked. "Nothing's the same. I'm not the same."

"Of course you aren't. Listen, did you ever try to walk on high-heeled shoes when one heel's broken? That's what it's like when you lose a partner. Everything's out of whack." She stood and smoothed the comforter where she'd been sitting. "What do you do about it? Either you get the heel repaired, or you buy a new pair of shoes. But you don't go dancing until you get it fixed. You're a lovely young lady with your whole life in front of you. I'd suggest you start shopping for that new pair of shoes!"

She winked at Emily. "Now I'm going to take this key and lock the door behind me. I'll bring it back first thing tomorrow."

"Thank you, Mrs. Lawrence. I'm so grateful."

"Don't be, dear. Someday I may ask the same favor of you!"

Lying in the dark, Emily heard her neighbor walk slowly down the stairs and through the front hall to the door. In the stillness, she could even hear the key turn in the lock, and Mrs. Lawrence's shuffling footfalls on the brick walk. She groped across the bed until her hand found Fiber's sleeping body. She gently pulled him closer.

He nuzzled her softly and sniffed at her tears. Then he nestled into the crook of her arm and sighed. Stroking him, Emily realized that he'd already forgotten his brush with death. And why not? He was still alive. He had survived.

And so would she.

But without Jack. For sixty days she had not felt the luxury of being cherished by another person, the joy of having a loving hand stroke her body. It was like *she* was dead too — not just grieving, but numb. When Gary had touched her earlier in the evening, she had not felt an emotional charge, neither desire nor revulsion. She had felt *nothing*, a big gaping chasm, a hole in her heart.

In fact, she couldn't even remember the sensation of physical love. Had this body she had been dragging around since Jack's death ceased to feel? Desperate and dispirited, she slipped her hand under her pajama top and let her fingers glide over her ribs to the soft slope of her breast. She pressed her palm against her nipple, rubbing it, gently at first, then with growing fury. Nothing! She felt nothing! It was only flesh, cold and dead, no different than a slab of meat in the butcher's case.

Disgusted with herself, she flung back the covers and jumped out of bed. Fiber sprang up, instantly awake and wary. She stomped into the bathroom and turned on the light. Its glare was blinding

after the darkness of the bedroom, and she shielded her eyes, groping in the cabinet under the sink. The first drawer held brushes and
hairpins, not what she wanted. The second drawer was filled with
soaps and shower gels and bath oil. No.

She flung open the third drawer, and there she found the long,
thin needle she used to remove splinters.

She held it up to the light, her eyes becoming accustomed to the
glare. The needle's tip was blackened with carbon, the result of earlier efforts to disinfect it with a match before using it to extract a
splinter or pry out an ingrown hair. She didn't care about sanita-
tion now, only sensation. Even pain would be preferable to this utter lack of feeling.

She stripped off her pajama top and let it fall to the floor. Holding the needle firmly between her thumb and forefinger she jabbed
it into the smooth skin on the inside of her arm. A prick, nothing
more, not real pain. She jabbed again, this time at her upper arm,
then higher, at her shoulder. She looked at her reflection in the mirror and continued to poke at her arm. Ten times, twenty, thirty.
Each tiny thrust left a tiny freckle of blood, a map of her frustration, but no pain. Why could she not feel! Was something wrong
with her? Would anything ever be right again?

Sampson sat in his Volvo, exhausted and shivering, waiting for the
hot air to blast from the heat vents. What was he doing here, spying
on a woman he barely knew? When he'd tried to get closer to her,
his curiosity had nearly gotten her dog killed. And still, he had not
had the courage to confront her. All he needed to do was knock on
her door, introduce himself, and tell her that he had been the recipient of her husband's heart. That in a way, part of her husband still
lived in him. That he was grateful to her and to her dead husband

for giving him the gift of life.

The problem was, he felt more than just thankful to this woman. He felt a gravitational pull to her, an attraction he didn't understand. It wasn't a physical attraction, at least not a sexual thing. With all of the drugs he was taking, sexuality was only a memory. What was it that drew him to her?

Yes, she was beautiful, he'd noticed that in the hospital the first time he'd seen her, before his transplant. There had been a subtle, soulful quality that had shone through the horrific veneer of catastrophe, a vulnerability that he knew all too well. And because he understood that inner demon, which was no demon at all, only a delicacy which was exquisite and rare, he was especially afraid of pressing her. But that was still no reason to stalk her like some kind of deranged serial killer.

He watched the old neighbor woman come through the front door and trundle down the walk. A moment later, the upstairs light went on in what he suspected was the master bathroom, and he saw a shadow cross the room. He waited, watching, until finally the light was extinguished and the house became dark and still.

Sam watched a few minutes longer, staring at the darkened windows, imagining what it was like inside, what it would be like living in the handsome wooden house, climbing into bed and snuggling close to a sleeping wife. What it would be like to be Jack Barnes.

Finally, he slipped the Volvo into gear and drove away.

16

It was after two when the telephone rang, but Emily was still awake, the events of the night replaying themselves on a Möbius strip in her mind.

"I'm calling for Mrs. Emily Barnes," a deep male voice said. "This is Officer Brad Tompkins, Clearview Police."

Emily sat up abruptly, unconsciously pulling the covers around her as though Officer Tompkins had walked into her bedroom. "This is Emily Barnes," she said cautiously.

"I'm sorry to wake you, ma'am. It's about your son, Jonah Keller."

"What about Jonah? Is he all right?"

"Yes, Ma'am. He's fine, a little worse for wear, but he'll live," Officer Tompkins said. "We picked him up a couple of hours ago. We were responding to a call about a disturbance at *Piercing Kingdom*, down at the beach. Your son was part of it. Did you know he was out at this hour, Mrs. Barnes?"

"Well, no," Emily admitted. She had put Jonah on the bus for Oceancrest the evening before. Why on earth would he be back in town? "What happened? Is he hurt?"

"Like I said, he got into a scrape with a rough crowd, but our men pulled him out before he got too beat up. Why don't you come on down to pick him up, and we'll have a little chat."

"Yes, of course. I'll be there as soon as I can." She started to hang up.

"Mrs. Barnes?"

"Yes?"

"He told us to call his father first, but we got a machine. That's why we called you. Maybe you want to try to reach your husband, if you have another number or a pager."

She couldn't help feeling stung. "Ex-husband," she corrected. "Sure, yes, I'll get hold of Matt," she said. "We'll both be there as soon as we can." And she hung up.

↺

There was no answer on Matt's line, so she drove to his house. The neighborhood was quaintly suburban, the house a '50s ranch style which, to Emily, meant no style, especially compared to her own beautiful craftsman bungalow. She rang the bell.

The front light went on, and a moment later the door swung open. Lauren stared at Emily with sleep still in her eyes. She was wearing a flimsy nightgown which floated around her body, revealing more than it hid. *So this is what Matt left me for*, Emily thought. She could hardly blame him — Lauren's body was voluptuous and lean at the same time, the type both men and women admired.

"Emily?" Lauren wrapped her arms around her torso for warmth, and the nightie bunched prettily under her breasts. "What's going on?"

"Sorry to wake you. It's Jonah. They've got him down at the police station, and I thought Matt would want to go with me to pick him up."

Lauren stared at her dumbly, trying to process this information.

"The police station? What happened? Is he hurt?"

"I don't think so. They were kind of vague. I didn't even know Jonah was still in town. Was he staying here?"

"Um, no." She shivered. "God, it's freezing. Why don't you come in."

"Thanks." Emily stepped through the door, and Lauren shut it behind her. They stood awkwardly in the hall, the air between them heavy with forced civility. A baby's thin wail wafted down the stairs. "I'm really sorry to disturb you," Emily said. "They told me they tried to reach Matt, but there was no answer."

"We've been turning off the phone at night so that it doesn't wake J. B. Matt used to get so many calls from his patients' parents. You know how anxious some parents are."

Emily smiled weakly. "Tonight, I am particularly aware of that. Um, is Matt awake? We should really get down there."

Lauren shuffled uneasily, twisting a strand of hair around her finger. "Actually, he's not here." The baby cried louder, and she looked up the stairs. "I'd better get him. Can you wait a sec?" She disappeared before Emily could ask why Matt wasn't home with his family at 2:30 on a Tuesday morning. And why the subject made her so uncomfortable.

When Lauren returned, she was wrapped in a bulky chenille robe and carrying little J. B. The baby was still screaming, his face red with fury at having been awakened at this odd hour. "Sorry," Lauren said, "he's a regular tyrant when his schedule gets disrupted, aren't you, little guy?" She bent to kiss the baby on the top of his head, but he pushed her away, his blue eyes focused on Emily. "Was Jonah this grumpy?" Lauren asked.

"Lauren, where's Matt? I don't mean to be rude, but *Jonah* is in *jail*. We need to get him out."

"Sure, I understand, but, um, what I mean is ..." she stammered, "... thing is, he told me he was going up to Oceancrest, to take Jonah out to dinner and talk about ... about you know, him coming to live with us." She looked stricken, as though she knew this subject was taboo. "But if Jonah's down here, then where is Matt?" She started to cry. "I don't know what's happening any more!"

Emily took a deep breath and let it out slowly. "Look, there's probably a good explanation. I'm sure Matt will be home soon, and he'll explain. Will you have him call me when he gets here? I'll keep my cell phone with me. He's got the number." She backed up toward the door.

"I'm really sorry," Lauren sniffed. "He hardly ever does this!"

Hardly ever? Emily didn't want to expend her limited store of energy wondering what frequency *that* implied. She started to back out the door. "It's okay. Just have him call me."

"Okay, absolutely. Give Jonah my love. Or whatever," Lauren called, as Emily ran to her car.

$\circlearrowleft$

The Clearview Police Station was ablaze with light and pulsing with activity. Emily gave her name to the officer at the front desk, and in a moment a short, compact man in jeans and a polo shirt stepped through the door which separated the offices from the main reception area. His hair was buzz cut, spiked with gray, and he was wearing a shoulder holster but no gun.

"Mrs. Barnes?" Emily stood. "I'm Brad Tompkins." He handed her his card. "How're you doin'?"

"I've been better," Emily said. "What happened?"

"Come on back. I'll tell you about it." He hitched up his jeans and led the way. "Coffee?" he asked as they walked past the machine.

"No thanks," Emily replied. The last thing she needed was more acid in her stomach.

She followed him through a brightly lit maze of desks in a small, open bullpen. Officers, some in uniform, and others, like Tomp-kins, in street clothes, and civilians mingled freely. The atmosphere was more like that of a high school classroom between periods than a police headquarters.

"Mrs Barnes?"

Emily turned and saw a familiar face, but she couldn't place it.

She must have looked puzzled because he said, "Ray Wilson." When she still looked blank, he added, "I met you at the hospital... after your husband's accident."

Emily's heart fell, as the memory engulfed her. "Yes, of course. How are you?"

Officer Wilson smiled, "Fine, thanks. And you?" She tried a smile, but her mouth would not cooperate. "I heard about your husband," he said. "I'm very sorry."

"Thank you, so am I."

He looked at Officer Tompkins and then back at Emily. "I don't know what brings you down here at this ungodly hour, but I hope this guy is taking good care of you."

She gave him a weak smile. "I'm sure he will."

Tompkins led her to a partitioned area at the rear of the room. He took a handful of files off of a none-too-clean folding chair and stacked them precariously atop a cabinet. He brushed off the chair with his hand, and said apologetically, "I don't think there's any-thing contagious on it. Have a seat."

He leaned nonchalantly against the cabinet, and the whole thing tilted. As though in slow motion, the stack of files listed, then fold-ers cascaded to the floor, the contents spilling together.

"Aw, Christ what a mess!" Tompkins growled. He and Emily both stooped to pick up the co-mingling of reports, crime scene photos and filings, time sheets, and requisition orders. "Suppos-edly, they're upgrading our computer system so we can be a paper-less office," he said without irony, shuffling papers together by the handful and stuffing them into folders at random, heedless of where they actually belonged.

Emily was horrified to see case records treated with such indifference. "It looks like you've got a ways to go," she commented.

"No kidding." He stood up. "Just leave it. Someone on the day shift can worry about it." He motioned to Emily to sit again and kicked a few stray papers out of the way so he could perch on the edge of the desk. "Your son — "

"Jonah," she supplied.

"Jonah," he echoed. "When we spoke on the phone, it sounded like you were surprised to hear he was in town."

Emily nodded. "He goes to school in Santa Barbara. I drove him to the bus myself Sunday night and watched him get on. He's never done anything like this before."

"At least he hasn't gotten caught doing it," Tompkins pointed out.

He was right. Most weeks she only talked to Jonah once or twice. In between, who knew where he was or what he was doing? She'd assumed Oceancrest was supervising his activities. But the school was progressive, and it prided itself on its Honor Code, which left it to the students to uphold the rules, without constant supervision. "He's a good boy," Emily said defensively.

"I'm sure he is. But in fact, we picked him up on a handful of charges: malicious loitering, destruction of public property, assaulting an officer, resisting arrest," he enumerated the charges on the fingers of one hand. "Still, he seems like a nice kid, and frankly, I don't want to toss him into the snakepit with the rest of the vipers we rounded up tonight. I want you to take him home."

"Thank God." Emily breathed a sigh of relief.

"But I thought you ought to know the company he's keeping. Have you heard of *Piercing Kingdom*?"

Emily shook her head. "No."

"Do you know a girl named Laura Felix?"

"Yes, she's ... a friend of Jonah's. She had dinner with us last weekend, on Jonah's birthday."

Tompkins nodded wearily. "She works there. We picked her up too. She's trouble, but she's not the problem."

"Who is?"

"It's not a 'who,' it's a 'what.' The age-old story: drugs. We found dime bags at the scene. All three officers agreed on this, but unfortunately the stash disappeared before we could grab it or trace it to any one person. My guess — and it's just a hunch — is that your son came down from Oceancrest to buy or sell. A dangerous business all the way around. Have you had any clues that he was into drugs — changes in behavior, a drop in his grades, new friends ..."

All of the above, Emily thought. But Jonah's future depended on the goodwill of this stranger, and she didn't want to say or do anything that might change his tolerant attitude. "Not that I can think of," she answered lamely.

He shook his head. "In a way, it's harder to understand why a kid from a nice family gets into dealing. I'm sure you give him spending money, pay his tuition."

Emily nodded eagerly. "Of course. He's never mentioned that he needed money."

"Sometimes it's not about *need*, like being hungry or having a habit to support," Tompkins went on, "which is the case when we talk about some of the kids from South Central. For them, it's an escape route from the hell of their everyday lives. But for a boy like your son ..." He ran his hand over his chin, which was grizzled with two days' growth of beard, "it's probably more of a cry for help. He wants somebody to pay attention to him. 'Course, I'm not a child psychologist."

"His father is," Emily said.

"Really? That would be ..." he skimmed the papers in his hand. "Matthew Keller, 254 Sycamore Lane?" Emily nodded. "I tried to reach him — I guess I told you that."

"Yes, and I did too. I drove by his house on my way here."

"And?"

"His wife didn't know where he was. In fact, she thought he was up at Oceancrest with Jonah." Emily felt a pang of guilt, airing facts about Matt's private life to a stranger, but she was angry. Where was he when his son needed him?

Tompkins nodded slowly. "Sounds like there are a few crossed wires at home. Any other problems you can think of that might have contributed to Jonah's behavior?"

Emily sighed. "This is a difficult time for us, I'm afraid. My second husband, Jonah's stepfather, died two months ago in an auto accident. I've been, I guess I've been, well, distracted. Then, last weekend, Jonah told me he has decided he wants to go live with his father, with Matt, and he knows I'm not happy about it. So yes, there were — are — other problems."

Tompkins was watching her closely. "To your knowledge, does your ex-husband want the boy to live with him?"

"Very much, or at least that's the impression he gave me. I don't know what his disappearing act tonight means, though." She looked at the floor, unable to meet Tompkins' gaze.

They sat in silence for a moment. "Tell you what," the man said brightly, "let's take a walk on back and get your son. I'm sure you want to do that." He rose, and Emily got to her feet too.

Together they walked back through the bullpen. Emily had to hurry to keep up. "I'm still not getting a clear picture of what happened tonight," she said.

"We keep a bead on this *Piercing Kingdom*. Tattoos and body piercing — they're related to the drug culture. Not that every kid with a pierced nose is a user, but pretty much everyone who is into drugs has some kind of body decoration.

"So, like I said, we keep an eye on the place. Tonight your son comes in, maybe to make a delivery, maybe to see his girlfriend — I guess you could call her that — Laura Felix. You said you know her?"

"Not well. I just met her for the first time on Jonah's birthday, last weekend."

"Anyhow, he comes in, finds her playing tonsil hockey with another kid, a known user, the two boys get into a scuffle, and suddenly there are drugs on the scene. We don't know whose they are, but we're pretty sure they belong to your son or this other kid. So we gotta bring all three of them in." He stopped walking. "The fact is, we could run 'em through the system, make a mess of their lives. But we don't want to do it, Mrs. Barnes."

She nodded, grateful, but terrified.

The officer tapped on a thick door which had a small window of tempered glass in the center of it. "We made calls on the other two," he said. "Laura Felix was just picked up by her sister. The other kid's name is Kevin Harper. We're waiting on his folks." He knocked on the door. An officer's face appeared in the window. He saw it was Tompkins and pushed the control to release the door. It clicked open.

Tompkins stepped back to let Emily enter. The room was a windowless cell, lit with fluorescent lights and smelling of Lysol. It was large enough to hold a dozen people comfortably, but right now it had only two inmates: Jonah, sitting on the bench on one side of the room, and another boy, older and hulking, slumped against the wall as far away from Jonah as possible.

Jonah looked up at his mother, then quickly turned his head away. But in that brief glance, she saw agony in his eyes and the bruises on his face — his left eye was puffy and shot with streaks of purple, and he had a crusty gash on his chin. From the look of the towel in his hand, the bleeding had only recently stopped.

Her instinct was to run to him and throw her arms around him, but she forced herself to stay where she was, to allow him his pride in front of his rival. She walked slowly to him and put her hand on his shoulder — she should be allowed that much, shouldn't she? Through his muscular shoulders she felt the delicacy of his bones, and her heart ached for him. How fragile he seemed for a 14-year-old, certainly no physical match for the boy across the room who outweighed him by twenty-five pounds at least. She'd never thought of Jonah as a fighter. He must have been provoked ... or had his anger been fueled by drugs?

"Jonah, are you all right?"

He nodded miserably, without looking at her. "Can we go now?"

She looked at Officer Tompkins. He bobbed his head. "Yes," she said to Jonah.

He stood, crooked with pain, favoring his right leg. When he started for the door, he walked with a limp. Emily bit her lip and stuffed her hands into her pockets so she wouldn't be tempted to try to help him.

"Ta ta, turdface," the other boy sneered.

"Asshole!" Jonah shot back through clenched teeth.

The other boy stood. "Who're you callin' an asshole, asshole?"

Jonah pretended to scan around the room. "Looks to me like you're the only one here, shit for brains."

"Jonah!" Emily said sharply, horrified by his language, and afraid Officer Tompkins might change his mind about letting him go.

"Leave me alone, Mom," Jonah said, his voice cracking on the word "Mom."

"Leave me alone ..." the other boy mimicked in a falsetto voice, and then, an octave lower, "Mom." He made a sound in his throat, like a cat purring. "What a pussy!"

"Kevin! That's enough! Shame on you!"

Everyone in the room turned to see who had spoken. To her amazement, Emily recognized the woman she'd seen in the hospital when she had gone to visit Andrea Leventhal, the one whose brother had been in the cardiac ward. What was her name? Diana Harper, that was it.

"Mrs. Harper?" Officer Tompkins confirmed.

She ignored him and approached her son. "I swear Kevin, I am sick to death of coming down here in the middle of the night! Don't we have enough troubles without this?" she said. The boy looked bored and annoyed, and did not reply.

Diana turned to Emily and gave her a surprised, sad smile. "Why hello! We seem to meet in the strangest places," she said. "This is your son?"

Emily nodded. "Jonah, Jonah Keller."

Diana stared at the bruise on Jonah's face. "Did Kevin do that?"

"I'm sure it was just as much Jonah's fault," Emily said, still trying to make the mental adjustment to this coincidence.

"It was not!" Jonah complained. "He started it."

"Liar! He jumped me, the little fuck!" The boy, Kevin, lunged toward Jonah, but Officer Tompkins came between them.

"You say there were drugs involved in this?" Diana asked the officer.

Tompkins nodded. "Can't tell for sure whose they were, but lucky for everyone, someone else snatched them and ran. Consequently, we have no evidence."

He looked first at Kevin and then at Jonah. "So these boys get a freebie tonight. Consider it a wake-up call, guys," he said. "Next time I throw your asses in jail. Got it?"

Neither boy spoke.

"Got it?" Tompkins bellowed.

"Got it," they both mumbled.

"Then get the hell out of here, and let your families get some sleep!"

Everyone shuffled out of the room. Diana jerked Kevin's arm to hold him back so Emily could pass through the doorway. "Ladies first, tough guy," she said sternly.

"Right," the boy said, and came to an exaggerated halt.

Diana looked at Emily. There was such sadness and defeat in her eyes. "I am truly sorry," she said. "Wherever Kevin goes, there just seems to be trouble. I hope your boy will be all right."

"Thank you. How is your brother doing?"

Diana smiled bravely. "He got out of the hospital last week as a matter of fact, and he's getting stronger and feistier every day. Thank God for that!"

⟳

The moment Emily started the car, Jonah reached for the radio dial. Emily grabbed his hand. "No music tonight, mister," she said, "we're going to talk." Jonah withdrew his hand and slumped down into his seat. They drove a few blocks in silence.

Emily thought about the night Jonah was born. The recollection was so vivid, she almost felt as though she were sitting up in the hospital bed, Matt perched next to her, his arm around her proudly, as, haloed with light, the nurse walked in and presented her with a bundle wrapped in a light blue blanket. "He's a perfect boy," she had told them. "I see a lot of babies in here, and this little fellow is one in a million. You can pin your hopes on him, I guarantee you that."

Emily had assumed the nurse said that to all new parents. But it didn't minimize the impact of her words. Because at that moment every parent had to feel what she and Matt had felt: the awesome and limitless potential residing within their newborn son, whose eyes looked at the world without judgment or bias, a human heart that held no sorrow or loss, a soul that was tarnished by neither guilt nor gratitude. To think that this pure spirit was entrusted to her! It had been the most exquisite moment of her life.

Now, fourteen years later, she looked at Jonah and deeply saddened to realize how that purity had eroded. Each second he had been alive had required a judgment to be made, and inevitably, with each choice, other options disappeared. How could she possibly know this person sitting beside her, a boy who was the sum and substance of myriad influences, some positive, some negative?

She was furious with him — and fed up. But for the sake of the memory of that moment of his birth, when all things were possible, she resolved to try one more time to reach him.

"Well?" she said at last.

"Well what?"

"Are you going to tell me about it?"

"About what?"

"Jonah!" She started to weep, not for what had happened that night, but for all that had already been lost in his first fourteen years.

"C'mon, Mom," he whined, "don't cry. It's nothing."

She looked at him in amazement. "I get called in the middle of the night because my son is in jail for making a public disturbance and possibly for possession of drugs, and you call that nothing?"

"I wasn't *in jail*," he said in the new patronizing tone he used with her. "And it wasn't drug possession. It didn't belong to me, anyway."

He sat up straighter and looked out the window. "Where are we going?"

"Home."

"I want to go to Dad's."

"He's not there."

"Lauren's there, isn't she?"

Emily bit her lip, devastated that he would rather be with Lauren than with her. "Aren't you wondering why I came to pick you up instead of your father, since you told the police to call him first?"

"You said he wasn't home."

"Do you know where he is?"

"Out of town?" he asked cautiously.

"Good guess. Lauren said he told her he was going to Santa Barbara, to take you to dinner. What do you know about that?"

Jonah shrugged. "Maybe he got hung up at work again. Big deal."

"Again? You mean this has happened before?"

"Sometimes. Maybe," he amended. "So what? I still want to go there."

"We're going home," she said firmly, struggling to keep the tremor from her voice.

"Great," Jonah said. "You might as well have left me at the jail."

↻

It was nearly dawn when they got to the house, too late to go back to bed. Jonah stormed up to his room and slammed the door behind him. Emily stood at the bottom of the stairs for a few minutes, listening, wondering what he was doing, wondering what *she* should do.

Her whole body ached with fatigue, but she knew she wouldn't be able to sleep. She had to do something to burn off her anger, frustration, and anxiety. It was still dark, earlier than she usually ran, and a raw wind was blowing. She would have to outfit herself in gloves, hat, knit headband, sweatshirt, and hooded windbreaker, as well as a day-glo safety vest for herself, and one for Fiber. But, still, the prospect of waiting in the cloying warmth of the house until it was light, trying to ignore the suffocating tension, was infinitely less appealing than the thought of jogging through the frigid streets in the dark.

It was four miles to Ann's condo at the beach, eight round trip, further than she normally ran. But once she got there, she was sure she could convince Ann to drive her home, and she needed to talk to someone. Who else could she disturb before six o'clock?

No noise was coming from Jonah's room, so rather than disturb him, she wrote a note saying she'd be back by seven, and slid it under his door. Then she bundled into her gear, called Fiber, and set out for the beach. No Walkman this morning — too many discordant thoughts were swirling around in her head, and they were much more compelling than any fiction.

There was an eerie calm to the city streets. Although light would soon be seeping into the night sky, the streetlamps still blazed. Gusting wind whipped the trees into a frenzy and forced her to zip the cap-billed hood of her parka up to her chin, narrowing her field of vision to what was just in front of her. But fortunately, she would only be running against the wind for about a mile. Then she would turn south toward Ann's, and the wind would be at her back. It would be a nice change, she thought, going with the flow, instead of fighting against it.

Fiber was uncertain about this breach of routine. His senses tweaked by the wind-whipped air, and his field of vision constricted by the darkness, he ran close to Emily's side, feet barely touching the ground, trusting her lead. When they came to the first intersection, Emily called out "Stay!" so she could check in both directions for cars, and he froze in mid-stride, hindquarters nearly overtaking his front legs as he skidded to a halt.

"Good boy," she praised him, and thought about her other "boy," the one who was not quite so good. There were so many possible explanations for Jonah's shocking change in behavior. She listed them one by one: the mere fact that he was a teenager, hormonal flux, sexual angst, the fact that he'd been living at boarding school for nearly two years, her divorce from Matt, Matt's remarriage, the birth of Matt's second son, J. B., her own marriage to Jack, Jack's death, and finally, the most worrisome explanation, the possibility that Jonah was using drugs.

She felt sick considering the probability. Adolescence was an emotional minefield. How could a parent even hope that a child could successfully navigate past the danger without falling prey to some tragedy? She thought about the fetus, still safe in her womb. Would she have the strength and the courage to bring another child into a world so fraught with anguish, let alone to do so without a partner?

Emily ran on and on toward the rising sun. By the time she neared the beach, the streets were beginning to shed their dark cloaks, and she felt an easing of tension. To watch light fill the sky always gave her a feeling of mastery over the day, and of optimism. There was still much to be grateful for.

She began to make a mental list of positive things: she was going to have Jack's baby; by the time he or she was born, she would be back on sure footing again, ready and able to give whatever she could to this new life. Jonah was safe with her now; there was no way she would allow him to live with Matt, she was his mother! She would drop everything and devote herself to him, help him find his way, and stay beside him to be sure he didn't get lost again. She had mentioned to Ann her desire to consult with the food service staff at the hospital, and Ann had encouraged her to do it. The thought of doing some good for the needy was uplifting.

As Emily approached the security gate to Ann's parking garage, it swung open to expel an early-morning commuter. Emily waited until the car passed and led Fiber in through the gate before it closed, saving her the annoyance of having to use the intercom at the front door. This way she could just go up in the elevator and use the hidden key to Ann's unit, which she knew was under a flowerpot beside Marilyn Macy's welcome mat, two doors down.

The run had worked miracles for Emily's spirits and had relieved her aching body. She felt refreshed, almost normal. As she got off the elevator on Ann's floor, she looked at her watch. It was still early, and Ann wasn't a morning person. Before she woke her friend, she'd fix herself some coffee, and see if Ann had anything interesting to eat — she was suddenly ravenous.

Ann's condo was typical of the beach units built in the early '70s: the entrance was in the middle, with a narrow living room and master bedroom fronting the sand, and the kitchen and second bedroom in the back, each with only small, high windows to let in the light off the street, since there was no view.

The condo was silent, the lights out, so Ann was no doubt still sleeping. Emily decided to take a shower. If she wasn't mistaken, she'd left a pair of sweats and perhaps even some toiletries here when she'd stayed the week after Jack's accident.

Without taking off her gear, she tiptoed down the hallway, Fiber by her side, and shut the door to "her" bedroom. Fifteen minutes later, flushed with warmth from the hot water and comfortably dressed in the sweat clothes she had found in the closet, Emily padded back out to the kitchen. There was still no light leaking out under the door which led to Ann's room, so Emily decided to wait another half hour before waking her. It was such a relief to be in this comfortable refuge. Nobody knew she was here, so no more bad news could assault her. The idea of having a cup of coffee and curling up and reading the paper in the living room chair which faced out over the sand sounded wonderfully appealing. She went to the kitchen to put the water on to boil.

The kitchen was a mess. No surprise there. This was one of the big differences in Ann's and Emily's styles: Emily needed to putter, always organizing, labeling, and cleaning out drawers. She wouldn't even try to relax if the house was not in perfect order. Ann, on the other hand, was oblivious to clutter, and loved to kick back with her feet up, no matter what the state of her housekeeping.

While she waited for the water to boil, Emily started straightening up the kitchen. There were no dinner dishes, but there were cognac glasses and a half-eaten chocolate cake, which Emily recognized as being left over from a brunch they'd catered in the Valley.

Ah, but there were two forks on the counter, so Ann had not binged alone. Holding the cake platter in one hand as she swept the counter free of crumbs with the other, it suddenly dawned on Emily that whoever had been using that second fork might still be here with Ann. In the *bedroom* with Ann!

Then she saw the running shoes, kicked under the kitchen table, as though whoever had been wearing them wanted them off and out of the way in a hurry. Ann was entertaining a male visitor! Emily didn't recall her having spoken of a new man in her life, but it was certainly possible. Had she been so focused on her own problems that she'd missed such a tantalizing piece of gossip?

Now that she thought about it, she couldn't remember having had a real conversation with Ann for the longest time. Sure, they'd worked side by side at Party Line, had the usual discussions about menus and staffing problems, paying bills and attracting new business. But nothing personal, virtually no girl talk, for weeks. Practically since Jack's death.

Was there a new love in Ann's life?

Emily bent over to pull the shoes out from under the table and when she saw them up close a frisson of uneasiness fluttered across her heart. The shoes looked familiar, yellow and white Nike Air-soles with long red laces. She tried to remember when she'd seen such shoes.

"Oh Jesus!"

Emily spun around. Ann was frozen in the glare of the kitchen light, clad only in a man's shirt, which hung open over her body. She pulled it closed, crossing her arms defensively. "Emily! You scared the shit out of me! What are you doing here?"

"Nice welcome," Emily said. She was still holding the shoes. "I went for an early run and I didn't think you'd mind if — "

"I do mind!" Ann snapped.

"Sorry, it didn't occur to me that you would be entertaining."

"Well I am, and I'd appreciate it if you'd make yourself scarce!" She grabbed the shoes from Emily and started walking toward the front door. "Do you mind?"

Emily was silent. Ann wasn't usually so secretive about the men in her life. "Look, I'm sorry, but what's the big deal?"

"Privacy is the big deal." Ann opened the front door and started to push Emily through it. "Just go, we'll talk about it later, at work."

"Excuse me!" Emily said. "I ran here."

"So run back." Ann said.

"It's four miles."

"Oh, for God's sake, you run farther than that all the time."

She started to shut the door, but Emily braced her body against it. "Ann!"

"What?"

"Do you mind? I'm barefoot out here. All my gear and my dog are in there."

Ann sighed and opened the door. "Well, don't move. Just stand there and I'll bring them out to you. Fiber? Here boy!" she called to him in a loud whisper.

"Is it someone I know?"

Ann whipped around with such a horrified expression on her face that Emily knew she'd hit paydirt. "It is! Who is it? Someone from work? Is it Lew? Just tell me!"

"You don't want to know."

"Yes I do."

"No, trust me, you don't."

A toilet flushed. Then the door to Ann's bedroom opened, and the man she had been entertaining walked down the hall toward them.

It was Matt.

17

*A*gainst her better judgment, Emily allowed Matt to drive her home. "We need to talk," he insisted after they'd gone a few blocks in stony silence.

"I don't want to hear anything you have to say," she told him. She was facing out the window, ignoring him much the same way Jonah had ignored her on the ride home from the police station — was it only three hours ago? Once again, Emily marveled at the roller coaster ride her life had become.

"You *need* to hear this, whether you want to or not." Matt stared at her, trying to catch her eye, and almost missed the on-ramp to the freeway. He swerved right at the last minute, cutting off a Cadillac, and Emily had to grab Fiber before he slid onto the floor.

"Jesus, Matt. You have the sensitivity of beef jerky! In case you don't remember, Jack died in an automobile crash." She pulled Fiber onto her lap, and he leaned against her, panting nervously.

"Sorry," said Matt, and he slowed to merge with the traffic. "This is such a complicated mess. I didn't mean for it to get out of control."

"Famous last words," she murmured. Her eyes caught a small bunch of dried flowers glued to the dashboard. Lauren's handiwork, no doubt. She fingered a rose and one of the petals crumbled. *Such a fragile thing, a relationship*, she thought.

Matt cleared his throat. "I'm going to be honest with you — " he began.

"That will be a novelty." She pulled another petal off of the rose, crushing it to dust between her fingers.

"Something happened at Jack's funeral. Lauren and Jonah wanted to go home, but I could see that Ann needed help cleaning up, so I offered to stay. We started talking, and you know how these things are."

"No, Matt. How are they?" Emily asked. "You've known Ann for a decade. Why now?" *And why did it have to be my best friend?* she added silently.

The highway was clogged with morning commuters, and Matt had to keep his eyes on the road, inching forward with the flow of traffic. "If you ask me as a man, I guess I'd say that the opportunity presented itself and we were both in the mood," he said, staring at the road ahead. "If you ask me as a psychologist, I'd say that in some ways, Ann was a substitute for you," he finished softly.

"A substitute for me!"

"Just because we're not married, doesn't mean I don't care for you, Emily. And I could see that you were hurting. I wanted so badly to comfort you."

"How dare you blame this on me," she snarled. "Or worse, on Jack's death. Face it, Matt, this only has to do with you and your gargantuan libido. For God's sake, you've got a wife and a baby, *and* a teenage son."

"They don't know anything about this," he insisted.

"So that makes it all right?"

"No, but it doesn't hurt them if they don't know, does it?"

The primness in his tone infuriated her. She stroked Fiber and tried to keep her temper in check. "Actually, I think they *do* know, or at least they have a pretty good idea," she said.

His head whipped around. "Why? What do you mean?"

"You told Lauren you were going to drive up to visit Jonah at school last night, right? Well, when you didn't show, our son left campus. He probably hitchhiked down here and spent the evening at *Piercing Kingdom*. Do you know it? Apparently, it's a lovely spot down at the beach, with a real wholesome clientele — junkies, hookers, drug dealers, dropouts, bikers, delinquents. Want to know what happened? He got into a fight with another kid over a girl and a bag of drugs, and ended up in jail."

Matt opened his mouth to interrupt, but she held up her hand. "Let me tell you the whole thing," she said. "The police called *me* to come and get our son, because they'd already tried you and got your machine. So I drove by your house, sure you'd want to go with me to bail Jonah out of jail. First, Lauren told me she didn't know where you were. Then she blurted out that you'd told her you were going to take Jonah to dinner and stay overnight in Santa Barbara."

Emily glared at Matt. He was staring at the road ahead, gnawing on a hangnail. "She was very upset, Matt. And so was Jonah, by the way. He tried to cover for you, but it came out that he knows you've used him as an excuse before, and that you sometimes don't show up when you're supposed to. Does he know why? What do you tell him? That you're working late with a patient? Because if he knew what was going on, it would break his heart. You don't have to be a child psychologist to see that Jonah depends on your marriage to Lauren. It's his solid thing to believe in. What's going to happen to him when he finds out it's a sham?"

There was a long silence. "I don't know what to say," Matt finally admitted.

"Well, think fast, because you're going to have to say something to Jonah in about four minutes."

"A confrontation at this point in time wouldn't be wise," Matt said in his professional voice. "You say he needs to believe in me. Well, I can't destroy that."

"Matt, aren't you listening? It's already destroyed," Emily said. "You destroyed it the first time you cheated, whether he knew about it or not, because you stopped being the person he thought you were. He's not stupid. He senses something's wrong. That's probably part of the reason he's been getting into trouble lately. He took some hard knocks last night."

"What do you mean?"

"The fight — the other kid was older and bigger, and it shows."

"Oh God!" Matt ran his hand over his face as though to brush away this news. "Anything serious?" he asked.

"By serious, do you mean maiming, disfiguration, permanent damage? No, I don't think so, at least not physically. But emotionally, your guess is as good as mine. Or better, I suppose, since after all, you are a child psychologist," she added dryly.

Matt pulled his truck into Emily's driveway and turned off the engine. He rested his forehead against the steering wheel, his eyes closed. She knew he was posturing, hoping to draw on her pity, and she was not about to fall into that trap again. "Oh, and it was swell of you to tell him I was pregnant, especially when you agreed I should be the one to break the news to him."

Matt opened his mouth to reply, but she held up her hand to silence him. "I'm sure you have an explanation for that too, but to tell you the truth, I don't want to hear it," she said briskly. "Now one of us needs to drive Jonah back to school, and I think it should be you. It will give you time to talk."

She got out of the truck before Matt could object and slammed the door behind her. The wind was still gusting, so when Emily opened the door to the house the stillness inside was even more pervasive. No lights were on, so Jonah was still sleeping, or at least he hadn't yet come downstairs. Emily flipped on the light switch and went to the stove to turn on the burner for the kettle.

Matt entered and stood just inside the door, as though he were afraid to come in any further. He watched her, his hands stuffed into the front pockets of his jeans. Like a kid, like Jonah in fact, he kicked the toe of his running shoe against the leg of a kitchen stool. "Coffee would be great," he said hopefully.

"*After* you talk to Jonah," she said, not looking at him. She stooped to pick up Fiber's bowl and walked with it to the refrigerator.

"He's probably still asleep," Matt said.

She took out a cold breast of turkey and removed the plastic wrap covering it. "So wake him up. He needs to get back to school. If you leave now, you could be there by ten. He's going to miss his first class as it is." She began to shred the turkey into Fiber's bowl.

"But I have a full day," Matt whined. "I've got patients starting at nine and going straight through until seven. It's too late to cancel now."

"Then Lauren will have to take him."

"But — "

"Hey, you keep telling me I'm too controlling. Well, as of this minute, I'm backing off. If you want custody, you're going to have to deal with these things, Matt. Now just go talk to your son."

Matt bowed his head and walked toward the stairs. She watched him, then knelt to set Fiber's bowl on the floor. "Here you go, boy. Enjoy."

The kettle whistled, and Emily spooned coffee into two single-cup filters. She set them over the mugs, then slowly poured in the water, the ritual and the aroma of coffee calming her jangled nerves.

"Emily!"

Matt's shout startled her and her hand jerked, upsetting one of the filters and spewing coffee grounds and scalding water over the counter and onto her sweatshirt. "Damn," she muttered, reaching for the sponge.

"Jesus, Matt what — " she began.

"He's not in his room," Matt interrupted, bursting into the kitchen. His voice registered concern and relief.

"He's probably in the bathroom," she said, concentrating her attention on the spill.

"I looked there too, and in your room. Emily, he's gone."

"Shit!" she growled under her breath, and threw down the sponge. She pushed past Matt, and took the stairs two at a time. Sure enough, Jonah's room was empty. His bed was rumpled, but there was none of the teenage clutter that seemed to accumulate in Jonah's wake, no other signs that he had been in the room — except the note she had left for him, telling him she had gone for a run. It was crumpled into a ball next to the wastebasket. She picked it up and carefully put it in her pocket.

Matt was standing at the door watching her. She brushed by him again and went into her room. She picked up the phone.

"Who are you calling?" he asked.

"The police."

Matt took the receiver from her. "That's not a good idea. He's in enough trouble as it is."

"Which is why we should call them."

"You think they'll just slap his wrist and let him go next time? Hardly. Do you want our son to have a police record at age fourteen?"

"Of course not."

"Then come on, let's see if we can find him. He's probably close by. You were only gone, how long, an hour?"

"More like two. He could be anywhere by now."

"Not without a car."

Automatically, they both looked down toward the garage, as though by magic they could see through the walls if Emily's car was still inside. "He wouldn't," she said. "He doesn't have a license."

"It wouldn't be the first time."

"You mean he's taken your car before?"

"Not exactly."

They charged toward the stairs. "What do you mean, 'not exactly?' " Emily asked as they ran down.

"A few weekends ago he drove down to the 7Eleven for a chili dog and was back before we knew he'd gone."

"How did you — "

"The smell in the car. Some of the chili spilled onto the carpet. God, it was pungent! For days!"

Fiber raised his head from his food dish as they rushed past him to the door connecting the garage to the kitchen. Emily flung it open. The Toyota was gone.

They walked back into the kitchen. Matt swung his leg over a chair and slumped into it. Emily brought the two mugs of tepid coffee to the table and sat down next to him. They sipped thoughtfully.

"You shouldn't have left him alone, Em," Matt chided.

She was indignant. "What do you mean? He's fourteen years old. Haven't you ever left him alone in your house for an hour or two?"

"Not after he had a night like the one you described."

"Oh? Has he had many of those?"

"That's not what I meant."

She was fuming and had to fight for control. "Let's just think about where he might have gone, okay?" She leaned back in her chair and reached for the pad and pen next to the phone to start a list. "School," she said, and wrote the word at the top of the page.

"He knows that's the first place we'd look. If he's running away, he wouldn't go anywhere near there."

"So that rules out your house too." She'd written *Matt's house* on the list and crossed it off as well. "But you should let Lauren know what's happening. Maybe he called there before he left … wondering if you'd showed up," she couldn't help adding. She handed Matt the portable phone. He took it from her, but set it on the table.

"Call her!" Emily insisted.

"I need to think about what I'm going to tell her," he said.

"How about the truth?"

Matt glared at her. "There's more to the truth than just a statement of facts," he said.

"What kind of psychobabble is that?"

"This thing with Ann. I don't know. It's complicated." He lowered his head sheepishly. "It might be more than just a fling."

"Oh, spare me!"

"I can't help it," he whined.

"You can too! That's what it means to be an adult, that you control this type of urge."

"But it's hard. Have a little sympathy."

"I do," Emily replied. "For Lauren." She grabbed the phone and began to dial.

"What are you doing?"

"Calling her."

"Come on, Emily. It's my life." He lunged for the phone, but she whipped around, putting her body between him and the receiver.

"You're a parent, Matt. Everything you do or don't do affects your son too. Both of your sons."

"Lauren, hi," she said into the receiver. "It's Emily." Matt crossed his arms on the table and put his head on them. *Good, let him suffer*, she thought.

"Yes, I picked him up," she said, answering Lauren's question about Jonah. "No, he was all right, just a little worse for wear. He got into a fight down at the beach, but they didn't press charges. I brought him home about five this morning, and then I went out for a run. When I came back, he was gone. I was hoping maybe he'd called there."

She listened for a moment. Then looking at Matt, she said, "Don't panic. I'm sure they'll both turn up soon. Will you call me if you hear anything? From either of them. And I'll call you if I do.

Try not to worry." She hung up and sat staring at the phone.

"Thanks," Matt said. "I owe you one." He reached out to squeeze her hand, but she pulled it away.

"Your wife is a wreck, you jerk," she told him. "You should be holding *her* hand, not mine!"

"As soon as we find Jonah," Matt promised. He put his hand on his heart. "Scout's honor."

Emily shook her head and went back to the list. "Okay, we know he's not at school and he's not at your house." She thought a minute. "Maybe he went to see that girl, Laura."

"The tattooed lady," Matt said with a weak smile.

"Did you know he was dating her?" Emily asked.

"No. I just met her on his birthday, same as you."

"Did you pick her up that night?"

Matt shook his head. "Yeah, but not at her house. When we stopped by that place to get Jonah's tongue stud adjusted, he went in, and she came out with him, like it had all been planned. It was a complete surprise to us."

"I guess I could try calling the store. Maybe they would give me her number."

"I hardly think it would be open this early."

"Wait a minute. The other kid that got picked up with them — Jonah was so angry at him, they almost got into a fist fight at the station. What if he went after him ... "

"How are you going to get his number?"

"Information. His mother's name is Diana Harper."

○

Jonah drove slowly, trying not to draw attention to himself. That would be the last thing he needed, to get picked up for driving without a license! He knew where he was going because he'd heard Kevin give the police his address, and although it was across town, it wasn't far from where they'd lived when he was a kid.

How had things gotten so screwed up? When he tried to make sense of it, the images disintegrated into white powder and blew away, leaving him in a bleak, pulsating void, like something in a Wes Craven flick, which threatened to swallow him whole and expel him like a fresh dog turd.

It had all started so innocently, with that rogue e-mail message he'd gotten right after his stepfather had died, from a guy who used the name *Crud*. He'd written that he had something of Jack's, and suggested Jonah meet him at *Piercing Kingdom* to talk about it. Jonah had been pretty sure it was a prank, because the message had so many slang words in it. Anyway, no adult he'd ever met would use the name *Crud*, even on-line, or hang out at *Piercing Kingdom*.

But what if he did have something of Jack's? He might even have stolen it. What if it was something of value? Jonah hadn't thought it would hurt to at least meet the guy, so he'd agreed to go.

As it turned out, he was right. It was a prank, or at least Jack's name had never come up, and when Jonah had tried to bring it up, the guy Crud had changed the subject. Crud's real name was Kevin. He was the kind of guy Jonah usually steered clear of, older, tougher, with a chip on his shoulder. But for some reason he took a liking to Jonah and they'd shared a joint. It was good stuff. Then he'd introduced Jonah to Laura. And that was all that mattered.

She was very hip and beautiful, and she had flirted with him in front of the other people in the store. That really blew his mind. Once they were all high and feeling very chummy, Crud and Laura had told Jonah about the *really* good stuff, the stuff they sold to people they liked a lot. Maybe Jonah would be one of those people?

They hadn't done any business that first night. Laura and Kevin had said they wanted to get to know him first, to make sure he was cool. And suddenly *being* cool in their eyes had become the most important thing in his life.

After that, he'd started hanging out at *Piercing Kingdom*. hitching up from school during the week and keeping Laura company while she worked, or going on deliveries with Crud. Laura seemed hot for him, and she'd dared him to get his tongue pierced. He'd been reluctant, but he'd known it was a test of his coolness, and he didn't want to look like a sissy in front of her.

When the little chrome ball was clamped into place, he knew he'd passed the test with flying colors, because they'd set up his first buy.

But it had gotten all fucked up. He'd given Crud and Laura $500 he'd scraped together, and they had given him five sealed envelopes. But when he'd opened one he'd found it was filled with grass — not marijuana, but green grass, like his mother's front lawn! And when he called them on it, they'd both laughed at him, in front of everybody. He'd gone ballistic and jumped on Kevin. That's when the police had stormed the place and stuck all three of them in handcuffs and dragged them down to the police station. What a dumb ass he'd been!

Well, he wasn't going to let Crud stiff him. He wanted his $500 back, damn it, and he was going to get it!

↻

Sampson pulled back the curtain and watched Kevin rake the front lawn. The wind was still blowing furiously, and the boy's attempts to keep the leaves in a pile were futile. But he kept at it, attacking the lawn with fury, as though the rake were a weapon, clawing at the fragile new growth of dichondra and uprooting the blades of grass, gathering the scythe-like leaves and sturdy brown pods which continued to hail down from the eucalyptus tree.

Diana fell into the chair beside Sam with an exaggerated sigh. "This isn't doing the garden any good," she said.

"It's not *for* the good of the garden," Sampson said, not taking his eyes off his nephew.

"Sam," she persisted, "look at him out there. Not only is he going to catch his death, but he's doing permanent damage to the grass. I've been babying that dichondra all winter."

He turned to look at her. "You've been babying Kevin too," he said softly. "He's had it too easy. He's soft."

"You're saying my son, who we just brought home from the police station for getting into a fight over some drugs at a piercing parlor, is soft?" she snorted.

Sam took her hand. "Look, sis, I don't profess to know that much about kids, and anyway, he is *your* kid, yours and Rod's, not mine. But I've had plenty of time to look at my own life, and this much seems pretty clear to me: Mom and Dad were real good to us. They taught us a lot of important things, but I think they held us back by being too protective of us. I grew up thinking it was better not to try, rather than to try and fail. And look at me. Look where I am! Still living in the house I grew up in, still letting someone else make the rules, still stuck in this emotional quicksand, afraid to do a damn thing, because I might fail. It's not right, Diana."

"But your heart," Diana said, "you were never healthy. How could you — "

"Ah, yes, the tragedy of my poor, flawed heart. Don't you see? All these years I've used that excuse, but sometimes I think it might be the *symptom* not the *cause*. Face it, sis, I'm an emotional cripple. And I don't want Kevin to end up the same way."

Diana bristled. "I resent that! Rod and I have been good parents. We sacrificed everything for our Kevin and Grace Claire! Rod wanted to be an architect. It was his most cherished dream. But when I got pregnant, he dropped out of school and got a contractor's license instead, so he could start earning money right away."

"Don't you think I know that?" Sampson said quietly. "Anyway, you're just proving my point. It was the easy way — "

"It wasn't easy," Diana cut in, her voice brittle. "It was hard. It was devastating to Rod to give up his dream!"

"Okay, easy is the wrong word. But it was safer, don't you see? By dropping out of school, he could always tell himself he *could have been* an architect. What if he'd tried to go to grad school and failed? What if he'd found out he didn't have a shred of talent, or that he didn't like the work? And look at you, sis ... " His voice softened into a caress. "You've devoted your entire life to caring for everyone else — Mom, me, Rod, the kids — instead of doing for yourself."

"Maybe this is what I wanted."

"Is it?" He leaned back in his chair and stared at her. "In my whole life, I've never asked you what your fantasies are. You're my sister, and I don't even know what you dream about."

"I'm not a dreamer, Sam, I never was. Well once...."

The phone rang, and Diana got up to answer it.

He leaned in closer. "What? There is something, isn't there? Sis? Tell me!"

She smiled and looked down at her hands, all of a sudden shy. "Don't you remember how I used to love to ice skate? For a while I thought maybe I could be another Peggy Fleming." She waved the thought away and picked up the phone. "Hello? Yes? Why, hello, Mrs. Barnes."

Sam recognized the name and sat up straight, suddenly alert.

Diana covered the receiver with her hand. "It's the woman whose son got picked up last night with Kevin," she whispered to Sam.

"I thought you said the kid's name was Keller," Sam persisted.

Diana shushed him and said into the phone, "No, we haven't seen him at all." She moved to the window. "No, my son's been here all —" She pulled back the curtain again to observe Kevin in the front yard. "Hold on. As a matter of fact, it looks like your son has just arrived!"

Diana flung the receiver at Sam. "Give her directions how to get here," she said, and ran out the door.

○

Jonah and Kevin stood ten feet apart, facing off like stray dogs. The wind whipped the fallen leaves across the grass around them, and above them, the eucalyptus tree listed and moaned. Although Kevin was bigger, Jonah was quicker, and in his face Diana could see a determination she'd never seen in Kevin.

But her son had a weapon: he brandished the rake in front of him like a club, swinging it from side to side, forcing Jonah to keep his distance. Sam came up behind his sister. "Kevin, stop it!" he shouted. But either Kevin didn't hear, or he was ignoring the command.

"Come on, asshole, come and get it," he taunted, poking at Jonah with the rake.

"Motherfucker!" Jonah shouted back. "Why'd you do it? What did you get out of it?"

"I got five hundred bucks, didn't I?" Kevin snickered. "It was a gag, man. Can't you take a joke?"

"Not to me," Jonah screamed. "You've screwed me royally! Drop the rake and fight fair!"

"What are you, a glutton for pain? Or are you just a dumb fuck? You'd never win, wimp."

"Oh, yeah? Try me."

"Kevin!" Sam ran across the grass, his heart pounding. "Stop it now!"

Kevin lunged at Jonah, but Jonah jumped out of the way, postured, and leveled a karate chop to Kevin's wrist. The rake fell from his hand, and Jonah grabbed it. Grinning in triumph and feeling his dominance, he swung the rake in a wide arc, ferociously slicing the air between them and now forcing Kevin to jump back.

Off balance, Kevin slipped on the piled leaves, and he went down heavily. He screamed in pain, his ankle bent at an unnatural angle.

Jonah poked him with the handle of the rake. "Get up and fight!"

"My ankle," Kevin whined, "It's goddamn busted!"

"What the hell do I care, you ... crud!" Jonah cried. He hoisted the rake as though to clobber Kevin.

"Stop!" Sam roared.

Startled, Jonah wheeled around, swinging the rake as he turned. He had no idea that Sam was right behind him, and when he did see him, it was too late to stop the blow from striking Sam full across the chest.

"Oof!" Sam felt a crushing pain and fell hard. Diana's scream was the last sound he heard before he blacked out.

○

Emily stood at the entrance to the Surgical Waiting Room for a moment, summoning the courage to enter. The newly remodeled area was a definite improvement over the basement cell where she had spent the last day of Jack's life. Just the fact that it was on an upper floor of the hospital and not in a bunker helped. People streamed by the double doors, a constant parade of life that was both a diversion and a reminder that hospitals were sites of healing and recovery.

The walls of the room were painted a cheery pale yellow, and comfortable chairs were upholstered in compatible tones of rose and teal. There was a television in one corner and a computer set up in another, and a full-time volunteer was on duty at a reception desk to answer questions and mediate between anxious relatives and the surgeons operating on their loved ones. It was all very civilized, but nobody was fooled. The life-and-death tension in the room was palpable, and there was nothing an interior decorator or, even a nurse, for that matter, could do to make it go away.

Diana Harper was sitting alone by the television. Her back was to Emily, and she was hunched forward, lost in her own thoughts, like everyone else in the room, waiting to be summoned.

Emily watched her and tried to think of what she could say to the woman. When she and Matt had arrived at the Harper's house, they had found Emily's car parked out front, but no one had answered the door. A neighbor had told them what had happened.

"You're sure it was the other boy who hit Mr. Sampson?" Matt had asked the woman. "Not his nephew?"

"Saw it with my own eyes," she had insisted. "Gave Sam a whack in the chest and when he went down, the child bent over him, like to hit him again! Then when Diana came out, he jumped that hedge and took off down Arbor. You that boy's folks? Well, it's none of my business, but shame on you! Kevin, he's no angel, but you don't see him walloping a poor sick man like Sam, then running away."

Still watching Diana, Emily took out her cellular phone and dialed. "Matt, it's me. Anything?" her voice was somber, contained. "Okay, you have my cell number. Call me the second — " She saw Diana rise and approach the volunteer. "Okay, okay," she said into the phone, and snapped it closed.

"I'm so very sorry, Mrs. Harper," the volunteer was saying to Diana in a calm voice, "but I don't know anything yet. I told you I will call you the second I hear from the doctors."

Emily watched Diana drag herself back to her chair and sit once again, her expectations clearly one notch lower. She felt the woman's terror, and she wanted to reach out to comfort her. But what on earth could she say or do to make things better?

She approached Diana and stood in front of her, waiting in silence until she looked up. Diana said nothing, but her expression acknowledged Emily's presence. She glanced at the empty chair beside her, and Emily sat down.

"It's not your fault, or your boy's," Diana said before Emily could speak. "I know he didn't mean to hit Sam. It was an accident. Besides, he tried to do CPR. I had to pull him off so I could do it myself. We all took classes years ago when we found out how bad Sam was."

She paused, no doubt remembering how long ago that was, how many years they'd been fighting this battle. "Anyway, the doctor told us to expect some setbacks. It's almost inevitable."

"What exactly is wrong with him?" Emily asked.

"You don't know?"

Emily shook her head.

Diana sighed and rubbed her hands together, rocking in her seat as though trying to keep warm, despite the fact that the waiting room was stifling. "It all started with cardiac dysrhythmia — that's an irregular heartbeat — they found it about five years ago. It's not necessarily a life-threatening problem, so they put him on a drug called amiodarone. It helped regulate his heartbeat, but it affected his lungs, so he had to go off it.

"The next thing they tried was propafenome. It worked for a while, but pretty soon he started getting PVCs — premature ventricular contractions, which made him panic and sent his heartbeat off the map. The doctor kept him on the propafenome but added propranolol, which blocked the adrenaline surge that caused the PVCs, and the combination of the two seemed to work for a while." She shook her head. "Listen to me, spouting off all these medical terms like some grocery list. And I was a high school dropout!" She paused. "You really want to hear all this?"

Emily nodded, imagining what it would be like to live with someone whose body was the stage on which a life-and-death drama was being played out. Was that what her life would have been like, if Jack had survived his accident?

"Despite all the drugs, Sam's arrests kept coming," Diana was saying. "Of course, we were constantly struggling with dosages, and each time he had an episode, we were scared stiff that he would survive but be cut off from oxygen for so long that his brain would be damaged, and he would become a vegetable. They finally told us the only solution was to find him a new heart. So they put him at the bottom of the list, and we began the wait." She blew her nose. "He was such a damn good sport about it. Started calling himself the Tin Man, and singing that song, '*If I Only Had a Heart*.'" Diana sang the words in a lilting soprano.

Emily looked startled. "The Tin Man?"

Diana nodded. "You know, from *The Wizard of Oz*. He was the one who needed a heart, remember?" She turned to look at the television. An enthusiastic game show contestant, costumed to look like a can of sardines, was jumping up and down and hugging the host. He kissed the model who was posed atop a Harley Davidson and put the helmet on his own head. Diana kept her eyes on the screen as she continued, unaware of how pale Emily had become.

"They finally convinced us that the only answer was to implant an AICD. That's an automatic implantable cardioverter defibrillator, this box the size of a Walkman." She illustrated the size with her hands. "Can you imagine having a chunk of machinery like that *inside* your body? It monitors the heart rhythm and delivers an electric shock if the V-tach — that's the ventricular tachycardia — goes too high, and it's supposed to bring the rate down to a normal rhythm."

Emily sat very still, trying to concentrate on what Diana was saying. But her mind kept returning to the night before Jack died, the first time she'd seen the man in the wheelchair with the obscene bulge in his chest.

Diana continued, "They told us it wouldn't be painful, that Sam would hardly feel the shock *if and when* he ever needed one. To make a long story short, after nine hours in the operating room, a procedure that was the equivalent of open-heart surgery, and two weeks in recovery, they let him out with this *thing* under his rib cage that stuck out like a huge deformity. I never told Sam this, but it made me sick to look at it. Sometimes he'd be wearing just a thin shirt and you could see it bulging out in front. Not only that, but it had a tube open to the outside, so the risk of infection was very high."

"Diana, when did your brother get his new heart? Do you remember the day?" Emily interrupted.

"How could I not? It was a Sunday afternoon, February 3rd. We decided that from now on we'd celebrate Valentine's Day on the 3rd, because it was the day Sammy got his heart."

Emily's hand went to her mouth, covering it as though to hold in the sob which was caught in her throat. Her eyes glistened with tears. It was all so clear to her now, the reason Diana's brother had seemed familiar when she'd seen him lying in the hospital bed.

Diana was unaware of Emily's reaction. "Anyway, the appearance of the AICD wasn't the worst part. He'd been home barely a week, and one night he was helping me put away the dishes from the dishwasher — I mean, how heavy is a dinner plate? Anyway, all of a sudden he goes kind of still, like he's resting you know? And then *KAPOW!* It was like some giant invisible force threw him against the wall. He just crumpled to the floor and then *KAPOW!* Again! Like something you'd see in the movies. It took us both a couple of seconds to realize that the damn defibrillator had gone off. It was set to trigger when his pulse got to 135. His poor heart was so weak that just lifting the dishes got it up that high. Let me tell you, it was terrifying. And I can only imagine the pain it was causing poor Sammy."

They both heard the phone ring. Diana watched the volunteer pick it up. "So he went back into the hospital to wait for a new heart. They said he'd move high up on the list if he did that, because it would prove how critical he was. Finally, after 106 days, they found a compatible organ. We were ecstatic. We thought it would be the end of all his health problems, that we could all get on with our lives. But it hasn't been like that. When you saw him in the hospital, he was there because he'd had a rejection episode. That one was bad, but today's was worse."

"Why?"

"In some cases, the body just plain rejects the new heart, no matter what the doctors try to do. Then sometimes, even though they do tests, they don't have all that much time. And once in a while, after the transplant, they find that the donor heart is flawed. Wouldn't that be divine justice — Sam finally gets a heart, and it's as worthless as the old one!"

Emily was silent for a long moment. "I don't think that's the case," she murmured.

Diana drew back. "Look, I know you're trying to be sympathetic, but don't give me that 'everything's going to be all right' crap," she snapped. "There's a very good chance everything is *not* going to be all right. That's just the way things are, and we've got to find a way to live with it."

"That's not what I meant. I'm saying I don't think you have to worry about the donor heart being weak."

Diana cocked her head. "Oh, really? Are you a cardiologist, or do you just think you know everything?" she asked coolly. She rose and turned away, and started to walk toward the volunteer's desk.

"I know the donor who gave your brother this heart. He was a very healthy man."

Diana whipped around. "What did you say?"

Emily stood. It seemed important that she be at eye level with Diana at this moment. "I said, I know the donor who gave your brother his heart."

"Nobody has that sort of information. They purposely don't tell you."

"They didn't have to tell me. I just know."

"How's that?"

"Because the donor was my husband."

18

*H*e had the dream again.

He was walking along a hot arc of sand, toward a rocky spar that jutted out into the bay. Then he was sprinting at the edge of the water, sweat pouring from his body, his heartbeat accelerating to keep pace with his footfalls on the wet sand, until suddenly, he turned toward the gentle surf and dove headfirst into the waves.

His overheated body buckled with the shock of the cold water, the contrast so intense it felt like an electric current coursing through him. He gasped for breath and swallowed water instead. But it wasn't water, it was thick and viscid, like melted chocolate. His arms flailed in the murky liquid, so weighted by its density that he could only move in slow motion. The ocean was congealing around him, forcing his arms down to his sides. He fought against the pressure, but his body was too weak. It was all he could do to stretch his neck upward trying to reach the surface of the water. It was so close, just a fraction of an inch away! All he would need was just one burst of strength, one strong push, and he would be able to break through.

But it was too much effort. He was going to drown, he knew it.

And once he accepted this, oddly enough, he felt relief. He stopped struggling, content beneath the surface, letting his body drift deeper, weightlessly, at one with the sea.

Suddenly a flame jolted through him, a sensation not of pain but of power. It thrust him up and out of the water, and he emerged gasping for air, grasping for life. His eyes burst open, nearly bulging out of their sockets with the brightness of the light. He tried to shield them from the glare, to slide back into the comfort of the dark water. The easy way, he thought, the safe way.

But another jolt forced him up and out again. This time, he saw masked faces grouped around him.

"Got him!" a voice said.

"Pulse rising," said another.

"Welcome back, Mr. Sampson."

Sam could see the mouth of the closest face moving beneath its mask, the concern in the eyes magnified by a pair of wire-rimmed spectacles. "We didn't think you were coming back this time," the voice said.

"Here I am," Sam mumbled. He realized he was wearing an oxygen mask, and he tried to raise his hand to remove it. But his arms were leaden, utterly unresponsive to his will.

"It's a good thing. Because if this equipment didn't get you going, we were ready to open you up again and do a manual massage."

At a nod from the doctor, one of the nurses pulled down Sam's mask. "Where am I?" he asked in a gasping breath. She quickly replaced the mask, covering his mouth and nose, and he inhaled deeply.

"Your home away from home, Mr. Sampson, Westside Medical Center. You don't remember anything?"

Sampson moved his head slowly from side to side, feeling his brains sloshing around in his head with the movement. He was fully awake now, but still water-logged from the dream, as though he had been swimming for hours against the vast currents of the ocean.

"Your sister said you were hit in the chest with a rake. Guess your new heart didn't like it, and it went into V-Tach. Then it stopped. Completely. Luckily someone knew CPR. Saved your life. You've got a lot to be thankful for."

Sam drank this in. He looked at the nurse, and she raised his mask again. "Dr. Greshom?" he breathed.

"On his way from Ojai. A golf tournament. He was only on the fourth hole when we paged him, so he'll be mad as hell. But he should be here any minute."

"The heart?" Sam asked, the words trailed off as his lungs ran out of air.

"We don't know, Mr. Sampson. It appears stable now, but we'll let the experts decide."

"He looked so different in the hospital," Emily said to Diana. "He was much heavier."

"The prednisone. It's a steroid. It puffed him up like a balloon."

"His hair — what I saw of it — was almost blond, and straight when I saw him the first time."

Diana nodded. "And after the transplant, it grew in black and wavy. We were all surprised. But they say that happens sometimes, depending on the — "

She stopped in mid-thought, choosing her words carefully. "Did your husband ... was his hair ..."

Emily nodded. "Dark brown, almost black. Wavy, but not very thick. He was just starting to go bald on top. I used to tease him that he'd be hairless before he turned forty. He said — " Emily's eyes sparkled with tears as she remembered Jack's words. "He said going bald would be a fate worse than death."

Diana put her hand over her mouth to stifle a sob. "I'm so sorry, so very sorry he died," she whispered.

"You didn't know him," Emily replied. "You shouldn't feel bad for him."

"For you," Diana managed to say. "I feel bad for you." She reached out and took Emily's hand, squeezing it hard.

"But I'm glad," Emily forced the words out, "... I'm glad Jack saved your brother's life. If he'd known, he would have been glad too. He was that kind of man."

"Mrs. Harper?"

The volunteer was standing behind her desk, beckoning Diana. "I've got Dr. Greshom on the line for you." She held out the receiver.

Diana looked at Emily and rose. Automatically, Emily rose too and walked with her to the desk. "Hello, Dr. Greshom," Diana said. She reached for Emily's hand and grasped it tightly while she listened. Emily watched her eyes for clues to what the doctor was saying, but she could not find any in Diana's distraught expression.

Finally Diana said, "I understand. Thank you, doctor." She hung up. "He's stable. For now," she told Emily. "But they need to keep him in the I.C.C.U. for a few days so they can monitor the heart and give him megadoses of prednisone." Her mouth twisted into a relieved half-smile. "That'll mean another wardrobe, three sizes bigger."

Emily smiled, and Diana's face softened. "Dr. Greshom said I could see him for a minute, so I guess I'll go up."

She began to gather up her things, stopped, and looked at Emily. "Do you think he knows who you are?"

Emily had been asking herself the same question. "I don't know. It must be more than a coincidence that our paths have crossed, but wouldn't he have said something to me or to you?"

"Sam never says much to anyone. He isn't the talkative sort."

The two women walked toward the elevators. Emily said, "When Jack died ... your brother gave me a package of Lifesavers. I didn't understand why, but now I think I understand. He was asking ..."

"For someone to save his life," Diana confirmed. "And your husband did it."

The light went on over the elevator doors, and the crowd of people who were waiting to board pressed forward. Diana turned to Emily. "Do you want to come with me? To see him?"

Emily paled. "Oh, no, I couldn't ..." She paused, groping for the right words. "I mean, I have to get used to the idea of knowing. It's — whew — a little overwhelming. Maybe later."

"I understand. Should I say anything to him?"

"Let's wait, at least until he feels better, do you think?"

"Of course."

The two women looked at each other, then spontaneously leaned forward to embrace.

"I don't think there's any way we could ever thank you," Diana said.

"Not me," Emily told her. "Jack. And the way you can thank him is to keep your brother healthy. And your son," she added. "I hope his ankle will be all right."

Diana's expression darkened, and Emily saw what she didn't say, that she was afraid her son was a lost cause. "Kevin will heal, he's as strong as an ox," she said. "And your son ..."

"Hopefully Matt's found him by now. I'll call from the car. Please, let me know how your brother — how Sam — is doing."

The elevator doors were closing. "I don't have your number," Diana called.

"I've got yours," Emily replied. "I'll call you."

○

The wind had died down, leaving the air crisp and vacant. Hurrying through the parking lot to her car, Emily was infused with a Christmas morning kind of joy, a sense of renewal. For months, Jack's death had been like a dull, dark cloak she had been forced to wear, a shroud so impermeable to light and air that at times she could barely breathe.

But now she felt as though the cloak had been swept off. Something positive had come out of the tragedy: a man had been given a chance for a new life. And he was not just a name on a hospital roll, but a person she had met, even talked to. The fact that the miracle of the transplant was now tangible made her feel empowered, and suddenly she believed that there would be an end to the hopelessness and despair she had been feeling, that she would not forever feel like an innocent victim of Jack's accident.

The long line of cars trickled slowly out of the parking structure and into the bright sunlight. As soon as she was in the clear, she dialed Matt's number. Lauren answered. "Hi, it's Emily," she said.

"Oh, hi," Lauren said in a chipper voice. "I tried to call you a while ago, but it wouldn't go through."

"I guess it didn't ring. Have you heard from him?"

"Yeah, he called a little while ago. He hasn't found Jonah yet, but he told me everything."

"He did?" Had Matt actually admitted he was having an affair with Ann, and if so, why did Lauren seem so happy about it? "What did he say?"

"That Jonah wasn't at school when he went up there last night," Lauren said.

"When Matt went to Oceancrest?" Emily repeated, pretending she didn't know this was an outright lie.

"Yeah, he said he drove all the way out there and Jonah wasn't at the dorm, never showed up at all. I guess he's in some kind of trouble, but Matt didn't tell me what. He said he spent the night looking for him. He didn't call me because he didn't want me to worry. I told him about the police, that you'd picked Jonah up and taken him to your house, but he said he'd talked to you already, and that Jonah ran away."

Emily had to bite her tongue. Matt had made it sound like it was her fault Jonah had bolted. She wanted to set the record straight with Lauren, but she decided it would take a lot less energy to just go along with the story for the time being. "Where's Matt now?" she asked.

"Still out looking for Jonah," Lauren said. "He told me he'd call me as soon as he finds him."

"Please, will one of you call me if he does?" Emily asked. "I'll keep the phone with me."

"Okay, sure," Lauren said.

Emily pulled into the right lane and turned toward the beach. She only knew of one other place to look for Jonah. She dialed 411 on her phone. When the operator came on, she said, "The number for *Piercing Kingdom*, please. And the address, if you can give it to me."

○

Piercing Kingdom was one large room, tricked out with colored spotlights, mirrors, and the type of fancy display cases which, in another part of town, might have held pearl necklaces and charm bracelets. Here they featured chrome and stainless steel studs, rings, staples, and decorative body piercing pins. The air was saturated with smoke, and it throbbed with a heavy metal beat.

Emily ducked under a black canopy to enter the store. A teenage boy stood just inside the doorway handing out flyers. His jacket was decorated with studs and zippers, and a swastika was shaved into his short hair. He shoved a flyer into Emily's hands without looking at her. *Smoking is a Human Right,* the title said, and further down in big letters, *DEATH CIGARETTES,* with a skull and crossbones under it. Emily handed the paper back to him. "No thank you," she said.

"Want some help?" a salesgirl from behind the counter called, smiling at Emily through black-lipsticked lips. She was having long

Taking Heart

strands of colored yarn woven into her raven black hair by a young man with skin so dark that the contours of his face were nearly invisible. "Are you looking for a gift or something?"

Emily had never seen anyone so emaciated. Her jersey dress was stretched like a second skin over her chest, ribs, clavicle, and shoulder blades, and ended barely an inch below her pubis. Emily could see through the sheer fabric that she was not wearing any underwear, and her legs were so thin that they barely seemed sturdy enough to hold her upright. There was a decidedly unhealthy pallor to her face, a pale greenish cast which was exacerbated by the extreme lighting and the ink black of her hair. *Where are these children's parents?* she wondered.

"Thank you, no. I'm looking for Laura."

"She's with a customer," the girl said, nodding her head at Laura and a girl in a sundress, who were on the far side of the shop examining some jewelry pinned to a black velvet drape.

"I'll wait then, thanks a lot," Emily said.

"Hey, I can help you," the girl said. She pulled a cigarette out of a pack sitting on the display case, tapped it, and stuck it between her lips. "It's not like we're on commission or anything." She lit the cigarette and inhaled deeply.

"Um, I'm not really looking to buy anything. I just want to talk to Laura. It's about something personal."

The girl snorted as though to imply that she couldn't imagine Emily and Laura having anything personal to discuss. "Whatever." She blew out a long puff of smoke and turned her attention back to the hair weaver.

Laura still hadn't seen Emily. She was yawning with boredom, looking on as the girl in the sundress examined one piece of jewelry after another, shaking them to hear them jingle — or at least Emily supposed they were jingling; she couldn't hear the sound over the music — then holding them up to her nose, her ear, her lip, as though trying to decide where they might look best.

283

Emily realized this could go on forever. "Excuse me, Laura?"

Laura turned her head lazily toward Emily, then raised her eyebrows. "Jonah's mother, right?" Emily nodded. "Wow, it's like surreal seeing you here."

"It *feels* a little surreal too," Emily admitted.

Laura stared at her. "Did you, like, want to buy something for Jonah? I know what he's saving for if you want to see it. As a matter of fact, I picked it out."

Emily gulped back a grimace. "Um, thanks, but I really came to talk to you."

Laura crossed her arms in front of her chest defensively. Her tattoo seemed to wink at Emily as she flexed her biceps. "What about?"

"I'm wondering if you've seen Jonah. He's ... disappeared."

It could have been Emily's imagination, but a silence seemed to descend on the store. Laura said, "Look, his dad called a while ago. Like I told him, don't ask me. I don't have a clue, I swear." Her eyes flickered over Emily's shoulder at something behind her, then back again. "It's, like, not my problem. I hardly know him!"

Everyone in the store was watching now. "Laura, this is a very serious situation. I don't know what you have to hide, but — "

"Look lady, I practically got canned after what went down last night, so don't drag me into this. I need this job, okay?"

"Drag you into what?" Emily persisted.

Laura stared at her, stone-faced.

"Laura, I know my son is in trouble. Maybe you aren't interested in helping him, but are you telling me you aren't even willing to *talk* to me so that I can help him?"

Laura hung her head. "Shit," she mumbled. She looked up at Emily. "Okay, okay. But not here," she said in a whisper.

"When do you get off?"

"Seven-thirty."

"Do you know the *Daisy Cafe?*" Emily asked softly. Laura nodded. "Come at eight. Please."

○

The *Daisy Cafe* was only a few blocks from *Piercing Kingdom*, but it was a world away in atmosphere. Rather than the neon hair, grunge, and body decoration which proliferated at the piercing shop, the *Daisy Cafe* drew the khaki pants and woven handbag generation, people still young enough to think they were hip, but too old to really *be* hip. The parking lot was crowded with their Jeep Cherokees, custom vans, and fully loaded motorcycles. A smattering of racing bikes was locked to a rack in front.

The atmosphere was casual but upscale. Although there was a small dining area for people who preferred to be served, most of the clientele were perched on stools around high round tables, drinking coffee out of colorful ceramic mugs and eating "to go" cakes, breads, and salads.

Emily bought herself a coffee and a portobello mushroom sandwich and found an empty stool near the door on which she could perch and keep an eye out. She wasn't entirely sure Laura would show, but assuming she did, she didn't want the girl to get spooked by the makeup of the crowd. By sitting near the door, Emily could snag her immediately and hopefully whisk her away to a corner where they could talk undisturbed.

She'd finished half of her sandwich and was considering whether to eat the second half or to save it for tomorrow's lunch, when Laura appeared. Despite the hour, she was wearing dark glasses. Her green hair was covered by a Mighty Ducks baseball cap, and she was wearing leggings and an oversized sweater which hid most of her piercings and tattoos.

She shuffled over and dumped her purse on the floor. "Hi," she said, staring down at Emily's plate as though she hadn't eaten for a week — as thin as she was, perhaps she hadn't.

"Hi, " Emily said. "I almost didn't recognize you."

Laura grinned. "Pretty good disguise, huh?"

"If you're concerned about being seen — " Emily began.

"It's cool. No one I hang out with would be caught dead here."

"Well, thanks for coming."

Laura shrugged, her eyes still riveted on Emily's sandwich.

"Would you like something to eat?" Emily asked.

"I don't have any money," Laura said, wringing every bit of pathos out of the words.

"My treat," Emily replied.

"Cool."

She waited while Emily pulled out her wallet and extracted a twenty dollar bill. Then, without another word, she shambled over to the counter and began an animated conversation with the server. As Emily was finishing the last of her mushroom sandwich, Laura returned, her tray piled with pizza, onion rings, two pieces of fudge cake, and a bagel. She set the tray on the table and went back to pick up a milkshake. The cashier gave her back the change, and she dropped it into her purse.

"Shall we move over there so we can talk?" Emily asked, indicating a quiet corner.

"This is fine, "Laura said. She slid onto the stool and began to eat with feral intensity, hunched protectively over her food, shoveling it into her mouth in portions so big she had to chew with her mouth open.

"I'm going to get another coffee," Emily said, an excuse so she wouldn't have to watch Laura stuff herself. "Do you want one?"

Laura didn't look up from her food, but said, "Yech, I hate coffee. I like my acid straight, in little green tabs," she smirked, and pulled a gummy strand of hair from her mouth. "But I'd take some jasmine tea." She wiped her hand on her sweater. "Long as you're up, could you bring me some of those ketchup thingies too?"

Emily got the coffee and tea, the ketchup and some napkins and brought them back to the table. "Thanks, Emily." Laura squirted ketchup on her onion rings and ignored the napkins, licking the excess off of her fingers.

"Can we please talk about Jonah?" Emily said. She was immediately sorry she'd phrased her question so meekly, so she added, "Laura, do you know where he is?"

Laura lifted both hands in mock surrender. "I don't have a clue, I swear." She went back to eating.

Emily persisted. "He obviously considers you a friend. You must know something."

Laura just shrugged.

"Okay, let's start at the beginning. How did you even meet him?"

Laura swallowed and sighed. "Like, I'm like at work, and he just keeps showing up. Bang! He's there, right in my face all the time. You can imagine how thrilled I was." She rolled her eyes. " I mean, it's not as though we had anything going between us. He's cute and all that, but he's a baby!"

Emily nodded, relieved, but still saddened to think that her son had a crush on this tawdry girl who didn't even like him. Poor Jonah.

Laura went on, "I just felt sorry for him, y'know, for what Kevin did."

"Kevin Harper? What did he do?"

Laura eyed her and took a drag on her cigarette. "I don't know if I should tell you."

"Laura, you came here. You must have wanted to tell me."

"Yeah, well, I told Kevin I hate it when he hoses people like that. I mean it's fun for a while, but it gets old real fast."

"Laura, what did Kevin do?"

"He played this joke on Jonah, a gag I guess you'd call it. See, what he does is, he gets peoples' e-mail addresses off the Internet, and then he sends people threats and other scuz and gets 'em all riled up."

"Why did he pick Jonah?"

"He didn't really. This is what went down. Like, see, Kev's uncle had a heart transplant, and he paid Kevin to go on-line and find out whose heart he got. So Kevin did. He's really smart with all that computer stuff.

"Anyway, Kevin found out that his uncle got your husband's heart, and all this other stuff about you all. So he decides to e-mail Jonah and pretend he's got some dirt on the dead guy, maybe ask for a little dough, I don't know exactly what he said this time." She shrugged. "I guess Jonah wrote back and they got jamming."

Laura nibbled on an onion ring, waiting for Emily to respond. For a moment she was too horrified to speak. Finally she said, "What kind of 'dirt' did he tell Jonah he had on Jack?"

"I dunno. Some bullshit like he owed Kev some money for some drugs he'd bought, something like that. And if Jonah didn't pay what was owed, he was gonna come after you."

"Me?"

Laura nodded. "It was so bogus, I can't believe Jonah fell for it."

"How did you get involved?"

"Kevin told him he could get even by making some deliveries for us."

"Drug deliveries?"

"Duh."

"Was Jonah doing drugs?"

"Doesn't everybody?"

Emily wanted to object, but she was afraid Laura would stop talking. "I still don't understand how you were involved."

Laura looked at her like she was an imbecile. "I buy, I sell." She shrugged. "Everyone has to make a living, and I sure can't keep myself in meth with what I make at *P.K.*" She stood and gathered up what was left of her food. "I gotta go."

"Wait." Emily grabbed Laura's arm. Laura tried to wrest it away, but Emily held firm. "What happened last night?"

Laura's mouth twisted into a half-smile. "Jonah got pissed 'cause he didn't like the quality of the grass he bought from us. Then some asshole called the cops, and they managed to get there before Kevin totally beat your son to a pulp. So he was lucky in a way."

Emily released her grip, and Laura jerked her arm away. "Why are you telling me this? Aren't you afraid I'll go to the police?"

"Not really. See, I can get witnesses to say that the dime bags belonged to Jonah, and they'll send him to JuVe. As a matter of fact, my guys'll say anything I tell them to. Something you stiffs don't understand — the people who buy from us, they like, do anything we want 'em to. Anyway, if things get too hot, I can disappear, just like Jonah did. I've done it before. As a matter of fact, I'm doing it now. So long, Emily." And she walked out the door.

Emily drove to the corner of Jessup and Dover and parked under the elm tree before she dialed Matt's number. He answered on the first ring.

"Emily, I just called you. There was no answer," he said.

"I'm not at home," Emily replied. "I told Lauren to give you my mobile number."

"She must have forgotten."

"Did you find him?"

"No." Matt sounded as dejected as she'd ever heard him. "But he left a message on my office machine. He said he was laying low for awhile, staying with an old teaching assistant from school, someone named Jasper. Does that ring a bell?"

"He was Jonah's big brother his first year, but he graduated two years ago. Jonah hasn't even mentioned him since then. What did he say?"

"That he was fine, and he would call us when he got some things taken care of."

"What things?"

"He didn't explain."

"Matt we've got to go get him!"

"Emily, let's give him a little time. He's running scared right now. It'll be better in the long run if we don't force him to come home before he's ready."

Emily was silent.

"Em?"

"I don't know, Matt. How can I *not* move heaven and earth to find my son?"

"Let me tell you a story. I saw a woman at the mall with a handicapped child, a kid about twelve or thirteen, in a wheelchair. He was strapped in, some muscular problem. Anyway, it was cold in there, so the mom handed the kid a sweater, and then stood back, watching as he tried to put it on. Something so easy for most people, but for the handicapped kid, putting on this sweater was next to impossible. It was excruciating to watch him struggle, really pathetic. Finally a guy passing by couldn't stand it. 'Damnit lady,' he said, 'why don't you help your son?' And the woman just looked at him and replied, 'I am.' Do you get my meaning, Emily?"

"I hear you."

And despite herself, Emily did.

19

*Wh*aaack!
Emily's racquet met the ball, and with satisfaction she heard the solid sound of a perfect connection. She watched the woman across the net swing hard at the ball, too hard, and saw it sail over her head, out of bounds. Set point!

Months before, when the Santa Glen Wellness Community hired Party Line to cater its annual Tennis Round Robin, Ann had suggested that she and Emily compete in the tournament as well. "We can wear aprons over our tennis whites," she'd said. "It'll be great publicity, exactly the audience we want to reach."

Usually they made a good team: Emily was more athletic, but she had no interest in the rivalry of the game, while Ann threw herself into the sport with a competitive abandon that Emily could only admire. But today Ann's performance was off. Instead of keeping her eye on the ball, she darted frantically about the court, looking over her shoulder at Emily, as though to make sure she was holding a racquet and not a shotgun.

Emily, too, was distracted. Despite Jonah's call saying he was okay, and Matt's assurances that he would come home on his own, her anxiety about him was a constant hum in her ears, a light blinding her vision, a heaviness in her body. He was only fourteen! Fear for his safety snaked tightly around her chest, constricting her lungs so that her breath emerged in short gasps. But despite the fear and her reluctance to believe anything Matt told her, she forced herself to glean some wisdom from his insistence that they wait for Jonah to come home on his own terms.

Emily shook her head and tried to clear her mind, to focus on the game at hand. She positioned herself near the baseline and bent at the waist, concentrating on the opponent across the net, waiting for the woman's serve. Just a few yards in front of her and to her left, Ann, too, was bent at the waist, holding her racquet in both hands, as though it were a baseball bat, ostentatiously shifting her weight from foot to foot the way the seeded players did at Wimbleton and the U.S. Open. The ball sailed over the net, and Emily moved forward to retrieve the volley. But before she could complete her stroke, Ann ran in front of her, slashing at the ball with a two-handed swing and slamming it into the net.

"40-15."

"Sorry, I thought it was mine," Ann mumbled, going back to her position at the net.

"You think they're all yours, don't you?" snapped Emily. They both knew she wasn't talking about the game.

"I said I was sorry," Ann replied.

"As if that makes it okay!"

They had not spoken about Matt. They'd met at the court, and when it was time for their game, they'd put on their Party Line aprons with coldly polite nods to each other and handshakes for their opponents, but no conversation.

Now Emily found herself obsessing on her view of Ann's bare legs and pink-pantied rear end, which was clearly visible below the hem of the apron over her tennis dress. She was tight and compact, as though she'd been vacuum-packed, her figure more pronounced because of her short stature. Her long red hair, held back from her face by a wide, white band, billowed about her head as she bounded around the court. With an inward smile, Emily wondered if Matt had ever seen his mistress in her headdress of orange juice cans.

Thwack.

The ball sailed over the net with much too much height. Automatically, Emily repositioned herself to slam it back over the net. "Get it Em!" she heard Ann call, and she felt an overwhelming desire to smash the ball right into her partner's pink-pantied rear.

But she controlled her anger, funneling it into her backhand, and clobbered the ball, sending it back over the net in such a forceful flat streak that instead of running toward the ball, the two opponents ducked out of its trajectory.

"Game and set!" called the referee.

Ann ran to Emily's side and gave her a hug, but Emily stiffened and did not return it. "Great one!" Ann crowed, ignoring Emily's coldness. "You really aced it. You're on fire today."

"I wonder why," Emily murmured, looking right into Ann's eyes. She saw her partner deflate, her enthusiasm become remorse.

"Hey, if I had it to do over — " Ann began.

"You did. Over and over and over, according to Matt," Emily replied as they crossed the court to begin the second set.

"Touché," Ann said.

"Wrong sport," Emily snapped.

"Jesus Christ," Ann hissed when they were out of earshot of their opponents, "it's not as though he's still your husband. Isn't that what divorce means, that the two people are free to play the field?"

"Number one, Matt may be divorced from me, but he is still married to Lauren, so that reasoning doesn't apply. And number two, you are I are still partners. In a way, it's like *we're* married. So I'd think you might have at least told me you were seeing him." She ran back to get an overhead lob, but saw that it was going long and let it drop.

"Out of bounds," called the referee, and Emily looked pointedly at Ann. "My sentiments exactly!" she said.

The referee threw a new ball to Ann, and she stepped up to take her service. "I knew you'd freak out if I said anything — which is exactly what happened!"

"Why did you have to *do it* at all? I mean, remember, I *know* Matt. He's an okay lay, but he's not *that* good."

"It's a little like tennis," Ann replied, "how well you play depends on the skill of your partner." She threw the ball into the air and served it solidly into the net.

"Thank you for illustrating my point," Emily said dryly.

Ann raised a second ball. "Anyway, it's all relative. You've been out of circulation for a while, kiddo. Let me tell you, the pickings are pretty slim these days." She threw the ball into the air and jumped up to meet it with her racquet. This time she aced it.

"Great shot!" Gary Forrester shouted, waving at them with enthusiasm. Despite the cool spring weather, he was wearing a bathing suit and matching terry cloth-lined shirt, open to the waist, which showed a little too much belly.

"I rest my case," Ann whispered out of the side of her mouth, then flashed a disingenuous smile at him. She raised the ball, setting up her serve.

"How do you know?" Emily asked. "Are you sleeping with Gary too?"

Ann dropped her arm. "Could we please talk about this after the game?"

"The ball's in your court," Emily replied.

Emily laid her head back against the rounded tile curbing of the outdoor Jacuzzi in Ann's condo complex, thinking about Jonah, her cell phone within reach should Matt try to reach her with news. It was late, and she didn't expect to hear anything more from him, but just in case, she was ready. She longed to put her arms around her son and protect him from the world, but she knew in her heart Matt was right. They had to wait for him to come home on his own terms. But it was hard, so very hard.

"Irish coffee is the perfect food," Ann said, handing Emily a mug and slipping into the water.

"How so?"

"It contains all four food groups: caffeine, sugar, fat, and alcohol. Cheers." Ann clinked her mug against Emily's, and they both sipped and soaked in silence.

The night air was still and cool but scented with spring. Jazz from somebody's balcony mixed with the sound of the distant waves and undulated over Emily's frayed nerves. She let her hand move under the surface of the pool, swirling the water so that it lapped at her chin. With her eyes closed, it felt like Fiber's affectionate kisses. "If I lived in this building, I'd be in here every night," she murmured.

"No you wouldn't," Ann said. "The fact is, this hot water is a breeding ground for STDs."

"What are STDs?"

"You've been single for more than two months and you haven't heard of sexually transmitted diseases?"

"If you're worried about catching one, what are you doing in here now?"

"I happen to know that the pool guy comes on Thursdays and he chlorinates the shit out of it, so tonight's the best night. Tuesday or Wednesday, I wouldn't put my baby toe in this water. The bacteria are as big as Koi."

"Ew, gross."

"You wanna know what's even more gross?"

"I doubt it."

"Some guys bring dates down here for a romantic interlude, and they release their little *'tadpoles'* right here in front of God and the rest of the condo complex."

"Stop!"

"They do! On a calm night, sometimes I can hear their mating calls from my unit." She let out a series of moans of ecstatic abandon, escalating in volume, and climaxing with an orgasmic scream.

"Ann!" Despite herself, Emily started to giggle.

"I'm serious. Once I came down here early in the morning to swim — that was when I was in my athletic phase, remember?"

"Athletic phase? You mean that three-day stretch after you joined Gold's Gym?"

Ann ignored this. "I was walking by the Jacuzzi and I saw this *thing* floating on the surface." She made a face. "It looked like a leaf, only it was glow-in-the-dark green. Wanna know what it was?"

"No."

"A condom! And there was something red at the bottom of the pool — it looked like a dead animal, I swear. I made the gardener fish it out with a rake. He didn't want to, but I made him. It was a pair of Speedos! Some guy had gotten naked and literally *forgotten* his bathing suit when he got out! How drunk do you have to be? I'm glad I wasn't around to see ..."

As Ann rambled on, Emily's thoughts drifted. The mention of the red Speedos had brought to mind the trip she and Matt had taken to Europe to celebrate the completion of his Ph.D. She'd been five months' pregnant with Jonah, so they'd known the trip would be their last before they assumed the responsibilities of parenthood and his psychology practice, and they'd promised each other that they would make the most of it.

After ten days of touring the south of France, they'd arrived in

St. Tropez. It was late June, and the beach was crowded. Telling her he'd forgotten his bathing suit, Matt had gone off to buy one, and he'd come back wearing the briefest possible strip of crimson cloth, so tight that it outlined every male curve.

In response, she'd reached back and unsnapped the bra top of her two-piece maternity suit and flung it aside, revealing her pregnancy-engorged breasts. She smiled, remembering how daring they'd felt. In fact, no one had taken the slightest notice of them, because everyone else on the beach had been similarly dressed — or rather, undressed.

She felt something brush against her leg and jerked back to reality. It was Ann's toes tickling her thigh. "Dollar for your thoughts?" Ann asked. "I know the going rate's a penny, but if the expression on your face is any indication, whatever you were daydreaming about is worth a lot more."

Emily fixed her eyes on Ann's expectant face. "We need to talk about you and Matt."

Ann rolled her eyes and slid down in the water with a sigh. Her mouth was just above the surface. "What good will it do to slog through all that?"

"I want to clear the air."

"So call the E.P.A. Did you know the smog level in LA has declined by 40 percent in the past twenty years?"

"Ann!"

"Okay, okay. What do you want to know?"

"Was it your idea or his?"

"Oh, come on! Next you're going to be asking me if he wore a condom."

"Did he?"

"What business is it of yours? The man is not currently related to you in any way. Granted, he is married, but not to you. And you don't even like his current wife, unless I was daydreaming and missed some freak bonding experience."

"He's still Jonah's father, so it impacts on Jonah if his father is having affairs."

"Not *affairs*, plural. Affair, singular. Only me."

"What makes you so sure?"

Ann sputtered in surprise, speechless.

"Did you think you were the first?" Emily pressed. "That was why we broke up in the first place — well, it was the straw that broke the camel's back anyway."

"You never told me that. How could you not have told me!" Ann took a gulp of Irish coffee to compose herself. "Anyway, it really doesn't matter. The fact is, Matt and I were attracted to each other, we were horny, we did something about it."

"So you don't think it has anything to do with me."

"You think the only reason Matt would sleep with me would be because he's pining away for you? Thanks a lot, but I think I can safely say he wasn't thinking about you when he was with me. Believe it or not, I have been known to attract and hold a man's full attention."

"It wasn't Matt I was referring to," Emily said softly.

Ann had to think about that for a moment. Then she sat up straight in the water, causing a minor tsunami in the tub. "You mean you think I slept with *him* to get back at *you* for something?"

Emily just looked at her and said nothing.

"You're my best friend! Why would I purposely do something to hurt you?"

"That's the second time you've called yourself my best friend."

"Well, aren't I?"

"I thought so. I want you to be. But with all the other men around, if you weren't out to hurt me, why else would you choose Matt? He's not even remotely your type."

"I don't have a type. What I have is a healthy libido, and sometimes I like to take it out and exercise it. Look Em, I'm 42 years old and counting, and I've never been married. Unless I want to live alone the rest of my life — and I don't, believe me — I've got to actively seek out potential candidates. Like I said earlier, they're not exactly a dime a dozen."

"Ann, another woman's husband is not an ideal candidate for marriage. You know that!"

Ann got out of the Jacuzzi and wrapped a towel around her. "All right, all right. I admit I didn't sleep with Matt because I wanted to marry him." She paced back and forth at the lip of the pool, hugging the towel tightly around her body.

"It didn't have anything to do with me, and it wasn't because you wanted to marry him. So you're telling me that you risked our friendship, and Matt risked his marriage, purely for sex?" Emily shook her head. "No, I don't buy it. Not for a minute. You just finished telling me that there are plenty of guys in this building alone if all you wanted to do was get laid. And even Matt isn't going to screw up his marriage to Lauren for a night of jollies."

They stopped talking, waiting while a mother passed by, wheeling a stroller with an infant in it. "Hi, Ann," the woman said.

"Hi, Leslie," she replied. "How's Travis?"

The woman yawned and smiled. "As precious as a four-month-old who only needs four hours of sleep a night can be."

Staring at the happy family, Ann seemed to deflate. She flopped down on a lounge chair and sighed. "You really want to hear this?"

"Yes!"

"Okay." She chewed on her thumbnail, her eyes downcast. "I want a baby in the worst way," she said, without looking up.

"What?"

"I said, I want to have a baby," she said more loudly. "And who better to ask to father it? He's obviously got good genes, and think how close we would be. Our children would have the same father."

Emily was speechless. She got out of the Jacuzzi and sat beside Ann, shivering in the night air.

Ann went on. "It sounds crazy now, just blurting it out like that, but it seemed to make sense at the time. Jack's death hit me hard, Em, harder than you realize. It made me see how transient and fragile our lives are. What if I died? Who would care?"

"I would," Emily said sincerely.

"Yeah, but you've got your own life. I need something that's mine. If not a husband, then a child."

She sighed. "That night, after Jack's funeral, sure, I'd had too much to drink. And maybe it was nuts of me, but if you want to know the truth, it felt right. Then later, when you told me you were pregnant, I was thrilled. It was going to be perfect. You and I would both be moms and our babies would be born at practically the same time. It was all I could do to not tell you right then and there."

She started to pace again. "The problem was, I didn't get pregnant. Or rather I did, but I lost it almost immediately. I didn't tell anyone. Nobody else knew about it except Matt. So I just called him and asked him to come over to try again. He agreed. And that was last night."

She stopped walking in front of Emily. "So, does it have to do with you? Yes, but only in a good way. I wanted our children to be close, so I chose Matt to be the father." She shrugged. "Was that so wrong?"

Emily rose. "No. Not wrong. Misguided maybe. With a little sprinkling of fairy dust on your thought process. But not wrong." She put her arms around Ann. "I'm sorry, my friend," she said.

"*You're* sorry? For what?"

"For forgetting that Jack's death didn't just affect me. You, Matt, Jonah, even Gary — all of your lives were changed too. I guess I never really thought about that."

SIX

20

A current of pain shot up from Sam's groin, and his body jerked involuntarily. "Am I hurting you?" the pretty Hispanic nurse asked as she delicately adjusted the tube which snaked from a penile catheter to a bag clamped to the mattress.

"Just my dignity," Sam said. He closed his eyes so he didn't have to see his flaccid organ listlessly draining urine into the cruel shaft of plastic taped to its tip.

"I can call a male nurse if you want," she said.

"What's the difference?" Sam replied. There *was* a difference, but it wasn't a male/female thing, not anymore. The problem was that the nurse was new. The more seasoned nurses handled this odious task with brisk disregard; it was the deference this one accorded the chore which humiliated him, not the practical fact of what was being done to him, a reality to which he had long ago become inured. In the years of his illness and the months of his hospitalization, he had lost all sense of privacy about his body. Every inch of it had been probed, pierced, scrutinized, and discussed. Each secretion had been examined and measured, every cavity explored, all functioning parts put through their paces. If at first it had seemed odd to hear a group of interns discussing the color of his stool or the texture of the purulence oozing from the incision in his chest, it no longer phased him. The issue now was making sure each nuance was duly observed and documented so that no mistakes were made and the correct treatment ordered.

The evolution of this attitude had been inevitable: during his first stint in the hospital after the emergency which had revealed the depth of this heart disease, he had been obsessive about trying to preserve his modesty and blindly trusting of the omnipotence of the medical staff. Now he knew better than to waste his energy trying to keep his gown smoothed over his genitals. It was better spent in vigilance toward the caregivers. He knew they didn't purposely ignore him or give him the wrong medication — the mistakes were the result of inexperience, overwork, and the fact that medicine was an art, not a science.

As if to prove this point, he saw that the nurse was heading toward the bathroom with the full urine bag. "Excuse me, Inez?"

"Yes sir, Mr. Sampson?"

"How much today?"

It was a polite way of reminding her that she had neglected to measure the amount of urine and enter it on the chart which tracked the output of his kidneys and liver. So far, they and his other organs had continued to pump and secrete properly, despite the repeated failure of their cousin, the heart. This was a good sign. But if they stopped functioning, it was critical that the problem be recognized immediately, because it would be a sure sign that his heart was failing.

Inez shot him a sheepish glance. "I'm going to check it right now," she said, and she returned to the room to fetch the measuring pitcher.

"I forget, do you measure it before or after you extract the sample for tests?" He knew the answer to this, but couldn't resist the added reminder.

"Before, Mr. Sampson, and I'll take the sample down to the lab myself."

"Thank you," he said, and lay his head back on his pillow and closed his eyes. It was hard work being this sick.

○

Sam must have dozed off, because when he awakened, his bed was surrounded by white-coated doctors. He heard their voices and knew they were talking about him, so he kept his eyes closed, feigning sleep, hoping to learn more about his condition than they would tell him to his face.

"Dr. Stone, how would you interpret the findings of the last blood panel?" Sam recognized Dr. Greshom's voice, resonant with confidence before the student doctors, at ease in this world of disease and dying.

A woman's voice answered, tentative in comparison to the assured tenor of the senior doctor. "The patient is in a declining state. Indications are not positive for a recovery."

"Be specific, doctor," Dr. Greshom barked. "This man is in critical condition. His life could depend on your diagnosis."

The woman's voice trembled as she recited the medical findings from Sampson's chart. "Patient has early signs of coronary atherosclerosis developing in the new heart, with substantial occlusion of the left anterior descending and right coronary arteries. There are also fibro-obliterative changes of the smaller arterial branches and moderate ... "

It came as no surprise to Sam that his life was hanging in the balance. What he wanted to know was what, if anything, could be done about it.

"... the long-term prognosis is poor," she concluded, in answer to his unspoken question, "unless a replacement heart can be satisfactorily transplanted."

"And if the patient does indeed undergo a second transplant, what is a realistic expectation for survival? Dr. Miren?"

"Hard to say, doctor," a man answered. "Liver, kidneys, and lungs are still functioning, but below optimum performance, due to the stress the body has encountered from the repeated episodes of tachycardia and the antirejection medication. A lot would depend on the patient's will to continue fighting."

"Are you implying that we, as doctors, can only be as successful as the attitude of the patient allows us to be?" Dr. Greshom's voice was shrill with sarcasm.

"In fact, studies have shown that without the will to survive, any patient — "

"What studies? What patients?" Dr. Greshom was angry now. Sampson had heard him blast this new trend in thinking before. He was from the old school, and his mind was closed to the findings of current research which implied that medicine was equal part art and science, and that successful treatment depended on the intangible essence of "human spirit."

"The Chinese concept of *chi* — "

"Chi, you say?" Dr. Greshom cut in. "I say that *chi* is short for *chimerical*. Do you know what that means, Dr. Miren? Do you know the word? It means existing only as the product of unrestrained imagination, fantastically improbable."

"But sir, for centuries the Chinese have — "

"If you want to practice Chinese methods, Dr. Miren, there is a very logical solution: *Go to China*! While you are here at this hospital, under my tutelage, you will concentrate on the tangible, practicable, and documented methods of Western science, not what is euphemistically called 'alternative treatment.' There is no alternative to established medical procedure. Is that understood?"

There was silence.

"Is that understood, Dr. Miren?"

"I hear what you're saying, sir."

"Very well. Now — "

"But Dr. Greshom, as doctors, doesn't it behoove us to utilize all the wisdom available to us, be it Eastern or Western, medical, spiritual, or scientific? Because isn't our duty to treat people by whatever means are available to us?"

A gentle voice had spoken, but it was filled with conviction. Sam smiled to himself, pleased to hear someone stand up to Dr. Greshom. He opened one eye just a crack so he could see the speaker, a young man of about twenty-five with a healthy head of shoulder-length hair, pulled back into a neat ponytail. His expression was as earnest as his words.

"Come on, Dr. Ohanian, do you really think pulverized reindeer horn is going to cure cancer?"

"No, but in fact, recent studies have shown that the phytoestrogens in soy can and do fight cancer."

"Well, in that case, maybe we should tell the National Cancer Institute to close up shop. What do we need them for if cancer is cured?" Dr. Greshom snapped. He turned to the group. "Let me ask you this," he continued, "Which would you rather have working for you, the vast resources of Western medicine, honed by the greatest minds of the century, or the wishy-washy wistful thinking of some shaman who wouldn't know a stethoscope from a syringe?"

Dr. Greshom snorted in derisive laughter, no doubt expecting the other students to join him. Sam heard a few titters, but for the most part, the students were silent. Whether this indicated their lack of agreement with Dr. Greshom's myopic philosophy, or merely their fear of standing up to him, Sam couldn't tell. But he was outraged to hear his own physician bullying the next generation of doctors into adopting his tunnel vision.

"Why don't you ask the patient that question?" Sam said, and then he opened his eyes. He was pleased to see the shock on Dr. Greshom's face. The interns looked from Sam to Dr. Greshom, waiting for their leader's response.

"Mr. Sampson, did we disturb your sleep?" Dr. Greshom asked politely.

"I wasn't asleep actually, only resting. But I'm awake now, Dr. Greshom, awake and pissed off to hear that as my doctor, you aren't planning to do whatever the hell it takes to help me survive."

"I'm sure you would agree that I have done everything in my power as a surgeon — "

"As a surgeon, yeah, but as a physician? It doesn't sound like it."

"As I told you after I removed your diseased heart, Mr. Sampson, the transplant was a success. No other treatment could have saved you. I as a physician did not fail you. Western medicine did not fail you. It is *your body* that has failed to accept the new organ. Short of transplanting a second heart, there is nothing we can do."

Sam knew he had only enough energy for one more sentence, maybe two, so he paused to summon up the strength to make them count. "Are you willing to just sit back and watch me die to prove your point, doctor?"

Dr. Greshom's face turned crimson, and he took a moment to compose himself. When he spoke, his voice was controlled. He directed his words to the students. "As you know, the drugs we give our transplantation patients do have some unavoidable side effects, one of which can be increased anxiety, a sense of impending doom."

"If I understood what you were saying earlier, Dr. Greshom, it's not just a *sense* of doom, it's real. I *am dying*, right?"

"I hope we will — "

"Am I or aren't I?" Sam repeated as loudly as he could.

"Mr. Sampson, if you are unhappy — "

"Unhappy? Yes, I'd say I was unhappy to be dying. Don't you think I should be?"

" — with the treatment I am giving you," Dr. Greshom continued over Sam's retort, "you have every right to select another doctor to direct your medical care. However, you might find it rather
difficult to locate one who is willing to accept a terminal case. Doctors, shall we continue with our rounds?"

"Why? Because it would hurt their reputation if I died?"

Dr. Greshom spun on his heel and led the student doctors out of
Sam's room. Several hurried after him, but others, embarrassed by
the exchange, followed more slowly, shaking their heads in dismay.
One lingered by Sam's bed. It was the young man with the ponytail.
He took Sam's hand and squeezed it.

"I'm sorry if what I said upset you, Mr. Sampson," the man said.

"No," Sam said, his voice a whisper, "you made me think. I'm
not afraid of dying, I just want to go peacefully."

"Of course you do. Everyone should have that right."

Sam looked into his eyes. "You really believe that?"

"I believe in using every treatment available to keep a patient
alive, Mr. Sampson. But I also believe that sometimes a patient's
life is over before his body ceases function. The two events don't always happen simultaneously. And when this is the case, my personal belief is that it is up to us as doctors to … ensure that the end
is not tormenting or prolonged."

Sam nodded, his eyes glistening.

"Mr. Sampson, I don't want you to think I'm … Dr. Greshom is
an awesome surgeon. He has brilliant hands."

Sam read the name on the man's badge. *Aram Ohanian*, it said.
"But Dr. Ohanian, speaking as a patient, I wish he had your soul."

○

Emily fought the urge to wake up, sleep a reprieve from anxiety
about Jonah. But maternal instinct pried her eyes open with unre-
lenting fingers. She turned onto her side, running her hand over the

smooth, empty plane of the blanketed bed, still expecting to see and feel Jack there.

What would he have said about Jonah's predicament? What would he have told her to do? Despite his inexperience with children, his advice to her had always been instinctively sound, because, as she often told him, he still thought like a little boy.

And what would he have thought of the man who had received his heart?

Part of her was curious and eager to talk to this man, Sam, now that she knew the truth. But another part of her was reluctant to face him, to look into his eyes knowing a part of Jack was there. Would she be resentful of the person who still lived because Jack had died?

But he was in the hospital again, and might not continue to live, because Jonah had clobbered him with a rake. If he died, it would be on her conscience.

And if he died, Jack's heart would die along with him.

There were so many jagged pieces to this puzzle: Ann's and Matt's betrayal, and their reasons for it; Jonah's disappearance in both body and soul; Jack's death, which effectively changed who she was as a person. She felt as though her life was a broken mirror: what was reflected back was abnormal and distorted. The harmony she craved and had worked so hard to achieve was gone. Could it be restored? Would she ever get them back? Could she live without it?

Without Jack?

She realized she was crying again. Dear Jack. He'd only been dead two months, and already his memory had settled into a protected place in her heart. She had a vague recollection that their marriage had had its imperfections, but she could no longer remember what they were. Was that good or bad? Did it signal recovery or denial?

If only this thing with Jonah hadn't happened. If only Jonah were here....

No! Jonah could not take Jack's place. She shouldn't use him as a substitute. She had to experience the pain and loss in order to heal. But it would be such a relief just to know that her son was safe, that at least *he* was not alone, and that he was not in danger, not afraid.

Her thoughts returned to the man in the hospital. Seeing him, talking to him, would be difficult. But it would take her to the next plateau in her acceptance of Jack's death. She would go visit him. Today. Now. The sooner it was over, the better.

But how could she face him? What could she say?

She stood in front of the glass doors to the hospital, imagining them whooshing shut behind her, sealing her in. Her instinct was to turn and run, to escape this place before the taint of tragedy could reinfect her. Steven Sampson was no relation. She'd hardly even had a conversation with the man. She didn't know if he was married, or how old he was, or what color his eyes were. Why should she open herself up to the pain of seeing Jack in him, of caring whether he lived or died? It would be so easy to just turn around and walk back to her car, to go on with her life!

But even as she thought these things, she knew she would not turn away. She had no blood tie to Sam, but in some ways their connection was even stronger. If he died, or rejected Jack's heart, it would be like losing Jack all over again. And because of the part Jonah had played in this scenario, she would feel responsible for his death. She *needed* him to survive!

But she still didn't know what she was going to say to him.

○

She approached the volunteer monitoring the telephones at the reception desk on the eighth floor. Beyond her were double doors marked *Intensive Care Cardiac Unit. No Admittance Without Authorization."*

"May I help you?" the woman asked, with just the right amount of sympathy in her voice.

"Yes, I'm wondering if you can direct me to Mr. Sampson's room."

The volunteer skimmed her list. "I don't see his name." She looked up and saw the concern on Emily's face. "Oh, that doesn't mean anything. This happens all the time. Are you certain he'd be in cardiac?"

"Yes, definitely. He's a heart transplant recipient. It was an emergency."

The volunteer's face brightened. "Well, that explains it. He'd be in the E.R."

"But he was up here. I'm sure of it."

"On this floor?"

"Yes."

"When did he come in?"

"Two days ago."

"Hmmm," the woman mused, "this is a puzzle."

"Please, I'm afraid he might be ... he is very ill."

The volunteer picked up the phone. "Don't you worry, if he's here, we'll find him," she said with maddening lightness, as though Emily had lost a pen or a favorite sweater. She started to thumb through the procedural notebook as though in it she might find some rule or regulation which would explain Sam's disappearance.

Emily couldn't wait. She wheeled around and headed for the double doors that separated the I.C.C.U. from the rest of the floor.

"Wait!" the volunteer called after her. She stood, then came around the desk as though to chase after Emily. "You can't go in there without an escort," she called.

"Watch me!" Emily said, and burst through the doors.

Inside, there was a palpable sense of urgency. The staff members moved with somber purpose, barely noticing Emily as she passed. There was no clique of nurses chatting at the door to the supply room, no wise-cracking orderly joking to make a patient laugh. The beds were in glass cubicles surrounding the nurses' station, a circular hub of activity and information.

A veteran of the system now, Emily walked boldly up to the desk and found Sampson's name on the wall chart, and noted his room number, 819-B. Without hesitating, she strode to the cubicle with that number and looked at the namecard. On it, in blue wax pencil, was scribbled *Sampson, Steven*, but a curtain was drawn around the bed so she could not see in. She composed herself. This was the moment of truth, the moment she would stand face-to-face with the man who had Jack's heart.

She tapped lightly on the glass. There was no sound; perhaps he was sleeping. She opened the curtain a crack, and her heart sank.

The bed was empty. Not just empty, but stripped of sheets and blanket. The cubicle too was empty, devoid of personal effects and equipment. She stared at it in horror and disbelief. *No*, she whispered to herself, *please God, you can't take him from me twice!*

She ran out into the hall and stopped an orderly pushing an elderly patient swaddled in blankets in a wheelchair. "Excuse me, is this Mr. Sampson's bed?"

The orderly's face was expressionless, disinterested. "Whatever it says on the card."

"But it's empty," Emily said.

The orderly shrugged and walked on.

"Please, do you know where he is?"

"Sorry, lady," he said.

"They took him this morning," a muffled voice said, and Emily realized it had come from the patient in the wheelchair.

"Where?" Emily knelt next to him to hear better. "Where did they take him?"

"Gone," the patient said. "I saw him go." He coughed, a deep hacking knife of a cough, and bent double with an agonizing gasp of pain. *Where did he go?* Emily wanted to ask him, but how could she ask a dying man to define what he meant by *gone*?

In desperation, she approached the nurses' desk. The nurse on duty was a tall, imperious woman with a nose as sharp as the pencil she was using to fill out forms. "I'm looking for Mr. Sampson, bed 819-B. He's not in his cubicle, and the bed has been stripped. Can you tell me where he is?" Emily blurted out before the nurse could speak.

The nurse narrowed her eyes. "This is a sterile area, madam, and you are not properly gowned. Do you know the risk of infection you are causing?"

"I want to know where Mr. Sampson is!" Emily insisted.

The nurse clenched her teeth to keep her anger in check. "Are you a family member?"

"No, not exactly. But — "

"It's quite an exact thing," the nurse persisted. "You either are or you aren't related."

Emily bit her lip to hold back frustration. "We are related to the extent that my husband's heart was transplanted into Mr. Sampson's body." She was surprised by her own vehemence, surprised and emboldened. "He was here two days ago, but you people seem to have lost him. Now I would like very much to know where he is!"

The nurse stared at her for a moment, unsmiling, her eyes unnervingly steady. "One moment, please," she said, and picked up the phone. She turned away from Emily and spoke softly into the receiver, words Emily couldn't hear. Then she turned back to Emily and smiled without warmth. "Someone will be with you shortly. If you'll have a seat in the ..."

"I'll just wait here, thank you."

The nurse opened her mouth as though to object, then clamped it shut again. "Suit yourself," she said, and went back to her work.

Had the nurse called a supervisor to help locate Sam, or a security guard to cart her away? Adrenaline coursing through her body, Emily could hardly bear to stand still as she waited to find out. She forced herself to breathe deeply and kept her feet planted on the floor, obstinately staring at the nurse, hoping the woman could feel the heat of her silent anger.

"May I help you?" a voice said from behind her, and Emily turned. It was Elaine Greenberg, the woman from *The Organ Bank*. She recognized Emily immediately and extended her hand, composed but wary. "Mrs. Barnes! How nice to see you."

"Mrs. Greenberg, can you help me please?" Emily tried to keep her voice from breaking. "I'm looking for a transplant patient. His name is Steven Sampson. They called him the Tin Man."

"I — I," Elaine Greenberg sputtered.

"I already know he was the recipient of my husband's heart," Emily interrupted. "He came in on an emergency two days ago, and he was put on this floor. Can you tell me where he is now?"

"Well ... this is quite irregular," Mrs. Greenberg fumbled. "I don't know where you've gotten your information, but — "

Emily gritted her teeth. She wanted to grab the woman by the lapels of her Escada suit and shake the information out of her. But instead, she clenched her hands tightly, feeling a perverse relief as her fingernails dug into her palms "That isn't the issue!" she spat. "If you can't or won't tell me where he is, I'll find someone who will."

The nurse rose menacingly, the shadow of her authority looming over Emily. "Mrs. Greenberg, would you like me to call for help?"

"The only help we need is someone who can tell me where this patient is!" Emily said, her voice almost a scream. "I want to know what happened to Mr. Sampson!"

"Hey, what's going on?" a calm voice asked.

Emily wheeled around, braced to do battle. It was Dr. Andrea Leventhal. They both drew back in surprise. "Andrea, thank God!"

"Emily? What are you doing here? What's wrong?"

All three women started to speak at once, each pleading her case to this higher authority. Andrea Leventhal looked at each of them in turn, and then in her quiet but commanding way, raised one hand signaling for silence. "Mrs. Greenberg, Nurse Olsen, let me just have a word with Mrs. Barnes," she said, and linking her arm through Emily's, she gently guided her down the hall, away from the other women. Emily felt the strong, sure fingers close around her arm, and her anger dissipated. Tears of relief welled in her eyes.

"You certainly got Nurse Ratchet and Florence Nightingale riled up," Dr. Leventhal said with a sympathetic smile. "What did you do? Smoke a cigarette in the ladies room?"

"The man who got Jack's heart — I met him a few days ago. Actually, I'd met him before, here, the weekend Jack died. But I just found out that he was the recipient. He was readmitted a couple of days ago, and when I came to see him today, his room was empty! Nobody will tell me where he is. Dr. Leventhal, Andrea, I'm afraid ... maybe he, maybe Jack's heart ..." she trailed off.

Dr. Leventhal had stopped walking. "And our fine staff wouldn't give you any information? Good grief!" She removed a two-way pager from her pocket and punched in a code. "What did you say his name was — I mean *is*?" she said emphatically.

"Sampson. Steven Sampson."

"And he was brought in when?"

"Two days ago. Tuesday."

Dr. Leventhal made an entry on her pager, then waited. "Hmmm," she said looking at the readout. "This says he's been re-classified, but it doesn't say how. That's either good news or bad news. Or, it could just be that no one's entered the information into the computer. Do you know who his doctor is?"

Emily had to think. "I remember it was a name that sounded like a famous author, Greene, Grimes, no Grishom!"

"You mean Greshom? Gerald Greshom? Older guy, balding, with glasses and a gleam in his eye?"

"I don't know. I never met him."

"Okay, let me page Gerald, and we'll know soon enough. Don't worry. We'll find Mr. Sampson for you. And if it's any consolation, the staff is pretty good at entering "deceased" in the computer. It's the releases and reassigning of rooms that they get screwed up." She smiled. "Because there are serious consequences if you lose a body, but hardly any if you misplace a patient."

Dr. Leventhal hurried down the hall toward Emily. Her white coat was unbuttoned, and it flapped behind her, revealing a cheery pink polo shirt and khaki pants. Nothing about her demeanor signaled bad news, so Emily's heart lifted.

"It was just a stupid paperwork mix-up," the doctor explained. "The beds in the I.C.C.U. are so damn expensive, and his insurance company is contesting payment on a previous hospitalization. So the accounting office made us move him out. They put him on Seven temporarily, which is orthopedic. Can you believe it? I yelled and screamed, mentioned the possibility of a lawsuit, and got them to find him a room on Nine. It's where we put VIPs and patients who are willing to pay extra for added service — like edible food, for example. I told them it was the least this hospital could do after a mix-up like that. Losing a patient! It could have been a public relations nightmare."

Emily put her hand on her heart and released her breath in one long sigh. "Then he's not in danger?"

"Doesn't sound like it, or else they would have kept him here. Let's go up to 'Lifestyles of the Rich and Famous' and see."

The ninth floor was definitely an improvement from floors one through eight. Instead of linoleum, a muted rose-colored carpet covered the hallway. The walls were painted a slightly lighter shade of pink, the color of an infant's skin. Contemporary photo landscapes were hung at evenly spaced intervals along the corridor, which made it appear wider, the atmosphere less sterile. Dr. Leventhal approached the nurses' station, and the nurse raised her head. "Hi, Mary," she said. "I hear you've got a new arrival from Eight, via Seven, Sampson's the name."

"Yes, doctor," the nurse replied respectfully, "he's in 958-A."

Dr. Leventhal turned to Emily. "Do you want me to come with you?"

"No, but thanks. You're a lifesaver."

"Hey, I'm a doctor. It's my job." She squeezed Emily's arm and backed toward the elevator. "If you need anything else, I'm sure Mary will take care of you. She's one of our treasures." She winked at Mary, and Mary smiled.

"Is it okay for me to go see him?" Emily asked the nurse.

Mary nodded. "His sister was with him, but she just went downstairs a minute ago to get something to eat. She said he was complaining that we didn't have cable TV, so I'm pretty sure he's awake."

Emily started down the hall, then stopped and walked back to Mary. "How is he?"

"If they let him out of I.C.C.U., he must be better than he was," Mary said. She pulled a clipboard from the cabinet beside her desk and skimmed the top page. "But I don't want to give you any misinformation. You'd better let him tell you, or Doctor Greshom."

Emily nodded and started down the hall again. The nurse called after her, "He seems like a fighter, Mrs...."

"Barnes," Emily said. "Emily Barnes. Please call me Emily."

"Emily," Mary said. "And if anyone's going to beat the odds, it's the ornery ones."

A chill swept down Emily's spine. *Beat what odds?* she thought.

21

The door to Sam's room was open. As Emily approached, she could see him lying in bed, his eyes fixed on the television, the remote control clutched in his hand. The curtains were drawn against the afternoon sun, and the fluorescent light over his head was on, bathing his face in stark, white light, as though he were a portrait in a museum. But instead of the rich, painterly tones of Rembrandt or Degas, Sam's features were tinged in gray, the color of the sky on a winter day. His face was puffy, his eyes sunken, his hair flat and oily against his scalp. The word cadaver rose in Emily's throat, but she quickly swallowed it and tried to look at the positive side: the news was good! Jack's heart had not failed its new host. Sam was alive.

Emily stepped back so she was out of his line of sight and ran her fingers through her hair, tucked in her shirt, straightened the lapels of her jacket. Then she rapped lightly on the open door and stepped forward.

"Are you accepting visitors?"

She watched Sam's eyes slowly swing around to find her, and saw his expression transform from annoyance to surprise, then descend back into a guarded reserve.

"Remember me?" she asked, her voice an octave higher than normal. "Emily Barnes."

He smiled then, and the features of his face seemed to soften. "Yeah, sure," he said breathlessly. "You're the wife of my heart."

So he did know.

Now that the truth was out in the open, conversation should have been easier, but it wasn't. They both felt the awkwardness of the situation and looked away.

Finally, Sam took the initiative. "Come in," he said. "Excuse me if I don't get up."

She stepped into the room and stood stiffly at the foot of the bed, still at a loss. It was peculiar to say the least, to be visiting a man who was hardly more than a stranger, while he was lying in bed in a faded hospital gown with his thin, unfamiliar arms exposed.

She must have blushed, because he pulled the sheets up higher on his chest, and said, "I should put on a robe."

"No, no, it's fine, I'm just not used to ..."

"Talking to a man in bed who isn't your husband."

"Right."

This much conversation robbed him of his breath. He closed his eyes and sucked on his oxygen for a few seconds before looking at her again. Then he patted the side of the bed. "Here," he said. "Too hard to talk when you're there."

Emily walked to the chair by the side of the bed and sat on the edge of it, holding her bag on her lap. "Your sister must have told you that I figured it out."

He shook his head. "Your face."

"You could see it on my face?"

He nodded.

"Am I that transparent?"

He smiled and touched his chest. "I know you here."

Emily turned her head away, embarrassed.

"Sorry," he said. "Stupid. Drowning in drugs."

Emily collected herself and smiled at him. "It's okay. This is just so odd. I know part of my husband is in you, and somehow I think I should be able to see it. It's silly ..."

"No," Sam said. "I'm different." He took a deep breath. "He's inside me."

They sat in silence, letting this sink in.

"Tell me about — "

"Jack. His name was Jack."

He nodded and took a breath. "So damn sorry," Sam said his voice ragged with emotion. "I wouldn't have — "

They both knew what he was trying to say, that it was agony for him to think of all she had lost — and through her loss, all that he had gained. "I know," she replied. "But it makes me feel better that at least one good thing came out of Jack's death."

"How did he — "

"An automobile accident. A terrible crash. He was ... horribly injured. His poor, beautiful body ... I think it's better that he didn't survive like that."

They sat in silence again. Then the silence became too long, uncomfortable. Sam sucked on his oxygen, struggling to think of a way to break the tension. "Did Jack like Mexican food?" he said at last.

Emily's face broke into a smile. "Burritos," she said. "They were his favorite. Actually, he loved fast food of any kind. But for Mexican, he always went to this place called Sergio's Szechuan. They make a seafood burrito Jack used to love. Crab, shrimp, and a whitefish mousse with black beans and plum sauce. Very spicy. Why?"

"I think I got his stomach, too."

Emily laughed, and the sound was a healing balm for them both.

"Tell me more. About Jack."

Emily sighed. "Well, let's see. He was thirty-seven. His birthday is — was — in November. He was a Scorpio, so you know how that is — very passionate, very volatile. Very ... strong." She thought for a minute. "He was handsome — dark hair, not quite curly, but wavy if he didn't get it cut often enough, which he didn't. He had green eyes that turned blue when he wore a blue shirt, and an olive complexion — he always looked tan. Of course, he was outside a lot. He loved sports, especially golf. He played golf at least three or four times a week."

Sam made a face.

"You don't love sports, I take it."

Sam gestured to his body. "Speaks for itself, doesn't it?"

"What do you do?"

Sam snorted. "Besides lie here?"

"I mean before."

"Musician. Jazz. Drums."

Emily's mouth gaped. "Jack loved jazz. According to his brother, when he was growing up, it was his dream to be a drummer. But he gave it up when he realized he didn't have the talent." Her eyes filled with tears. "Think how happy he would be if he knew ... that his dream came true."

Before Sam could control it, tears filled his eyes too, and slowly they spilled down his cheeks. Emily came closer and touched his cheeks gently with the edge of the sheet. "Are you in pain?" she whispered.

"Damn body wants to fight it out," he sputtered. "Don't know why."

"What does the doctor say?"

Sam's lips curved into an ironic smile. "That I'm terminal."

Emily took a step back. "He told you that?" she whispered.

Sam nodded once and closed his eyes. "Unless I have another transplant." His breath was getting shorter, and he paused before each word. "But-people-don't-usually-win-the-lottery-twice."

There was so much more to say, and above all, he ached to touch her. But he could not summon the strength. He felt himself sinking lower, lower still. And then his body went limp.

"Sam?" Emily bent to him, and she could see his eyeballs moving behind his closed lids, a clear indication that he hadn't stopped breathing, that he was just asleep. She pulled the sheet up to his chin and smoothed the blanket. "Good-bye, Sam. I will see you later," she said. And she thought she saw the hint of a smile on his thin lips.

○

When Diana stepped out of the elevator, Emily was waiting to go down. Without hesitation, the two women fell into each others arms. Their hug started as a simple greeting, but as they held each other, emotion began to flow between them, and they clung to each other, rocking, tears streaming down their faces.

Finally they broke apart, wiping their cheeks.

"Did you — " Diana asked.

"Yes," Emily replied.

"Did he — "

"He knew."

"His body won't stop fighting it," Diana said in a choked voice. "I'm so afraid."

"But Jack's heart is strong! It won't fail him," Emily insisted, wanting it to be true.

"The doctor said it's just a matter of time."

Emily's voice was just a whisper. "How much time?"

Diana just shook her head and started to cry again. "So here we are," she said at last, "back where we started seven months ago. Only it's worse, because Sam is lower on the list. And the problem is ..." she trailed off, staring into the distance. Then she took a deep breath and continued. "The problem is, obviously, they can't take this heart out of his body until a new one becomes available. So he's in danger every minute. Not only that. Since he rejected one good heart, there's no reason to think he wouldn't reject another one, so he's a low priority."

She turned to Emily, dry eyed and solemn. "All we can do is hope for a miracle."

$$\circlearrowright$$

Emily pulled to a stop under the elm tree and turned off the engine. The tree was in full leaf now, providing a canopy under which she could observe the intersection. She hadn't planned on coming today, but something in Diana's words about the need for a miracle had drawn her to this spot. Why? She guessed it was because she was beginning to understand that life itself was a miracle, both the giving and taking of it.

For perhaps the hundredth time, she pictured the accident in her head — saw Jack's Mustang flying down the road, the blue of his shirt mirroring the morning sky, the smoke from his cigar trailing behind like the white wisp of a jetstream, the sun glinting off the hand-polished surface of the car, creating a halo of refracted light around both vehicle and driver. Knowing Jack, he was driving faster than was prudent to make up for the time he'd lost driving back to the house to retrieve the key card for the Club gate.

Probably he'd been listening to one of his Oscar Peterson CDs, the volume tuned to an ear-splitting decibel to counteract the rush of wind. Most likely, he was thinking about his upcoming golf game or one of his investments, but time and again, she'd wondered if a fleeting thought of her had crossed his mind before the impact, a fugitive mental caress. She doubted it. Jack was not a man to dwell on his feelings. Sometimes she'd railed at his ability to look at their love the same way he did any of his other assets: since the initial investment had been made, all that remained was to collect the dividends on a predictable and regular schedule.

But she realized how lucky she'd been to love a man who never doubted his love for her. It was a rare gift.

She wondered at what point he had noticed the dog in the street — or if he had actually seen the animal at all. Perhaps, as sometimes happens, he'd only perceived an object in the road out of the corner of his eye as he passed, and by the time his full consciousness had been engaged, he had already made the fatal error, stepped on the gas instead of the brake, and initiated the accident.

Had there been an instant when he had realized he was about to die? Or had he been watching the dog in the rear view mirror, feeling relieved that he had been able to avoid hitting it, not realizing that he was careening toward a collision?

It was agony, but once again, she imagined the moment. Yes, she vaguely remembered hearing the distant screech of brakes from the house and having the awful, vivid awareness of violent impact, the premonition of catastrophe. At the time, she'd dismissed the sounds as someone else's tragedy, certain that her loved ones were safe. Ah, how wrong she had been!

She thought about Sam. The Tin Man. He, too, was careening toward death, but much more slowly. And while Jack had most likely been unaware of his peril for more than an instant, Sam had lived with the knowledge of this for endless days and nights.

Was it better to go quickly, as Jack had, or to have time to prepare? Or *could* you prepare for death?

When she had looked into Sam's face, she had seen the answer to her question. He knew what was coming, and he was making himself ready.

22

S am could feel it — the news was not good.

All day, the nurses and the technicians had gone about their tasks briskly, smiling at him with encouragement as they worked. But it was obvious that they were holding back some critical information. There was reluctance and restraint in the way their hands gripped his body as they held him forward to change his gown, a gentleness which felt tentative. And this tentativeness translated into fear, fear of death. Although the hospital staff was trained to work with the sick and dying, taught to give care despite contagion, diseases, and disfigurement, they could not help it if the knowledge of death's nearness seeped out through their fingertips and shone in their eyes. He saw it, and he knew they knew he did.

He tried to sit up straighter, that small effort costing him dearly in precious strength. "How am I doing?" he asked, wanting not the truth but some reassuring lie to cling to.

"That's what you should be telling me, mister," an ebullient nurse replied without looking at him. Her eyes were on the plastic pouch filled with his urine. She looked like Madame Curie, holding the amber sack up to the light, staring at it intently, then jotting a figure down on his chart — at least she was attending to business without his nagging. Her name badge was askew on her prodigious bosom. *Marisa Bennet,* it read.

Sam took a sip of oxygen and said, "Well, if it's up to me, Marisa, I'm doing fine, and I want to go home. Shall I get dressed?" He made a move as though to rise, but it was an empty gesture. Not only was he literally wired down by the myriad machines surrounding him, but he hadn't nearly the strength he needed to hoist his body up and out of bed, and they both knew it.

"What, you don't appreciate our hospitality?" Nurse Bennet teased with a cheeriness so forced that it undermined her determination to comfort him. "Gosh, Mr. Sampson, you're hurting my feelings."

"If all that hurts are your feelings, consider yourself lucky," Sam mumbled. But she did not appear to hear.

There was a tap on the door, and an orderly entered wordlessly with a tray of Saran-wrapped food. "Room service for Mr. Sampson," he said.

"Not only that, but you'd miss your gourmet breakfast if you left now," Nurse Bennet smiled. "Just set it over there, Hector. I'm almost through."

Hector slouched into the room and set the tray on the nightstand without acknowledging Sam.

"I hope those Eggs Benedict have plenty of Bernaise sauce on them," Sam said. The orderly didn't turn around. "And you remembered my champagne, right?" Hector's mouth softened into a smile as he shuffled out of the room, stepping aside for an intern to enter, a young Hispanic doctor with a day's growth of beard.

"Hey, Tin Man, what's up?" the doctor asked. "You like this place so well you come back to visit, man?" He took Sam's chart from the nurse and skimmed it. She pointed to a notation and whispered something to him that Sam couldn't hear.

"Couldn't stay away, Doctor Chavez," Sam said. "Wanted to know what happened between you and Senorita Munoz."

The intern looked up and frowned. Sam held his breath, thinking he was reacting to the chart. But then his eyes became dreamy, and he said, "Ah, the one that got away. You know how it is, man, interns have too many late hours. Days would go by, and I wouldn't even get home. When I did see her, sometimes I was too tired to even ... I'll tell you, it's a sad thing when a man can't even stay awake for that!"

"Tell me about it," Sam commiserated.

"She got engaged to a guy who owns a chain of flower shops, you know? At least when *he's* late, he brings home roses."

"Yeah, but what good will he be if she needs to have her appendix out?"

"You said it, man." Dr. Chavez leaned over Sam, looking into his eyes. Sam tried to make eye contact with him, but the young doctor wasn't looking at Sam the person, he was looking at Sam the heart transplant recipient. He wasn't being unkind in this, but professionally his interest was in the mechanism, not the man. "How do you feel, Tin Man? Any pain?"

It felt like an elephant was sitting on his chest, and when he lay on his back too long he'd be consumed by orthopnea, making it almost impossible to breathe. But Sam knew better than to mention this. He had learned early on to never tell an intern anything, even if he was a nice guy like Chavez. Why? Because he didn't want or need their inexperienced interpretations of his symptoms; too much got lost in the translation. So he saved his explanations for his own physician. "The only pain I've got is a pain in the ass from lying in this damn bed."

"Hey, like they say, it beats the alternative," Dr. Chavez said. "Can I get you anything?"

"Yeah, a six-pack of Heineken. Or better yet, make it a case. I'm dying of thirst — and I do mean dying!"

"You know the drill, Tin Man. Since your heart isn't pumping hard enough to give your kidneys the juice they need to eliminate the fluids, we've got to restrict your intake. Otherwise, you'll blow up like a hot air balloon." He flipped the cover back on Sam's chart and handed it to Nurse Bennet. "Anything else?"

"Yeah. How long do I have before this heart explodes?"

The intern shifted uncomfortably. "Dr. Greshom will be here sometime this morning to discuss — "

Sam tried to sit up straight. "Hey, this is my *life* we're talking about. Can't you just give me a hint? Am I on my way out? For God's sake, I feel like I am, but no ... one ... will ... tell ... me ... a ... damn ... thing!" The length of this speech sucked all the air from Sam's lungs and the words came out in a wheeze that exploded into a coughing fit, each hack propelling a frisson of pain through his chest.

And then the heart began to roar, a jungle beat that pounded so loudly it drowned out all of the other sounds in the room. He began to gasp for air, and his body thrashed wildly, trying to provide it.

"He's going into tachycardia again, Doctor," the nurse said. She ran to the bed and tried to pin down Sam's arms, immobilizing him so he wouldn't hurt himself or dislodge any of the intravenous lines.

"Page Dr. Greshom," Chavez said, "and we'd better give him a shot of amiodarone."

Sam groaned. Although his body was out of control, he could still think clearly, and he knew that although the amiodarone would relieve the arrhythmia and stop the seizure, it could also cause lung problems later and possibly congestive heart failure, hardly a good trade-off.

He wanted to protest, to stand up and shout, No!
No more drugs or surgery or fear!
Let me die in peace.

But, of course, he could not speak, and the medical staff wouldn't have listened if he could. This whole process was not about *his* will to live, but about *their* drugs and treatments, the so-called miracle of modern medicine. It was not about saving his life, it was about ensuring that the transplant was a success. He closed his eyes and concentrated on the heart, visualizing the throb of the muscle as its beats reached a crescendo. Why was his body fighting against the good organ, the second chance he'd been given?

A vise clamped down on his chest, and a lightning bolt shot out to his shoulders and arms. "What's the pain on a scale of one to ten?" The nurse's voice cut through the dense fog that enveloped him.

"Twenty," he mouthed, clenching his teeth against the next spasm. "*Aaaugh!*" His scream was involuntary. He felt lightheaded and nauseated.

"Here it is, doctor," he heard the nurse say.

Sam gasped, and his whole body bucked as the electric heat of the drug shot into his vein. But he still couldn't breathe, and rising nausea burned the constricted passages of his throat.

Then he was moving into that space beyond pain where sensation became a simple, dazzling brightness. He had been to this place once before, in the far distance of his consciousness, and he remembered it with curiosity and rapture. He imagined he could raise his hand to grasp the light, and he yearned to draw it closer. But it remained just outside of his reach. He wondered, was the brightness life, or was it death?

He would know soon enough.

$\circlearrowleft$

"I want to see where you live."

Emily turned from the television to look at Sam. Had he spoken, or had she just imagined it?

They had been watching a cooking show — Sam's idea. When she'd arrived, he'd told her to turn it on, saying he hoped it would stimulate his flagging appetite. She suspected the real reason he wanted the TV on was that he was having increasing difficulty breathing and speaking, and since they were essentially strangers, silence between them was awkward.

"Sam?" She walked over to the bed. His eyes were closed, his skin pale, almost waxen, his body bloated with steroids to stave off rejection. Although he lay utterly still, she could see his eyeballs darting back and forth under nearly translucent eyelids.

"Sam?" she said again.

"See where you live," Sam repeated, without opening his eyes.

"I'll bring pictures."

He shut his eyes and shook his head weakly. "Dying man's last wish," he gasped.

"Stop it. You're not dying." Her words were hollow with false conviction.

Sam opened his eyes and looked at her with a weary intensity, holding her tight with his gaze. "Bet?"

"Come on," she said, turning away to break the mood. "I don't want to do this."

"Me either."

"Sam, I'd love to take you to my house," she said. "You know I would. But how would we manage with all this?" Her eyes swept the room, cluttered with monitoring devices and life-sustaining machinery, a new unit every day, it seemed. "Besides, I don't think Dr. Greshom would let you."

"Ask."

She went first to Andrea Leventhal, her expert on all questions medical, of which there seemed to be many these days.

"Isn't it crazy?" Emily asked. "He's much too sick. And what if a heart becomes available?"

"Realistically, I think Sam knows, and you know too, that he's not at the top of the list. There are four other cardiac patients in this facility alone who haven't received a first transplant, let alone a second. Anyway, they'll give him a beeper," she told Emily. "If a heart does come through for him, they'll let you know. You don't live that far away. You can get back in time."

Emily shook her head. "It just seems so risky. Why would he want to take the chance?"

"It's a pretty normal response, don't you think? And actually, you could interpret it as a positive sign. If he has enough energy to *want* to do something, anything, that's good, you see?"

"But he's so weak. Doesn't he need to conserve all his energy to stay alive?"

Andrea looked into her eyes. "Say what you really mean, Emily."

Emily sighed. It took her a moment to find the courage to speak. "What if his heart stops while we're out there? What if he dies when he's with me?" she whispered.

Andrea nodded. She'd known this was the real issue, and she knew how hard it was for anyone to admit it. "Emily, this may sound harsh to you, but I'm sure he's thought about it. And if he's willing to take the chance, well ..." she shrugged. "Isn't it his decision?"

"I just don't want ..." Emily began, but had to stop. She took a deep breath. "I'm afraid."

Andrea put her arm around her shoulder and gave her a squeeze. "Of course you are. It's an enormous burden when someone is willing to entrust you with his passage. But it's also the most meaningful gift they can give."

"Why don't we invite Diana to come with us?" Emily asked.

Sam shook his head "no," saving his strength for the hours ahead. He'd insisted that the nurse shave him, and he was wearing freshly pressed clothes that felt strangely stiff on his body. Just getting dressed had taken the better part of the morning.

"He's stabilized," the nurse assured Emily as she snapped the paper face mask over Sam's nose and mouth, "so he should be fine. See you later, Tin Man. Have fun." She patted Sam on the shoulder, and the orderly wheeled him out of the room.

They rode down to the garage in silence, and Emily brought her car around to the door. The orderly pulled Sam out of the wheelchair, and Sam shuffled the two feet to the car, his legs threatening to buckle with each tiny step. The excitement over this outing made his eyes brighter than they had been in days — or was the brightness a sign of an inner conflagration, Jack's sick heart ready to explode?

"Let's at least go by the house first and see your mother," Emily pleaded.

"After," he said. "If."

He motioned to the orderly to close the car door, and waited, staring straight ahead, until Emily rounded the hood and got into the driver's seat.

She thought about what he meant: *if* he had the energy; *if* he didn't have to rush back to the hospital because a heart had come in, or for an emergency; *if* he didn't die first.

"*When*," she said firmly. "I'm going to call them and let them know we're coming." She reached to pick up the cell phone, but Sam put his hand on hers. Although his touch was light as a feather and the flesh cold, she felt it as a fiery weight.

He took as deep a breath as he could, his whole body seeming to inflate with the effort. "Today, just you and me. Please."

"Okay," Emily whispered. "Okay!" Then she smiled, trying to

make light of it. "I'm flattered. This is the first date I've had …" She didn't want to say "since Jack died," so she finished, "in months."

He grinned. "Years for me," he said.

She drove slowly through the darkened expanse of the parking garage with one arm outstretched in front of Sam's chest, turning the corners in slow motion, as though Sam were a potted plant or a freshly frosted cake that might tip over. She braked so a car could back out of a parking spot, and while waiting to drive on, she glanced over at Sam. Although it was a brilliantly sunny day in late April, he was bundled up for a Minnesota winter: hat, gloves, muffler, wool coat buttoned to the neck. He was staring ahead out the windshield at the dazzling spring day.

"It's gorgeous, isn't it?"

He mumbled something she couldn't hear.

"What?" she asked, leaning close so he wouldn't have to shout.

"Put the top down!"

"Sam, no. You'll catch your — it's too cold. It's barely spring."

He only had to look at her for her to read his thoughts, that when summer did arrive, *if* he were still alive, it was likely that he would be too sick to realize, let alone appreciate it. "Okay," she said. "We'll go topless. Just don't ask me to buy you some Raybans and a pair of Speedos." She pushed the control, and the automatic top began to rise, folding back onto itself until it was a compact bundle resting on the shelf behind the seat. She stepped on the gas, and they slowly pulled into the street.

It was one of those dazzling California days when blue sky and warm air conspired to create the sensation of floating in a warm bath. Such a day was always uplifting, but to see Sam's face as the gloom of the parking garage gave way to the brilliance of the morning, even Emily, who had never admitted to a belief in God, felt the presence of a higher being. Sam's grave illness, which had demanded their utter, somber attention inside the hospital, was left behind, as though it resided in that imposing edifice and not in his body. The dark cloud of concern about Jonah that had been hanging over her own head also floated away momentarily, and she felt peaceful, radiant joy. It was not possible that death and disease and worry could exist in an atmosphere such as this! She and Sam looked at each other and began to laugh.

Their exhilaration was contagious — when they stopped for a red light, a man in a wheelchair looked at them and smiled. A child holding her mother's hand waved, and Sam waved back. A dog barked at them and tugged at its leash to get to the car.

When the light turned green and they drove on, Sam lay his head back against the headrest and closed his eyes. Emily saw a teardrop streak down his cheek. "Is it too windy? Are you all right?"

"Better than I've ever been," Sam said. And when he looked at her, even though his mouth was still covered by the face mask, she could see in his eyes that he was smiling. Impulsively, she reached over and took his hand, squeezing it gently. The bones felt as brittle and fragile as a sparrow's wing. Without a word, Sam raised her hand to his mouth and kissed it tenderly. She couldn't feel his lips through the gauzy cotton of the mask, but she could feel his emotion, and it touched her deeply.

Rather than take the freeway, which would have been quicker, but windy, loud, and intense, Emily drove west on placid surface streets. She remembered a street she'd noticed recently which was lined with early-blooming jacaranda trees, and she detoured to find it. The trees were just reaching full bloom, their purple plumage cresting overhead to form a canopy of flowers. Fallen blossoms carpeted the sidewalks, and at one house a gardener was using a blower to clear the path, the air lifting the delicate blooms so that they billowed in ethereal clouds around him, like a swarm of lavender butterflies. As they drove slowly past, some of the flowers wafted over them and settled on their laps. She took a handful of them and sprinkled them over Sam's head. He picked up a single blossom and nestled it behind her ear.

"This is a miracle," Sam said, as they drove slowly on.

"I know," she replied.

"How long do these trees bloom?"

"Not very long. Only a few weeks, I think," she answered. "Why?"

"Bury me under one," he said.

For a long time, Emily was silent. "Boy, you really know how to bring down a party," she said at last.

"Please."

"Okay," she replied. "If that's what you want."

"Something else," he said.

"Shall I make a list?"

"Take me to the place where Jack died."

Abruptly, Emily slammed on the brakes. The car behind them had to swerve to avoid running up their bumper. Its driver sat on his horn, then swung around the Toyota to pass. "What are you trying to do, kill someone?" he yelled as he went by.

Emily ignored him. "Why?"

"Pay my respects," he said. Then he closed his eyes.

○

They weren't far from the site of the accident. Emily didn't say anything, just pulled the car to a stop where she usually did, on Jessup at the on-ramp to Highway 138. When the car stopped moving, Sam opened his eyes and looked around.

"Here," he said. It was not a question.

They sat without speaking, watching the sporadic ebb and flow of traffic. Most cars came to a complete, safe stop before crossing the intersection to get on the freeway. But a few were more daring, slowing only to a rolling stop before accelerating across the street to the on-ramp. One car, a tiny Mazda Miata, ignored the stop sign altogether and avoided a collision with the BMW sedan coming the other way merely by dint of its small size and the German car's superior braking system.

"I never asked — " Sam began, but he didn't need to finish for Emily to intuit his question.

"He was on his way to play golf — he played every Saturday. This is the way he always came, ever since we moved here. They told me a dog ran into the street. Not out in the middle, but just in the gutter over there, to do its business. It was early, before eight, and maybe a little foggy. There was a Pespi van coming through the intersection. The driver thought Jack might have been going a little over the speed limit, but not much. He wasn't a reckless driver, but sometimes he didn't pay enough attention to the speedometer.

"He must have seen the dog suddenly, out of the corner of his eye. You know how that happens — you flash on something too late to be able to tell if it's a danger or not, and you react by reflex.

"But I guess he stepped on the gas instead of the brake." She closed her eyes. "I've imagined it a million times: what he might have been thinking about, whether he had time to realize he wasn't going to hit the dog after all, if he knew he'd stepped on the gas pedal, how much pain he felt ..." her voice trailed off.

"One night when I came out here, I saw the dog and its owner. He didn't know who I was, or that Jack had died. He thought it had just been a bad accident, and that he'd been a hero because he'd called 911."

"You didn't tell him?"

"I couldn't."

"Of course not."

They sat in silence, staring at the intersection, imagining the progression of events that morning.

"The paramedics arrived in minutes, and they had him at the Medical Center within half an hour. I got the message about two hours later. You know, it's eerie, but when I think back, I vaguely remember hearing the crash. But how could I? Our house is more than half a mile from here. But somehow I do think I heard it, and then I put it out of my mind because I was so sure everyone I loved was safe, untouchable."

"You couldn't protect them."

"I know."

After a moment, she went on. "The police called me at work, and I went right to the hospital. He was in surgery for seven or eight hours. I don't think the doctors expected him to live, but it was impossible for me to believe he would die. I'd never even thought about it. Do you know what I mean? When I heard about the accident, it seemed like a story people were telling me. How could I possibly believe it? I didn't, really, until they let me see him that night."

She realized she had a viselike grip on the steering wheel. She had been holding it so tight and so long that her hands ached. She released it and let her hands fall into her lap.

"I don't know if he knew I was there or not." She paused. "I don't know if *he* was there or not," she amended. "I hope he wasn't, because his poor, precious body was so very devastated. I wouldn't admit this to many people, they'd say I was cruel and unloving. But I've thought about it a lot, and I've decided it was better that he died. Better for him. Better for me. There, I've said it."

Sam took her hand, still white with tension, and rubbed it between his own. "I agree," he said. "Not about Jack. About me. When it's time, it's time."

Emily started the engine. "I take that as a subtle hint that we should move on," she said, her mouth toying with a smile. "It's nearly lunchtime. Are you hungry?"

"One more stop."

Emily looked at him and sighed. "Don't tell me — you want to see where he's buried, right?"

"Right."

"Sam, isn't it too much for one day?"

"Emily, I have to."

○

Emily hadn't been to the gravesite since the memorial service — in her mind, Jack wasn't there; it was only a symbolic resting place. But as they neared the Club, she found herself curious and eager to see the site. The key card for the Club gate was still in her glove compartment, so they were able to enter the grounds without difficulty. She drove to the clubhouse, parked, and went inside. Sam could see her talking to the pro, and in a moment they both came out. The pro slid into one of the waiting golf carts and drove it over to Emily's car, glancing at Sam out of the corner of his eye.

"I'd drive you, Mrs. Barnes, but I really can't leave the shop for that long."

"No, this is great. Thanks, so much," she said.

"Hey, Jack was a great guy, an original. It's the least I can do."

Emily helped Sam out of the car and onto the front seat of the cart. "Jack had friends," Sam mused.

"I think he tipped well," said Emily, waving to the pro as they drove off.

"Golf was his sport?"

"He played at least three times a week. But before that, he was fanatic about scuba diving. Then he had an accident and almost drowned, so he stopped diving."

"What happened?"

"You really want to hear this?"

Sam nodded.

"He was out with one of his friends, down in Palos Verdes, by the cliffs, at one of those small, isolated beaches. Anyway, it was summer, late in the day, and the water was choppy, the way it sometimes gets. They'd been diving awhile and Jack got out of the water to get something from the car, I think. But his friend wanted to stay and harvest some abalone he'd found.

"Jack was coming back to the shore from the car, and all of a sudden he saw his friend flailing his arms, madly signaling for help. And then he went under. Jack ran to the water, jumped in, and swam out to where he saw him go down, but there was nothing, nobody there. He didn't have his tank on, didn't even have his fins or his mask on, but he dove down over and over again, looking for the guy, getting more and more frantic with each dive.

"Finally, he was so exhausted he had to go back to shore and call for help. He was swimming in when suddenly something pulled him from below, jerked him right under the water. He was taken by surprise, he was exhausted, and he didn't have his gear on. So he went down, and all he could think was, 'I'm going to die.' And then he passed out."

They had arrived at the stand of eucalyptus trees on the eighteenth fairway. Emily pulled the cart to a stop. "This is the place," she said. "We put the ashes right under that tree. See where the grass is a little lighter in color? That's because it's newer."

"Emily, finish the story."

She sighed and went on. "It was a practical joke," she said, "one of those stupid, macho, guy things. The friend was just pretending he was drowning, as a gag. He didn't realize that Jack didn't have on his gear, or at least that's what he said later. But Jack almost died. Luckily someone on the beach knew CPR, and they brought him back.

"After that, like I said, he didn't dive much, even though he had loved it. He said he'd only go again when he found someone he trusted enough — not just with his own life, but someone he'd be willing to die for."

Sam said nothing, remembering Jonah telling him that Jack had promised to take him diving for his birthday. He wondered if Emily had known this.

"You're getting a chill," Emily said, seeing how pale Sam had become. "Let's get going." She looked at her watch. "It's almost lunchtime. Aren't you hungry yet?"

Sam thought a moment. "Where did Jack like to go for lunch?"

◯

Sergio's Szechuan was jammed, and Emily had to drive around the block to look for a parking spot. "There," Sam said, pointing to an empty handicapped stall. "I'm eligible."

Instead of waiting her turn at the back of the line, Emily went right up to the window and tapped the first person in line on the shoulder. He was a hulk of a man, a young Latino with a gold front tooth. "I'd like to ask a favor. Would you please let me go ahead?" she asked politely.

He gave her a once-over with a leering smile. "What 'chu say? You want some *head*, lady?" he sneered.

"Hey! Wait your turn like everybody else," another person said.

"If it were for me, I would. But see my friend in the car?" She nodded at Sam, and the teenager turned around. Sam had put his face mask back on and was lying back against the seat rest. "He's very, very sick. He doesn't have much time."

"None of us do, lady," said a voice in line.

"No, I'm serious," Emily persisted. "He's terminally ill. I have to get him back to the hospital."

"If you think you're going to butt in this line, you must be *mentally* ill," someone else said, and there was laughter.

"What's his problem, lady?" the Latino asked. He was somber now, staring at Sam.

Emily turned away from the hecklers to face him. "He had a heart transplant a few months ago, and now his body's rejecting it.

342

He's on the list for another heart, but his chances of getting one aren't very good. He just wanted to taste one of Sergio's burritos before he went back to the hospital. It was the only thing he asked for."

"So hook him up to a fast food I.V.," said another voice from the crowd.

"Next!" the order taker called.

"Go on," the Latino boy said. "Get your fuckin' burritos." He stuffed his hands in his pockets and stepped back so she could go in front of him.

"Hey! That's not fair!"

"Don't let her crash!"

The man looked at Emily. "My cousin, he got shot. The bullet went straight through his lung. They said he needed a transplant," he said, "but they couldn't get him one in time."

"I'm sorry," said Emily. She stepped up to the window and placed her order.

$\circlearrowleft$

Although she'd only been gone a few minutes, Sam was asleep again when she got back to the car. She set the box of food on the seat between them and turned on the engine. But before she pulled away from the curb, she raised the convertible top and latched it into place. No sense in exposing Sam to the elements when he wasn't even awake to enjoy the sensation.

Emily kept her eye on him as she drove the short distance home. His body was completely given over to sleep, like a child who had been kept up past bedtime. He didn't wake up as she merged into traffic, didn't respond to the intoxicating aroma of Sergio's Szechuan, or to the scream of a police car which passed with sirens blaring. When she turned sharply to go into the driveway, his whole body listed against her, and she had to hold him upright with one hand while she steered with the other.

She pulled to a stop and used both hands to settle him back against the seat. His head lolled forward onto his chest, and she gently lifted his chin. "Sam," she said softly. "We're here."

There was no response.

"Sam," she said more loudly, and when he didn't respond, she felt a surge of panic. He couldn't be — was he — could he have — "Sam!" She said sharply and shook him violently. "Wake up, damn you! Wake up!"

Her body coiled into a tight knot of fear. It wasn't possible. How could death take him so silently? Tears of horror and disbelief filled her eyes. She held his head in both of her hands. "Sam, please don't die. Please no!" Her words escaped in a plaintive wail.

Slowly, as though it was a great effort, Sam opened his eyes. Relief coursed through Emily's body. "Oh, Jesus," she said, choking back tears and nervous laughter. "Oh dear God, you scared the shit out of me!"

"What happened?"

"I thought — I was afraid — "

"That I'd died?" he asked.

She nodded. "It's a terrible thing to say, I know. I'm sorry." Then she started to sob. "I'm so sorry. I really am."

He let her cry for a minute, gently pushing a strand of hair away from her face as tears flowed freely down her cheeks. "If it happens, it happens, and that's it," he said softly.

"How can you be so casual about it?"

He took a couple of deep breaths, then spoke quickly. "I'm going to die. I'm not afraid, and I don't want anyone else to be. The difference, I guess, between my death and Jack's, is this time, right now, I get a chance to say good-bye. And I'm grateful for that."

"Sam — "

He took her hand. It was the first time he'd touched her. "Emily, the world's not going to screech to a halt when I die. I'm not saying I'm glad it's happening, but I accept it." He shrugged. "You can't imagine what a relief it is."

"But — "

"Can we please go in? If I'm going to check out, I'd rather not do it in the car. Besides, my burrito is getting cold."

23

E mily had planned to take Sam through the front door, but
that would have meant having him walk another twenty
feet, and she did not want him to waste his energy. She came
around the car and opened his door, extending a hand to help him
out. "Let's just go in the side door," she said. "I always do."

Fiber was standing in the kitchen waiting for her arrival, his
small body taut with excitement and welcome. But when he saw
that she was not alone, instead of running to her, he took a step
backward, growling softly, his divining rod of a tail stiffly lowered.
He ignored Emily and stared straight at Sam, tensed and ready to
react if the stranger made any hostile movements.

Emily said, "Since Jack died, he thinks he's a Rottweiler, especially around strangers. Let me go in first." She scooted around
Sam and entered the kitchen, kneeling in front of the dog. "It's
okay, Fi, come here!" She patted her leg, encouraging him, but the
dog held his ground and started to bark furiously, his front paws
lifting off of the floor with each yap.

"Sorry," she said, rising, "Just ignore him."

"No, wait." Slowly, carefully, Sam knelt down, his legs wobbling as his weak muscles tried to hold the unfamiliar crouch. He grabbed the edge of the counter to steady himself. "Here boy. Fiber, is it?" Emily nodded. "Fiber, that's a good dog. Come here."

Hearing his name uttered in a strange but nonthreatening voice, Fiber stopped growling. He raised his muzzle and sniffed the air warily, but finally took a tentative step forward. Sam reached his hand out. "That's a good boy. Come here. I'm not going to hurt you, or your mistress."

Fiber approached cautiously, his body tensed, ready to flee. "Thatta boy," Sam said softly. "Be friendly, and I'll share my burrito with you."

"Oh, I left them in the car," Emily said. She turned to go get them. "You be nice," she warned Fiber, and he tipped his head as though to say, *Who me? Aren't I always?*

She retrieved the box, and when she returned to the kitchen, to her surprise, Sam was sitting on the floor and Fiber was licking his face, his tail measuring his ecstasy in exuberant wags.

"You should feel honored," she said. "He's never this nice to strangers, especially on his own territory."

"Maybe I'm not a stranger to him," Sam said, "heart to heart."

Emily's jaw dropped. "You mean, you think he can tell?"

Sam shrugged. "Is it so improbable?" He scratched Fiber under the chin, and the dog closed his eyes and whined softly.

"Shall I show you around, or do you want to eat first?"

"I'd like to see the house. But do you mind if I look around on my own?"

"Well, no," Emily replied. "But why?"

How could he explain that he wanted to see if he could feel if Jack's heart was at home here? "Just curious," was all he could say.

"Okay, I'll be in here if you need anything," she said. "I'll cut up some fruit for us. Do you like pears, apples, or bananas?"

"Bananas, " he said, "as long as they come in a banana cream pie."

◌

Sam shuffled through the dining room to the living room, trying to drink in all of the details of furnishings, atmosphere, and essence. It all seemed startlingly familiar to him, the wide-planked peg-and-groove floors, carpeted with oriental rugs, the amber light spreading rays of warmth into the room, the rich smell of leather and the heady perfume of roses which he'd somehow known would be in a vase on the coffee table. But he didn't try to fool himself that this sense of déjà vu was a gift from Jack's heart. He merely accepted with gratitude the sensation of belonging to this place, a comfort he realized he'd never felt in his sister's home. Gingerly, he lowered himself into the wing chair facing the fireplace. The cushion was firm but soft beneath him, already contoured to his exact shape.

"Sam, I'm just going to take Fiber out in the yard for a minute. Are you okay?" she called from the kitchen. She watched him sink into Jack's chair and felt peaceful just knowing he was there.

"I'm fine," he said. "Just taking a breather."

The room seemed to close in around him, enveloping him in a world that was at once familiar and new — the pillows carefully plumped up on the sofa, the wood laid in the fireplace, ready to light if the weather turned cool, the leafy branches of the coral tree outside of the window, brushing gently against the window. When he closed his eyes he could imagine coming home to this room and to this life, Emily in the kitchen preparing supper, the dog at his feet, chewing contentedly on a bone.

But as he fantasized, instead of relaxing into a contented rhythm, the metronome of his heart began to beat like a pagan dance. Again! He tried to stand, to fight his way out of its grip, but each palpitation drove him further back into the chair, demonstrating that it was the master and he the slave. *Hold on,* he told himself, *this is nothing new. You know this rudiment. Let it play through.*

Suddenly, he was back in the dream — the dazzling sun of the sandy cove, the water lapping at his feet as he ran, following the arc of the shore. The harder he ran, the more shallow his breathing became. His feet were blistering in the hot sand, and his body raged with the searing burn of the sun. His mouth was dry, so very dry; a crust of white formed in the corners of his cracked lips, and his tongue poked out from between his teeth like a snake's. The water was so close he could smell its cool release, but he continued to run in the burning sand, fighting the pain and the desperate need for liquid replenishment.

Then, without warning, the world tilted, and he was running straight into the water, diving through the waves, kicking hard to propel himself into the depths. The ocean was crystal clear, and within the space of a few strokes, he saw a submerged form — it looked like a child, a boy with long hair, buoyant as flames, rising and falling around a porcelain face.

Then, with a clarity that only comes in dreams, he understood who this child was and that he had been sent to save him. He extended his arm to grasp the undulating hair, using it to pull the boy from this watery grave up to the safety of the surface and the beach. But it wasn't easy. Fear made the boy flail his arms as though in anger, as though he did not want to be saved.

But everyone wanted to be saved, to live; he was sure of it. He cried out to the child, forgetting that he was underwater, and the water gushed into his mouth and lungs. Choking and gasping for air, he knew he must rise to the surface, but he wasn't going to go without the boy.

◌

When he opened his eyes again, Emily was kneeling next to him. There was an aura of radiance around her — or was it the light streaming in from the window behind her? Mercifully, his heartbeat had retreated to a more normal pace, and he could smile at her and pretend everything was all right, that he had just been resting as he had earlier in the car.

"Cat nap," he explained. "Very comfortable."

Her tense expression relaxed. "I'm glad," she said. "The burritos are steaming. Do you want to eat in here, or in the dining room?"

"Dining room," he said. "But could I look upstairs first?"

"Okay. Let me just turn off the oven, and I'll help you."

"I'm fine," he insisted, "See?" And he did his best to pull himself up out of the chair without assistance, to prove his fitness, even though he knew it would deplete the precious store of energy he had left.

Apparently, Emily was fooled by his show of strength, or else she just wanted to believe that he was all right, because she went back to the kitchen saying, "Jonah's bedroom's on the right, ours — the master suite, that is — is down the hall to the left."

Sam waited until she disappeared before he started up the stairs, because he didn't want her to see how difficult it was for him to make the climb. Taking a deep breath, he gripped the wide mahogany banister with both hands and very slowly pulled himself up the first riser. Due to the physical therapy sessions he'd been forced to endure, he knew the best way to climb stairs: to step on the riser with his right foot, pull himself slowly up, bring his left foot up to rest alongside the right foot. Then repeat this process, taking as much time as necessary between steps, until he reached the top. It was tedious, but he had to make the climb. Not for his own sake, but for Jack's. He was taking Jack's heart home to rest.

Sam did not know that Emily was watching him. Even if he'd turned back to look — and he didn't, not once — he wouldn't have seen her, because she was hidden from his view. But she saw him struggle, ached to help him, could hardly restrain herself from running up the stairs behind him and putting her arms around his frail body, so tortured by pain and bloated with chemicals. Oh, how she wanted to help him! But she held herself back. Like Jonah, he needed to make peace with himself by himself.

Even if it was the last thing he did.

The phone rang, and reluctantly she abandoned her vigil to answer it. Sam didn't turn around to see her go, but he felt the absence of her watchful, caring eyes on him, as though the crutch which had been holding him up had been knocked out from under him. He was nearly to the top of the stairs, but he faltered now and had to rest. Was it only two weeks ago that he had been exercising *for the sheer joy of it*? Now each step was agony, each breath a labor.

He only knew he had to keep going. And that he *would* keep going. Through the years of his illness, he had long since stopped trying to second-guess his instincts. How many times had he known, utterly and completely *understood in his core* that within the next hour or day his heart would begin another terrifying riff? It was the same sort of prescience that alerted travelers to cancel their reservations on an airline that subsequently crashed. The fact that he was so tuned in to this inner drumbeat was probably the reason he was alive at this moment — that, and the skillful work of the doctors, nurses, and technicians who had orchestrated his transplant.

But the geniuses of medicine could only do so much. They knew, and he knew, that Jack's heart was now conducting the music. All he could do was listen to the beat and follow the rhythm.

Finally he reached the top of the stairs, and he rested there, leaning hard against the railing, hearing Jack's heart pounding against the walls of his chest like some damn demon with a battering ram. The pain was intense and frightening, but Sam reveled in it. He was still alive. He had done the right thing by coming here: Jack's heart *knew*.

As much as he wanted to see the boy's room, he was driven by a manic urgency toward the master bedroom. Time was his enemy, and this realization forced him to push past the pain and the debilitating sense of exhaustion, to focus only on achieving his goal.

The distance was short, about ten paces for a healthy person, perhaps thirty shuffling steps for someone with a sick heart. Sam forced himself into a six-point rhythm: left foot forward — rest, rest. Right foot forward — rest, rest. The little dog charged up the stairs and streaked by him into the bedroom. Sam heard the jangle of his collar as he leapt onto the bed, then off again. He appeared in the doorway to the bedroom, head cocked to one side, waiting, wondering why it was taking Sam so long to get there.

I know, pal, it's a real pain in the ass, Sam thought, but did not waste his energy saying.

Finally — and in Sam's mind, it was a finale, the last few steps he could take — he reached the door to the bedroom. He leaned against the doorjamb with his eyes closed, dizzy and gasping for air, wondering with each inhalation if it would be his last. He didn't dare look at the room yet, focusing all of his remaining strength on regaining his equilibrium. He felt as though he were standing at the gates to heaven, about to cross the threshold of eternity. Odd that he of all people, a man who had shunned religion and ignored the question of God — which was worse than denying His existence, since denial would have implied an acknowledgment of at least the *potential* for His existence — was now thinking of heaven and eternity. Perhaps this was part of the process of dying — and he was dying, of that he had no doubt.

He felt a gentle weight fall on his foot, and he opened his eyes. The dog was standing before him, wagging his tail. Once he had Sam's attention, he looked down at the stuffed toy he had just dropped on Sam's right foot, a somewhat bedraggled, slightly chewed dog with angel's wings. Then he jumped up onto the bed, wagging his tail, a clear invitation for Sam to join him.

Sam looked around the room. It was eerie, but he had a clear sense that he had been there before. It wasn't what he saw, the details of flooring, furniture, and fabric, but the way he felt the sensation of comfort and well-being. The early afternoon light was stronger here than downstairs, and it filtered through the branches of the coral tree just outside, streaking in through the window, uplifting and warming him. Fear and pain could not possibly survive in the presence of this brilliance, he was sure, and so Sam felt his spirits rise.

Now that his goal was in sight, he felt a resurgence of energy, his final reserve — what was there to save it for now? He started to walk again, this time toward the bed. Steadying himself on the dresser as he passed, he noticed a picture in a silver frame and stopped to look at it. It was a wedding photo of Emily and Jack. It was the first photograph he had seen of his benefactor, and he stared at it hungrily.

He had been curious about Jack's physical appearance, but Emily had not been specific. Perhaps she'd thought it would depress Sam to put a face on the man whose death had prolonged his life. So in the absence of a picture, Sam had visualized a Tom Selleck look-alike, a handsome, healthy, vigorous man whose heart was so strong that it had survived the death of his body. But the man in the picture was small, barely larger than Emily. While she looked beautiful and bridal in a veiled hat and a tailored beige suit, he was wearing a raucous tie, wide and clownlike, splashed with bright colors. She was smiling decorously into the camera, but he was grinning madly, his arm raised behind and above her elegant hat, preparing to pour a glass of champagne over her.

He shuffled the few remaining steps to the bed, holding the photo in his hand. He touched the spread, a soft woven material. Slowly, he lowered himself until he was sitting, then he stayed there, resting, getting the feel of the mattress. It was like a cloud, firm but pliant, some kind of foam. It called to him, begging him to lie down.

He thought, *This is the place I have come to die.*

He lay back, and then, strangely, the dog came and lay quietly beside him, the dog-angel toy still in his mouth. "Good boy," Sam said, stroking him contentedly. And then he closed his eyes.

Emily was coming up the stairs when she heard the crash, the tinkle of broken glass. She took the remaining risers two at a time and ran to the bedroom. Sam was lying on the bed with his eyes closed. At first she thought he was asleep. And he was, in a way, hovering in that ether between life and death. Fiber was by his side, an expression of bafflement on his face. Her wedding photo lay on the floor, obviously released from the grip of Sam's outstretched hand. The dog stood when he saw her, guiltily wagging his tail.

"Sam? Are you all right?" she said softly, trying not to panic. When he did not answer, she approached and sat on the edge of the bed by his side. His face was relaxed and peaceful, his mouth slightly open. She cautiously picked up his hand, fearing it would be cold and stiff. But it was pliant and warm. A good sign. She shook him gently. "Sam, Sam," she repeated, liking the sound of his name. She pressed her head to his chest, and thought she could hear a heart beating, but it might have been her own.

What should she do? Try CPR? Or was he carrying some emergency medication? She should have asked the doctor. This was exactly the situation she had feared. But now that the worst had happened, she wasn't afraid any more, simply anxious to do the right thing. But what was the right thing?

The only thought she had was to call the hospital and ask for Sam's floor. Mary, the nice nurse who seemed to take a special interest in him, answered the phone. When Emily told her what had happened, she asked for the address and told her to sit tight, the ambulance was on its way.

24

*A*n instant later — or so it seemed to Emily — the doorbell rang. She hadn't taken her eyes off Sam, hadn't removed her hand from his neck, holding on for dear life to the fragile pulse beating there.

She ran down the stairs to let the paramedics in. But it was Gary Forrester standing at the door. "Hi," he said, "I came to drop off — "

"Gary!" Emily craned her neck to look past him, but there was no ambulance in the driveway, no paramedics coming up the walk. "Come help me!"

Gary turned to look back at the street, confused by her blank expression and her total indifference to his presence. "Are you okay?" he asked.

Leaving the door open, Emily charged back up the stairs. "I'm waiting for the paramedics," she called. "I think my friend is dying!"

Fiber was standing on the bed barking when she ran into the bedroom. Sam's position had not changed, but his eyes were open.

"Sam!" she cried, running to his side. "Are you okay? God, you gave me a scare."

His face had a blue tinge. He was shivering and clammy to her touch. "Damn dog woke me up," he managed to gasp.

Gary appeared in the doorway. "Em — I ..." He stopped when he saw Sam on the bed. "Geez, for a minute I thought it was Jack. Who ...?"

"This is Sam ..." She took his hand and rubbed it between hers. "He's the man who has Jack's heart," she said, smiling bravely. "Sam, this is Gary, an old friend of Jack's."

"Any ... friend ... of ... Jack's ... is ... a ... friend ... of ... mine," Sam said, struggling with each word.

"How long has he been like this?" Gary asked.

"Just a few minutes," she said, not taking her eyes off Sam. "Sam, can you breathe?" She seemed to have lost her own ability to inhale.

Sam opened his mouth to speak, but no sound came out, only a gasp for air. And then his body went limp.

"Sam!" Emily cried. She pulled the pillow out from under Sam's head so he was lying flat on the bed. "Gary, help me!" She pinched his nostrils together and opened his mouth, leaning close to him. "Push on his chest, hard!"

Gary hesitated. "Come on!" she commanded.

Gingerly, Gary lay his hands on Sam's chest, one on top of the other, and pushed down. "Harder!" Emily said. Gary pushed again, this time with more force. Emily bent down and put her lips on Sam's mouth. She felt the hard chill of his lips, tasted the taint of decay. She came up for air.

Thinking it was a game, Fiber pounced playfully on Sam and then stuck his snout at Emily, licking her lips as she lowered them to Sam's. "No!" she cried and pushed him away. "Get back!"

Surprised at her harsh tone, Fiber retreated, and Emily repositioned herself to give Sam another breath. "Again!" she called to

Gary, and she bent her head to Sam. *Don't die,* Emily prayed, *please don't die.*

Was it her imagination or was the color returning to Sam's face? She stared down at him, hoping for a reprieve, and in that instant, Sam's face became Jack's.

It was Jack lying there on the bed.

And this was the chance she had never had, to save his life. Her energy restored by the realization that she didn't have to stand by helplessly, that she could affect the outcome of this crisis, or at least try, she bent again to give her breath to the dying man. *I will keep you alive,* she thought. *Please don't die, Jack.*

Fiber heard the paramedics first and leapt off the bed, barking furiously. Gary followed him to the top of the stairs. "We're up here," he shouted.

Footsteps echoed on the wooden stairs. Emily lifted her head, and two paramedics appeared in the doorway. They didn't wait for permission to enter, but approached the bed with authority. One reached for Sam's wrist, while the other slipped an oxygen mask over his nose and mouth.

"Heart attack?" the first asked.

"Rejection, I think." Emily panted. "He's had a transplant."

"Okay, let's get him moved."

With swift ease, they transferred Sam onto a portable stretcher and secured him to it with Velcro straps. As Emily and Gary watched, they wheeled him out of the room and carefully lifted the stretcher down the staircase.

"I'll stay with Fiber if you want," Gary offered.

"Thanks," Emily replied. "I'll call later." And she ran down the stairs and out the door. Once the paramedics had Sam loaded, she climbed in the back. One of the medics got in after her; the other shut the doors and went around to the driver's seat.

"How is he?" Emily asked.

"His heartbeat's pretty erratic, but at least it's pumping," the paramedic replied. "What's your husband's name, ma'am?"

"Jack," Emily said, without thinking, "Jack Barnes." But then she saw that the paramedic was typing the name on a small computer. "But this isn't my husband. This isn't Jack. This is Sam. I mean Steven, Steven Sampson. " She took Sam's hand and rubbed it between her own. "But it's Jack too."

The paramedic looked confused.

"He has my husband's heart," she clarified.

And my own, she thought.

○

"He's still unconscious, but stable for the time being," Dr. Greshom told Diana. Emily had called her from the ambulance, and the two women had been waiting together in silent vigil while the doctors attended to Sam. "But I can't give you a long-term prognosis," he continued, "because there isn't one. Unless we can find him a new heart, I'm afraid he will not survive more than a few days, a week at most."

Diana began to cry. "I can't believe this is happening again! Oh, Sam." She leaned against Emily and wept bitterly. "He doesn't deserve to die."

Dr. Greshom's face remained impassive. "Nobody does, Mrs. Harper." Then he softened. "There is a positive side to this emergency: because of the severity of his condition, he moves higher up on the list, so if a donor heart comes in and it's compatible, it's his — unless another potential recipient who has not yet been given a first heart takes a turn for the worse."

"Why is that?" Diana asked.

"We have to give precedence to first-time recipients for obvious reasons, one being that there is a greater likelihood that this patient's body will reject again, since it has done so already. Sometimes the host body simply refuses to accept a new organ, and it's not as though we have hearts to spare. In any event, it all depends on whether a donor is found in time, and if the heart is compatible."

"What will happen to Jack's heart?" Emily tried to steel herself to the idea that one way or the other, Jack's heart was going to be removed from Sam's body, that this final part of her husband might die.

"We'll take a look at it once we get it out, see how badly it's been damaged by the rejection mechanism of Mr. Sampson's body. If the damage is minor and correctable, we might be able to make a few adjustments and give it to one of our older, high-risk patients."

"I don't understand," Diana said.

"It's a relatively new program here, maybe a tad experimental for some. The fact is, some harvested organs are not in perfect condition and may not last more than a few years. Normally, damaged organs are not transplanted into a person like your brother who lacks only a healthy heart to live a long, healthy life. But to a person in their seventies or eighties, or a person with other debilitating ailments — diabetes, AIDS, some forms of cancer — people for whom even a few extra years would be a gift, even a damaged heart would be better than no heart at all.

"But the final decision is up to the donor and the recipient — that is, we need permission from Mr. Sampson to use the heart again, and we need to make sure the potential recipient is aware of the risks.

"This brings up another issue," Dr. Greshom said somberly. "If we do not find Mr. Sampson a new heart, there will be the matter of his other organs which, like the heart, could be life-saving to other patients, if they are harvested in time. If he doesn't regain consciousness it will be your decision to make."

A nurse came into the room. "Excuse me, doctor, could I have a word?"

Dr. Greshom stepped away to speak to her. He turned his back to the women for privacy.

Diana put her hands over her mouth and shook her head violently back and forth. "I can't think about that while Sam is still alive," she whispered.

Emily's heart ached for her. "I understand. But think how valuable Jack's heart was to Sam. You know how good he would feel to be able to help someone else live."

"I can't think about it," Diana sobbed.

The doctor returned, overhearing. "Maybe you won't have to right now, Mrs. Harper. Your brother has regained consciousness."

○

"I need to remind you that his condition is still critical," Dr. Greshom warned the women as they approached Sam's room. "He could go quickly, or he could linger. But the chances of his making a full recovery at this stage without a new heart are ... well, I don't want to rule out the possibility of a miracle, but it would definitely take one." He pushed open the door.

Sam was barely visible at the center of a ring of life-sustaining and monitoring equipment. Gowned and masked and warned to keep their distance, Emily and Diana came closer. Emily ached with the memory of visiting Jack in a room like this the night after his accident. As Jack had been then, Sam was very, very still, as pale and ephemeral as a cloud. His eyes were closed, and his lips clung to a tube, through which air was being forced into his lungs, saving him the effort of breathing. Except for the infinitesimal rise and fall of his chest with the ebb and flow of oxygen, it looked like Death had already paid its visit. Indeed, it was surely waiting close by.

But when Diana took her brother's hand and squeezed it, he opened his eyes. "Sam," she said. "It's Diana, little brother. I love you, Sammy."

Although his face remained expressionless, his eyes slowly closed and then reopened, clearly a grateful acknowledgment of her compassion.

"They're going to find you another heart," Diana continued. "Dr. Greshom said you're at the top of the list, so don't worry. You just have to hang on."

With enormous effort, Sam moved his head a fraction of an inch to one side, then to the other, and closed his eyes. Diana was worried. "What is it, Sam? What is it?"

He raised his hand slightly off the bed and motioned that he wanted to write something. Emily got a pen and paper from her purse. She tried to put the pen in Sam's hand, but he couldn't hold it. So she wrapped her hand around his and let him guide it on the paper. In wobbly handwriting, he wrote the single word "NO."

Diana looked at Emily. "No what?" she asked. "No, you can't wait? I understand, sweetie. They're doing their best to find you a new heart. We're all praying."

Sam wrote again on the pad. His effort was labored and slow. Finally, when he dropped the pen, they saw that he'd written "more" after the word "no."

"Of course, there's more," Diana said. "You can't give up, Sam. You have to be strong."

"Sam, *you* don't have to do anything, the doctors will take care of you," Emily chimed in.

Sam closed his eyes. Very slowly, his hand moved onto the paper on which he had written, pointing to the words there.

"That's enough for now," the doctor said. He ushered them out into the hall. "Do you have any more questions?"

Diana was dry-eyed. "If he doesn't get a new heart, how long does he have?"

"Diana, don't torture yourself," Emily said.

"I need to know." She looked at the doctor. "How long?"

"As I said earlier — "

"How long?" she demanded.

Dr. Greshom sighed. "He could have an extreme episode at any moment. But the chance of that should be diminished by the medication we are giving him." His beeper sounded, and he removed it from his belt, squinting to read the message on the small screen. He squeezed Diana's arm. "I'll be back to see him tonight," he said, and hurried off down the hall.

Diana stood staring after him, her mouth agape. A nurse put her arm around her shoulders. "Why don't we go to the visitors' lounge?" she asked. "I'll get you a cup of tea."

Diana allowed herself to be led away. But Emily noticed Elaine Greenberg stepping out of the elevator, and hung back.

"Mrs. Harper," Elaine Greenberg called to Diana.

Emily intercepted her, shaking her head. "Not now," she said. Her voice was soft but firm.

"It's my job, Mrs. Barnes, you of all people should appreciate that." She tried to walk around Emily, but Emily blocked her way.

"*You* of all people should appreciate the importance of timing, Mrs. Greenberg," Emily replied. "There is still a chance that Mr. Sampson will recover."

"Of course you want to be hopeful, but — "

"Yes, so please allow us to have hope."

"Still, Mrs. Harper should be made aware of her brother's wishes," Elaine Greenberg called after her.

Emily stopped walking, then turned and slowly walked back to Elaine Greenberg. "What do you mean?"

"Mr. Sampson signed the donor papers days ago. He's giving his organs to us, I just have to coordinate — "

"I will take responsibility for seeing that she knows Sam already signed the papers," Emily said.

"But — "

But Emily had already turned to walk away.

"Poor Sam," Diana said when Emily joined her in the visitor's lounge. "He isn't thinking clearly. The drugs must be affecting his brain."

Emily thought about what one of the orderlies had said to her after Jack died. *I told him if the fight was too difficult or if there was too much pain, that you would understand and still love him, even if he let go.* "Diana," she said aloud, "I think you have to consider the possibility that he *is* thinking clearly."

"What?" Diana was taken aback.

"He may be tired of the fight. Not only the constant fear of rejection, but of living with the side effects of the drugs and the pain. Don't you think it's possible that he may be asking for your permission to die?"

"How dare you!" Diana cried. "Just because you have nothing left to lose."

"That's not true," Emily said quietly. "I have Sam to lose too. But in the end, it's his decision."

25

*E*mily awoke gasping for breath, suffocated by a sense of impending doom. She lay still, blinking in the darkness to allow cognition to catch up with intuition, and finally, it did: Sam was in the hospital, dying.

A split-second later, the phone rang. She knew before she picked up the receiver that it would be the Medical Center calling. It was. But it was not the call she expected.

"Is this Emily Barnes?" the voice on the other end asked.

"Yes," she said softly, steeling herself for what she knew was to come.

"One minute please, doctor would like to speak with you."

Get on with it, Emily said to herself, waiting for Dr. Greshom to come to the phone. *Tell me that Sam has died.*

"Emily?"

It was a woman's voice. "Andrea?" Emily asked. "What — are you — is it Sam?"

"No," Dr. Leventhal said. "It's not Sam." Her voice was even, but Emily knew her well enough now to hear anguish behind the words. Instinctively, she braced herself, for what she did not know.

"It's Jonah."

"Jonah!" Emily sat up straight in bed. "What happened? Where is he?"

"He's here," Dr. Leventhal said. "There was an anonymous 911 call and paramedics picked him up down by the beach. He's ... I'm so sorry to have to tell you this. It was a drug overdose. We're still trying to figure out what the substance was ..."

"Is he alive?"

"He's in a coma. We have him intubated. There may be organ damage. We're trying to assess it now."

"Oh, Lord," Emily threw back the covers and leapt out of bed. "I'm coming," she said, tearing off her nightgown. "Andrea, don't let him die!"

With an unearthly sense of calm, Emily backed the car out of the driveway and turned in the direction of Westside Medical Center. She thought about how familiar the route had become. Three months ago she had received the urgent call about Jack's accident, had sped to the hospital, unable to think, barely able to breathe. And now it was happening again. But this time she was dry-eyed and controlled, as though that first stunning tragedy had had a purpose after all: to prepare her for this even greater horror.

She picked up the car phone and dialed Matt's and Lauren's number. After two rings, Lauren's sleep-graveled voice came on the line.

"Lauren, it's Emily. Put Matt on, please."

Lauren was instantly awake. "What is it? What's wrong?"

"Jonah's in the hospital. He overdosed, they don't know what drug — " She skidded to a halt, halfway through a red light. Then, seeing that there was no traffic in either direction, she stepped on the gas and sped on through the intersection.

"Oh, my God, Oh my God!" Lauren cried. "Emily, Matt's not here! He's on a retreat. I don't even know how to reach him. I'll come! I'll meet you there."

Despite her own distress, Emily pitied the anguish in Lauren's voice. The last thing she needed was to have to worry about Lauren. "No, don't." Emily said, "Stay there. I'll call you back when I know more. If you find Matt, tell him I'm at the Medical Center."

She pressed the *end* button and immediately dialed Ann's number. It took Ann three rings to answer.

"Hello?" Ann's voice was muffled, dreamlike.

"Ann," Emily said sharply, "let me speak to Matt."

"Emily? He's not — "

"Put him on, Ann. It's an emergency. It's Jonah."

"Ohmygod."

She heard some murmuring and shuffling, then finally Matt's familiar voice came on the line. "Emily? What is it? What about Jonah?"

"He's in the hospital. An overdose."

"Is he okay?"

"It sounds bad. He's on life support. They think there might be some organ damage."

"Jesus, God!" Matt said.

"Yes, I think prayer is a good idea," Emily said grimly.

"Will you pick me up?" Matt asked. "I don't have my car."

She could see the parking structure of the hospital looming ahead. "I'm almost there now," she said. "Have Ann bring you." And without waiting for a reply, she pushed the *end* button.

$$\circlearrowright$$

Andrea Leventhal was waiting for Emily at the admittance desk. She wrapped her arms around her. "My friend," she whispered in Emily's ear. "I am so sorry this is happening to Jonah, and to you."

"How is he?" Emily asked.

"He's in a hepatic coma. That means whatever he took has shut his liver down. We are assessing the damage now."

"But shouldn't you do something, some treatment, if he's in such a precarious — "

"I've called in our liver specialist, Jim Rudolph. He's the best, believe me. If there is no change in twelve hours, I presume he will want to operate."

The nurse put a sheaf of papers on the counter. "You will need to read this, Mrs. Barnes, and sign at the bottom of each page."

Emily bit her lip to keep her emotions in check. "Can I see him first?"

"Come with me," Andrea said, and pushed through the double doors labeled "I.C.U. Staff Only."

"It was just luck, if you can consider anything about a tragedy like this luck, that I was on duty when he was brought in, and that we weren't swamped," Andrea said. "If it had been last Saturday night, forget it. There was an explosion at one of the refineries in El Segundo. Every E.R. on the West Side was — there he is, there's Jim."

A tall man in green surgical dress was coming down the hall. "Dr. Rudolph, this is Emily Barnes, the patient's mother," Andrea said. "Emily, Jim Rudolph."

He nodded to her, his eyes sympathetic, then he turned to Andrea. "Let's take a look at what we've got," he said. And together they went into Jonah's room.

Emily had never seen her son so still. He lay on his back, his arms at his sides, his eyes closed. Startlingly, his skin was tinged yellow. "Jonah, darling." Emily stepped closer, and the nurse tried to restrain her.

"It's all right," Andrea Leventhal said, and the nurse retreated.

Emily stood at the head of the bed, looking down at the face of her dying son. How could this child be wrenched away from her? She reached out a hand to stroke his face, and her heart clutched when she felt the nascent stubble of beard on his cheek. "I love you, darling," she said.

"Mrs. Barnes, I'd like to examine Jonah, if I may," Dr. Rudolph said softly.

"Yes, please," Emily replied.

"It would be best if you waited outside."

How could she leave? But Andrea was gently taking her arm and pulling her away. Reluctantly, Emily let herself be led back to the reception area.

○

Matt and Ann jumped to their feet when they saw Emily approaching. "How is he?" Matt asked. "Where is he?"

"It's his liver," Emily told them. "It stopped working The specialist is examining him now. If there's no improvement in twelve hours, they'll operate, to see if they can repair it."

"Jesus," Matt gasped, as though all the wind had been knocked out of him.

"Emily, I'm so sorry," Ann wailed.

"So am I," Emily said. "So am I."

"I should have seen that he was hurting, that I wasn't giving him enough attention," Matt said in a voice choked with anguish. "I'll never forgive myself if he dies."

"This isn't about it being your fault, or your forgiving yourself, Matt," Emily said. "It's about Jonah living or dying. We just have to pray that he isn't taken from us."

"Can I see him?" Matt demanded.

Andrea stepped forward. "I'll take you back, Mr. Keller. We'll see if Dr. Rudolph has finished his examination."

"Who are you?" Matt asked.

"Sorry, I'm Dr. Leventhal," she said. "Come with me."

Left alone, Ann and Emily stood awkwardly together, neither knowing what to say. Finally, Ann spoke. "Em, for what it's worth, Matt and I are breaking it off. I went to the doctor and found out my ovaries are shriveled up like prunes. So I can forget hoping I'm going to get pregnant. Anyway, trying to use Matt as a sperm bank, that was just a misguided ego trip on my part, and I regret every minute of it. I'm just … so very, very sorry. Can you ever forgive me?"

"That seems so unimportant now." Emily wrapped her arms around her friend and they stood that way for a time. "Ann, I want you to be godmother to my baby," she whispered.

"What?"

"I mean it. I want you to be godmother to this little guy," she patted her stomach.

"Oh, Em," Ann said, " I don't deserve — "

Emily brought her finger to her lips. "Please, we need you to be our family now."

○

"His ALT level is more than three times the normal level," Dr. Rudolph told Emily and Matt when the tests were concluded. "Also, his bilirubin is elevated in the blood. That and the level of serum albumin concentration indicate virtually no liver function. His condition is severely critical."

Emily tried to concentrate on what Dr. Rudolph was saying, but there was blood on the doctor's green surgical shirt, and she couldn't stop thinking, *this is Jonah's blood. This is the blood of my son.*

"We still don't know what drug caused this condition. It could be something as simple as a combination of a large dose of acetaminophen taken with alcohol, or other drugs such as chlorpromzine, phenytoin, even vitamin A or niacin, although the history you gave the nurse doesn't indicate that he was taking any medication, or that he had any specific ailments requiring drug treatment. So it is baffling."

"A few months ago, Jonah started hanging out with some kids who were into drugs. Maybe someone gave him something tainted or mislabeled," Matt said.

"I'm sorry to say it, but it happens more often than you'd like to think. In any event, the only option left to us at this point is to remove the damaged organ and transplant a healthy liver. But unfortunately, we can't just go to the organ bank and pull one out. The term *organ bank* is kind of a misnomer. There are long lists of people waiting for — "

"My husband was an organ donor," Emily interrupted. "We know about the lists and the shortage of organs."

The doctor nodded. "Then you also know we need to find a liver that's compatible."

"How much time is there, doctor?" Matt asked.

"I can't say. As you know, he's in a coma now. He could linger in that state, or he could go any time."

Emily and Matt sat staring blankly at the doctor. "Is there anything else we can do? Anyone we can call?" Emily asked.

The doctor shrugged sadly. "I wish I could tell you — "

"What if you took a piece of my liver," Matt said. "I've heard that the liver regenerates, isn't that so? Can't I give him some of mine?"

"Matt, you know you can't. I can't either." She turned to the doctor. "We got hepatitis on a trip to Mexico. Both of us. That makes it impossible for us to be donors, doesn't it?"

"I'm afraid it does, Mr. Keller, I'm sorry."

◯

"Em, do you mind if I have a minute alone with him?" Matt asked.

They were sitting on either side of their son, waiting, praying for a miracle. Emily bit her lip to keep her emotions in check. There had been no change in Jonah's condition and, according to the doctor, a minute might be all the time he had left. But how could she deny Jonah's father a private good-bye to his son? "I'll go find some coffee," she said. "Do you want some?"

"No, nothing," Matt said. "Thank you." She nodded and got up to go. Matt grabbed her hand. He had tears in his eyes. "No, Em, really. I mean it. Thank you for bearing this child, for giving him life. Thank you for sharing him with me. You know how much I mean it."

She squeezed his hand. "I know, Matt," she said.

The hospital was quiet at this late hour, almost peaceful. As Emily walked down the hall, she knew she would remember every detail of this night: the close, warm air of the hallway, the odor of disinfectant on the linoleum floor, the hushed laughter of the nurses, cheerful to be going about their tasks without the audience of worried relatives, omnipresent during the day.

"Can I get something for you, Mrs. Barnes?" one of them asked as she passed the reception desk.

"I'm just going to the cafeteria to get some coffee," she said.

"Gosh, it's locked up tight at this hour," the nurse said. "They close at 7 P.M., if you can believe it."

"It doesn't matter. I just need to go *someplace.*"

"I don't know if you're religious, but on the first floor, in the east wing, there's a small chapel. I go there sometimes, when I need to clear my mind."

"Thanks," Emily said. "Maybe I will."

She got in the elevator and pushed the button for the first floor, not realizing until the doors were closed that the car was going up. She closed her eyes and leaned against the wall. It didn't really matter whether she went to the chapel or stayed in the elevator car; the image of her son lying in a hospital bed so near death was all she could see. With Jack, the doctors had worked for hours to save his life, but in the end nothing they could do could save him. But Jonah's life *could* be saved, they had the expertise and the equipment. But without a healthy, compatible liver, nevertheless, he would die.

The elevator doors opened, and Emily glanced up to see what floor she was on. Eight. Sam's floor. She realized she hadn't even thought about Sam since she'd gotten word of Jonah's overdose. Was he still here?

She stepped out and moved aside as an orderly pushed an empty gurney into the elevator. The nurse on duty was occupied, taking curt instructions from a resident, so Emily was able to slip past her, down the hall to Sam's cubicle without being noticed.

The lights were out, but she saw with relief that the monitors behind the bed were registering steadily. Sam was alone, but the room was filled with evidence of Diana's love — a hand-crocheted quilt on the bed, framed photographs on the nightstand, a CD player and a stack of cassettes on the bureau. Taped to the headboard was a child's drawing. "Get well soon, Uncle Sam," it said at the top. "Love, Grace Claire Harper."

Emily moved closer to the bed. Sam's breathing tube had been removed from his mouth, and he was receiving oxygen through two plastic tubes running into his nose. This was a good sign!

She stood in the dark, thinking of all this man had gone through to stay alive. Had it been worth it to him, the pain, the agonizing emotional strain, the roller coaster ride of his illness? He had fought so long and so hard. And for what? A few extra months of life?

"Oh, Sam," she whispered. "I wish I were as brave as you." And she began to cry.

"Why are you crying?"

Emily looked up, incredulous. "Sam? You're awake?"

"Come," he said.

She walked to the head of the bed and sat in the chair. "Do you feel better?"

He tried to smile, but his mouth barely moved. "Picture of health," he said. Then he frowned, and very slowly he raised his hand to her cheek and wiped away a tear. "What?"

"It's Jonah," she said, and the relief of releasing her grief made her legs weak. She let her body crumple onto his bed. "He overdosed, and his liver shut down," she said. "He's in a coma."

"Transplant?" he asked in a whisper.

She shook her head. "You know the story: there's not an organ available, and they're not giving us any hope of finding one in time. He could go any minute. In fact, I've got to get back. I just left to give Matt a chance to ... to say good-bye to him."

She stood to go. "At least ... at least Jack will be there waiting when he arrives. Jonah doesn't do too well in new situations. I'm glad that he'll see a familiar face, someone who loves him."

Sam watched Emily drift out of his room. He knew it would be the last time he saw her, but he didn't try to say good-bye. His fingers groped across the bed until they found the call button for the nurse. He pressed it twice, saw the red light come on over his head, and closed his eyes. For the first time in a long time, he felt at peace. It was all starting to make sense.

A nurse appeared. "Mr. Sampson? Do you need something?"

"Please call Dr. Ohanian."

"Dr. Ohan — you mean that young resident with the ponytail?"

Sam nodded.

"Let me help you myself," the nurse said. "What do you need?"

"Dr. Ohanian. I need Dr. Ohanian."

26

*M*rs. Barnes, Mr. Keller, I have news!"

Sitting on either side of Jonah's bed, Emily and Matt looked up, their eyes bleary with grief and lack of sleep.

"We have a liver," Dr. Rudolph said. "If it's a match, your son has a chance."

Emily and Matt rose to their feet and hugged each other, and then they reached out to embrace the doctor. "Thank God!" Matt said. "Thank God!"

The doctor held up his hand. "Before you get your hopes up, I've got to tell you that this organ may not be perfect."

"I don't understand," Matt said.

The doctor nodded. "Let me explain. The donor was not a healthy man, and there is no way of telling if the liver is fully operational. It is functioning, yes, but it may not be in optimum condition. We can wait and hope that a healthy liver comes in, but we are in a race against time, and the odds are against us. I will tell you honestly that some doctors and some hospitals do not advocate the transplantation of questionable organs for obvious reasons: it is a difficult surgical procedure with its own risks, and it is an expensive one. If the organ fails, it is everyone's loss. However if it *doesn't* fail....

"Our philosophy at Westside Medical is to offer the family the option — you see, some patients aren't even eligible to go on a list to wait for a perfect organ. I'm talking about the very elderly and patients who have other ailments, such as diabetes, which put them at high risk. So this program offers them at least a chance.

"I am suggesting the possibility of including your son in the program simply because he is so young and healthy — he is too vital to let him just slip away."

"If he has this transplant now, does it mean he would be ineligible for another liver, a perfect one?" Matt asked.

"That's a good point. If the surgery is a success, but the organ proves defective, he would go back on the list. But of course he would be at the bottom. Also, you'd have to sign a release, indemnifying the hospital, stipulating that you are aware that the organ may not be healthy — in case he doesn't survive the surgery. "

"Doesn't survive," Matt mumbled in horror.

Matt and Emily clung to each other with tears streaming down their faces. "How can we make this decision? It's too hard!" Matt cried.

"I'm sorry I can't give you better options. But you must decide quickly: either we continue to wait and hope, or we move quickly to transplant the liver we have. Because if you don't want to use this organ, we will find someone else who does."

Emily spoke first. "Matt, it does sound very risky, but it's a chance for Jonah to live. I think we should let Dr. Rudolph try it."

"Em, how can we risk it?" Matt was floundering, looking to her to be strong.

"How can we not? Matt, I know you agree with me. The doctor can't say it in so many words, but it's not just *a* chance, it's Jonah's *only* chance. Do you want to just sit by and let him die? Isn't it better to at least try something?"

Matt lay his head on Jonah's inert body. "You're right," he said softly. "Okay."

The doctor nodded at a nurse waiting at the door, and she entered with the surgical team behind her. "There are papers to sign, so we'd better get started," Dr. Rudolph said. "We'll need to get Jonah prepped immediately."

Emily bent to kiss Jonah's cheek. "Don't be afraid, honey. We'll be there when you wake up."

Matt knelt by Jonah's side. "Good-bye son. God be with you."

○

Lauren was waiting for Matt in the reception area. She wrapped her arms around him and led him to the couch. "He's going to be okay, baby," she said. "I'm sure of it."

Emily watched Matt surrender to the succor of his young wife and felt a pang of loneliness. Where could she go? Who would share her anxiety? Who would understand her terror and give her comfort? There was only one person she could think of, and he was close by.

She took the elevator to Sam's floor. It was mid-morning, and the floor nurse was monitoring all visitors.

"Excuse me," she said, "you've come to see ..."

"Steven Sampson."

The nurse frowned. "I'm terribly sorry, Mr. Sampson is no longer with us."

"Not again! Where have you put him this time?"

The nurse was taken aback. "We haven't *put him* anywhere. Mr. Sampson expired at 4:55 A.M.," she said.

"No!" The word came out in a choked scream.

"I'm very sorry. But he was terminal, you know. Sometimes it's a blessing — "

"No! It is not a blessing!" Emily cried, and pushed past the people in her way until she was at the entrance to Sam's cubicle. Sure enough, the bed was empty, fresh sheets were stacked on the mattress, and the battalion of monitors behind the bed stood a silent guardian.

○

Somehow Emily remembered that the night nurse had told her about the chapel on the first floor, and through a daze of grief, anxiety, and disbelief, she found her way there. She sat in the front pew, her knees almost touching the small altar, put her head in her hands, and cried.

She cried for Sam, for the fact that he had lost his long, arduous struggle, and that she had not been there to ease his passage.

She cried for Jack, that he, too, had died alone and before his time.

She cried for Jonah, that his young life was hanging so precariously in the balance.

She cried for all of the people she had known whose lives ended before it was rightly their time to go.

"Mrs. Barnes."

Emily looked up. A young doctor with a ponytail was standing beside her, but in the dim light she couldn't make out his face.

"My name is Aram Ohanian."

The name did not register with Emily. She just stared at him.

"Have you had any news about your son's transplant?" he asked.

Her head whipped around. "How did you know about Jonah?"

"The Tin Man told me."

"But he's — "

Dr. Ohanian nodded. "He's gone, yes. But I saw him before he went. D'you mind if I sit down, Mrs. Barnes?"

Emily slid over so the young doctor could sit next to her. "He was some kind of a guy, the Tin Man."

"Yes, he was."

"Right to the end."

"You were with him when he died?"

Dr. Ohanian hesitated. "Well, I was, yes."

"I hope he went peacefully," Emily said.

"That he did, I guarantee it."

They sat in silence for a moment.

"He asked me to give you this." He put a roll of Lifesavers in her hand. "He told me to tell you that they were for your son."

"For Jonah?"

"Mrs. Barnes, I think he wanted me to tell you this, but it's hard to know how to say it." He took a deep breath. "Let me put it this way: the Tin Man was dying and he knew it. A few hours, a few days. It was just a matter of when, so he chose his time. He chose to go this early morning."

Emily's eyes widened. "How do you know it was his choice?"

"He pulled the plug — so to speak — himself. Let's just say I put it within his reach."

"But why?"

"Your son needed a liver. That was one thing the Tin Man had that he could give. He wanted me to tell you ..." he stopped and reached into his hip pocket. "Here, I wrote it down." He withdrew a crumpled piece of paper. "May I read it to you?"

"Yes, please."

"*Emily,*" he read, "*In my life I never took the trouble to do any-one any good, so I'm glad I could at least do some good in my death. I've told The Organ Bank people that I want Jonah to have my liver. I don't know if it's in great shape, but at least it works. Maybe it'll keep him going long enough to get a better one, or until those doctors come up with a cure. Now I'm no hero, so don't mourn me, and don't think you have to thank me. It's Jack's gift, really, Jack's gift to Jonah. I was just the way station. You can't imagine how good it feels to go, knowing that. Take heart, Sam.*"

Epilogue

*T*he memorial service was brief, and nobody wore black. It took place on a glorious July day, and what everyone would remember was the procession to the burial site — Party Line had hired a jazz band to lead the mourners from the gate of the cemetery to Sam's final resting place, a distance of nearly half a mile. So at a nod from Ann, strains of *Precious Lord, Take My Hand* floated over the lush green hills of Forest Lawn, as the musicians moved forward. They walked slowly, in deference to the mourners in wheelchairs: Jonah, still recovering from his surgery, rode in one pushed by Matt and Lauren; Sam's mother was in another, pushed by her grandson Kevin, somber, and surprisingly stripped of all visible body piercings, and behind them, nearly a dozen transplant recipients from the Medical Center.

The hospital staff was also well-represented: Drs. Greshom, Ohanian, Rudolph, and Leventhal, and enough interns, nurses, and technicians that someone thought to wonder who was still at the hospital to take care of the patients.

Diana and Emily walked arm-in-arm just behind the band. Both were dry-eyed and smiling. Because as much as there was to mourn, there was also much to celebrate. Sam's life had ended, but other lives had been saved. And the new life taking form in Emily's womb was healthy and growing, a manifestation of optimism and love.

Sam was to be buried under a jacaranda tree in full bloom, and one had been planted expressly to mark the spot. As the procession approached the site, a light breeze blew, and the tiny lavender flowers danced in the air like a swarm of butterflies, finally settling lightly atop the grass.

There were no formal speeches or prayers. But after Sam's coffin was set into the ground, a young woman in her thirties stepped forward. She was wearing dark glasses and a wide-brimmed hat.

She looked out over the crowd and removed her glasses, too nervous to speak for a moment. Finally, she began. "I was blind for seven years. I had an accident. You can't imagine what it was like to have my sight taken away from me. Then, last May, Steven Sampson gave me his corneas. Now I can see you all standing here. I can see the trees and the grass and the birds and the sky. He gave me back the world! Thank you, Mr. Sampson."

She dropped a roll of Lifesavers on the casket and stepped back. A man on crutches hobbled forward. His arm and shoulder were covered in a sleeve of heavy plastic filled with air, like an inflatable mattress. "My house caught on fire, and my arm was burned real bad. The pain was unbearable," he said. "They told me it would take months and months for my skin to grow back. Months and months of excruciating pain. I didn't think I could live through it. But thanks to Steven Sampson, I've got some grafts going. The arm doesn't look so hot now, but the doctors think the grafts are going to take. Thank you, Tin Man, for giving me back my good right arm." He took a roll of Lifesavers from his pocket and dropped it onto the coffin.

A young couple stepped up to the gravesite. "Our daughter is sixteen," the man said. "She was on dialysis for two years. Complete renal failure. Now, thanks to Mr. Sampson, she has a functioning kidney. She isn't quite strong enough — yet — to be here today to honor him, but on her behalf, and for ourselves, we say thank you, Tin Man." The man nodded to his wife, and she dropped a roll of Lifesavers onto the coffin.

One by one, others stepped forward to thank Sam for his gifts: his pancreas, some veins, his intestines, even some collagen.

Finally, Emily and Matt took their places on either side of Jonah's wheelchair. Jonah looked to Emily for direction, and she nodded to him. He stood and walked forward to stand by Sam's grave.

"Someone gave me some bad drugs — well, all drugs are bad, but these were deadly, and I O.D.'d," Jonah said. "My liver shut down. I should have died, but I got lucky. The Tin Man saved my life. I'm going to appreciate things a lot more from **here on out.**"

Diana walked up and stood beside Jonah's wheelchair. "My brother Sam had a bad heart. He was sicker than a dog for five years. I can't tell you how many times we rushed him to the hospital, sure he wouldn't survive.

"But he kept bouncing back.

"Only each time he'd bounce a little lower. Finally, the good people at *The Organ Bank* found a new heart for him. And it saved his life. I never knew the man who died so Sam could live, but I can tell you this: Sam understood that his heart was a gift, and the only way he could thank God for such good fortune was to pass along that gift.

"And that's just what he did. All of you who have come today to honor my brother, well, I hope you feel the same way he did. You've each been given a gift. A gift of life, a gift of soul. In one way or another, it's up to you to pass it along."

She started to step back, then stopped and looked out over the assembled crowd. "I've been praying hard, trying to think what Sam would have wanted to say if he had been here. And what came to me was something our grandmother used to say to us when we were sad because a friend had moved away, or when one of our pets was lost." Her voice faltered and she looked down, waiting to regain control. When she raised her eyes again her face was serene.

"Nana would tell us, you've got to hold the things you love with an open hand." Diana paused. "I didn't really understand what she meant then. But I think I do now."

Again Diana looked out over the crowd, this time seeming to catch each person's gaze with her own and hold it for an instant. "Be loving, everyone," she said at last. "Be grateful for what you have. And be joyful for what you can let go."

Slowly, she raised her hands, opening her palms to the sky. "Good-bye, Sam. Go with love."

ACKNOWLEDGMENTS

This book was nurtured by the support, encouragement, and assistance of dear friends, for which I am deeply grateful: John and Nicola Barber, Angela Dyborn, Carol Ellis, Michele Lansing, and Connie Linn read and commented on early drafts, as they have on each of my novels. A new pen pal, Mitch Hider, combed through the final draft with eagle eyes and surprised me with what he uncovered.

Dr. Barbara Levey, Dr. Jerry Levey, Carol Pugh, and Jon Pugh read this novel in manuscript form and gave me professional and personal insights which enhanced the accuracy of the story.

John Deep transformed the manuscript into a book, and Noreen Morioka and Sean Adams of AdamsMorioka captured my words visually and translated them into an image for the dust jacket. Heine Prato kept harmony in our household so that the atmosphere was conducive to creativity. My family provided an emotional safety net for me when the sadness of the fiction I was creating became too real. And, as in every facet of my life, the guiding light of my husband Roy's love provided dazzling inspiration.

Now that the story is written, I can breathe a sigh of relief, grateful that it *is* fiction and not the reality of my own life. But having dwelt in Emily's world for so long, I come away feeling deeply fortunate for the abundance of joy, love, good fortune, good friends, and good health that has carried me through the first five decades of my life.

A NOTE ABOUT THE TYPE

The text of this book was set in Sabon, a typeface designed by Jan Tschichold (1902 — 1974), a well-known German typographer. Known as a contradictory perfectionist, in his youth, Tschichold was a great advocate of Bauhaus philosophy and avant-garde design, while in later life, his enthusiasm and fervor for asymmetric typography, rectilinear design layouts, and lower-case sans-serif fonts was replaced by a more balanced and larger historical view. Created in 1964, Sabon is a beautiful classic serif typeface family, based on the original designs of Garamond for the Roman and Granjon for the italic, with many subtle and elegant technical improvements. Without question, in terms of type design, the creation of the Sabon typeface family was the pinnacle of Tschichold's life.